ROAD TO THE BREAKING

BOOK 1

CHRIS BENNETT

Road to the Breaking is a work of historical fiction. Apart from well-documented actual people, events, and places that figure in the narrative, all names, characters, places, and incidents are the products of the author's imagination, or are used fictitiously. Any resemblance to current events, places, or living persons, is entirely coincidental.

Publisher's Cataloging-In-Publication Data
(Prepared by The Donohue Group, Inc.)

Names: Bennett, Chris (Chris Arthur), 1959- author.
Title: Road to the breaking / Chris Bennett.
Description: Second edition. | [North Bend, Washington] : [CPB Publishing, LLC], [2021] | Series: Road to the breaking ; book 1
Identifiers: ISBN 9781733107938 (trade paperback) | ISBN 9781733107945 (ebook)
Subjects: LCSH: United States. Army--Officers--History--19th century--Fiction. | Inheritance and succession--Virginia--History--19th century--Fiction. | Slaveholders--Virginia--Fiction. | United States--History--Civil War, 1861-1865--Fiction. | LCGFT: Historical fiction.
Classification: LCC PS3602.E66446 R63 2021 (print) | LCC PS3602.E66446 (ebook) | DDC 813/.6--dc23

II

To sign up for a
no-spam newsletter
about
Road to the Breaking
and
exclusive free bonus material
visit my website:

http://www.ChrisABennett.com

DEDICATION

This book is dedicated to my dear aunt,
Jeanette Gay Petersen (Aunt Gay!),
without whose assistance, wisdom, and timely advice
this book would not be half the book it is (literally!)

It is also dedicated to my grandmother,
Mary Lou Pember,
who helped instill in me a lifelong interest
in all things having to do with the Civil War,
and my parents, Craig and Marilyn Bennett,
for teaching me the love of reading books,
among many other good things in life.

And to my three children, Nick, Rachel, and Josh,
who inspire me to always try to achieve more,
and to be the best I can be at whatever I dream of doing.

And last, but never least, my wonderful wife, Patricia,
for putting up with me during all the long nights,
and encouraging me to keep at it,
no matter the obstacles,
and to always believe.

Contents

*"It was a time of such suffering and death,
it caused the breaking of all the old ways.
Some for the good, and some for the worse.
Nothing came through 'The Breaking' unchanged,
and all that once was,
even to the greenness of the earth,
was broken during that time,
and was never again the same."*

– Billy Creek, Indian Scout, U.S. Army 8th Infantry

CHAPTER I. IN THE HEAT OF BATTLE

"Carry the battle to them.
Don't let them bring it to you.
Put them on the defensive and
don't ever apologize for anything."
– Harry S. Truman

Thursday March 15, 1860 – South of Fort Davis, Texas:

Captain Nathaniel Chambers raised his right hand and reined in his horse, signaling the blue-uniformed mounted column to a halt. Within a few yards the fast trotting troop came to a stop. The choking cloud of dust that'd been trailing behind now swirled up around them as they stilled their horses on the road.

A rider approached hard from the opposite direction— Lieutenant Jason Stewart, officer of scouts. Through a cloud of his own dust, the lieutenant reined to a stop in front of his captain, snapping a crisp salute. Nathan Chambers returned the salute. He couldn't help noticing the hint of a grin on the handsome young face of the lieutenant, covered by a fresh coating of sweat and dust. The grin touched the corners of his light blue eyes, sparkling beneath long blond hair flowing out from under his hat.

Nathan assumed the grin meant good news. "Mr. Stewart."

"Captain."

"What's the word on our *friends*, Lieutenant?"

Stewart could no longer suppress a broad smile, "We have them, sir! The Comanche are just the other side of that draw, and we're gaining fast!"

"They're slowed by the horses they stole?"

"It seems so, sir. And I don't think they're yet aware of our pursuit; lucky thing we were already out on patrol when they raided Marfa, or we'd not be to this point until sometime tomorrow. Our Tonkawa scouts have overtaken them without being seen ..."

1

It was now Nathan's turn to smile. His own dark eyes echoed Stewart's enthusiasm and excitement at the thrill of the hunt and the growing anticipation of battle, though he was ten years and several thousand slogging army miles the senior of the twenty-three-year-old lieutenant.

"Excellent, Mr. Stewart! Fall in next to me. Let's move out and close with them, shall we?"

"With pleasure, sir!" Stewart yanked the reins to turn his horse.

Something warm and wet struck Captain Chambers hard in the face. The sudden shock of the blow took his breath away. He looked down at his chest. A thick, sticky liquid mixed with reddish chunks splattered the front of his blue tunic. A second later he heard the distant report of a rifle, coming from the ridge to their left.

He looked up to see the young lieutenant pitch forward from his mount, a red, gaping hole where his handsome face had been. The lifeless body hit the dirt of the road with a thud, and a red puddle oozed outward around his head. Stewart's horse screamed and bucked with shock and fear, the acrid smell of its master's blood filling its nostrils.

"Dismount! Take cover!" Nathan shouted. He rolled off his horse and glanced back to confirm his men were doing the same, dismounting on the opposite side from the source of the gunfire. They knew this simple strategy could save their lives, the large body of their mount a living shield against incoming fire.

Bullets whistled in, followed by the echo of multiple rifle-shots. *Boom … boom, boom … boom*! Down the line someone let out a loud grunt, and a shout of pain, "Ah! *Damn* … I'm hit!"

Lead continued to zip past, pounding into the dirt of the road amongst men and horses, spraying out stinging sand and rock fragments in every direction.

The soldiers scrambled to vacate the deadly roadway. They saw gun smoke rising above the ridge to the left of the road. The slope continued downward on the right side into a deep, steep-sided ditch, affording them immediate cover. The soldiers, gripping reins, pulled their horses down the bank in a slipping, sliding, chaotic scramble of dust, dirt, and falling, rolling bodies — human and equine.

Their frantic efforts kicked up a thick veil of dust in the hot, dry, gravel road bank. The ditch proved deep enough to cover the backs of the horses, but the steep bank rising on the far side prevented their escape in that direction.

Well-trained, experienced soldiers responded to the enemy without orders. Several men, pre-assigned the duty, rounded up and secured the company's horses, while the others rushed to the lip of the ditch and returned fire.

"Goddamn the murderous bastards!" Nathan snarled, yanking his cavalry saber free from the scabbard at his left hip and starting up the ditch bank. The raging fire in his belly demanded he answer whoever had killed Jason Stewart, and he meant to do so with the sharp steel edge of his sword. He surged halfway up the bank, intending to charge across the road and on up the hill, knowing his men would follow with or without orders.

But halfway up the ditch bank he stopped and stood still, wavering. His sword hand quivered. He closed his eyes, squeezing out a swelling of tears, and took a deep breath. *No ... no! Not this way ...*

He shuddered, then shook his head. *God knows it's not the way ... too many men will die ...* He forced the image of Lieutenant Stewart's lifeless, bleeding body from his mind.

Sheathing his sword, he strode back to the bottom of the ditch and turned toward his men spread out to his left. He cupped his hands and shouted, "Cease firing!"

The men repeated and carried out the order on down the line until the only sound of gunfire was that coming from the distant unknown enemy further up the hill.

"*Lieutenant Jones!*" In a few moments, a young man came scrambling over to where the Captain sat, up against the ditch bank, his back toward the enemy. Nathan noticed this young officer held his pistol. Nathan had never bothered to unholster his own pistol, knowing it was useless at this distance. The Lieutenant crouched in front of the Captain, trying to duck his head while attempting to salute, "Sir!"

3

"Mr. Jones have Sergeant Wiggins spread his men out along the ditch bank to our right and have Sergeant Clark do the same to our left. Have them keep a sharp eye out for any attempt to flank us while I check on our casualties. Oh ... and, please do just put that sidearm away, before there's an accident."

To Nathan's surprise, the man didn't respond to his orders. Jones stared open-mouthed, slipping the revolver back into its holster and securing the flap without taking his eyes from the Captain. "But, sir ... you are ... *wounded?*"

Nathan looked down at his chest for the first time since scrambling from his horse and into the ditch. The blood and gore that'd splattered his tunic was now caked with a thick coating of dust.

"Not *mine*, Lieutenant. I'm afraid this was from poor Mr. Stewart. He didn't make it off the road."

Jones stayed where he was for a long moment, slack-jawed, staring up at the Captain.

"Let's move, Lieutenant!"

"Oh ... yes, sir!" Jones shook his head as if to clear the evil image from his mind. He snapped a quick salute and scrambled off to pass his orders along to the two sergeants.

Nathan followed in his wake to check on the casualties. He came to where one of the wounded soldiers lay on the ground. He recognized Private Sanders from A Company with Private William Jenkins hovering over him, tying off a bandage wrapped around the wounded man's left shoulder. William was a scholar who'd studied at a prestigious college back east before joining the Army. With his shy demeanor, spectacles, and bookish habits, Nathan had thought him the most useless soldier possible, until he'd put his learning to good use—his medical knowledge in particular. And, to everyone's surprise, it turned out he could fight!

Nathan leaned over, saw Sanders was conscious, and met his eye. "Mr. Sanders ... how're you feeling?"

"G ... g ... good, sir." Despite the heat he shivered, and his face was as white as a newly laundered sheet.

William turned to the very large man next to him and said, "Stan, kindly remove your tunic and hand it to me. Sanders is going into shock. I need to keep him tightly covered and warm."

"Warm? Is hot enough to melt lead out here, William," Stan said in a thick Russian accent.

"C'mon, Stan … no time to argue."

Stan turned and looked down at Sanders, then shrugged, and unbuttoned the brass buttons of his tunic. He peeled it off and handed it over to William, leaving himself in just his gray undershirt, soaked through with sweat. He looked over at Nathan and grinned, "But Captain will be giving me Company punishment—out of uniform in face of enemy!" He laughed.

Nathan shook his head and rolled his eyes. Stan was just … Stan, and there was nothing anyone could do about it. But Stan was one hell of a fighter, so the officers were willing to overlook the rest.

Stan's tunic made a fair-sized blanket for Sanders … Stan being one of the largest men Nathan or any of the others in the regiment had ever known. The Captain was a large man, at six-foot-three and over two hundred pounds, well-muscled in his arms and chest. But Stan towered over him by a full head, was much broader in the chest and shoulders, and outweighed Nathan by nearly a hundred pounds—a true giant of a man.

William tightly wrapped the wounded man in the tunic. After a few minutes Sanders stopped shivering and Nathan thought he saw some color come back to his cheeks.

Nathan stood and stepped back, signaling William to join him.

"Sir?"

"How is he?"

"Bullet hit up high on his left shoulder. Went clean through and through. Broken bones, certainly, and a good deal of pain, but not much blood, thankfully. He should make it, sir. But he's certainly out of the fight, being unable to stand."

"And Private Chancy?" Nathan pointed over to where another man lay, holding his head in his hands, a dozen feet away.

"Unable to walk, sir. Seems his horse rolled over him when tumbling into the ditch … most likely a broken leg. I was just getting ready to splint it. Oh … and one horse was hit. Appears to be a glancing blow across one flank, and probably not serious, but may not be ridable. No one else has been hit at this point … except Lieutenant Stewart, of course. I was just trying to figure a way to go check on him, without getting myself killed in the process … but I heard he was hit in the head. Is he … presumed dead, sir?"

"Yes, yes … he is most *certainly* dead, Mr. Jenkins. A man doesn't survive a bullet going clean through his head and coming out his face!"

"*Oh!* Yes, of course not, sir!"

"Keep up the good work, William. Well done. And … thank you."

"Thank *you*, sir!"

Nathan checked in on Private Chancy, who was in good spirits despite a great deal of pain from his leg, which to Nathan's eye was certainly broken; God never intended legs to bend *that* way!

He continued down the line, exchanging greetings with the men.

"Hello, Mr. Thompson. Mr. O'Brien … enjoying our little outing?"

"Oh, aye sir! It's been as lovely a little ride as one could hope for. Though the neighbors are none too friendly, I find," young private Jamie O'Brien answered in his thick Irish accent. He grinned at the Captain.

Nathan chuckled. "True enough … well, I guess we'll just have to see what we can do to improve their disposition, won't we?"

"Aye, sir! I'll be agreeable for doing just that, sir!"

"Mr. Allen … having a pleasant afternoon, I trust?"

"None better, sir. But if you have a bottle of whiskey about you, I'd be grateful for a little sip. Just to wet my whistle, it being so gall-durned hot out here … you understand, sir?"

Nathan smiled and slapped the man on the back, moved along, sharing similar banter with the other men as he went along.

He had a sudden memory of his first commanding officer and mentor, Captain William Montrose Graham, striding up and down the lines, saber in hand, exuding unflappable courage for his terrified young troopers as bullets screamed past them.

I can also put on a show to give the men confidence, Captain Graham; but where are you now when I could use it myself? he whispered to the specter of his old captain.

℘ℓℑℭℜ℘ℓℑℭℜ℘ℓℑℭℜ℘ℓℑℭℜ

The soldiers pinned down with their captain in the dry West Texas ditch were from nearby Fort Davis, which housed nearly four hundred men. The Fort guarded the east-west road from San Antonio to El Paso, against Indians, Mexican bandits, or outlaws threatening the lawful civilian commerce in the region. But now, unexpectedly, the hunters had become the hunted. For the better part of an hour they lay in the ditch taking sporadic incoming gunfire.

A bullet hit just inches from Sergeant Jim Wiggins' head. It pounded his ears with a concussive hiss, kicking up dirt and sand, covering him in a spray of grit that pelted his face and neck and slid down inside the front of his shirt. "Shit!" he spit the dirt from his mouth and tore off his hat, slamming it to the ground. "Goddammit all to Hell! I've had just about enough of this!" He scrambled up the ditch bank and lay prone on his belly. He aimed his rifle up toward where a small puff of gun smoke drifted into the air. He squeezed off a round in response, the loud *boom* ringing in Nathan's ears where he sat a few feet away.

"Damn their mangy flea-bitten hides!" Wiggins spun back around and slid into a squatting position. He immediately began reloading the rifle. First, he retrieved a paper cartridge from his belt pouch. Tearing the paper surrounding the powder with his teeth he poured it into the barrel of the rifle and plugged the Minni ball in on top. In one smooth motion, he pulled the ramrod from the rifle and poked it all down. Finally, he re-cocked the hammer, adding the percussion cap.

Jim Wiggins was a sturdily built man, slightly under six feet. Despite his youth, still in his early twenties, his barrel-chest, bull-horn voice, and dark, rusty red hair and beard made him the archetypical army drill sergeant.

"You heard the Captain's order, Sergeant. Stop wasting ammunition," Lieutenant Jones said from his position a few yards from Nathan.

"Yes, sir. It may be wasteful, but it sure do make me *feel* better! Getting mighty tired of just sittin' here, bakin' in the sun is all, *sir!* Itchin' to make it hot for them fellas up there." Wiggins turned and spat more dirt from his mouth. He turned toward Nathan and the two shared a look.

Nathan gazed back up the hill toward their enemies. After a few minutes, he turned back to his sergeant, "Mr. Wiggins … something's not adding up here …"

"Sir?"

"Before he was killed, Lieutenant Stewart, may God rest his soul, reported the Comanche were past yonder draw and moving *away* from us. And our scouts were watching them. So … how can they possibly be on top of *this* hill?"

"A different bunch from the horse raiders, maybe? Positioned here earlier to ambush us as we followed?"

"Could be … But there's another thing that's not making sense here."

"Like what, sir?"

"Like maybe these aren't Comanche after all. Think on it …"

Sergeant Wiggins tipped his hat back on his head and looked up at the sky, scratching his itchy, sweaty scalp, picking out tiny bits of sand and grit.

"Well, sir … now you mention it … the last Comanche ambush I stepped into weren't nothing like this-here. Knives and spears flying everywhere. Men fighting hand-to-hand, rolling on the ground, kicking, shouting, cursing. Blood splattered all about. Damned happy I was to have a bayonet at the end of my rifle that day!"

"And today?"

"Well … seems to me these-here fellas are happy letting us roast slowly in the hot sun or picking us off one at a time … at their own leisure and convenience, of course."

"Exactly. And the Comanche I've fought were always keen on preserving their precious lead and powder. They'd not waste it shooting at an enemy who's not even showing himself."

As if to emphasize Nathan's point, another round ricocheted off the bank of the ditch above their heads, pelting them with sand and gravel, but otherwise leaving them unscathed.

"Okay … so, if not Comanche then *who*, sir? Surely not Mexican soldiers this far north?"

"No … outlaws, I reckon. Most likely that nasty bunch of horse thieves and cut-throats we've been trying to track down for several months now. That Moat Kangly bunch who've been causing so much trouble down along the Rio Grande."

"Makes sense, sir. Likely they made a deal with the Comanche to buy the stolen horses off 'em and have been sitting here waiting to see if we'd come a-following."

While they'd been talking, Lieutenant Jones had moved over to listen in on the conversation. "Sir, if you're of a mind to take the fight to them … I've done a little reconnoitering. There's a draw over on the left side of that ridge. We could send some men up that way and see if we could flank them and drive them off that ridgeline."

"Yes, I saw it too, and it's a thought, Mr. Jones. But … I fear that fellow up there knows it too. If I were him, I'd place an ambush about halfway up and massacre anyone who tries sneaking up that draw. What say you, Lieutenant?"

"Yes … likely so, sir, now you've pointed it out. Then what? Sit here all day, cooking in the sun, or until they tire of the sport and just … melt away?"

Nathan didn't bother answering the rhetorical question. Instead he sat on the ditch bank, gazing absently at the ground between his boots. He pulled out his belt knife and began slowly stirring the small rocks and dirt between his feet with the point.

The sergeant and lieutenant knew well enough to leave him alone and let him ponder the problem. The Captain was not only the highest ranking and most senior among them, he was also a veteran of that now legendary war down in Mexico. A real, shooting war with whole batteries of cannons and thousands of soldiers on both sides.

The sporadic incoming gunfire continued from the rocky ridgeline. The slope between them and their unknown assailants was steep and strewn with large, man-size rocks that'd rolled down from the top over the millennia. Between the rocks were clumps of sage brush, and ragged patches of thin, dry grass, about knee high.

But the slope was not terribly steep. It would not require climbing hands over feet. Nathan Chambers calculated the time it'd take to reach the top, the cover they'd have during that time, and the number of rounds the enemy could get off during such a climb.

After a few moments he stood up, sheathed his belt knife and clapped the dirt off his hands and the seat of his pants.

"Well, gentlemen, I reckon the United States Army is paying us a good day's wage to wrangle these scoundrels. I don't much enjoy sitting here idly while our enemy decides when it's convenient to slip away. I prefer to earn an honest day's wage, for an honest day's work. And I'll be damned if I'll let them get away with murdering our Lieutenant Stewart!"

"Yes, sir, the Lieutenant was a fine man, and it's a damned shame that needs answering," Sergeant Wiggins answered with a scowl, spitting to the side. "And I agree we should earn our pay, sir … and more's the better if it's at the expense of them fellas up there!"

Lieutenant Jones nodded but said nothing. For a moment he appeared teary-eyed, unwilling or unable to speak of the recent gruesome demise of his comrade and fellow officer, still laying up on the roadway where he fell.

"*Sergeant Clark!*" Nathan called out.

Tom Clark came toward them at a quick trot, hunkered over to keep his head below the top of the ditch. He stopped in front of the Captain, snapping a quick salute, "Sir?"

"We've just been discussing our situation, and I'm thinking these may be outlaws, not Comanche. Opinions?"

"I agree, sir. These fellows aren't acting much like Indians. Not aggressive enough, by my way of thinking. Content to sit back and take long-range shots at us—to little effect. I've never seen Comanche that patient. Too eager for blood … or to make a clean getaway."

"Mr. Wiggins, how many hostiles above us?"

"I've counted twelve guns, so far, sir. But if I was him, I'd have a few more up that-there draw as you suggested. So I'd say fifteen to twenty, give or take."

"All right. We've been trying to catch that damned Moat Kangly for months now, if this is him. But whoever he is, I don't care for the thought of him skulking off right from under our noses after murdering Mr. Stewart. Let's see if we can't close the noose on him and turn this ambush around. Sergeant Clark …"

"Sir?"

"Send four of your men over this way. Take the rest and move as far around to the left as you can without being seen. Mr. Wiggins …"

"Sir?"

"You will pick seven men to provide covering fire."

"Sir!" he responded with a salute.

"Mr. Jones …"

"Yes, sir?"

"You and I will lead the remaining … eight men, I guess … in a direct assault up the hill. These outlaws seem to enjoy sitting back taking potshots at us … let's see how they like a good hard fight coming right at them! And … *by God*, I promise someone's going to hang for the despicable murder of Jason Stewart!"

"Yes, *sir!*"

"Tom, as soon as Jim starts his covering fire, I want you to lead your men wide around to the left to see if y'all can work your way up around the side of that ridge. Avoid the draw but see if you can get around behind them to cut off their escape. We'll give you ten … no … make that fifteen minutes head start, then we'll start our charge. In the worst case, if you can't get there in time, we'll drive them off the ridge and get out of this damned sun! In the best case, we can cut them off from their horses and maybe finally have a reckoning with our old *friend* Moat Kangly."

"Sir! We'll do our best!" Tom snapped a salute, and turned, scrambling back to where his men awaited.

"Sergeant Wiggins, pick your men and prepare to fire. Once we get three quarters the way up, leave off firing and charge on up after us. Mr. Jones, have the remaining men fix bayonets."

"Sir!" they both said, at nearly the same time.

Four men came trotting over from Tom Clark's group. Two joined Jim Wiggins' riflemen—Stan, the gigantic Russian, and William, the scholarly, bespectacled private who served as Company doctor. The other two, baby-faced fellows who looked younger than their twenty years, joined the Captain's assault group—Jamie O'Brien, a red-headed Irishman and resident gunsmith; and Georgie Thompson, a blacksmith from Pennsylvania; both of whom Nathan had chatted up earlier.

Nathan pulled his assault team together for some quick instructions. "Y'all know pretty well what to do already, but I'll say it anyway: better safe than sorry. Firstly, stay spread well apart side to side, at least five yards between you and the next man. Give yourselves room to move around; no sense letting them take out two of us with one shot!"

Nathan had a sudden vision in his mind's eye: the devastating assault on Molino del Rey during the Mexican war. He shuddered. He'd been a green second lieutenant, fresh from the Academy. Though they'd won the battle, he'd lost his beloved commanding officer, and dozens of other good men in the terrible slaughter. He could still see it like it was yesterday—men marching forward shoulder to shoulder. A methodical, frontal assault over open ground against a dug-in, well-armed enemy. Whenever a man went down, the officers yelled at the remaining men to form up ranks and keep marching. As they advanced, more and more men fell, bullets zipping through the air, the wounded screaming in pain as they fell. Smoke obscured the view, burning their throats and choking their breath. Then came the terrifying roar of cannon fire. Grapeshot and canister, cutting men down in swaths, their bodies hideously torn and mangled. Chaos, fire … red, bloody death everywhere!

He shook his head to clear away the terrible memories. He never wanted to repeat those dreadful mistakes. A frontal assault, if called for, should be hard and fast, the enemy given as little time to react and as little target as possible!

"Move as fast as you can up the hill, but don't go in a straight line. Move back and forth, erratically, so they can't get a bead on you. Duck behind cover when it presents itself, but for *God's sake*, whatever you do, don't *stop* behind it! If you do, you'll give them time to find the range, and you'll get pinned down and stuck there. Or you'll get killed trying to poke your head out for a look.

"If anyone goes down, don't stop to help. You'll only get yourself killed too, and that won't help anyone! Sergeant Wiggins will come along behind us in short order with Private Jenkins and company. They'll take care of anyone who gets wounded along the way.

"And lastly, don't waste the one shot you have. You won't have time to stop and reload. You'll hear the lieutenant and I firing off the occasional pistol shot, to give them something to think about. But don't get all excited and waste your rifle shot. Remember, we've got six pistol shots to your one rifle. If it helps, remember your history lessons from the good old Battle of Bunker Hill, and *'don't fire 'til you can see the whites of their eyes!'*"

This last line brought smiles, and several chuckles from the young men gathered around. It was an old saw they'd heard a hundred times since childhood. But they'd never imagined living out that scene for themselves in real life!

"And I would be remiss, gentlemen, if I didn't recall the proper passage from the Good Book as we prepare for battle. From Deuteronomy chapter three, verse twenty-two: *'Ye shall not fear them: for the LORD your God, He shall fight for you.'*" This brought appreciative smiles from several of the men. Others nodded their heads or tipped their hats to their captain, but they spoke not a word.

He dismissed them, and they spread themselves out along the edge of the ditch as ordered. The private named Georgie turned to his friend and said, "Well Jamie, what do you think of our chances on this one?"

"What? Oh, don't you worry, *boyo*, by gosh! Didn't ya hear? The *officers* it is! They be a-leadin' the charge, and they ain't *whankers*. If there was any *real* danger in it, they'd send us in ahead and follow along safely after, don't you know!"

They shared a chuckle.

Down along Sergeant Wiggins' line, Stan turned to his friend William and said, "Hey, William. Why you thinking we got picked for to be doing the shooting, and not for doing the running?"

William turned and looked up at his friend, squinting through the bright sunlight reflecting off his glasses. "Probably because you are so ridiculously large, the enemy wouldn't even have to aim to hit you ... and me? Well, they're likely afraid I'd lose my glasses and spend the rest of the fight wandering around looking for them."

Stan laughed out loud, slapping William hard on the back.

"Hey, you miscreants! Hold it down there!" Sergeant Wiggins growled. But Stan chuckled, noting the look of amusement on their Sergeant's face and the smile in the corner of his eyes.

Nathan took one quick last look at his men to make sure everyone was in position, then signaled Sergeant Wiggins to begin firing. He'd ordered sequential firing, rather than volley fire, to keep the enemies' heads down as much as possible.

After the first shot was fired, Tom Clark led his men off to the left, hunched over to avoid being seen, but moving at a fast trot. Nathan pulled out his pocket watch to note the time.

Fifteen minutes passed, with Sergeant Wiggins' men firing off their shots in a steady rhythm. Gun smoke drifted lazily in the still air, its familiar, acidic odor filling their nostrils.

Nathan clicked his pocket watch closed and tucked it back in his tunic pocket. He drew his cavalry saber with his right hand and un-holstered his Colt revolver in his left. He closed his eyes and drew a deep breath, taking a firm hold on the rage that burned inside him. When controlled it could be a powerful weapon; when *not* ...

Lieutenant Jones, taking his cue from the Captain, pulled out his own saber and revolver. Nathan nodded to Jones and without a word charged up the ditch bank, the lieutenant right behind him. The eight privates scrambled up next, bayonets thrust forward. The group moved across the road and started up the hill at a run.

Jones couldn't resist a quick glance over to where Lieutenant Stewart's body lay in the middle of the road. The blood had soaked in and dried to a dark stain on the surrounding ground. He snapped his eyes away, immediately regretting having looked.

Under his breath, Nathan uttered another Bible verse that came to mind, as sharp as a knife blade, *"Blessed be the LORD my strength, which teacheth my hands to war, and my fingers to fight!"*

༄༅ྀ༅ྀ༄༅ྀ༅ྀ༄༅ྀ༅ྀ

They climbed the hill at a steady run, zigzagging from side to side as instructed. Below, Sergeant Wiggins and his men continued to lay down a steady covering fire from prone positions at the edge of the ditch. The bullets from the enemy zipped past and banged around them as they ran, but so far no one had been hit. The soldiers firing from below were apparently having the intended effect, preventing the enemy from taking careful aim.

Nathan scampered over rocks and around bushes, having now covered a quarter of the distance. He glanced to his left just in time to see one of his men go down. Nathan didn't know who the man was or how badly he'd been hit, but he couldn't stop to check. Moving up the hill and engaging the enemy was all important; to stop or slow down, meant death.

They were now within seventy-five yards, then fifty. The bullets from his own men below continued to rattle off the rocks above in a most encouraging manner.

The gunfire from below suddenly stopped. This meant Jim Wiggins and his men were on their way up the hill, bayonets fixed. Their covering fire had become too dangerous for their own men climbing the hill in front of them. Nathan was now close enough to see figures peering out from behind rocks above him.

15

He took shots at them as he ran, the big Colt held out straight in front of him in his left hand. There was little hope of hitting anything, climbing uphill as he was, with no chance to steady his aim. But he fired anyway, to force his enemies' heads down, if he could.

He could feel his legs tiring, but he forced them to keep pumping. His breath was coming in great gasps.

As he neared the top of the hill, he noticed the gunfire from above had stopped. *"The enemy will just melt away ..."* he remembered Lieutenant Jones saying. Where was Tom? Had he made it around the ridge to cut off the enemy's retreat? Nathan burned at the thought that the enemy might escape justice. It gave his legs new energy, and he surged ahead.

He topped the ridge, squeezing himself up between two large rocks, then stopped to take a quick look around. He was panting, and his legs ached from the effort. But he was eager to move on. Then Lieutenant Jones appeared, with seven of the privates. They looked winded and red in the face, but fierce and determined.

"Come, men; I'll not have them escape us now, *by God!*"

Nathan leapt down from the rock, and without looking back, ran across the relative flatness on top of the ridge. It was rolling and covered in tall scrub brush, preventing a view beyond more than a few yards in front. He heard gunfire and shouting ahead.

They crested another low rise, and a scene of chaos opened before them. Men and horses were entangled—struggling, fighting, stabbing, wrestling on the ground. They ran forward and found Tom Clark's men had arrived, barely in time. Some bandits had already mounted horses and made their escape, dust trails rising into the air.

He stepped forward and saw one soldier take a rifle butt to the face and collapse. But another soldier ducked an outlaw's slashing knife and neatly stepped forward, planting his bayonet in the center of the man's chest with a *thud!*

The fight could have gone either way until Nathan and his men arrived. The Captain and Lieutenant jumped into the fray, slashing with their sabers, while the privates charged forward with a shout, bayonets to the fore.

One outlaw, a skinny youngish looking fellow with only the slightest hint of a beard, suddenly stepped back from the fight, dropped his rifle, and held his hands up. "I'm done … don't kill me!"

It was the crack that burst the dam, his fellows quickly doing the same, weapons thrown down and arms held high.

All except one … a large, evil looking man with dark hair and a full beard. Even without the long, wicked scar under his left eye Nathan would have recognized Moat Kangly from his portrait on wanted posters scattered all over the territory. The leader of the outlaws scowled at his men and backed away from them. He held a huge Bowie knife, like a short sword in his thick hand, and appeared determined to continue the fight single-handedly, if necessary.

But Nathan stepped up in front of him and pointed his saber at the ground, "You are outmanned, and your men are finished. Will you not yield, sir?"

Kangly didn't immediately respond. He glared at Nathan, and they locked eyes. Men on both sides watched, wondering if their two leaders would fight it out, man to man, blade to blade. But Nathan Chambers' coal-dark eyes had an unflinching intensity that many men found intimidating, backed by an iron-hard will that would not be denied.

After a few moments Kangly relented, lowering his knife, "Why not?" he shrugged.

"Wise choice. But … before I place you under arrest, I would know which man among you murdered my lieutenant down on the road."

Kangly gazed at him again and paused as if trying to decide whether to answer. Suddenly he broke into a leering grin, "There's only one man here could've made such a shot … in fact I doubt one man in ten thousand could've made it. Not that I like to brag. A judge may see me hang for it, but still … one can't deny the skill of the shot. And … I've never had the *pleasure* of killing an army officer before. At least I'll have time to enjoy the thought of it while I'm awaiting the noose."

17

Nathan's eyes widened, his nostrils flared, and his face turned red. His body quivered slightly, and for a moment he looked toward the sky.

Without a word he stepped forward, pointed the Colt at the center of Kangly's face, clicked back the hammer and squeezed the trigger. The pistol jumped with an ear-ringing concussion, shockingly loud in the post-battle silence. The outlaw's lifeless body, eyes still wide as in shock, toppled backward like a felled tree, hitting the ground with a thump. Gun smoke swirled up around Nathan's face. "You'll have no sick pleasure at our man's expense … *sir!*"

No one moved or spoke. Nathan holstered his pistol and sheathed his saber. His face was stern but had resumed its normal color. His body no longer shook. The anger was spent.

As Nathan turned away Sergeant Wiggins came rushing up with his men, bayoneted rifles in hand. He looked down at the body of the dead outlaw, "Damn, sir! Seems I've missed all the fun!"

Two of Wiggins' men, Stan and William, were supporting a third man between them—Private Simms, the soldier who'd been hit off to Nathan's left while they were assaulting the hill. He looked pale and wobbly and had a blood-soaked cloth wrapped around his head.

Sergeant Wiggins and his men moved forward to help the other soldiers round up the prisoners, securing their weapons and horses.

Billy Creek, their Tonkawa Indian scout, who'd suddenly appeared in their midst, knelt next to Kangly's body. He stood, and turned to Nathan, handing him something. It was the outlaw's great Bowie knife. Billy had pulled it from Moat Kangly's dead grasp. "A keepsake for you, Captain," he said with a grin, holding out the handle.

Nathan took the knife, looked at it curiously, and said, "Thanks, Billy. But … what will I do with the thing?"

Jim Wiggins strode by, and answered the question for him, "Well, sir, if nothing else, I reckon you can use it to hold the papers down so's they don't blow off'n your desk … when you get to be a general!"

"Heaven forbid!"

Billy Creek smiled and made a short snorting kind of laugh, turning away.

ʕ๏ɚ)ɞ)ʕɞ)ʕ๏ɚ)ɞ)ʕ๏ʕɞ)ʕ๏ɚ)ɞ)

The brief battle was over. They estimated three or four outlaws had escaped. Five were killed, including Kangly; and seven surrendered, most of whom were wounded to varying degrees. On the Army side, only Lieutenant Stewart had been killed, but five had suffered wounds that would require immediate treatment, one being potentially life-threatening.

On the long, slow ride back to the fort Nathan ruminated about the battle, which despite the victory, had left a bitter taste. True, they'd won and had suffered no more killed, for which he was truly grateful. But the untimely death of the bright young Lieutenant Stewart left a sadness he knew wouldn't quickly fade.

And more than that, he was frustrated and angry with himself for losing control of his temper and killing Kangly. The man's cruel words and evil leer had burned through the restraints on his rage like a hot flame through a piece of dry twine.

It was a demon that'd haunted Nathan since early childhood, for as long has he could remember. Though normally easy going and good humored, he was intensely competitive with an overly keen sense of right and wrong that could trigger an uncontrollable rage. He could still remember several childhood friendships ending in blood and tears—rarely his own. Twenty-some years later, he still shuddered at the evil images when they came unbidden to his mind's eye.

It was this temper, in his teen years often directed at his father, that'd finally led his mother to send him away to school in the North. He'd never struck his father, but he could remember wanting to frequently. Even now looking back on it, he felt a knot in his stomach … *What if I'd have attacked him … really hurt him; my own Daddy? I can't imagine ever getting over it. God knows some other later things were hard enough …*

Only a few men he'd served with had ever seen that truly dark side of him. *None of the current group of men, thank God.* Oh, they were aware he had a temper, and had seen him commit acts of extreme violence when provoked. But they didn't know the whole truth. None of them knew about … *El Diablo Blanco.* He pushed down that evil memory through sheer force of will, for the thousandth time.

Childhood outbursts were one thing—black eyes and bloodied lips. But upon entering adulthood during his first year of boarding school, what manifested suddenly turned deadly.

Johnny Miller, the classroom bully, had mistaken Nathan's easy-going, friendly attempts to fit in with his new classmates for softness; he'd decided Nathan would be a good target for abuse. Nathan, keenly aware of his past problems controlling his temper, had tried hard to suppress his growing anger. For weeks he'd ignored the taunting and prodding. But the abuse from Johnny continued unabated; and even worse, other classmates began to tease Nathan, misinterpreting his lack of reaction as fear or weakness.

But the more Nathan tamped down the anger, the more it built up inside him, until the fateful day the bully pushed him one step too far—over the edge into an abyss of rage.

On that day, the boys lined up in the courtyard as usual, preparing for the short walk across to the cafeteria for their midday meal. Without warning, Johnny gave Nathan a hard shove from behind, spilling his books to the ground and nearly knocking him over. Johnny laughed out loud, taunting Nathan. "Well, looks like someone's awfully clumsy. Can't even stand still without tripping, eh Nathan?"

He had laughed. Several of the other boys had laughed with him. It was the last time they laughed at Nathan.

Without a word, he turned and punched Johnny hard in the face. Johnny staggered back. Blood spewed from a broken nose. But one punch wouldn't quench Nathan's raging fire. He launched himself into the bully, both fists swinging, knocking him to the ground. He jumped on top and continued the attack. It was shocking, ferocious, and bloody.

Such extreme violence was rare in schoolyard fights, which were typically more about posturing, taunting, and a few poorly aimed punches, before the schoolmaster stepped in to break things up. A few bumps and bruises, a black eye, or a fat lip were normally all there was to show for the scuffle.

But this time it took the schoolmaster and several of the stronger schoolboys to pull Nathan off and restrain him, still cursing and thrashing, until the dark fit had passed. Johnny laid on the ground moaning and crying, his face a bloody mess, a wrist broken from trying to fend off the blows.

Nathan still shuddered when he thought of it, even all these years later, knowing he would have killed Johnny if they hadn't pulled him off. He still believed Johnny had deserved it, but it hadn't been his proudest moment!

Only the timely intervention of one of the old schoolmasters, Mr. Wilson, had saved Nathan from expulsion. Mr. Wilson took Nathan under his wing and spent many hours after class with him talking about how to channel the anger into productive activities rather than suppressing it; he'd already experienced what would result from that wasted effort!

That year spent in Mr. Wilson's classroom had probably saved his life, he now believed. Otherwise the anger likely would have led him to an early tragic end. Now, after all these years, he still used those lessons Mr. Wilson had taught him. Little tricks, to keep him from killing someone when he could feel the rage building.

But the tricks didn't always work; there were times when he couldn't contain it or safely vent it. It frightened him …

And though it made but little difference whether Kangly died out in the wilds from a gunshot or was hanged properly back at the fort, Nathan knew it meant he was not entirely in control of his own actions. And it was one more black mark on the wrong side of his personal ledger with the Almighty. One more in a long list of demerits for which he must somehow make amends.

Chapter 2. Messages from Home

"A man travels the world over
in search of what he needs,
and returns home to find it."
–George A. Moore

Tuesday April 3, 1860 – Fort Davis, Texas:

Captain Nathaniel Chambers strode across the parade ground toward the command post office. A stranger watching might have guessed he was the commander of the station by the way he carried himself, even without the crisp, army captain's uniform. His head held high, surveying his surroundings with a steady gaze; he was the very picture of the man in charge.

With his tall, athletic physique and his lean, handsome face, he was a man women noticed, and men admired. But he wasn't vain about his appearance having done nothing to earn it. This was a gift God had granted him, along with his keen eyes and a sharp memory for the smallest details. And only God knew the reasons why.

He took in every detail as he crossed the field. The parade ground of Fort Davis was nothing more than a bare, dusty, weed-filled patch of open earth between a hodgepodge assortment of buildings.

A brown and gray striped lizard skittered across the ground in front of him as he walked, catching his eye. The next instant the lizard disappeared in a sudden, shocking blur of motion. A brown speckled bird, looking something like a malnourished rooster, tore away at a great pace, the lizard's tail dangling from the side of its beak. A "Road Runner" the locals called the strange bird, Nathan recalled. The name fit, he decided. He'd never known the creature to fly, but that never stopped it from moving about at a great pace.

He decided calling this place a "fort" was a stretch. No walls, no stockade, and no particular plan or layout he could discern. Not even sited on a decent, defensible piece of high ground.

The Army established the fort after the 1849 California gold rush created an unexpected crush of east-west overland traffic. Secretary of War Jefferson Davis tasked Brevet Major-General Persifor Smith with establishing a fort in the area to guard the southern roads from outlaws and Indians.

Nathan shook his head in perplexed disbelief when he gazed up at the steep rock walls surrounding the fort. General Smith had located his new fort within the walls of a box canyon to protect it from the howling Texas winter winds. But the very canyon walls intended (in vain) to protect the fort from the wind, also provided ideal cover and high ground for any enemy who might attack it.

This basic flaw made necessary the endless, and unpopular, patrols of the surrounding ridgelines. They kept watch 365 days a year, day and night, regardless of the weather.

And because the Army had never decided whether to make the fort temporary or permanent, it had evolved haphazardly. They'd erected new buildings as needed, using materials easy to hand.

For many enlisted men, Fort Davis was just another duty to slog one's way through. For most officers, it was a purgatory. A place to waste away a once promising military career in the middle of nowhere.

But Nathan Chambers enjoyed the outdoors, the challenges of an unforgiving natural environment, and one's unrelenting human enemies, juxtaposed to the manly comradery of the officers and men. There was no place he'd rather be and nothing else he'd rather be doing. He'd been an army officer his entire adult life. It was what he knew. The only thing he'd ever done or ever wanted to do.

He neared his office, and took a deep breath of air, already warm, though it was still early morning. He reveled in the clean, dry, crisp smell of sagebrush in the air. Around him the usual hustle and bustle of fort business was getting started, troops leading their horses to the paddock after returning from a night's patrol or leading them out into the bright daylight for a long day in the saddle. Other men, without specific patrol duties were marching, rifles on shoulders, drilled by their sergeants ensuring they had something *useful* to do.

He entered the office and took a moment to enjoy the sudden coolness the thick stone walls provided after his brisk walk in the hot sun. He hung his hat on a hook on the wall, and approached the desk where Sergeant Tom Clark, his aide-de-camp, stood at attention.

As usual, Tom's uniform was clean and neatly pressed, and his light brown hair smartly trimmed. His close-shaven face wore a serious expression, as was proper when at formal attention, but Nathan detected a smile at the corners of Tom's eyes.

Nearly a head shorter, and fifty pounds lighter than Nathan, Tom was nonetheless a tough fighter, courageous and resourceful on the battlefield. He was equally skilled in the command office, juggling the endless duties as the post's quartermaster with seeming ease. Tom was Nathan's favorite in camp—in his opinion, a thoroughly efficient, trustworthy, and honorable young man.

"At ease, Tom. And good morning. Please ... sit," he pulled up a chair himself and sat next to Tom's desk. "Any mail?"

"Good morning, sir. Yes, the usual dispatches ... and this," he handed Nathan a yellow colored envelope. It was a telegram, sealed and marked on the outside in bold ink:

> *Personal and Confidential. For the eyes of Captain Nathaniel Chambers only, U.S. Army, Fort Davis Texas.*

The Captain took it and looked at both sides. But he could divine nothing from the envelope. So he shrugged, and scooping up the rest of the mail, moved off into the back room where he had his desk.

A few minutes later, he strode out, grabbed his hat, and exited through the front door. The door banged closed leaving Sergeant Clark completely stupefied.

Hmm … that was passing strange … never before seen that. I wonder if it has something to do with that personal telegram? Well … I'm sure I'll hear about it later, whatever IT is.

But Tom did *not* hear anything later; the Captain never returned to the office. It left Tom wondering and stewing, forced to handle fort business by himself, including making any required command decisions.

ഇ৯৩ﬡ৩ঙ৩ﬡ৩ঙ৩ﬡ৩ঙ

Nathan strode back to his personal quarters, the telegram held in his left hand. He re-read it for the fifth time, as if he might somehow eke more information from the terse message with another reading.

> *March 23, 1860. Dearest Nathan. With heavy heart I regret to inform you of your father's passing by sudden collapse. Letter to follow. Love A.C.*

It was now April 3rd. The telegram had taken just under two weeks to travel to Fort Davis from Houston, the end of the telegraph line from the East. There had been talk of it extending to San Antonio and Austin, but it hadn't happened yet.

The message was as shocking as it was terse. His father, Jacob Chambers, was a giant in his mind, though he'd not been a large man. He'd been stern and serious, a man in control of his own world, demanding unquestioning obedience from servants and family members alike—and usually getting it, Nathan had to admit. Except … from his only son. Nathan had rebelled from an early age, and now … now he was thousands of miles away and hadn't been there when his father died.

Conflicting emotions struggled inside him. He'd never been close to his father … at least not that he could remember. He could recall saying "yes, sir," and "no, sir," so often it seemed like the only thing he'd *ever* said to his father. But he could not recall any kind words nor warm moments.

Not so with his mother. "A.C." was Abigail Chambers, always called just "Miss Abbey" back home in Virginia. She was as warm and kindly as her husband was cold and severe. It was an odd contradiction. He'd not thought on it much before, but now realized his mother must also have suffered under her husband's severe regime. It occurred to him to wonder how she really felt about Jacob's passing. He had a hard time imagining any softness or special kindness ever passing between them. He'd never seen it, he was certain. *Maybe that's why I was an only child.* He scowled and shook his head at his own irreverent thoughts.

Then he experienced a sudden, chilling realization about the impact on his *own* life and future. *Momma knows nothing of business, Daddy would never have allowed it. She's incapable of running the great family farm by herself. And … there are no other close family relatives to help her …*

ᏸᏬᏇᏣᏸᏬᏇᏣᏸᏬᏇᏣ

The next day when Nathan arrived at the office, he carried on in the usual manner. If Tom had expected an explanation of the previous day's oddness, he was left disappointed. Nathan never mentioned it and proceeded back into his office to conduct the day's business as if nothing at all unusual had happened.

Though Tom noted a more serious tone to the Captain's voice, everything else appeared the same. *Very odd. He acts like nothing has happened, though clearly something has …*

Five days later another telegram arrived … with the same wording on the outside, "Personal and Confidential ..." But this time Tom noticed Captain Chambers' reaction was more restrained, as if he'd been expecting it. After reading the new telegram the Captain did *not* storm from the office as he'd done before, but stayed seated at his desk, continuing the business of the day.

When Nathan stepped out, several hours later, Tom asked, "Is there anything I can do for you, sir?"

"No, thank you Tom. There's nothing I need just now." But the severe look on his face belied the calm words.

Back in his office, Nathan tried to get through the morning's paperwork—mission reports from the previous day's returning patrols, and a stack of orders for men heading out the next day. But he found he was having a hard time focusing. His mind kept

26

going back to his Momma's telegrams. He reached over and picked up the most recent one, re-reading it again:

> *March 30, 1860. Nathan dear am very sorry to ask. But don't know what to do with farm by myself. Please come home! Love A.C.*

"Damn it … *damn it, Daddy!* Why did you have to up and die, leaving me this dilemma?" It surprised him he'd said it aloud. He felt foolish and quickly glanced out the door to where Tom sat in the outer office. To his relief Tom showed no reaction; apparently, he'd not heard the outburst.

Daddy certainly didn't choose to die unexpectedly, and even if he had, he wouldn't have done it just to sabotage my career. Or maybe he would have, come to think of it. But either way, it makes no difference …

Nathan had a sudden image of his younger self, an energetic, enthusiastic, strong-willed child growing up on the family farm on the western side of the Allegheny Mountains in Virginia. He could recall an insatiable desire for the next exploration or adventure. This rambunctious boyhood mischief typically ran afoul of his stern, serious, authoritarian father.

Ironically, a father who expected unquestioning obedience faced a strong-willed young son who questioned everything. And when young Nathaniel reached an age where his mother could no longer physically intervene, she sent him away to a boarding school up north. He wondered if his mother would've made the same choice if she'd known he would never come home again. *Not likely*, he decided, and for a moment felt a twinge of guilt and a sudden sadness for her.

The second telegram had *not* been unexpected. He'd expected his mother to give him a few days to come to terms with the shock of his father's death. And then, she'd beg him to return home, to take up the reins of the family business. The southern tradition demanded he take his "rightful" place as master of the household. Although he'd anticipated it, he did not immediately pen an answer.

He loved being an army officer and had no wish to be anything else. Farming was a thing he knew nothing about beyond what he could remember as a young boy. It'd be a difficult adjustment for him, living a sedentary life.

But the family farm, Mountain Meadows, had been in the family for three generations now. His grandfather had carved it from the raw wilderness over fifty years ago. It had eventually become a prosperous estate with several thousand acres under tillage.

And it was also a place of uncommon beauty, he had to admit. Heavily forested hills giving way to lush meadows where crops of all kinds flourished in the warm, southern sun. And just the right amount of rain in the springtime and snow in the winter to make trees grow enormous. Like nowhere else on Earth, he was sure. His grandfather had built the magnificent great house and his father had expanded it to almost twice the original size.

His momma had added her touches as well—beautiful furnishings and a flower garden that was the envy of the county. For a child it was a dream world of forests, rivers, and caves to explore; hunting, fishing, and endless boyhood adventures.

And now his momma had to run it on her own, something for which she had neither experience nor aptitude, as far as Nathan knew. Could he ignore her pleas and risk letting her lose it all? It was not only the family home, it was also his inheritance, and with the demand for cotton what it was, the farm represented a sizeable fortune.

And then a thought hit him he hadn't considered before, and in that moment he realized he'd pushed it back to the furthest reaches of his mind. Back to a place where he'd never have to think about it. Never have to consider what it said about his family, and by association, about himself. *What about … the slaves?*

 ΣΩΣΩΣΩΣΩΣΩΣΩΣΩΣΩ

Tom had feigned a nonchalant reaction to the Captain's unintended outburst. Sitting at his desk not ten feet away he'd heard the sudden curse, followed by *"… Daddy, why did you have to up and die, leaving me this dilemma?"*

Captain Chambers' father dead? *That* would explain the sudden, uncharacteristic behavior after the first telegram. Tom knew the Captain's personal story well enough to understand his family owned a large estate back in Virginia. He also knew the Captain did *not* get along with his father …

And the second telegram? The one the Captain seemed to expect … what could it have been about? And what did the Captain mean by his "dilemma"?

He chewed on it a few minutes; then it hit him. *Oh, no!* His mind spun with the implications—an impending disaster!

So that night after Captain Chambers left for the evening, Tom grabbed his own hat, and headed out the door, slamming it shut behind him. *Time to go have a talk with Jim.* He headed out to find his best friend and fellow sergeant, Jim Wiggins.

ཀ

For the next several days, Nathan struggled with his decision. On the third day following the second telegram's arrival Tom stepped into the Captain's office and stood in front of his desk.

After a moment Nathan looked up from the report he was reading. "Yes, Tom?"

"Sir … may I speak with you for a moment? On a … a *personal* matter."

"Of course, Tom. At ease. Come … sit." He gestured toward the empty chair next to the desk.

Tom sat, and without preamble began, "Sir … I must confess … I overheard you the other day, and then pretended not to. I heard you curse, and say your father had died, leaving you with a dilemma."

Nathan raised an eyebrow at Tom but said nothing.

"Well, first, sir, I would be remiss if I didn't offer my condolences on your loss."

"Thank you, Tom, I appreciate that. And I … I *apologize* for not telling you straight out. It was just such a shock. At first, I didn't know what to think, and then …"

"Yes, sir. I understand. No need to apologize; truly."

"Well, thanks for being understanding, Tom. Was there … *something* else?"

"Well, yes … there is. If you'll forgive me inserting myself into your personal business, sir. But I … I want to *help* you, sir."

"Help me?"

"The dilemma you spoke of … deciding between the Army and returning to Virginia."

"Tom … you've been reading my personal mail?"

"Oh *no*, sir! I would never do *that!* It just makes sense …"

"Yes … I suppose that must be obvious … But how do you propose to help me? Do you mean to talk me out of it, or are you more inclined to be rid of me?"

They shared a smile and Tom shook his head and rolled his eyes. Nathan had already heard all the horror stories about the incompetence of his predecessors at Fort Davis, leaving little doubt about Tom's preference in that regard.

"Sir, I don't intend to talk you into … or out of … anything. I came here to offer my assistance. I'm hoping I can help make the choice easier for you."

"It's a kindly thought, Tom, but how can you help?"

"Well, sir, it seems to me your decision is carefully balanced, on the very edge of a knife, so to speak. Just a little weight added to either side will tip it over the edge. I intend to offer that extra weight to the balance."

Nathan raised an eyebrow but said nothing.

"You're probably thinking I intend to tip the scales in favor of the Army. And believe me, I was sorely tempted to do just that. But … I don't think it's the *right* thing to do, sir."

"No?"

"No, sir. You're a man of honor, and honor demands a man look after his family first. And your family needs you back home, taking charge of the family's business. And comforting your poor, widowed mother, of course."

"Believe me, Tom, these past few days I've thought of little else …"

"Yes, I'd imagine so … but how I intend to help is … I intend to go with you!"

"Oh! Well, I … I appreciate the thought, Tom, but … *why?* You've a very promising career ahead of you in the Army. You're smart, brave, as competent in the field as you are in the office. A natural leader. I'm certain you can become a commissioned officer one day. In fact, I've been intending to write the letter of recommendation in that regard. There's no limit on how far you can go in the service."

"There, sir! *That's* the reason, right there! It's your own fault, Captain."

"My fault for *what?*"

"Before you arrived, this place was a hell-hole. Nobody wanted to be here. But now ... the men have pride in what they're doing. There's an infectious comradery ... an *esprit de corps*, as the French would say. Because of *you*, sir."

"Oh ... well, I don't know about all that ... I just do my duty in the way I see fit."

"Sir, I don't want to be here once you're gone. I don't want to watch things slide back to the way they were. I'd rather quit and become a civilian again. So if the right decision is for *you* to go, then ... I guess that means ... it's time for *me* to go, too. But also ..."

"Yes?"

"You're a career officer, sir, starting way back at West Point when you were just a young man. And ... no offense sir, but ... you've never had to run a business."

Nathan smiled and waved a hand, "None taken, Tom. I'm not ashamed to admit it."

"That's where I can help you, sir. I'm good at logistics, planning and such. My family ran a freight hauling firm back east, and I used to work in the business office before I got restless and went looking for adventure out west. And I've learned a whole lot more since becoming a sergeant in the Army and serving as quartermaster for some four-hundred men."

Nathan now had a thoughtful look and stared up at the ceiling as Tom continued.

"I can run a business, sir, and free you up to be ... well, a 'gentleman farmer,' I guess."

Nathan smiled at this, shook his head, and made a small chuckle. "I doubt I'll ever be *that*, Tom. I'm thinking if I return to

31

Virginia it might be best to just sell the farm and find a new home for Momma. And after that? I have no idea ..."

"If you decide to sell the farm, I can help with that too—I can figure out what everything's worth, help you find buyers—even negotiate the sale. And after ... well, you'll need to invest the money in something, and I can also help you with that."

"Well, that's very kindly offered, Tom. But I can't ask you to do all that for me. Especially since I still have no idea what I'll do, even if I decide to return to Virginia."

"You haven't asked me, sir. I ... I just ..."

Tom looked down at his feet, absently kicking at a bent nail head sticking up from one of the wooden floorboards, his face turning red.

"I want to go with you, sir. I ... I don't care where. Whatever you end up doing ... I want to be there doing it, too."

Nathan leaned back in his chair and stared toward the ceiling. He stayed that way for a long moment. Then he leaned forward, looked back at Tom and said, "Yes ... I'll admit I've been wrestling with this decision since the first telegram arrived. I've agonized over it nearly every waking hour, and through several sleepless nights.

"And ... just this morning I prayed on it, asking God to grant me the wisdom to make the right decision. I prayed he'd show me a sign to help me choose. And now ..." he laughed, shaking his head and smiling—the first warm, genuine smile Tom had seen in several days.

"Now I believe *He* has given the sign, Tom. It seems clear to me ... *His* gracious gift of your comradeship *is* the sign I've been looking for. Praise be to God." He bowed his head and was silent for a long moment.

Then he looked up, "And thank *you*, Tom. Thank you very sincerely, and God bless you!" He stood and extended his right hand.

Tom sprang to his feet and gripped the offered hand, shaking it with great enthusiasm. "No ... thank *you*, sir! Thank you for all you've done for me, and for agreeing to take me with you. You will *not* regret it!"

"I've no doubts about it, Tom. Well ... I guess that's that."

He sat again, and leaned back in his chair, once more staring up at the ceiling. He took a deep breath, slowly letting it out before leaning forward again.

"Tom, if you don't mind, as soon as our day's duties are complete this evening, I'd like to start planning *our* trip back to Virginia."

ஐஐஐஐஐஐஐஐஐஐஐஐஐ

Nathan read the new telegram again, for the ninth or tenth time. And though he could find nothing specific of concern in it, still ... something about it was making him uneasy. *Something* had changed since her last telegram, he was certain. He couldn't put his finger on it. The message gave him that strange, incomprehensible sense of dread or danger he often got out in the field before any specific threat materialized.

There was something his momma wasn't telling him. Something causing her fear. Not just the natural, expected worries about running the family business by herself ... something more ... something *dangerous* even?

> *April 19, 1860. Dearest Nathan. Am overjoyed and relieved you return home. Wondering how soon you depart and how long is journey? Apologies for impatience. Know you will ensure safe journey. I need your presence and support. You cannot arrive soon enough! Anxious for your expeditious return. Love A.C.*

Each time he read through it he tried to figure out what bothered him. There were certain words and phrases ... *"relieved ... how soon you depart ... impatience ... safe journey ... need your presence and support ... cannot arrive soon enough ... anxious ... expeditious return."* Though the words seemed innocuous enough when spread throughout the letter, put together they hinted at ... *something*. It gave him an odd, almost itchy sensation. Something was amiss, some unseen danger he couldn't quite name. He'd learned over the years to ignore such intuition at his own peril.

But he couldn't imagine what danger there could be in *civilized* Virginia. Could she be ill? He couldn't recall his momma ever being sick when he was a child. It was perplexing and maddening.

He sat down to pen an answering telegram. And though he'd ask her if all was well, something told him she wouldn't tell him anything of substance until he was safely home. She'd not want him putting himself in danger through imprudent haste. She knew from his letters over the years, traveling in the West when ill-prepared or improperly supplied was not just inconvenient and uncomfortable; it could very well prove fatal.

After he'd decided weeks ago to return home, he and Tom had moved the preparations forward in a steady, workmanlike manner. He now felt a sense of urgency that hadn't been there before. Though he didn't know why, he knew he needed to return home in the most "expeditious" manner possible.

෫෦෨ඏ෫෦෨ඏ෫෦෨ඏ෫෦෨ඏ

Monday April 16, 1860 – Greenbrier County, Virginia:

"Miss Abbey … your horse is ready, ma'am," Megs announced, stepping quietly into the library. A tall, thin black woman in her fifties, she was the head maid in the Big House and Miss Abbey's longtime favorite.

"Oh … thank you, Megs," Miss Abbey answered, looking up from the book she'd been reading. She smiled as she stood and straightened her dress. Miss Abbey was also tall and thin. She and Megs were of the same age and had been together since Miss Abbey had arrived at Mountain Meadows Farm thirty years earlier. But Miss Abbey's fair skin and shoulder-length straight blond hair were in stark contrast to Megs' dark skin, and closely cropped, tightly curled black hair. Both still retained the greater part of the natural good looks God had favored them with in their youth.

"Good day for a ride, ma'am. But you sure you don't want me to send one of the farmhands along with you?" Miss Abbey recognized a hint of worry in Megs' voice. She'd never asked that question before, knowing how Miss Abbey treasured a little private time on her weekly ride. But things had been … *different* lately.

"Thank you, Megs, but I shall be perfectly safe here on the farm, I have no doubt."

She tried to be reassuring, but noticed a concerned look on the familiar face.

They exited the library, crossed the wide foyer to the large front door, and walked out onto the veranda. Miss Abbey took the lead, with Megs a step behind and to one side. They crossed the veranda to the head of the stairs and stepped down to the gravel walkway. A short path led across a narrow strip of grass to the hitching post at the edge of the circular driveway.

The young groom named Cobb looked up at Miss Abbey and smiled as she approached. He had an easy, friendly manner and ready sense of humor, and she thought him a very handsome young man. She assumed he was popular among the young black women on the farm though she hadn't heard of any particular attachments.

"Good day, Cobb. I trust you're in good health this fine, sunny Monday?"

"Oh, yes ma'am! Never better; very kindly of you to ask. Nellie's also in good health and fine spirits today," he said, giving the mare a friendly pat on the side of her head.

"Hello, Nellie! Oh … what a fine girl you are! Shall we have our little ride?" she said as she reached out and gave the horse a scratch on the muzzle. Nellie seemed to enjoy the attention, rubbing affectionately against the proffered hand.

Megs reached over and tied a straw hat on Miss Abbey's head with a pink sash. Once her hat was in place, she moved around the hitching post and stood next to Nellie.

Cobb picked up a special stool from where it sat next to the hitching post and set it down beside the horse. The stool was built like a square block with a single stair on one side. Miss Abbey stepped up level with her horse where it was a simple matter to mount.

The grooms had outfitted Nellie with a sidesaddle, Miss Abbey's usual riding style. It allowed her to ride with propriety while wearing normal, everyday skirts. When she was a young girl, she'd preferred riding in the normal fashion astride the horse, wearing britches like a man. But after she married Jacob, he wouldn't hear of it. She'd been riding sidesaddle so long now she barely remembered how to do it the other way.

As predicted, it was a beautiful day for a ride. She took a deep breath of fresh air as she rode slowly away from the house and up the gravel driveway. The driveway made a circle next to the house before heading out between the slave cabins and farm outbuildings, then out through the fields and forest. Eventually it led all the way to the main east-west road, some four miles distant.

She'd not be going that far today, however. Her favorite riding spot was a side trail leading off from the driveway about two miles from the house. The trail led to a tall hill which afforded a grand view of the farm and the surrounding countryside. She'd ridden to the top of the hill often but usually preferred to stay on level ground in the wide field at the foot of the hill.

The field was a meadow nine or ten acres across and mostly devoid of trees with a pretty, little stream running down one side. And best of all, this time of year it was absolutely bursting with wildflowers of a dizzying array. Miss Abbey enjoyed slowly riding or even leading the horse around this meadow, losing herself in the myriad flowers for hours on end.

Today the field should be especially beautiful, she assumed, since many of the flowers had been on the brink of blooming when she'd ridden there a week earlier. Fair weather and sunny skies in the interim should have been the proper medicine for their earlier reticence, she decided. She was getting excited about seeing it, so after she turned off from the drive onto the side path leading to the meadow, she kicked Nellie into an easy trot. This part of the path between the drive and the meadow wound a narrow way through thick bushes and low-growing trees. But Nellie knew the way, and easily navigated the lazy curves of the trail.

They rounded another corner when Nellie skidded to a stop, nearly throwing Abbey forward off the saddle. But she was an experienced rider and kept her seat. Before Abbey had regained complete control, however, the horse backed a step, screamed, and reared high in the air. Again, she clung to the saddle, as the horse landed back on all fours. Nellie stepped backward, turned, screamed, and reared again. This time as Abbey struggled to maintain her perch, she heard and felt something snap and found herself sailing through the air!

As she fell, she caught a quick sideways glimpse of the thing that'd caused all the trouble: a large, gray and black striped snake coiled up in the middle of the path—a timber rattler!

She hit hard on her back, shoulders first, followed by her head. But after lying where she'd fallen a moment, she took stock of her situation. She'd landed in a thick bush and was now dangling at a forty-five-degree angle, with head down, and feet sticking up. She wiggled her feet and toes, and her arms and fingers, to make sure nothing was broken. And though scratched, scraped, and bruised all over, she'd apparently suffered no serious injuries. So she wriggled and squirmed her way out of her uncomfortable, impromptu nest. In a few moments she'd extracted herself from the bush and found herself on all fours back on the dirt trail. She stood and brushed herself off. Nellie was nowhere in sight, having bolted back toward the road.

Examining her dress, she discovered the fall had torn it in several places, and it had dark green smears in others, but happily no blood. She felt stickery pieces of brush and leaves tangled in her hair. *Must look an awful sight*, she thought, making a sour face.

She glanced back along the path toward where the snake had been. It remained coiled up in the center of the path. She stared at it a moment longer, puzzled by its behavior. She stepped forward, now curious, until she was fewer than ten feet away. The snake still made no movement, and she realized something was amiss.

She picked up a stick about three feet long, stepped forward and poked it at the snake. Still it made no movement. Strange. She stepped up and tipped the snake over with the toe of her shoe. As she suspected, the snake flopped over on its back. It was already dead. She knelt to examine it more closely, finding no marks of violence.

But why would a snake coil up in the riding path to die? If a predator killed it why were there no marks, and why wasn't it eaten? And if it had died of natural causes why wasn't it hiding under a bush as one might expect of an old or sick animal?

It was a puzzle, but she decided it was unlikely she'd be able to solve it. So she gingerly picked it up with the stick and flipped it over into the bushes off the side of the trail. There it wouldn't spook anyone else's horse.

She walked back the way she'd come on the trail. After a few minutes she came to the main road and turned in the direction of the house. She'd only walked a short distance when she heard a noise behind her on the road. She turned and met Nellie, trotting up the road toward her.

"So … there you are, my little miscreant! Afraid of a little snake, are you? Well, come here and let's have a look at you."

The horse walked straight up to her, and she gave it a quick once over, but discerned no injuries. The saddle was missing, though, presumably deep down in a bush near where Abbey had fallen.

So she took Nellie by the bridle and turned back toward the house, leading the horse. She walked along the road for nearly a quarter hour before reaching the edge of the cultivated areas of the farm. She'd not gone even halfway across the first field when a man stepped out onto the road in front of her. He was breathing hard as if he'd just run a race.

It was the head overseer of Mountain Meadows Farm, Allen Sickles. He was a tall, lean man in his early forties, with a thin face and long dark shoulder-length hair, and closely trimmed beard. Not a handsome man, in Miss Abbey's opinion, with his long, hooked nose and crooked front teeth that stuck out in an unflattering manner. He did, however, know how to run a farm—a man she desperately needed in Jacob's sudden absence.

"Miss Abbey! What has happened? I was out in yonder field and noticed you walking your horse with no saddle, so I came running to check if there was something amiss. Are you hurt? Here, let me take the horse from you, ma'am."

"Thank you, Mr. Sickles. We took a little fall, I'm afraid. A timber rattler on the trail."

"Oh, dear! That might have ended very badly, ma'am. But what of the saddle?"

"Strangely, when Nellie reared it gave way and broke off. A thick bush broke my fall, fortunately, so I have only scratches and bruises, and not broken bones."

"Oh, thank goodness for that, ma'am."

Even as he said this, another of the white farmhands, a young man named Zeke, came up to them. He was also breathing heavily as if he'd hurried to get there. He was still in his late teens, thin and lanky, with long, light-brown hair sticking out from under a straw hat. "Mr. Sickles ... ma'am. Is aught amiss? It looked to me you might need some help."

"Miss Abbey is all right, Zeke, but she took a fall and her saddle came loose. Here, take the horse and walk Miss Abbey back to the house, if you please. I'm going to look for that saddle and maybe kill that snake."

"You needn't bother about the snake, Mr. Sickles; it's already dead."

"Oh? Your horse kicked it, did she?"

"No ... it was very odd. After I extracted myself from the bush, I poked it with a stick and found it'd been curled up in the road, already stone dead."

Zeke pushed back his straw hat and scratched at his head. "Ain't never heard of a rattler dying in the middle of the road all curled up like that, Miss Abbey."

"Me neither," Sickles agreed.

"Yes. But apparently the snake didn't much care what we thought it should or shouldn't do!"

Miss Abbey smiled for the first time since being thrown from the saddle.

ॐ৯৫৫৫৫ॐ৯৫৫৫ॐ৯৫৫

Later that afternoon, after she'd taken a bath, changed her clothes, and Megs had brushed the stickers from her hair, Mr.

Sickles came to the house. He asked Miss Abbey to step outside for a moment. Megs came along as well.

He led them to the hitching post. The groom Cobb was there, but unlike this morning he was *not* in a happy mood. Miss Abbey's missing sidesaddle sat perched on top of the hitching post.

"Ah, you found it. Thank you, Mr. Sickles."

"Yep ... as you'd reckoned, it went down inside a bush, not too far from where you fell, from the marks and tracks. And I found that snake too. But ..."

"But?"

"Well, Miss Abbey ... it's all very odd ..."

"Odd? In what way?"

"Well, you say the horse never kicked the snake. And yet ... when I looked it over closely, I noticed something had caved in its head, like from a strong blow."

"Oh ... that *is* strange."

"And there's more, ma'am. The reason I asked you out here. After I found the saddle, I had a couple of the boys carry it back here, and when I examined it, I found this ..."

He lifted the side flap of the saddle to show the place where the cinch had originally been attached.

"Yes ... now I see why the saddle came loose. The cinch is broken."

"Not *broken*, ma'am ... look closer."

She leaned in to examine the cinch. At first glance it was just a broken leather strap, but then ... *she saw it!* At the break point, nearly halfway across the strap the break was neat and even ... as if ... "Someone has cut it!"

"Yes, ma'am, so it would seem."

"But ... why?" She looked at Sickles, who shrugged, then over at Cobb, who hung his head and wouldn't meet her eyes.

"Well ... I'm sorry to have to say it ma'am, but it appears ... well, may as well come right out and say it, Miss Abbey; it appears someone was fixing to do you harm. Someone who knew when you'd be riding that horse and knew where you'd be riding. That snake didn't curl itself up in the trail with a bashed-in head, and that saddle cinch sure didn't cut itself, neither."

He looked over at Cobb and scowled. The implications were clear.

"Cobb? Do you know anything about this?" she asked, a sick feeling rising in her stomach. It was chilling to think someone was actively trying to do her harm. Her growing anxiety and unease with all that had been happening since Jacob's death had now risen to a new level.

He looked up with fear and tears in his eyes. "Oh, *no*, ma'am! When I saddled up Nellie this morning everything was fine. The saddle was perfect. There ain't no way I would've put that cinch on all cut like that ... why, I'd've noticed it right away. I swears ma'am, that cinch weren't cut the last time I seen it. And I don't know nothing about who might've done it, neither. But ... ma'am ... I'm so, so very sorry you got throwed and was hurt. I feel ... awful bad about it. I would never do nothing to harm you ma'am; you're the nicest lady I knows, if you'll pardon my forwardness."

He seemed sincere, and clearly upset by it, so she was inclined to believe him, though he *was* the most likely suspect.

"Hmm ... was the animal ever out of your sight after you saddled it?" Sickles asked.

"Oh, yes, sir. I like to always be right on time for Miss Abbey's ride. So I'll saddle up Nellie first thing ... in case there's any problems with the tack that needs fixing or whatnot. Like if there was a worn cinch or something ..." he gave Sickles a meaningful look, before continuing. "After she's ready to go, I leave her in her stall for a bit while I go about my duties with the other animals; mucking out stalls, feeding hay, checking the hooves and shoes, and so on."

"Was anyone else in the barn at the time?"

"Oh yes, sir. Two other grooms, Sampson and Phillip. They was doing the same chores I was about."

"And were the barn doors open, so others might've come and gone without you noticing them?"

"Yes, sir. On a nice spring day like this-here, we opens wide the doors on both ends first thing so as to let the fresh air flow through the barn. Clears out some of the night smells, if you take my meaning. While I'm busy shoveling out a stall I reckon a whole army could march straight through that barn without me paying the slightest mind."

Sickles looked over at Miss Abbey and raised a questioning eyebrow.

She returned the look, and said, "I believe you, Cobb. But … Mr. Sickles, if Cobb didn't do it, then who?"

"I believe him too, ma'am; he's never been one of your … *disgruntled* types, like some of the others. I reckon one of the slaves may be nursing a grudge. And who better to take it out on than the mistress of the house, now the old master is gone?"

"Oh! Do you really think so? I can hardly believe it. I've always tried to treat everyone … *kindly* … and now this? I … I don't know what to think." She looked over at Megs and saw shock and concern that must've mirrored her own.

"Well, there's always a few in every bunch, ma'am. I have some ideas … like there's this fellow called Ned who was … *disciplined* … a couple years back and has been sullen and mean-like ever since. And there's a couple of fellows that seems to be close friends of his that might be of a mind to agree with him. I'll make some inquiries and find out if anyone has anything to say on it."

"All right, Mr. Sickles, though I'll not have anyone hurt trying to get them to say something. Do you understand me?"

"Yes, ma'am. I will just talk with 'em but won't be doing them no harm … unless I find out who done it. Then I'm like to lose my temper, ma'am."

"Well, before you do that, bring them to me, Mr. Sickles, if you please."

"Yes, ma'am. I'll do that."

ᘝᘓᘔᘕᘖᘙᘝᘓᘔᘕᘖᘙᘝᘓᘔᘕ

When she sat back down in the library, she noticed on the side table a folded piece of paper. It was a letter she'd been reading before being called outside to examine the saddle. She sat and picked up the letter, scowling at the thought of the content. It was from her neighbor, Elijah Walters. He was the son and heir of the late Percival Walters, who'd had a running feud with Jacob Chambers for years, starting when Nathan was still a young boy. After Percival had died a few years back and Elijah had taken over the Walters Farm, the feud had gone quiet. They'd hoped it had died with Percival. But now that Jacob had also passed, the son seemed determined to revive it.

It started with the discovery that he had started logging operations on the very piece of land that had caused the feud in the first place. Apparently, a surveyor's mistake when drawing up the original property lines had resulted in a small parcel where the Chambers and the Walters properties overlapped. The spot was heavily wooded with prime timber near the main road where it was easily accessible. So the parcel had potential monetary value, which was why neither Percival nor Jacob was willing to part with it.

Abbey considered the whole thing ridiculous, but Jacob would never agree to offer a compromise. Now, it seemed Elijah had decided to take advantage of Jacob's passing and seize the property. Abbey's strongly worded letter of protest—of which copies were sent to both the county courthouse and sheriff—had gone unanswered.

This was followed by a series of odd "incidents" that'd been highly disruptive to her household and business.

First, she received a letter from the cotton broker to whom they had sold their main harvest for more that fifteen years. The letter stated he would no longer do business with Mountain Meadows Farm due to *"an unfortunate change in business circumstances."* She guessed it either meant he didn't trust her to bring in the crops on her own, or Walters had pressured him to stop doing business with her. It was something Jacob would have handled easily, likely intimidating the broker into changing his mind. But to her it was a major inconvenience and would force her to locate and negotiate terms with a new buyer, something she was ill-prepared to do.

Then, she learned several of her longtime farmhands had been approached and offered jobs working at Walters Farm for higher pay. With Jacob gone she feared losing anyone, so she responded by giving everyone pay raises. So far no one had left, but Walters might continue trying to lure them away.

Then there'd been the mysterious fire out on the edge of one of the cotton fields. Though it'd been dry, there'd been no lightning, so a natural cause was unlikely. It'd hit just at sunset after the hands had come in for the evening. All farmhands, black and white had been mustered back out to fight the fire, which had taken half the night, ending in the loss of more than twenty acres of cotton. One of the white farmhands told her afterward he'd had a strong whiff of kerosene while fighting the blaze!

If the crop losses and expenses continued, they would quickly eat up the farm's savings, which had already been seriously depleted two years earlier when Jacob invested heavily in the new cotton gin and bale press. She feared and dreaded the thought of being forced to sell off some of the slaves to keep the farm afloat. She shook her head at the thought, *No, not that! Anything but that. To sell ... our people!? No ... it must not come to that!*

Then, only a week ago, on a routine trip to town for supplies, her slaves, and the farmhand who accompanied them, had been harassed by riders on the road. These men surrounded their wagon as they went down the road and spoke to them in a demeaning and threatening manner. Though the strangers never harmed anyone and eventually rode away, the Mountain Meadows men, both black and white, were badly shaken by it. The white farmhand said he recognized one of the riders from church—one of Walters' men.

And now this letter. No niceties, no pleasantries, and no mention of the logging or any of the other strange happenings. Only an offer to buy the Mountain Meadows property, lock, stock, and barrel, as soon as possible. It included a price, but even Abbey, despite her lack of business experience, knew it was a ridiculously low offer. She briefly contemplated responding and enjoyed the thought of giving Walters a piece of her mind, and not pleasantly!

But she decided not to bother. It would do no good. And besides, he'd not bothered to respond to her protest about the logging, so why should she bother responding to his nonsensical purchase offer?

She sat back in her chair and sighed a heavy sigh. Apparently, the Chambers-Walters feud was back on in full force, only this time she was caught in the middle of it.

Now she was starting to wonder if Walters' had instigated the saddle-cinch incident along with all the rest. Was it possible he had someone at her own farm working against her? A slave? Or one of the white farmhands?

The thought made her shudder, and she silently said a little prayer, *Dear God … please bring my Nathan home safely … and soon!*

Chapter 3. On the Border

*"You should reach the limits of virtue
before you cross the border of death."*
– Tyrtaeus of Sparta

Saturday April 14, 1860 – Fort Davis, Texas:

His official duties over for the day, Nathan was poring over a map of West Texas spread out on the table in his quarters while enjoying an evening sip of whiskey. The bottle helped serve as a paperweight to hold the map down flat. The knock on the door was expected, having become a regular part of the evening routine since he'd made his fateful decision.

"Come."

"Good evening, sir."

"Tom … come look at this map."

Tom hung his hat on an empty peg by the door and strode over to stand next to Nathan.

"Ah … familiar territory, sir."

"Yes … exactly what I was just thinking. And … every time we've traveled back to Army headquarters in San Antonio, we've ridden along the trans-Pecos road, up here …"

"Yes, kills two birds with one stone, so to speak, since we have to patrol the road anyway …"

"Precisely. But … look here. There are well-marked trails that take a more southerly route, brushing up against this northern hump of the Rio Grande, before heading due east to San Antonio."

Tom traced his finger along the route Nathan had indicated.

"I see it, sir, now you point it out. It appears to be a more direct route; the main road takes us quite a ways further north than we really need to go."

"Yes, that's what I was thinking. I have a mind to take that more direct route. See if we can't shave a few days off the trip, only …"

"Only?"

"Only it's wild country and rarely patrolled. Liable to be dangerous. And … just you and I this time; no troop of armed soldiers conveniently at hand if there's mischief. I'd like to save time if we can, but I fear it may be too risky …"

"Oh, well, sir, as for that … I've been talking with Jim about the hazards of the road back to the East, and …"

"*Jim?* Jim Wiggins? What does he know about all this?"

"Oh, everything, of course. He was the one who helped me figure out what was going on with you after those telegrams arrived. And … *oh*, did I forget to mention he was coming along with us?"

"Jim, too? Well, he's a good man, for sure … but Jim's an Indian fighter to the core; I've never seen a more natural-born fighting man, save maybe the Russian, Stan. What'll he do to keep his interest back in *civilized* Virginia?"

"I honestly don't know. But when I told him we were leaving, he refused to be left behind. He's spent his whole life in Texas, so I guess he's ready to see some new country. Anyway, as I was saying, we've been talking …"

"And?"

"Well, we were thinking a man of your station ought not to travel in the wilds without a proper escort. And then I remembered several of the privates were coming up for re-enlistment this month. If they were *gently persuaded* to decline the Army's *generous* offer, they might be willing to travel with us."

"Oh! That's a good thought. It *would* be nice to have enough guns along to dissuade potential trouble. So … have you recruited anyone?"

"Yes, I've already taken the liberty … and it's funny you mentioned Big Stan just now …"

Nathan's eyes widened, "*No!* You didn't?"

Tom nodded, and a grin began to spread across his face, "Yep … and his buddy, the 'doctor,' William Jenkins, too."

It was now Nathan's turn to smile broadly, and he reached over and patted Tom on the back warmly. "Well done! Well done, indeed, Tom! Now … let's take a closer look at that southern route …"

47

In the end, four privates and one of the volunteer scouts agreed to return with the Captain and the two sergeants to Virginia. Like Stan and William, the other two privates were also a pair of close buddies. The first was George Ethan Thompson, a blond, baby-faced young man who went by "George E."—to distinguish himself from his father, "George A." (for Albert) Thompson. But everyone just called him "Georgie." The other was Jamie O'Brien, a red-headed, freckle-faced Irishman who'd come over to America on a boat when he was a young boy. They'd come out to Texas together looking for adventure two years prior, from a small town in Pennsylvania.

Despite their youthful looks, the two had developed a reputation for toughness, and for keeping level heads in a fight. Nathan recalled they'd been two of the men who'd accompanied him up the hill in the fight with Moat Kangly and his bandit gang.

Since Georgie had been a blacksmith and Jamie a gunsmith back in Pennsylvania, the Army was only too happy to accommodate them. As their skills were similar and complementary in many ways, the two often worked together on the various odd mechanical jobs around camp. The Captain guessed they'd had their fill of wild western adventure and were ready to return to a more civilized country.

The last of their traveling companions was called "Billy Creek," though nobody knew his real name. When asked, he would laugh and say, "It doesn't matter; white men can't say it, anyway." He was one of their Indian scouts, a Tonkawa Indian.

His tribe was, for reasons the Captain did not fully understand, at odds with practically every other Indian tribe in the West—especially the belligerent Comanche. It was generally assumed the Tonkawa had become scouts for the Army out of pure necessity. They'd been in serious decline as a tribe, and their very existence was threatened by their more powerful and numerous Indian enemies. The blue-coated white soldiers could stand up to the Comanche and beat them in battle. This made them an ally the Tonkawa desperately needed. In the process, the

Tonkawa had become an extremely valuable asset to the Army; their knowledge of the land, flora, and fauna, and their tracking abilities were legendary.

Billy Creek had proved his value on many occasions. In addition to scouting, he was also a fierce fighter, despite his small stature. Billy's father had also served as a scout for the Army, and Billy had followed along, learning the family trade from a young age. So Billy, who was now in his early twenties, had spent most of his life in army camps amongst the white soldiers. He joked he knew more words in English than in Tonkawa ... especially the swear words!

When Nathan asked him why he wanted to go to the East, Billy shrugged his shoulders. "Something new to see, I guess. And ... no *Comanche. Ha!*" From a distance, Billy was indistinguishable from the other soldiers. He was short in stature and slight of build, but he wore the same blue uniform. He did sometimes wear a broad-brimmed hat with a single eagle feather protruding from the hat band, in recognition of his ancestry and his role as a scout.

Nathan wasn't sure what Billy Creek would gain from the trip east, or what he would do to occupy his time in Virginia. But there was no denying his wish to come along. And the Captain had to admit he enjoyed Billy's company, and was happy to have him, whatever the reasons.

ౠఞౚ౧ఞఞ౧ఞ౧ఞ౧ఞ౧ఞ౧ఞ౧ఞ౧

Planning the journey took the better part of a month. Nathan's uneasiness about what might be happening back home continued to grow.

He found himself getting snappish and having to apologize to Tom on more than one occasion. He felt badly about it, especially since Tom was doing the bulk of the arranging. But if Tom noticed Nathan's growing uneasiness, he said nothing, and didn't seem put off by it.

Both Nathan and Tom shared a high ethical sense that the Army should *not* pay for any of their personal needs once they were civilians, no matter how trivial. So they set out to furnish themselves and the men with everything they would need for the long trek east.

Tom calculated the journey would take nearly three weeks of steady travel. That assumed everything went smoothly and they weren't sidetracked along the way. Four or five weeks was more likely. And the modes of transportation would vary greatly — everything from horseback, to steamboat, to train.

There were no trains this far out in West Texas, although there were some farther east near Houston. But even those rail lines didn't connect Texas with the rest of the country. The railroad reached westward about seventy miles out from Houston and from there ran to the Texas Gulf coast. So from Fort Davis they would travel by horseback across most of Texas, until they reached the railhead at the town of Alleyton. The other end of the line was the port city of Galveston, from which they would catch a steamboat for New Orleans. From New Orleans, they'd be able to catch a train traveling due north through Mississippi to Tennessee. Then they'd switch to an eastbound train taking them to Virginia. The last leg to western Virginia would once again be mostly on horseback unless the rail lines had been expanded in recent years. They wouldn't know that for sure until they were closer to home and could acquire a local railroad map.

So they'd clearly need horses, an expense the Captain was obliged to pay, including for his own. He purchased his favored mare, Millie, from the Army—an officer's privilege. Tom did likewise, being very fond of his current gelding, Jerry.

And Nathan had little choice but to buy the large stallion that'd served as Stan's mount, it being one of the few animals strong enough to carry him. The creature was as physically imposing as its rider. But where Stan was typically jolly (except in a fight) the horse had a sour disposition and a reputation for biting and kicking the stablemen and other horses.

Stan had taken to calling the stallion "Groz." When the stablemen asked him what it meant, he explained, "Is short for Ivan *Grozny*. It means 'Ivan the Great.' He was first great Caesar of all *Russ*. In English you would say 'Ivan the Terrible, first Czar of Russia.'" The stablemen laughed, and *"Ivan the Terrible"* the stallion became.

For the most part, the men would wear whatever civilian clothing they'd brought with them when they joined up with the Army. Tom helped them acquire a few articles to fill in the gaps. Billy Creek, however, had nothing appropriate to wear for the trip east. He would no longer be able to don an army uniform, and his traditional Indian attire wouldn't do at all!

Of course, they'd also need food fit for travel that wouldn't spoil: jerky, hard-tack, and salted pork. Nathan also purchased a hunting rifle in the hopes they might supplement their dried goods with fresh game if the opportunity presented itself.

He decided to buy a revolver for each man, rather than a rifle. Though smooth-bored and short-barreled, giving it a relatively short effective range, the revolver *was* superior to the rifle in several respects. It was much easier to carry and keep close to hand while riding, so better in any unexpected action. And most importantly it contained six loaded shots to a rifle's one, giving its owner a lot more firepower.

ༀ⃟ᨏᨀᨅༀ⃟ᨏᨀᨅༀ⃟ᨏᨀᨅ

Two days before Nathan's replacement was due to arrive, he received another message marked "Personal." But this telegram wasn't from his mother. He shared the contents with Tom. It read:

> *Headquarters, Department of Texas*
> *San Antonio, April 22, 1860*
>
> *My Dear Captain Chambers,*
>
> *I was deeply moved when I received your letter resigning your commission. I certainly understand the duties of family. I often feel the pull of those obligations myself. My deepest condolences on the passing of your father. I had the pleasure of meeting him and your mother once when I was on official business in Richmond.*
>
> *Please be so kind as to give my condolences and convey my respects to your mother, a lovely and gracious woman.*

Although I am very sorry to be losing a fine officer and fellow Virginian, I wish you the very best of success in your new life as a civilian.

I am, very respectfully, your obedient servant,

R. E. Lee
Brevet Colonel, Commanding Department of Texas

"Colonel Robert E. Lee?" Tom asked. "I've never met him, though I have heard good things."

"Tom … you once said you thought I might be the best officer in Texas. Well, I can tell you for sure: as long as Colonel Lee is in Texas, I will *never* be the best officer."

"Yes, sir — if you say so, sir."

⁊ℭᏝℭᏝ⁊⁊ℭᏝℭᏝ⁊⁊ℭᏝℭᏝ

Thursday May 10, 1860 – near Del Rio, Texas:

They were now well on their way, finally, to Nathan's relief. Another exchange of telegrams with his momma had not served to lessen his unease; if anything, it did the opposite. He felt an urgency to move quickly that he could not shake, though he couldn't have given a good reason for it, had anyone asked.

They were five days' ride east from Fort Davis, about halfway to San Antonio. Though hot, and dusty, the ride had otherwise been a pleasant and uneventful journey.

In typical style, Jim would help ease the miles by entertaining the men with his off-color humor. His stories varied in length from simple one-liners to lengthy, complex adventures. He typically managed to insert at least one of their companions as the butt of the joke. His stories were highly entertaining, complete with humorous imitations of voices, both male and female, including foreign accents — Stan and Jamie, being foreigners, were particular favorites.

"Hey y'all, did you hear what Stanny-boy did last week?" he called out as they rode along, prompting chuckles, and sarcastic responses.

"No Sarge, what did Big Stan do last week?" Georgie eventually called out, giving the required response.

Stan, always the good sport, shrugged his shoulders giving a *who, me?* look.

"Well now, since you ask, I'll tell you," Jim continued, chewing on an unlit cigar he held in his teeth, smiling broadly.

"Well Stan, now he was on leave, and feeling a bit thirsty, but more than that, feeling a bit horny ..."

This of course prompted several snarky remarks from the audience, to which Stan shook his head and grinned.

"But you see, the problem was, Big Stan had done gone and lost all his money a-gambling with the men back at the fort. He had only a half dollar in his pocket. So, after thinkin' on his dilemma a moment, he goes on in to his favorite waterin' hole, and walks straight up to the prettiest barmaid."

To this Stan nodded his head in agreement, still grinning broadly.

"Well, our Stan ain't a man to waste many words, as y'all know. So he comes right out and says 'Hey, pretty missy, would you be coming up to my room if I was giving you one thousand American dollars?'"

This last part Jim said in his best Stan accent, prompting hoots of laughter, even from Stan.

"Well, as y'all can imagine, after only a moments' pause, the barmaid, she answers, 'Why sure, honey, I'll go up to your room for a thousand dollars.'" Jim told this part in his best, sassy-barmaid voice.

"'Oh, good,' says Stan, 'then would you be going to my room for two bits?' Now the barmaid looks highly offended and says, 'Sir, what kind of girl do you think I am?' But Stan, he shrugs his shoulders and says, 'Oh, missy, we've already determined this! Now we just haggle on price!'"

Stan snorted, and slapped his leg, pointing his finger at Sergeant Jim between choking bouts of laughter. "Oh, very good one, Sergeant ... is very good! I will have to say this next time I am in saloon talking to barmaid!"

Stan would typically come back with a witty story of his own. He smiled and shook his head, still enjoying Jim's joke. But it seemed nothing came to his mind, so several minutes passed with no retort.

Then Jamie called out, "C'mere, Stan. Tell us again how a big, dumb Russian like you came to be a fightin' Indians all the way round the world in Texas, America." Jamie could get away with calling Stan a "big, dumb Russian," because Stan usually referred to him as "the thick-headed Irishman."

It was a story most of them had heard at least parts of before though surprisingly not Captain Chambers. He found his curiosity piqued, so he listened with interest to the tale.

"Oh, well … is not much to tell …" Stan began in his usual manner, meaning he *did* have much to tell.

"When I was young man … fourteen years old … I was living in hard, cold part of Russia—most easternest part of that very great land—in place called Siberia. We lived in small village; really just lumber camp, with few common buildings—town hall, postal office, general store, and most importantly, *pivnaya*, what you Americans call saloon! At this time, I lived with my mother, two brothers and three sisters, in tiny, one-room log house. Papa had died few years before when big tree fell on head.

"I was already *very* large boy … not so big as now, of course, but much bigger than brothers who were older, and even bigger than most men of the town. And, like most ornery young boys, I liked to fight! Oh, how I liked to fight …

"Of course, I fight my two brothers, and all my schoolmates, but after time they refuse fight more. They say, 'Stanislav … you too big fight us boys. Go out and fight with men.'

"So, I go out to *pivnaya* where men are having much vodka. And I am being surprised when I try start fight—not one … but *three* men are thinking to teach young fool lesson and give big beating."

Stan paused here and smiled, looking around at the men before continuing his tale.

"Well, these men were stupid with too much the drinking vodka, while I am young and strong like bull. In end, I am one

54

giving lesson! Now I am happy, ornery, young man ... like little child gifted with new toy. So I come back to *pivnaya* night after night, until nobody wanting fight no more, no matter how stupid drunk.

"Finally, the *glava derevni* ... hmm ... 'master of village' you would say ... he comes to Momma and says, 'Tatyana, you must do something about Stanislav. He is scaring men away from saloon with his fighting.' But Momma was not knowing what to do. So she says, 'Stanislav, no more school for you, time to be working a job so you come home tired at night and stop fighting.'

"I am pretty sure she wanted me join men of village cutting big trees. But I was afraid of great tall trees ... the one thing bigger and stronger than me ... and was remembering one had fallen on poor Papa. So, when I hear of a harbor town ... twenty or thirty miles away on coast of great ocean, I thought that was for me. So I pack clothes in bag, and off I go.

"It was last time I saw Momma, may she rest in peace, though I wrote her letters sometimes."

"Oh, so sorry, Stan. Your mother has passed away then?" Georgie asked. He, like the Captain, had never heard Stan's full tale.

But William, who had heard the story many times rolled his eyes and shook his head, recognizing the familiar trap Stan had laid.

"My mother *dead*? Oh no, Georgie. Last time I got letter she was in perfect health. It's just this: once I left her house, she could finally *rest in peace!*"

Georgie laughed, but most of the others had heard it before.

After a moment, Stan continued. "So, when I arrive in small harbor town, I am cold, tired, and hungry. For once I am not wanting to fight, so maybe Momma was right after all. I walked around town looking for work. But when men ask what I know how to do, I say 'nothing,' so nobody gives me work. Finally, a man says, 'You may know nothing, but you are big strong young fellow, so you go down to ships and talk to man on big steamboat. He might need strong fellow like you.' So I go to waterfront and find big boat. There lots of men carry heavy loads onto boat, and

55

Captain says they are ready to depart next tide. If I want job go help men load boat. So I did.

"Next day I am on boat in middle of ocean and no land in sight. Never had I even seen ocean or big boat before."

"Were you very afraid?" Georgie asked.

"No, not afraid. No big trees on ocean!"

They shared a laugh.

"Anyway, ship is belonging to Russian-American Company, and we sail to place called *Alyaska* across ocean in land of America, where we go to hunt seals. At first, I am thinking ... is hunting, will be good job, but ..." Stan heaved his massive shoulders into a shrug and sighed, "Hunting seals is *not* like hunting other things. Better they should call it *killing* seals, or *slaughtering* seals, or *butchering* seals. There is no *hunting* ... men bash seals on head on beach where they move only slowly. Then they take out sharp knives and cut skins off, wanting only precious fur. Meat is left on beach to rot.

"I am not ... how you say it ... squeamish? I liked the *real* hunting back in Russia, but this ... this made me feel sick, and for first time something I see make me *rvotnoye*, how you say ... vomit? Yes, the murder of seals made me vomit. But the other men they laugh and say, 'you get used to it Stanislav.'

"But I *not* get used to. The seal, he looks at you with big eyes like pet dog, and you are supposed to bash on head," he sighed again, "is not for Stan.

"So when finally ship land in real town in *Alyaska*, called *Novo Arkhangelsk*, hmm ... this place local Indians are calling *Sitka*. Then I leave ship, and the Captain, he says, 'You can't leave, Volkov. You are part of crew. You must work until return to Russia, or you owe for price of passage.'

"But I laugh in his face, and say, 'Who will stop me? You?' and I walk away. But Russian-American Company owns town, and they send men to drag me back to boat. Then they learn how I like to fight!

"But man can't fight always, so I get on fishing boat going south down coast. When fishing finished, I got off on empty shore filled with only rocks. I walk and walk until I meet some Indians.

These Indians also fishers who treat me kindly. I live with them for year or more, catching fish.

"Then one day Indians travel to place of white men, neat little village of cabins next to great forest of trees for the logging, like in Siberia. I am very excited to meet them. It was two years or more since I have seen any of my own kind.

"Now, you can laugh knowing the world as you do. But remember, I am knowing nothing of great wide world. So you can imagine surprise when I start talking to these white men and they just stare at me. Then they say things to me, and I cannot understand any word they say. Like talk from Indians until I started knowing their words.

"But these new white men were not surprised like me. They talk together a moment. Then one nods, looks at me, points finger and says 'Russian.' It is first time I am hearing the word, but I learn it is their word for my people. Then man points to himself and says 'American.' This is first time I hear of white men in America not Russian. I learn later this man's name is Denny; he is boss of these *Americans*.

"They call little village *Seattle*; they say it is name of local Indian chief, though I never meet him. But … there is nothing for a young man to do in little town like this, except cut big trees, which … well, I have already said what I think of *that*. They made me to understand there was much bigger town further down coast. A place so big they have special word for it: *'city.'* They name this place *Port Land*, and soon I am able to get ride on trading boat heading down coast."

"'*City*' … is such tiny word for such big place. You men living your lives in great land of America are not knowing what this place called *Port Land* meant for me. Never before have I seen anything like this. People everywhere, moving about like ants in hill. Great ships coming and going always. And whole streets full of saloons, new kinds of alcohol I have never tasted before. And even some Russians are there, and they tell me all about the great city and the even greater land called America.

"And the *women*! By this time, I was not purely innocent, you will be surprised to be hearing!" He shrugged and put on his most innocent expression.

"Some young Russian missies had taught me things about the … pleasures of female kind. And Indian maidens had … taught more things …

"But I had not lost love for fighting, and here were endless saloons filled with endless stupid drunks to fight. I am surprised men say they will pay me to fight. Other men bet on who is winner. Soon I am paid fighter and am fighting for large group of people. And other fighters are not drunks, but paid, like me. I enjoy new challenge, but still … none of you puny Americans could beat me."

He grinned his huge, toothy grin, and slowly looked around at the other men. This time there were no sarcastic remarks. They could well believe it was true.

"Soon I am running out of men to fight. A man says he take me to new city called *San Francisco*, even bigger city where I can fight new men. So, I take ship to new city. *Port Land* was great, large city to me, but this new city was big beyond knowing. More of everything … ships, buildings, people, saloons, women, and *fighting!*

"At first all is well. Plenty good fights, plenty good money. Then in one fight something happens … I hit man and hear something like *snap!* Man drops to floor like sack of dirt, and not moving. Men say he be dead. I am not thinking much of it at first; you fight enough times, hmm … these things happen," he shrugged his shoulders.

"But people watching, gamblers and men paying fighters all leave quickly, with dead man's body lying on floor. I ask where they are going, and man says 'There be trouble. Police will come and throw you in jail. May even hang you.' I do not know what to think, or what to do.

"Then man walks up to me all dressed in blue, with bright brass buttons and fancy looking hat with gold braids. So I am thinking he is policeman, but he laughs and says no. Later I learn it is army officers' uniform, but at time I know nothing of such things. He is *not* afraid, but says 'Come with me, and I will help you with these troubles.' So ... I go. He takes me to place with many other men dressed like him. Lots of men, scurrying about, like they have important things to do, though I never saw anyone doing any.

"The man takes me to room with big desk and sits down behind. I sit in other chair. He says, 'I am going to send you to place where they will pay you to fight every day. And I promise they won't even care if you kill opponent; in fact, they prefer it!' Well, that sounded like place for me ..."

He laughed and looked around at the men, "Next thing I know I am wearing blue uniform, and am on wagon riding to hot, dry place called *Texas*. When I arrive, they hand me rifle and say, 'Here, Volkov ... now go fight Comanche Indians!'" he laughed again, shaking his head.

Jim grinned broadly, the cold cigar still between his teeth, "Well, you have to admit, the Army *does* have a great sense of humor!"

☙ℰℭ⅂☙ℰℭ⅂☙ℰℭ⅂☙ℰℭ⅂

They made camp early that day, just outside a small village on the Rio Grande called Del Rio. Although they were technically still on U.S. soil, on the north side of the river all the local inhabitants were Mexican. The company stopped to water their horses at a small stream a few dozen yards beyond the first of the houses. It was a pleasant stop, with a clear stream lined by a strip of green grass, and small trees providing welcome shade. In the distance to the east, the direction they would need to go, they could see tall barren bluffs baking in the heat of the afternoon sun.

Nathan decided to make camp next to the little stream. He still felt that nagging uneasiness about whatever was going on back home, with its inherent push to keep him moving. But he didn't especially like the idea of hiking up into dry, bare hills after a long day in the saddle.

He hoped they might also be able to acquire fresh supplies. So while the others were watering the horses, Nathan and Tom decided to walk in to the "town" to see how the locals would greet them. They left their pistols behind, assuming two unarmed men on foot would be more welcomed and less intimidating than eight heavily armed riders.

To their delight, the first inhabitants they saw were two young boys, aged maybe eight and ten. They were peeking at them from behind the corner of a wooden outbuilding.

"Hola niños! ¿Qué travesuras andan haciendo?" Nathan called out to them, asking in Spanish what kind of mischief the boys were up to. This was met by giggles from the two youngsters, the oldest of whom shouted back, *"Nada, Señor! ¡Nada!"* followed by more giggles.

"Que pasa! ¿Nunca han visto a un hombre blanco?" Nathan said, teasingly asking them if they had never seen a white man. Nathan could speak reasonably good Spanish. He'd learned it over the course of his many years interacting with Mexicans both in Mexico and in Texas, including several very close personal relationships. He found switching to Spanish often helped ease an otherwise tense situation. Tom could understand a few words he'd acquired from his time in Texas. But he'd grown up in the East with no exposure to Spanish, though he had studied French in school, which helped a little.

"Si, Señor. ¡Hemos visto hombres blancos, pero no a ustedes!" the older one answered, saying yes, they had seen white men, but not these *particular* white men.

"All right, fair enough," Nathan chuckled, reverting to English. *"Bueno salgan de allí,"* Nathan answered, gesturing for the boys to come out from where they were hiding. The boys giggled, but cautiously left their hiding place and approached them.

"Como se llaman?" Nathan asked the oldest his name.

"Mi nombre es Manuel," he said pointing to his own chest, and *"Mi hermano es Miguel,"* he said, pointing to his smaller brother. He paused and put his finger to his head as if thinking, "Welcome … to … our village … of … Del Rio," he said in slow, careful English.

Nathan laughed, and patted him on the back, *"Mucho gusto, Manuel! ¡Miguel!"* he said, tipping his hat to the boys. *"Mi nombre es Nathaniel. Mi amigo es Thomas,"* he said by way of introduction.

"¡*Su Ingles es excelente, Manuel!*" he added, complimenting the boy on his use of English.

"*Gracias, Señor,*" the boy answered, beaming from the compliment.

"*Manuel, nos puedes llevar a tu casa? Queremos hablar con tu papa,*" Nathan said, asking the boys to lead the way to their father's house.

"*Si, Señor, ¡sígame!*" Manuel said, turning and trotting up the dirt path.

The boys led them to a small house with adobe walls and wooden poles framing the roof. Several chickens pecked at the earth in front of the house, and they skittered out of the way as the boys trotted up to the front door. Manuel opened the door and without ceremony trotted inside, shouting, "*Mama, Papa! Hay unos señores grandísimos que quieren hablar con ustedes. Son buena gente y no tienen pistolas.*"

The boy's description of them made Nathan laugh. He translated for Tom, "Great big men who are very nice and don't carry guns!" They waited outside for the boys' parents to arrive.

The parents also proved friendly to the Americans. The man spoke reasonably good English, which explained the older boy's earlier greeting. They were happy to sell the men fresh supplies and even offered to bring them a warm, home-cooked meal, which Nathan accepted eagerly.

By the time Nathan and Tom returned from their excursion, the other men had almost finished setting up camp beside the stream, staking out the horses, erecting tents, and building a campfire. Although the sun beat down relentlessly during the day, it was still springtime. They knew from experience that as soon as the sun set it would take all the heat with it. The fire also helped to keep at bay the swarming insects that came out in force the minute the heat of the sun abated.

Nathan sat back against the trunk of a small tree, stretching his legs out appreciatively on the soft grass. He reached into his jacket and pulled out a cigar. He struck a match and lit it, the familiar warm sensation and aroma embracing him like an old friend.

Tom said, "A sip of whiskey would go nicely with that, sir."

"Yes … too bad your commanding officer forbade it." They shared a smile. Nathan had decided against bringing any liquor on the trip, preferring they all kept their wits about them out in the wild.

A few minutes later Georgie stepped up in front of him and gave a salute, "Captain, your tent's all set up for you now, sir."

"Thanks, Georgie … but you *do* know you needn't address me as 'Captain' any longer. We're not in the Army now, and by tradition only a rank of colonel or higher may use the honorary title once their service is ended."

"Well … yes, sir … but *no*. Me'n the boys've been talking on it, and … it just don't feel right to call you anything other. It would seem … *awkward*, sir, to call you by your given name, and 'Mr. Chambers' seems odd and too formal somehow. We all still think of you as our captain, sir, so we'd prefer to keep calling you by that, if it's all right with you. And we don't rightly care what the Army might think about it."

Nathan looked over at Tom, who'd been listening to the conversation and was nodding his agreement. He looked at Georgie and shrugged. "Very well, if it pleases you. I suppose we can say it's more of a … *nickname* than a title."

"Thank you … *Captain*, sir!"

Nathan sat and continued to puff on the cigar. Looking up, he saw Billy walking into camp. *Now, where has he been all this time?*

Billy had a scout's habit of coming and going without anyone noticing—anyone but Jim Wiggins. Jim always seemed to know where Billy was and what he was up to at any given moment. Nathan watched as Billy stepped up to Jim and said something to him. Jim turned and caught Nathan's eye, before striding purposefully over to him.

"Billy says riders come. Five white men, leading three extra horses, and … *a woman*."

Nathan knew Jim was concerned. In the wilderness, unknown riders likely meant trouble—serious trouble.

Nathan turned to the scout, "What sort of men, Billy?"

"Tough-looking men. Armed … pistols and rifles." Billy did not sound especially concerned, despite the potential danger.

"Lawmen? Texas Rangers, do you think?"

"Hmm … could be … but," Billy paused.

"But?"

"My sense tells me these are *evil* men, Captain. Bent on doing nobody no good. Except maybe themselves."

"And the woman … what of her?"

"A white woman … youngish, pretty maybe, but she hangs her head as if tired or … sad? Don't know. Couldn't clearly see her face."

"Is she bound?"

"No, sir. No bonds on her. But she rides in the middle of the group. If she tried to ride away, they could easily stop her."

"Sir, they'll be here in a few minutes, riding along the same road we came in on …" Jim began.

"Well, then let's be prepared to greet them. Disperse the men about the camp. Have them keep hands off pistols but unbutton holsters just in case. And spread the word; no one makes a move unless I do. Or they shoot me dead, of course," Nathan gave him a wry grin.

Jim, resisting the urge to snap a salute, spun around and trotted back to the others. The word was soon spread, and the men positioned themselves out around the camp, trying to appear nonchalant about whatever they were doing. Nathan continued to sit where he was, leaning against the small tree, not far from the campfire. He nodded appreciatively at Jim for his positioning of the men. It'd be difficult to get the drop on them, being spread around the campsite as they were. But they didn't appear especially threatening to the casual observer. Billy was again nowhere in sight. Back to scouting the newcomers, Nathan assumed.

He reached down and unbuttoned the flap on his holster, then leaned back to enjoy the cigar while awaiting the arrival of their "guests."

Before long they heard horses walking slowly down the road, just beyond the low rise leading to their camp.

Now within sight, the riders came on at a steady pace. When they drew even with the camp, just a few yards from where Nathan sat calmly smoking his cigar, they came to a stop.

Just as Billy had described, they were a tough-looking bunch, well-armed with rough, trail-worn clothes, dirty from a long ride. They were unshaven, and had long, scraggly looking hair sticking out from beneath broad-brimmed hats. White men, not Mexican or Indian, just as Billy had described. Nathan couldn't help but think, *not much different from our appearance right now,* and resisted the urge to rub his stubbly chin. He noted the newcomers had also removed the safety straps from their holsters.

The lead rider looked over and locked eyes with Nathan. He reached up and tipped his hat politely at Nathan but didn't smile. Nathan nodded his head in answer.

"Don't recall seeing you in these parts before, mister," the man began in a tone neither particularly warm, nor especially threatening. "What's your name, and what be your business?"

Nathan took another long drag on his cigar and then let it out slowly before answering. "The name's Davis," he said. It was not a complete lie. Officers were sometimes referred to by the name of their command, in his case Fort Davis. Something told him it would be wise not to give out his real name just now. "And these …" he said, waving the cigar in an arc, "are my men."

He gave the man a hard look.

"As for my business … I believe I'll keep *that* to myself."

The stranger stared at him for another long moment, then shrugged his shoulders and said, "Suit yourself, mister. Meant no offense by it … just curious is all. Name's … *Smith. Mr.* Smith."

"Well, *Mr. Smith,* pleasure to make your acquaintance. Will you and your men come down and share the warmth of our fire? And of course, your … *wife,* is it? She's welcome as well."

The man glanced at her, but she didn't look up. "She's my … *cousin* … taking her to visit our dear old auntie who lives just south of the border … ain't that right, *darlin'*?" he asked. But the woman continued to stare at the ground in front of her and didn't answer.

Very odd … Nathan decided.

"But as for your fire … we thank you, but no. We're anxious to cross the river while it's still light. Dear old auntie must not be kept waiting." He flashed a smile as if enjoying his own bit of wry humor. Nathan saw one of his front teeth was missing, replaced with a shiny gold one.

"Well, then. Good day to you, sir. Ma'am," Nathan tipped his hat in the direction of the woman. When he said "ma'am," the woman glanced up, and briefly met eyes with him. In that instant he felt a strong connection. It startled him, and he had to resist an urge to sit up straight and call out to her. She was trying to tell him something with her eyes, he was certain. But it was as if she spoke in a tongue foreign to him and he could not understand the words. And then she looked back at the ground, and the connection was lost.

"Good day to you, sir." The man with the gold tooth who called himself *Smith*, tipped his hat once again, and started his horse moving. The others followed, carefully eyeing Nathan and his men as they passed. Nathan watched until they were out of sight. He hoped the girl might turn and make eye contact again. But she never did.

When they were gone, Jim strode over and said, "Outlaws, or I'm a snake! And that girl … she's no *cousin*. A hostage, I reckon. I'd bet a bushel basket of ten-cent cigars on it!"

"Hmm … yes, I'm inclined to agree with you," Nathan answered, still staring down the road. "Jim … I'm sure he's already doing it, but please have Billy watch them cross the river and move on beyond. I'd rather not meet them again later tonight with my eyes closed."

"I agree with you there, Captain. An unsavory looking lot, I'm thinking." Jim turned and spit for emphasis.

Tom stepped up to join the conversation. The rest of the men had gone back to setting up camp and preparing for the eagerly awaited evening meal.

"What should we do, sir?" Tom asked. "Surely those are outlaws and have kidnapped the girl."

"Well, we may *think* that, but we don't *know* it for sure. If the girl had denied his story, or had called out for help, I would've shot that disreputable-looking gold-toothed fellow right out of the saddle. But she didn't, so now we don't know the real story. And probably never will, I suspect."

"You mean to just let them go?"

"We're no longer in the Army, Tom. There's nothing we can do."

"Well, yes, sir. But still … it don't seem … *right*, somehow."

"The Captain's right," Jim said. "We can't go chasing them men into a damned foreign country, outlaws or no. It's as good a way as I know of to get yourself kilt. Or end up a permanent guest of them Mexican Federales in some God-forsaken rat hole. No thank you!" Jim spat to the side, once again.

And so they reluctantly let the matter drop.

Jim turned and trotted off as ordered to make sure Billy was following the strangers.

☙☞☙☞☙☞☙☞☙☞☙☞

Fortunately, they soon had something more pleasant to occupy their minds. Their "hosts" arrived bearing the promised home-cooked meal. The young parents of the two little boys who'd earlier met Nathan and Tom came carrying two large baskets, each of which was covered with a white cloth. Nathan introduced them to the men as Fernando and Isabella. The men all took turns shaking hands enthusiastically with young Fernando. He was a rather short and wiry-looking man, who seemed somewhat overwhelmed by all the attention. He nodded politely and repeated "*Mucho gusto, mucho gusto*, nice to meet you, nice to meet you" over and over.

And they each took a turn bowing and expressing their gratitude to Isabella, who curtseyed politely in return, flashing them a lovely smile. She was an attractive young woman, a bit more on the heavy side than her husband. They both appeared to be in their mid-twenties, which put them at the same general age as Nathan's men.

"Hey, William," Georgie said, "ain't their names the same as the king and queen of Spain who set old Chris Columbus 'sailing the ocean blue?'"

"That was King *Ferdinand* not Fernando," William answered, for which Georgie received a good-natured elbow to the ribs, and a laughing "Told you so, boyo," from his buddy Jamie.

"King Ferdinand the Second, of Aragon to be exact," William continued. "But you are correct it was Queen *Isabella*. Queen Isabella the First, of Castile, in fact. She and King Ferdinand had married to unite the two disparate kingdoms of Spain and then rule them together. But they were not the first rulers Columbus approached to sponsor his expedition, having first proposed it to the King of Portugal, whose name was …"

But before William could say more, his breath was cut off by a strong whack on the back from Stan, "Yes, yes, William … we know you can teach us all the very interesting history lessons. But if you do, we will meantime be starving of the hunger while lovely food goes cold!"

There was laughter, and someone said, "Hear, hear!"

Of course the two little boys, Manuel and Miguel had tagged along, carrying various utensils for the meal. They were happily mixing in amongst the men, laughing and chattering in a confusing mix of Spanish and English. The boys seemed excited to try out the English their parents had taught them. But it didn't always come out as quickly or smoothly as they wanted, so they filled in the gaps with their native tongue.

The men settled down to enjoy the much-welcomed meal. It consisted of black beans, meat (Nathan suspected it was goat), and melted cheese, all wrapped in a flat, round piece of bread the Mexicans called a *tortilla*. They were also offered a Mexican beer, which their hosts called *cerveza*. It tasted a little different from what they were used to, but they thought it good. And after the past week on the trail drinking stale water from a canteen, it was a welcome change. They were soon joking, laughing, and singing boisterously around the campfire.

Stan, as usual, dominated the gathering. At one point he was bouncing the two boys up and down, one on each knee as he sang them a humorous song. It came out in a mix of English, bits of Spanish, and even Russian when he couldn't remember the proper words in the other languages. The little boys giggled with joyful enthusiasm, bringing smiles to the men.

Then Isabella called Manuel over to her and whispered something in his ear. Manuel smiled brightly, "Si, Mama!" and ran off toward the house. In a few minutes, he came trotting back holding something in his arms. When he got closer, they could see he held a small guitar. He brought it over to his papa, who looked up in surprise and laughed. "Okay, okay," he said, shaking his head and smiling. He took the guitar from the boy and settled it across his lap. He picked at the strings for a few minutes, making little adjustments to the tuners, and then suddenly started to strum the guitar. He was an excellent player, bringing smiles and nods of approval from the men. After a moment Isabella began to sing, her voice strong and sweet. The tune sounded familiar, but the words were in Spanish. Nathan, of course, could understand the lyrics—a ballad of two young lovers; but even the men not fluent in Spanish could get the gist, as the words *"amor"* and *"corazon"* used frequently throughout. Isabella met eyes with Fernando as she sang, and they shared a smile. Nathan had a pretty good idea who the young lovers in the ballad were. Nathan smiled to see the joy of love they shared; in the vast Texas wilderness, this simple human truth warmed his heart.

He rested his back against the tree that had become his regular seat at camp. He could feel the heat of the fire against his boots. He closed his eyes and listened to the sound of the guitar, and the young woman's lovely, exotic serenade. It brought his mind to another time … another young woman, also singing sweetly in Spanish, his head resting in her lap. But that was a lifetime ago, far away across a gaping chasm of time, heartache, and loss. He forced his mind back to the present; *best not to go there,* he scolded himself.

He looked up and could see the stars coming out in the evening sky, and he decided this was as fine an unexpected gathering as he could remember. He was sure the men felt it too. Such a sharp contrast with their life in the Army. Long stretches of routine and tedium, interspersed with moments of extreme danger and fear. This warm, human moment touched something deep down inside them.

He noticed Jim had his eyes closed and a blissful look on his face. William was staring at the fire as if lost in deep thought. Stan was waving a hand, and humming along to the tune, a broad grin on his face.

Jamie and Georgie were looking at the young woman and whispering something to each other, smiles upon their faces. It seemed to Nathan their eyes were watery, but whether it was from a long distant memory of a girlfriend, or a mother, or something else entirely, he didn't know.

He looked over at Tom, and they shared a smile. He leaned back again and idly watched the sparks from the fire drift up into the sky to merge with the stars, the lovely feminine voice providing the perfect backdrop to the beautiful scene. He closed his eyes once more, enjoying the sound of Isabella's singing.

He did not remember feeling sleepy, but woke sometime in the night feeling a slight chill on his face. He found someone had thrown a blanket over him as he slept. He pulled the blanket up over his ears, rolled over to a more comfortable position, and went back to sleep.

෨෪෬෫෨෪෬෫෨෪෬෫

The camp was astir well before dawn. The men were anxious to be on their way across the hot, dry hills lying directly in their path before the heat of the day set in with its intense anger. Nathan pulled on his boots, though he didn't remember having kicked them off sometime during the night. Their hosts were already there, pouring hot coffee from a large ceramic pot they'd brought out even as the sun was beginning to lighten the eastern sky. Nathan thanked them again profusely for their hospitality the previous night. For the food and drink, and especially for the music. He paid them the price they had negotiated for the food and supplies, and then half again more. They smiled brightly, nodding, and thanking him again and again. The men quickly had everything stowed and loaded on their spare horses and their single pack mule.

Nathan pulled himself up into the saddle. Fernando approached and said, "Thank you for your visit, and your kindness, Señor Nathan. We cannot remember ever enjoying guests more than we have enjoyed you and your men. Our *niños* shed great tears you will not stay longer and will not come out, as they do not like farewells. If ever you are passing Del Rio, we would be honored if you would visit us again."

"*Muchas gracias*, Fernando, we most certainly will. And if ever you have reason to travel to the East, you and your family will be most welcome in Virginia!"

He meant it sincerely, though he knew it was likely never to happen. Then he said his farewells to Isabella, thanking her in Spanish for the hospitality and the lovely singing. She blushed, smiling brightly, and once again he found himself recalling another young Mexican woman ... from another time.

They started their horses down the narrow dirt path that served as the road to the East. Stan looked back toward their camp and said, "Look, Captain!"

Nathan turned and looked back. The two boys had climbed atop the same wooden outbuilding they'd been hiding behind when he and Tom first saw them.

They waved and shouted to the men. He assumed it was a farewell, but it faded away in the distance. They smiled and waved back before continuing on their way.

They'd not gone far, less than a mile, when they came a fork in the road. Fernando had described it to them the previous night. The right fork led to the ford across the Rio Grande, and on into Mexico. The left-hand road led east into the hills, and eventually to San Antonio.

As they approached the fork, Jim called out, "Captain, Billy is coming up fast behind. Shall we wait?"

Without a word, Nathan raised his right hand, bringing the riders to a halt. They turned their horses to greet Billy's arrival. He'd been in and out of camp during the previous evening, but Nathan had not seen him all morning.

Billy rode straight up to Sergeant Jim and gave his report. He'd been used to doing this in the Army, Jim being named officer of scouts after the unfortunate death of Lieutenant Stewart. Billy saw no reason to change the routine now. He seemed to have little regard for their change in status from military to civilian. To him, the Captain was still the Captain, and Sergeant Jim was still the officer of scouts. That their uniforms had changed from blue to brown and gray seemed of little matter to him.

"More riders approach. White men again. Three this time, with one extra horse. These are also well-armed; all have pistols in holsters. Two carry rifles."

"Latecomers of the group from yesterday, do you think?" Jim asked.

"Could be. But I am *not* thinking so."

"Oh, why not?"

"These men seem … hmm … not so *wicked*. They are not ragged looking, and one seems much younger, and dressed differently, and not *hard* like the others."

"Not outlaws? Lawmen then, this time?" Nathan asked.

"Yes … I think, maybe. The two hard ones anyway. The other … I think not. They come. Wait here and you will see for yourself and can ask your own questions. I will return to the bush, so they will not see me."

With no further ado, Billy turned his horse and moved off the road into the thick scrub and small trees lining the roadway.

"Well, Captain, what do you reckon?" Jim asked, turning to Nathan.

"I reckon we'll take Billy's advice and wait. I'm curious what these riders have to say. I think we could spend the better part of a year out here and not see another white man. To see two different groups in as many days is passing strange. It seems unlikely it's just a coincidence. If I were a betting man, like you Jim, I'd lay odds these two groups have a connection."

"Hmm … and I'm thinking only a fool would take that bet, Captain."

So as before, this time without a word from their Captain, the men spread themselves out across the road and along its sides in preparation for their unknown guests.

Looking back along the road, they saw three riders approach, leading one extra horse, just as Billy had described. When the threesome came closer, the men could see what Billy had meant. One appeared to be the leader, about the same age as Nathan; he was clean cut, but had a hard look about him, with long mustaches running down the sides of his mouth. A second man had a similar clean-cut hard look, though he was younger. The third man looked younger than the others, probably still in his teens. He did *not* wear typical riding gear; his hat and clothing had a more *agricultural* look. But like the others, he did have a pistol holster strapped to his side.

The group closed to within spitting distance when, to everyone's surprise, the young man reached down and pulled out his gun. He pointed the pistol directly at Nathan, and demanded, "Where is she? Where's the girl? Tell me, or I swear by God I'll shoot you down where you sit!"

Nathan slowly raised his hands, palms outward. None of the men moved; they sat their horses stone still, waiting in tense silence.

"Put tha' thing away, before you be gettin' us all killed, *fool!*" the older stranger hissed at the youngster. Nathan noted a heavy, Scottish accent. He'd known several Scotsmen in the Army, so was familiar with the sound.

"Not 'til he tells me what he's done with my sister!"

But the leader moved his horse up next to the young man, reached over and grasped the barrel of the pistol, first pointing it toward the ground and then pulling it forcefully from his grip.

"Fool! Can ye nae see these ain' the men we been chasing?"

"How d'you know?"

"Well, for one, can ye nae count? Five men we been chasin', and these be seven."

"Others may have joined them. How d'you know this ain't them? This is where we'd hoped to catch them."

"If ye start payin' attention, ye may learn somethin'! These men ain' outlaws or I'm a toad! You can thank the angels they ain't or we'd be dead already. Look how they sit at the ready; disciplined, waitin' for their leader tae give the word. Nae outlaws have such control. Even most lawmen couldna' pull it off. Soldiers I'd say, though I canna' guess why they're riding out here without their uniforms. Well, how about it mister, have I missed my mark?"

"No, sir. You are correct." Nathan slowly lowered his hands, causing his men to relax … *slightly*. "We *are* soldiers, or rather *were*, up until about a week ago. We've finished our tour of duty and are on our way back East. My name's Chambers, late captain and commanding officer of the 8th Infantry out of Fort Davis. This is Tom Clark, and Jim Wiggins, who were my sergeants. These men are also from the 8th. Now, if you don't mind, I'd like to know who y'all are, and what brings you here—if your friend has decided not to shoot me first." He grinned, and tipped his hat toward the young man, who was now red in the face but silent.

"Captain Chambers o' Fort Davis? I've heard of ye. Good man, by all accounts. Sorry I am to hear ye be leavin' Texas. Our great loss, I'm sure. My apologies for the young'n's behavior, but once ye hear our tale, perhaps ye will forgive him his rashness. The name's Robert Ballantyne, Lieutenant and commanding officer, Texas Rangers up in Bandera County. This here's my sergeant, Henry Johnson. And this is Willie Taylor. He's a local resident of our county, and the reason we're here, or at least one of 'em. We're trackin' a band o' outlaws who robbed the bank in Bandera town, shot up the place, and rode out. Young Willie and his sister Sue, to their misfortune, happened to be in town when the shenanigans took place. Next thing you know young Sue's bein' scooped up for a hostage, and the outlaws're riding hard outta town. Poor Willie got himself kicked in the head and dropped like a stone. And now, here we are, hell-bent on freein' the girl, and bringin' them scoundrels to justice."

"But where are your other Rangers? Surely, you've not come here with only two men and a boy? Did you lose your men in a gunfight with the miscreants, or have you split up during your search?"

But before Lieutenant Ballantyne could answer, Willie snapped out, "I am *not* a boy. I am nineteen years of age, and fully a man, my good sir!"

Nathan turned and gave him a serious look. After a moment's pause, he tipped his hat toward the younger man once again. "Quite right, Mr. Taylor. I stand corrected. I can see you are indeed a full-grown man. Please accept my humble apology for my thoughtless insult."

Willie was taken aback by this unexpected response, sincere and gentlemanly politeness being the last thing he had expected under the circumstances. "Of course, uh … think nothing of it. And … and … I apologize to *you*, sir, for … for pulling a gun on you and … and for mistaking you for an outlaw."

This brought a smile to Nathan's face, who rubbed the nearly week-old growth of whiskers on his chin before answering. "Well, I reckon I can forgive an honest mistake." This response brought smiles to Nathan's men, who were also aware their present appearance was less than regulation.

Lieutenant Ballantyne continued his story. "Nae, Captain Chambers, I have nae lost my men. But as fortune would have it, Sergeant Johnson, myself, and one more o' our men were on our way back to Bandera. We'd been out escorting a pair of prisoners to a neighboring county. We were still about two day's ride out from Bandera when Willie came ridin' up tae us, all of a lather, and told us his sad tale. We debated ridin' to town and gathering more men, but I feared the trail would grow cold by the time we returned. So, in the end we decided tae send our third man back for help, while we started tracking the outlaws. We have left signs for 'em at every juncture along our way, but still, by now I expect they're a week behind us, at the least.

"We found the trail and tracked the outlaws for several days, but I began tae fear we were losin' ground on them. Since they were generally headin' south, I decided they must be plannin' on retreatin' into Mexico. It made the most sense, if they thought they might be trailed for the bank robbery, and with the girl … well, they might figure on escapin' across the border. So, remembering the ford at Del Rio I decided tae take a gamble, and foregoin' the slow process of tracking, I decided tae make a hard ride for the border. We were hoping to get here 'fore the outlaws and lay in wait. But now, rather than outlaws, we've found ye."

"Well then, all the more reason to forgive our friend Willie here for thinking ill of me. And … I may have news for you about the men you seek, and the girl."

With this, Willie perked up. "News? What news?"

"Before I say more … describe your sister to me, Willie."

"Yes, sir. She's only a year younger than me, thin and pretty, with brown straight hair just past her shoulders. Last I saw her she was wearing a brown, wool skirt, and white blouse. She had a straw hat on … oh, never mind … that fell off when they grabbed her. I … I *tried* to save her … I ran after the man who had her, but one of them rode up behind me and kicked me in the head. I couldn't walk or ride a horse until the next day. But soon as I was up, I bought a gun and rode out after them as fast as ever I could. Luckily, I ran into Lieutenant Ballantyne and his men or I would have never found them. I'm a farmer, not a lawman … I didn't even know where to look. But Lieutenant Ballantyne … he's a great tracker; he found their trail, and we've been following them ever since and … oh! I'm sorry, I'm just prattling on like a fool. Please, Captain Chambers, tell us your news!"

"Very admirable of you, trying to rescue your sister. As for my news, I believe y'all have just missed the men you seek. Yesterday we made camp back yonder, just the other side of Del Rio. Before sunset they rode through our camp. They had a young woman with them, who was much as you've described. She was *not* bound but rode amid a group of five men. Their leader is a thin, surly looking fellow, with long dark hair, short scraggly looking beard, and one gold tooth."

"That's them! Gold-tooth is the one who grabbed Sue. I'll not soon forget the evil smirk on his face as he wrestled with her. What happened after they rode into your camp, Captain?"

"They stopped briefly but never dismounted. The gold-toothed fellow said the girl was his cousin, and they were crossing over to Mexico to visit their elderly aunt."

"The lying scoundrel! And then what happened?"

"They rode on through camp. Crossed the border yesterday evening."

"And you didn't try to stop them? You just … let them go—my sister a hostage?"

Nathan reached into his pocket and pulled out a cigar which he proceeded to light.

But Lieutenant Ballantyne said, "Fool! Dimwitted sot! Stop insultin' Captain Chambers when he's the last man on earth who's deserving it! Do ye nae see? He nae had reason to stop those men. He *dinnae* know who they be, nor who be the girl. He dinnae even know if they was wanted men. He would have been puttin' himself and his men at great risk for nae good reason."

Nathan nodded to Lieutenant Ballantyne appreciatively and blew out a long trail of smoke.

Again, Willie bowed his head and appeared embarrassed. "Uh … yes. I apologize again, Captain Chambers. It's just … I'm dreadfully worried. Since our Momma and Papa passed a few years back, we two're the only family we got. When I think of my sweet young sister in the hands of … of … those beasts! It's … *unbearable*…"

Then Nathan turned to Lieutenant Ballantyne. "What now? Will y'all cross the border in pursuit? Or will you try to contact the Mexican authorities, to see if they will detain them?"

But the Ranger did not immediately respond. He walked his horse to where the roads forked and then stood in the saddle, looking down the road leading to the ford.

After a few minutes he turned back toward them and let out a heavy sigh. "I *dinnae* have faith in the Mexican government. They have nae reason to care about American bank robberies or hostages. Oh, it may be they'd be telling us they'd take care of it, all right, and would act the very picture of cooperation. But nae would e'er come of it.

"Nae, Captain. If we want tae catch those men and bring the girl back alive, Texas Rangers will have tae do it. There's nae doubt in my mind about that."

"Then … you'll wait here for your other men to arrive, before going after them?"

"If it were only tae pursue bank robbers, then it'd be an easy choice. I'd rather sit here waitin' on my men 'til perdition, than tae go in against such bad odds. But ... I fear for the girl ... what she may already be sufferin' at the hands of that bunch. And o' course ..." he paused and looked over at Willie, as if reluctant to say what was on his mind. He shrugged his shoulders and continued, "we have tae consider the possibility they may try tae sell her..."

"*What?!*" Willie squawked. "Sell her? Sell her to whom? For what purpose?"

But Ballantyne just scowled at him, so he shut his mouth, staring at his feet, shaking his head, and muttering to himself.

Ballantyne turned and looked Nathan hard in the eye, "I fear if we wait here for my men, we may nae recover the girl. But if the three of us cross the border alone, I fear we will fail in our mission and likely lose our lives in the trying."

They locked eyes in silence for a long moment. Nathan continued to puff on his cigar. Then he turned his horse and walked to the fork in the road. There he, like Ballantyne before him, stood up in his stirrups and gazed down the road toward the river and Mexico beyond.

After a long pause, he turned toward the Texas Ranger, and said, "I've ridden into Mexico twice before to make war. Once with the Army, and once ..." he paused, looked skyward and shuddered. "Once I rode alone and without the uniform. It was ..."

He closed his eyes and was silent for a long time, as if lost in distant memories.

"Well, anyway, I intended never to go there again ..." He sighed. Then he sat back down in the saddle, turned, and walked his horse back to where the others waited.

He stopped his horse in front of the men. "It's no longer our duty to go after these men. And ... I've not said anything before, but ... I feel something is *wrong* back home. I've begun to feel a burning urge to get there as quickly as may be, before ...? Anyway, I would *not* go to Mexico to chase some damned bank robbers. In fact, I'd not even cross the street on their account. There'll always be outlaws, and there will always be good men to fight them. But we've served our duty, and now … it's time to go home."

He paused for a moment, taking another puff on the cigar. No one spoke, and all eyes were on him.

"But this *girl* …" he paused. "This *girl* makes it a different matter. She's an innocent, held in bondage against her will. It's just … *not* … *right*. If I ride away … she'll likely die alone and desolate in a strange land."

He met eyes with Tom, who nodded. Nathan guessed Tom was making the same connection he was: the slaves back in Virginia were also innocents held in bondage against their will.

He sighed again, then continued, "So I'll ride with these men … to save the young girl or die in the trying. I'll not ask the rest of you to come with me. There'll be no shame in staying here and minding the camp until my return, or even in riding on."

He expected Tom or Jim to raise an objection but was surprised Georgie was the first to pipe up, "Well, hell, Captain! We never agreed to ride with you back to Virginia just to quit when the going got a bit tough! We signed on 'cause … well, 'cause you're our *captain*, and we're your *men!* So if you say you're gonna fight, well *then* …" he trailed off, blushing. He wasn't used to giving speeches, and hadn't intended to this time, but his emotions had gotten the better of him.

But the other men knew what he meant and nodded their agreement. A smile touched the corner of Nathan's eyes as he looked from one man to the next.

"All right, then. Willie … looks like we'll all be going over yonder to get your sister back."

"Thank you, Captain Chambers … and all you men … thank you very kindly … much obliged! This is most honorably done, and I shall be eternally grateful."

"Yes, yes. Let's wait and pull it off first, before you start in on that. Come, Ballantyne, let's return to camp at Del Rio, and make our plans. The locals may know of these men and where they're like to be hiding. If nothing else they can certainly tell us about the lay of the land on the other side; what towns and villages there are, where the Mexican military might be, and so forth. In the meantime, Billy can cross over and do a little scouting on his own."

"Which o' ye is Billy?" Lieutenant Ballantyne asked.

"None." Nathan answered. "Billy's our Indian scout. The man who's been following you for the past several miles, and who's even now back in those trees watching."

Then he looked over at Willie. "He's also the man with the rifle pointed at your back, who would've shot you out of your saddle if I'd given the signal." Nathan grinned, the cigar clenched between his teeth. Willie involuntarily flinched, ducking his head. He felt a sudden itch between his shoulder blades.

ক্রেডেওরেডেওরেডেওরেডেওরে

At the end of the day they found themselves back at their familiar campfire in Del Rio. This time there was no singing, and only a hastily prepared meal, although the little boys and their father had once again joined them in camp. Nathan, Tom, Jim and the two Rangers sat with Fernando, grilling him on everything he knew about the area on the other side of the river. Billy sat with them, listening intently, but not saying anything.

When Nathan asked Fernando if he knew the men who had ridden through Del Rio last night, he answered, "No, Señor Nathan. I do not know this man you call 'the golden tooth,' but I have seen him before. He and his men pass through the village a few times in the past month. They not stop, not water horses, not ask for food nor drink. They not speak with us of Del Rio, for which I am grateful. They look bad hombres to me, so I hide the niños and Isabella when I seen them coming."

Later, after Fernando and the boys had retired for the evening, they discussed all they had learned.

Nathan had found the information about Gold-tooth and his men to be the most interesting tidbit. "If they never stop for water or supplies, neither coming nor going, it must mean they stay somewhere just across the river. When coming into Texas they've not yet ridden far enough to have worked up a thirst. When returning, they're anxious to get across the border to their safe haven. And knowing it's not much further, they won't waste time stopping for anything on this side."

"That makes sense," Ballantyne said, "and seems good news. We may nae have to travel deep into Mexico; the better for us. But still, how dae you expect tae find them? Fernando described a village on the other side similar tae this one called … *Acuña*, was it? But he says the village is surrounded by any number of small haciendas spread all throughout the hills. Gold-tooth could be anywhere, on any one of them small farms. We *cannae* just go riding about the Mexican hills knocking on doors 'til we find our man!"

"True. *We* can't do it, but that's where I'm hoping our friend Billy will help us out. An Indian dressed in white man's clothes will be taken for a Mexican from a distance. And even up close, they'll assume he's a half-breed; and one more half-breed wandering about Mexico will hardly pique anyone's interest. But Billy's no ordinary Indian. He's a skilled tracker and man-hunter. If these men can be found, Billy will find them."

Billy looked up and nodded, a smile touching the corners of his eyes, but he said nothing.

"We may have to wait a while, though. Tracking is an art requiring meticulous attention to detail and considerable patience. Believe me, I've learned the hard way an officer poking his nose into it and prodding with questions will only make it take longer. Best to stay out of the way and let the man do his job."

"But how long will *that* take?" Willie ducked his head into the circle of officers, though he hadn't been invited.

"Billy can start across the river tonight. If I were to guess, I'd say we will have to bide our time here all day tomorrow. If we're lucky, Billy may return tomorrow evening, and we can lay our plans and start out the next day. If not … well, time will tell."

"*Ahhrgh!* A whole 'nother day!" Willie stomped off into the darkness.

But Billy did *not* return by the next evening, nor the day after. Willie was becoming more anxious and sullen by the hour.

The soldiers, used to waiting for their scouts and seeing no advantage to being in a hurry to risk getting themselves killed, were content to wait it out. They took turns on guard duty, but otherwise were happy to be out of the saddle for a few days. And though Nathan's nagging urgency to return home hadn't slackened, he'd been a soldier long enough to know some things just couldn't be hurried.

But Willie's anxious pacing and fretting was becoming an annoyance, so Nathan finally pulled him aside. "Have faith, Willie, and patience if you can. Billy's the best scout we've ever had. He'll return when he's learned what he set out to learn, and not before. It does no good to fret and pace; the best thing we can do is rest and be ready to ride out upon his return. If you pace yourself to exhaustion, how will you be of any help to your sister?"

He stopped his pacing and looked up at Nathan with watery eyes. "I feel I am less than useless to her in any event. If it weren't for the Rangers and you soldiers, I'd be as lost as a babe in the wilderness." His voice was beginning to choke with emotion.

"Then you must be thankful to the Lord God we *are* here. In my experience, such things are *not* mere coincidence. Think on it, Willie! In this great wide land, full of snakes, buzzards, and hostile Indians, you rode out with no idea where to go, or what to do. And then, as if by pure chance, you happen upon the very men you need to rescue your sister. And not once, but *twice*—first the Rangers and then us soldiers! No, take hope; it is clear God guides your footsteps, and likewise he will deliver your sister from this evil. In the good book it says, in Isaiah chapter 40, *'every mountain and hill shall be made low: and the crooked shall be made straight, and the rough places plain.'* A God who can do all that can surely bring your sister home safely. Have faith … all will be well."

"If God can do all that, why hasn't He already saved her? We are just men, and He is … *God!"*

Nathan sat and pulled out another cigar, lighting it and taking a puff before answering.

"It's a good question—one I've often pondered, as have many wise men, I think. It seems to me God prefers to use his servants, if possible, to carry out his wishes. Even as a general uses his men to fight a battle. If you were *meant* to find us, then clearly God intends *us* to carry out this duty on his behalf. And … some of us may've done things we're not proud of. Could be we *owe* God some service …" he trailed off, frowning, as if once again indulging in troubling memories.

But Willie seemed not to notice, "I guess that makes sense. God may be too busy moving mountains, *'making rough places plain'* and such, so counts on us mortals to help take care of each other."

"I think you have the right of it, Willie. Besides, I'm not keen on waiting around for God to solve my problems. I'm a man of *action*; put a good horse under me, and give me arms for the fight, and I'll be well satisfied! I believe God smiles on that kind of men."

ᔥᔥᔥᔥᔥᔥᔥᔥᔥᔥᔥ

The next morning, as they were finishing their breakfast, Billy returned. He was escorted by Jim, who had ridden to the river at first light to see if Billy might return. Billy's long-anticipated arrival stirred up the camp like an ant nest poked with a stick.

They dismounted and walked toward Nathan, Jim bearing a wide grin. Everyone in camp gathered around, eager to hear the news.

"Good news, Captain. Billy's found them!"

Nods of approval, and pats on the back from several of the men followed this announcement, but nobody wanted to interrupt Jim's story.

"Not more'n five miles from the river, at the far edge of Acuña village. They're holed up in … well, *damn me!* Like my Momma ain't never taught me no manners at all! It's *Billy's* story … so let *him* tell it."

Billy nodded to Jim and gave him a grin.

"Not much to tell. Not like tracking out in the wilderness. Too many people about. Mostly Mexicans … a few white men. Happily, no Mexican soldiers. Trick is to track but not look like tracking. Not easy without attracting attention. Not daring to ask too many questions.

"Found a dusty old bottle in a ditch ... once had liquor in it. I staggered around holding this bottle, mumbling to myself. Nobody pays any mind to an old drunk. And nobody thinks he's strange for staring at the ground.

"Found what I was looking for; one of the outlaw's horses had a bent shoe on his left front hoof. A clear track. Find that shoe, and I find the horse, and our prey.

"Bent-shoe horse is at a house selling liquor. The Mexicans called it 'candeeda,' or something like it."

"*Cantina*. That's what them Mexicans call a saloon," Jim offered.

"Hmm ... yes, could be. I sat by this cantina and watched, as if lost in my bottle. Gold-tooth and the others are there."

"What about Sue?" Willie asked, impatiently interrupting Billy's tale, "Any sign of her?"

Billy didn't immediately respond to Willy's question. He looked over at Jim, who nodded.

"No sign of the girl. Never came nor went while I watched. Dared not go in though. Likely she's inside."

"Damn! Let's go get her outta there! Captain! Lieutenant Ballantyne! Shall we not saddle up?"

"Just hold ye horses there, Willie," Ballantyne answered. "Like I said afore, shut up, pay attention, and learn! This here's the part separating success from disaster. Let the Captain do the job he has trained tae do. He's been dealing with the likes o' these jaspers since ye was a babe in diapers."

Nathan had everyone stand back and give Billy a little room, so he could draw out a map in the dirt. He wanted to know everything about the terrain surrounding the cantina. From long experience he knew Billy had recorded all the necessary information in his keen mind; it was just a matter of drawing it out. Billy described the cantina as about the size of a large house. Single story, with adobe walls, and a roof held up with rough-cut wood beams covered in thatch, much like Fernando's house. The building had a single door in the center of the front, and only one other in the back. It had only small, diamond-shaped, port-hole type windows, two on each exterior wall. It had an odd, asymmetrical shape as if it had been expanded and added onto over the years. From what he could observe from outside, Billy suspected the front part of the building contained the saloon, while the back part contained sleeping rooms.

Just a few dozen yards to the south was a pole barn, open on the side facing the cantina. It was low-roofed, but large enough to house many horses, under cover, out of the hot sun in summer and the biting wind in the winter. Billy had found the horse with the bent shoe there.

The cantina and its stables were located on the road leading south out of the village. It was about a tenth of a mile south of any other structure in the town, and several miles from any other building further south. A little muddy creek ran along the backside of the cantina, a few dozen yards away. Over the eons this stream had apparently carved the small canyon the cantina now occupied. The walls of this canyon weren't steep-sided, but rather rounded, as if the stream had wandered back and forth over the years. The resulting slope on the west bank, where the cantina sat, could be easily hiked. One could sit on top of the slope and have a view of the cantina below, only a few hundred yards away. On the opposite side, the east side, the canyon wall was closer but more broken and sharply eroded, creating several draws separated by jutting rock formations.

Nathan liked the sound of this. A few men with rifles on those slopes could completely control the exterior of the cantina below. And they could prevent anyone from reaching the barn to mount any kind of pursuit once they'd finished their business.

There was, however, still the problem of not knowing what the inside looked like, making their plan of attack more difficult. Billy said people were moving in and out in a constant flow. Mostly Mexicans, but also a few disreputable-looking white men. Many were armed. The men they were seeking appeared to be staying there, Gold-tooth for sure. Nathan assumed Billy was correct and there were bedrooms in the back.

Although they knew how many of Gold-tooth's men had ridden through their camp that night in Del Rio, they did not know how many other men Gold-tooth might have. And they didn't know how many of the Mexicans might take his side in a fight. If they just rode up and kicked in the front door, guns blazing, they could find themselves badly outnumbered, outgunned, and surrounded by enemies. Not a very appealing prospect.

Finally, they had to consider the problem of the girl. If she were close by when gunfire erupted, she had a good chance of being killed in the crossfire, along with any other innocent bystanders who might be inside.

No, Nathan decided, they needed to figure out a better plan. Clearly, they needed to get inside the cantina without violence, to reconnoiter the enemy's numbers and positioning. Then ideally get the jump on them before they suspected anything. Disarming the enemy without a gunfight would be optimal. If that wasn't possible, well ... he'd never shied from a fight before. And the Texas Rangers appeared to know which was the business end of a gun! Willie ... well, not so much.

Nathan and Ballantyne talked the situation over for the next several hours. They went through various options and ideas, with Tom and Jim offering suggestions and opinions as well. Willie watched and listened, but for once kept his mouth shut. The others either listened, or wandered off to take care of other duties, assuming their officers would figure it out in good time.

The scheme they finally settled on seemed a good one. It included a plausible reason for them being at the cantina and had a good element of distraction. It also took advantage of the fact Gold-tooth did not know the soldiers and the Texas Rangers had joined forces. He hadn't seen the Rangers at all and didn't know they'd been tracking him.

It also helped that Nathan had been cryptic about his business the one time he'd briefly conversed with Gold-tooth. He could also use that to his advantage.

The planning continued while lunch was prepared and eaten, and on into the early afternoon. Nathan and Ballantyne left nothing to chance, grilling Billy on every detail he could recall. Willie began to pace once again, but this time Nathan ignored him. Getting it right was more important than doing it quickly.

Finally, they completed their plan. Ballantyne briefly argued to launch it immediately, that they still had enough of the day left to pull it off. But Nathan was adamant that they give themselves the most possible daylight to work in, to ensure they'd be back in Texas before nightfall. He had no desire to spend a night in Mexico, and risk waking up to a company of Mexican soldiers!

So Nathan called them all together to go over it in detail. Each man would need to know his precise role. When he finally announced they would start at first light Willie groaned, but otherwise kept his mouth shut.

❧❧❧❧❧❧❧❧❧❧❧❧

That evening, as he sat in his usual spot against the tree, feet stretched out toward the campfire, Nathan smoked contentedly on a cigar. It occurred to him this delay meant he'd run out of cigars before they made it back to civilization in San Antonio, six days' ride away. This had become a pleasant routine, he had to admit. He was going to miss their little camp by the creek in Del Rio, once they finally left for good. This night, however, he didn't lean back and enjoy the stars.

Instead, he pulled out a small whetstone, and began to sharpen his large Bowie knife, the blade he'd taken as a trophy from the dead bandit, Moat Kangly. He wasn't sure why he'd begun to carry it. Maybe to remind himself what could happen if he lost control of his temper. Gazing at the knife he recalled the events that'd led to him acquiring it. An image of the shocked face of the outlaw, a neat bullet hole through the middle of his forehead, briefly flashed through his mind, and he shuddered.

He finished sharpening the blade and slipped it back into the simple leather sheath he had made for it.

Tomorrow he'd be riding with force of arms into Mexico—something he'd promised himself he would *never* do again. He leaned back, closed his eyes, and sighed a heavy sigh. He hoped this time would be different; maybe this time he could repay God, at least partially, for what'd happened before …

Then suddenly a Bible passage came clearly into his mind. He recalled it had been the very chapter and verse he'd spoken aloud the last time he had crossed over into Mexico.

> *The LORD thy God is he which goeth over before thee; as a consuming fire he shall destroy them, and he shall bring them down before thy face. So shalt thou drive them out, and destroy them quickly, as the LORD hath said unto thee.*

Chapter 4. In the Cantina

*"One is never really lost in Mexico.
All streets lead to a cantina.
All good stories start in cantinas."*
– Rudolfo Anaya

Tuesday May 15, 1860 – Acuña, Mexico:

The three riders came to a halt just outside the cantina. The sun was already beating down like a hammer, though it was only mid-morning. Nathan didn't know how long they might be inside, so once dismounted they let their horses drink from a watering trough next to the hitching post. A brief diversion, but Nathan had no intention of allowing the horses to suffer from heat and thirst. And besides, anyone watching this might assume the men had ridden farther and harder than they had. It never hurt to keep the enemy guessing.

The horses slaked their thirst, and Nathan resisted the temptation to glance up the hill to where the rest of his men and young Willie should be positioned by now. But it wouldn't do to raise the suspicions of anyone watching, and if the men were doing their job properly there would be nothing to see anyway.

They only allowed the horses a short drink before tying them to the hitching post and heading for the door.

Jim led the way, followed by Tom with Nathan taking up the rear. They'd come armed for battle; each man had two fully loaded pistols, one in the holster at his side and the other tucked into his belt. Except Nathan, who carried the pocket Colt in his vest pocket, it being too hot to wear a jacket; and the Bowie knife in its sheath on his left side, the side opposite the gun holster. They were expecting trouble and taking no chances. Besides, this show of firepower would be in keeping with their cover story as less than reputable businessmen.

Jim turned the handle on the thick wooden door and pushed. The door opened inward to reveal a dimly lit room, the only light

88

coming in through the small, diamond-shaped windows and a half-dozen or so oil lamps in sconces at various points in the room. This was typical in this part of the world where they generally sacrificed light for the sake of coolness.

They closed the door, and after a few moments their eyes adjusted to the darkness, and they immediately put their plan in motion. Nathan took a quick glance around the room as if looking for someone, and then strode up to the bar which ran all along the left side of the room. He noted Gold-tooth was there, leaning up against the bar off to his right, but he paid him no attention. Tom moved over in that direction, as planned, while Jim moved off to Nathan's left. Both men stepped up and leaned into the bar as if eager for refreshment. Nathan caught the barkeep's eye and signaled him to come closer.

Then, in voice intended to project across the room said, "*Pardon, Señor.* I'm looking for a man; a white man I'm supposed to meet here. His name is Barton." Though Nathan could have said this in Spanish, he chose English for the benefit of Gold-tooth and his gang. Also, he'd learned when dealing with Mexicans it never hurt to make them think he didn't know the language.

"No, Señor. I not know any white man of that name. But many men come and go in this place with never the giving of names. What is this man looking like?"

"He's about so tall, thin build, slightly older than me. Dark hair kept cut short, but with long mustaches. A hard look in his eyes; you know the sort?"

"Si, Señor. Many hard-looking men here, but I no think your amigo has been here."

"No amigo of mine. But I *do* have business with him. We're supposed to meet here today, this morning. Guess he's late. Well, goes to show how unreliable people can be."

He ordered a glass of whiskey, and with drink in hand, turned and looked around the room once again, taking his time. With his usual keen eye, he took in every detail. The number of tables and their positions, who sat at each, whether they were armed (most were), white versus Mexican. He identified each of Gold-tooth's men from memory and noticed them scattered all about the room, either by strategy or pure chance. He scanned the place from right to left, so he would end up looking at Gold-tooth. When he turned that direction, their eyes met. Nathan feigned a mild surprise as if seeing someone familiar but unexpected. He nodded to Gold-tooth and raised his glass in acknowledgment.

"Smith, wasn't it?"

"Yes, we meet again … but I'm sorry, I am a bad sort with remembering names …"

"Davis," Nathan answered, repeating the half-truth he'd told back in Del Rio.

"Ah yes, *Davis*. So, your mysterious business has led you to my favorite little watering hole."

"How's your old *Auntie* doing?"

"My what …? Oh, yes … dear old Auntie … fine, she's just fine. So happy to see her favorite nephew back in town after so long an absence."

Nathan smiled a knowing smile which Gold-tooth returned. Nathan tipped his hat and walked over to a table along the back wall in the middle. It was a round table of thick dark wood, scratched and stained from long use. He'd picked it for its strategic location. It would have a good view of the door and the rest of the room, and he could have his back to the wall. Two men sat at the table, one white and one Mexican. Fortunately for Nathan's purposes the white man was not one of Gold-tooth's, as far as he knew. *'Well, time to start our little game,'* he thought.

Nathan walked over to the table and stood looking down at the two men. They paused in their conversation and looked up at him. The white man said, "Is there something we can do for you, mister?"

"Yes, I want to sit at this table."

"There's plenty of seats, help yourself."

"No."

"Beg pardon? What d'ya mean, 'no'?"

"No; I don't want a seat. I want this table." Nathan was a large, physically imposing man, a stranger who'd entered the cantina with two other tough-looking men, all heavily armed. He was also a career army officer, used to giving commands and expecting them to be obeyed. He glowered down at the men, giving them his most stern, *don't cross me* look. Over at the bar Jim and Tom turned to watch. Each held a whiskey in his left hand but rested his right hand on his gun holster. Gold-tooth watched with interest, a smile curling up one corner of his mouth.

The men at the table stared up at Nathan for a moment, then looked at each other and shrugged. "No need to take offense, mister. We was just leavin' anyway, wasn't we Hector?"

"Si, si! We was just on our way out the door, Señor. The table, she is all yours!" They stood up, gulped the last of their drinks, and headed for the door.

Nathan sat in the chair vacated by Hector. It put his back to the wall. With a sweep of his arm he moved the empty glasses to the side and set his own glass down with a thump. A middle-aged Mexican woman came over and swept up the glasses to take them away.

"Just bring that bottle of whiskey back with you when you come, Señorita. I'm thirsty, and it could be a long wait."

The barmaid nodded and flashed him a smile, "Si, Señor Davis; si!" Nathan made a mental note; she'd been listening in on his brief conversation with Gold-tooth. Likely she knew all the secrets of this place. That might prove useful, depending on how things turned out this day.

Nathan leaned back in his chair, took out a cigar, and lit it. He resisted the temptation to take out his pocket watch and check the time. It was something an officer or a gentleman would do, not a disreputable horse-trader. And even though he knew when Ballantyne should arrive, "Mr. Davis" wouldn't know that, so there would be no reason for him to check his watch. So he tried to relax, enjoying the comforting aroma of the cigar, and the warm glow of the whiskey.

While Nathan waited at the table, Jim made a show of flirting with a younger bar maid, as if he hadn't been with a woman in ages. Come to think of it, Nathan decided, it wasn't far from the truth. Tom kept quiet with his head down in his glass of whiskey. From time to time he'd nod his head, as if drowsy from the heat and the effects of the strong drink. Both were pre-planned acts, but Nathan was confident no one else would know it.

After the planned time had elapsed, the door to the cantina opened, and in strode the two Texas Rangers. Nathan experienced what it must have been like when he'd arrived earlier, the doorway filled with a bright light in which nothing but the silhouette of a man could be seen. By habit everyone in the room momentarily stopped whatever they were doing to assess the newcomers.

After closing the door and waiting a few moments to allow their eyes to adjust, the two newcomers strode over to Nathan's table.

"Davis."

"Barton. You're late."

"Could nae be helped."

"Well, s'pose we get down to it."

"S'pose we should."

With nothing further said, Ballantyne, who was going by the name of Barton, took the seat to Nathan's left, and Ranger Johnson a seat two down from Ballantyne. Per the plan they left the seat to Nathan's right empty. They hoped to lure Gold-tooth into that chair, so he'd be next to Nathan's gun hand when it came time to get the drop on him.

"Ye got the horses?" Barton asked.

"Yep, fifty head, as agreed. Damned lot of nuisance getting them, too. Just'd get them rounded up when some whore-mongering blue-coat patrol would come by and we'd have to scatter. Or damned Comanche would raid us, and we'd have to buy back our own horses."

"How ye got 'em ain' nae concern o' mine. Everyone's got a sad tale only their momma cares to hear, and prob'ly nae even her."

"Yea, well, you're all heart, that's clear. Anyway, I got the horses. I assume you've got the coin to pay for them."

"Aye, I've got coin. Problem is, the situation down here's changed since we spoke before. Federales ain't so desperate for rides as they was. Price has gone down." There was an uncomfortable silence following this pronouncement.

"Barton" poured himself a glass of whiskey from the bottle in front of Nathan.

"We had a deal," Nathan growled, in a menacing tone.

"Deal's gotta change. I ain' gonna pay ye more for them horses than I can sell them for down south. I'd be cuttin' me own throat on that deal. If ye don't care tae haggle on it ye can take your chances back north where ye got them. Though … I expect ye 'customers' there might be a bit more curious about where they come from. Especially them that wears the blue coats and the tin stars if ye take my meanin'."

Nathan pushed back his chair and puffed his cigar, glowering at Barton. But Barton wasn't intimidated, folding his arms and staring back.

Nathan noticed the old barmaid was hovering around their table and those close by, and each time she returned to the bar she had a few words with Gold-tooth. He was not looking their direction, but Nathan felt confident the woman was filling him in on everything the strangers were saying and doing.

"What're y'all offering?" Nathan asked.

"Two dollars a head."

"What!?" Nathan slammed his fist on the table for emphasis, raising startled looks from several nearby patrons. There were now many eyes on them from around the room.

"You take me for a fool?! It'd be downright thievery at that price! I'd rather butcher the lot and sell the horsemeat to the locals. We'd discussed twelve dollars a head before. Two dollars! Only *two?!*" He shook his head in disbelief.

"Look here, Davis. I gotta make a profit on this business, and the men I'd arranged tae sell 'em to ain' buyin' nae more. So, I got tae drive these horses farther off south tae sell 'em. That's meanin' more fodder, more pay tae my men, and a less certain buyer where I'll have tae end up goin'. But … I'm a reasonable man. Seein's how we did discuss a higher price originally, let's talk about what price ye would be willin' tae accept for them fillies…"

It was all a ruse designed to take in Gold-tooth. They'd intended the horse trading to seem like a swindle by Barton, who'd offer a price ridiculously low. Much lower than the going rate in the area, and Gold-tooth would know it. Their hope was he'd see the horse deal as a way to make a quick profit by using some of his cash from the bank robbery. He'd offer Nathan a slightly higher price than Barton's, but still low enough to make a killing on the deal. The implication was Nathan and his men had been stealing the horses in Texas with the promise of a good price in Mexico. Now they had limited options with the law looking for them north of the border.

They began a round of haggling, with Nathan trying for a higher, more reasonable price, and Ballantyne, a.k.a. Barton, stubbornly refusing to go much above his original two-dollar mark. From the corner of his eye, Nathan could see Gold-tooth turn from the bar and watch from time to time, but he made no move toward the table.

The staged haggling finally worked its way around to the pre-arranged price, but there was still no reaction from Gold-tooth. Nathan resisted saying his final "yes" to the deal, and leaned back in his chair, smoking his cigar as if struggling with the decision. In fact, his mind *was* racing. *What now?* he thought. They had been sure Gold-tooth would bite at the chance to buy horses at a price guaranteed to make a big profit. But he seemed content to sit on the cash he'd just acquired from the bank in Texas.

He could think of nothing else to do, so reluctantly leaned forward and said, "All right, *deal*. But I'm still damned unhappy about it!"

Nathan was at a loss about what to do next. But apparently Ballantyne had been thinking on the problem and had come up with a new plan on the spot.

"Cheer up, Davis! It's nae like ye *paid* for them fillies, anyway."

Then he reached into his vest pocket and pulled something out. He set the thing on the table, and Nathan saw it was a deck of cards, which Ballantyne began shuffling. "I'll give ya a chance tae win back the money ye think I owe ye," He smiled as he continued to shuffle the cards.

"Hmm … the way this day has gone I'll likely just lose the more. But, well … why not? My luck is bound to change."

"Good lad."

Nathan thought he understood what Ballantyne had in mind, so he looked over to the bar, scanning down the row as if looking for his men. But Jim and Tom continued to ignore him, Jim with the young barmaid, and Tom with his bottle, so his gaze settled on Gold-tooth. "How about it, Smith? Care for a game of cards? See if you can help me win back my money from this swindler?"

Gold-tooth smiled, and tilted his head, gazing at the ceiling for a moment. "Why not?" he answered. "I've not had the pleasure of taking money off fools for some weeks now and find I'm missing the sport." He smiled, as if enjoying his own wit, flashing his namesake gold tooth in the process.

He came over to the table and took the seat to Nathan's immediate right. *So far so good,* Nathan thought. *Now we just need to get him to let down his guard for a moment. Then we can end our little play, grab the girl, and get out of here.*

Nathan offered him the bottle, and he accepted, refilling his glass. Nathan noticed he used his left hand to pour, keeping his right, gun hand free. Yep … it would not be easy to catch him off guard, Nathan decided.

Barton fanned out the deck of cards and held it out for each to take a card. "High card calls the game."

Gold-tooth drew first and showed an unimpressive nine of clubs. *Good, one of us will get to call it,* Nathan thought. But then Nathan drew a seven of spades, and Johnson drew a two of clubs. Since Barton held the cards, he let Gold-tooth draw his card out for him. A five of hearts!

Despite his mediocre draw, Gold-tooth had won after all and got to call the game. *Not a very auspicious beginning,* Nathan decided.

Gold-tooth said, "Draw Poker," and grinned his gold-toothed grin.

Nathan experienced a moment of anxiety; he'd have much preferred one of the older, more familiar games like Faro, or Monte. He knew the rules of Draw Poker; they were so simple a child could learn them in a few minutes. It was a relatively new spin on a game he had often played with his fellow cadets in his days at West Point. Back then they played Poker with only 20 cards: Ace, King, Queen, Jack, and 10 of each suit and exactly four players. The dealer gave each player five cards face down, which he picked up, careful not to show them to his opponents. Based on the contents of his own hand, he tried to predict its value versus those of his competitors and bet accordingly.

This new "draw" variant had become popular only in the last ten years or so. They now played with a 52-card deck. And they'd added a "draw" round, where each player could exchange any number of cards in his initial hand for new cards from the deck. After that they held another round of betting. These simple changes had, however, dramatically changed the game in ways not imagined by those who'd invented the new game.

The introduction of exponentially more combinations of hands made it impossible to predict what your opponent might be holding. This led to a whole new type of betting, not based on how good your hand actually was, but rather on fooling your opponents into thinking your hand was better or worse than it was. In fact, this new form of betting had so altered the psychology of the game that many people now simply referred to it as "Bluff." The element of chance had, to some extent, been replaced by one's ability to "read" other player's reactions. How they behaved when looking at their dealt hand, how many cards they exchanged in the draw, how enthusiastically they bet, and so on, all had meaning. Men who became expert at reading these "tells" had a great advantage over those who simply knew the rules of the game.

Based on Gold-tooth's confident grin, Nathan had a sinking feeling he was in serious trouble. Likely the outlaw had spent countless days and nights holed up with his fellow gang members, playing the game and becoming an expert at it.

Nathan, by contrast, had been an army officer the entire time this new game had been on the rise. Gambling of any kind was frowned on in the Army, especially among officers, it being considered ungentlemanly behavior that could lead to conflicts of interest—officers owing money to other officers. Not that there wasn't the occasional "friendly" game when a group of officers got together. But card games between officers and enlisted men, or even officers of varying ranks were strictly against military etiquette. Since he was the highest-ranking officer at Fort Davis, and the only captain, Nathan had rarely played the game, and had only seen it played a few other times.

But fortunately, Ballantyne, or "Barton," as Gold-tooth thought him, didn't seem worried, and immediately shuffled the card deck. It occurred to Nathan that lawmen also had a lot of time on their hands, with supervising prisoners and whatnot, and might also be proficient.

"Stakes?" Ballantyne asked, looking up at Gold-tooth.

He flashed a smile once again, looking over at Nathan. "Let's make it two bits to ante-in. And two-bits minimum raise, but never less than the last raise; I've no patience for piddling bets. Don't you agree, Davis?"

"Certainly. There's no sport in wasting time with miniscule amounts. But why not make it a half-dollar and have done?" Nathan tried to act confident and thought he'd take a stab at an early "bluff" of his own. But he had a feeling Gold-tooth had already read the "tell" of his initial sub-conscious reaction when the game was named.

Ballantyne scowled at Nathan, but Ranger Johnson shrugged his shoulders in acquiescence.

Gold-tooth, however, made no disguise of his amusement at these opening maneuvers, "Oh ho! Feeling confident suddenly— so soon after losing at horse trading? Perhaps it will *not* be so easy taking your money after all!"

A half-dollar ante was high stakes considering a common laborer might earn a dollar for a day of hard labor, and a skilled carpenter, or mason, two dollars. It *definitely* raised the game beyond the "friendly" level.

Things started out well enough, with Nathan winning the first hand with a pair of kings, netting him a five-dollar pot. He also fared well in the second with two pair, queens and sevens, carrying the hand. Ballantyne won the next round, but Gold-tooth never lost the smirk on his face, and Nathan worried they were being played by the more experienced man.

His suspicions seemed to bear fruit, as Gold-tooth won five of the next six. Three of these he'd won after the other men folded, so they'd not seen his cards. Was he bluffing? No way to know except by calling his bet and risking more money on a losing hand.

Nathan tried calling Gold-tooth on the next hand but lost again; Gold-tooth held the better hand. Nathan calculated how much money he'd brought with him, wondering if he would run out of money before they got the drop on Gold-tooth. But the outlaw closely watched Nathan's every move, and Nathan knew he couldn't draw his pistol on Gold-tooth while he was losing. It was a too-obvious move for the loser to pull a gun on the winner to re-claim his lost money, and Gold-tooth would surely expect it.

Also, there was an element of honor in it; Nathan didn't like the idea of "cheating" at cards, no matter what was *really* at stake. If he drew down on the outlaw now, it would look like he was doing so because he was a poor loser. To argue he did so only to rescue the girl would seem so much sour grapes.

But honor or not, Nathan realized he was in trouble and sinking fast. He could feel the sweat on his brow running down the side of his face but resisted the urge to wipe it away. He figured he had already lost somewhere around twenty-five dollars and had brought only thirty into the cantina with him. Ballantyne and Johnson had done slightly better, dropping out of losing rounds more judiciously than he. The idea was for Nathan to win; the Rangers were just there as cover. But Nathan couldn't afford to lose all that money; he needed it to replenish their supplies in San Antonio. And he had no way to get more before New Orleans where he had money on deposit at a bank.

Nathan decided to swallow his pride and take his chances. He planned how he would pull the pistol from his vest pocket and grab Gold-tooth at the same time. It would be tricky, and the likelihood of getting shot, either by Gold-tooth or one of his men, was high. The firm bulge of the revolver in his vest pocket reassured him. He'd have it out and cocked in less than half a second. He prayed that'd be quick enough.

On the next hand when it came his turn to bet after the draw, he reached into his coin pouch and realized he was down to his last dollar. To stay in the game, he had to at least match the last bet, which required him to put down a half-dollar. Instead, he announced, "I raise to one dollar, and I'm *all in*." "All in" was a term meaning he was betting the last of his money and a higher bet by another player couldn't force him out. The others could theoretically go on betting if they preferred, but they usually either folded, or called the bet. The two Rangers folded, not wanting to spoil Nathan's play, which left only Gold-tooth. Nathan had decided, win or lose, he'd pull the pistol and grab Gold-tooth the moment they laid down their cards. Although going out with a win would feel much better, he had only a mediocre hand—a pair of tens with a king high, so he didn't have much hope.

"All right, Davis. I call your bet." Gold-tooth laid another half-dollar on the table in front of him, grinning. "Show your cards."

The door to the cantina burst open with a bang, the intense bright light dazzling in the dimly lit room. A figure appeared in silhouette in the doorway. He couldn't make out the newcomer's features, but Nathan thought there was something familiar about him. He closed the door and then stood for a moment as his eyes adjusted to the dim light.

Nathan emitted a soft, involuntary groan as he recognized the face of young Willie Taylor, breathing heavily, standing just inside the door.

�****************�****************

Jamie and Georgie lay side by side in the tall, dry grass, staring down the sights of the rifles they'd borrowed from the Texas Rangers. It was less than two hundred yards from where they lay to the front door of the cantina. At that distance, they could hit a squirrel with no great difficulty; a man would be a ridiculously easy target. To their left lay Stan and William. William peered through the Captain's brass spy glass, while Stan spun the cylinder on his big Walker Colt pistol. They all surveyed the scene below, watching for any signs of unusual activity that might signal trouble for the Captain inside the cantina.

The plan had seemed a good one. If all went well, the outlaws would find themselves suddenly staring down the barrels of drawn pistols and give up without a fight. If not … well, then they would just have to deal with whatever came next.

In the meantime, the Captain had positioned the rest of the men on the hillside above the cantina, on the top of the gently sloping west side. They'd have weapons loaded and at the ready, so if gunfire broke out, they'd drive off anyone approaching the building. Or if the fight spilled out of doors, they could seize the initiative. And if need be, they could rush inside, guns drawn.

Willie was with them, mostly to keep him out of trouble. When he objected to this part of the plan, the Captain had calmly pointed out Gold-tooth had seen him during the bank robbery. So clearly he could *not* go with them into the cantina. This made perfect sense and seemed to mollify him.

Billy Creek's job was to sneak around the back, on the east side, with the Captain's hunting rifle. He'd work his way up onto one of the rock formations to be in position to cover the back door. They all had agreed he was the only one who could to do it without making undue noise or stirring up a telltale cloud of dust. An untimely slip or fall on the hard-scrabble canyon slopes could prove disastrous. Jamie assumed Billy had been in his position for hours by now though no one had seen him.

The men had been in place on the hill in time to watch the Captain, Tom, and Jim ride up and enter the cantina. They'd watched as Ballantyne and Johnson arrived a half hour later. That had been more than an hour ago. The sun beating on their backs had long-since soaked their shirts through with sweat, and still they waited. Jamie suffered Willie lying in the grass to his right. Unlike the soldiers, Willie was not a patient waiter. He fidgeted and fussed the entire time, emitting regular heavy sighs, interspersed with "How long should it take? It's been hours, what's happening down there? Jesus, the waiting; how can you stand it?" and so on, and so on.

Jamie turned toward Georgie, and said in a low voice, "Should I be shooting him now, do you think, and be putting him out of *our* misery?"

Georgie smiled, but shook his head, "No, it'd make too much noise and ruin the Captain's scheme. Otherwise, I'd vote 'yes'!"

"More's the pity. I for one am hoping the young lassie don't turn out as annoyin' as he, or I may regret havin' come to rescue the little darling."

"I can hear you, you know!" Willie whispered in a pouty tone. "If it was your sister down there, you'd be as impatient as me. And 'no', she's not nearly so annoying as me. She's a perfectly nice and sweet person ... to think of her down there with those ... those *men!*"

"Don't fret yourself none, boyo. The Captain may seem gentlemanly and all, but he's a stone-cold killer when it comes right down to it. Old Gold-tooth and his gang o' wolves've got no idea o' the lion that just walked into their den. Ain't it so, Georgie?"

"Oh yes, he's a hard one all right. The rest of us are just babes in diapers next to him. Why, I heard he was down to Mexico City killin' them Mexicans by the bushel basket while we was still a'home sucking our momma's tits! Don't you worry none about your sister, Sue; if anyone can get her out, the Captain can. And don't be forgettin' about Sergeant Jim! I ain't never seen a man enjoy a fight more'n that one! And Mr. Tom Clark's a cool hand in a fracas as well. No sir ... ain't nothin' to worry about."

"And them Rangers don't seem like no little sissies, neither," Jamie pointed out. "They appear able to hold their piss and liquor, when it comes down to it."

"Aye, I'd say 'yes' to that," Georgie agreed, nodding enthusiastically.

But their efforts were wasted on Willie, who'd stopped listening and resumed staring down the hill.

Another half hour passed, and by now Jamie was only vaguely aware of Willie's continued fidgeting, having grown somewhat immune to it.

Willie jumped up from where he lay, "I can't wait any longer. Something's gone wrong. They've been captured, or killed, or …" and he headed off down the slope at a run. Jamie lunged from his place of hiding, trying to grab ahold of Willie's shirt. But he missed and hit hard on his chest with a thump, cursing as best he could while trying to catch his breath.

Georgie took careful aim at Willie's back, and asked the group, "Shall I shoot him?"

For a moment nobody answered. Then Stan said, *"Nyet, NO! Dammit!* It would be making too much noise!" He stood, looking down at the others, and swore again, *"Blyad'! Der'mo! Eto piz'dets!* Damned fool! He's gone to poke bear in den; stir hornet in nest!"

"What now?" Georgie asked, "Captain told us to hold this hill and make sure no more bandits approached the cantina."

They stood and watched helplessly as Willie reached the front door and stepped inside. For a moment they held their breath, watching and listening. Then suddenly they heard a muffled *boom, boom!*

"Come, fellows, our captain is needing us!" Stan shouted, and he started down the hill at a run. The others jumped up and raced after him.

xxxxxxxxx

At first no one reacted with any alarm as Willie stood blinking in the doorway. His farmer's clothing and youthful looks were so out of place in the cantina Gold-tooth laughed out loud.

"What's the matter boy? You look like little Bo Peep lookin' for lost sheep!" he laughed, showing his gold tooth. That simple flash of gold set off a chain-reaction that swept through the cantina like a flash flood, leaving a trail of death and destruction in its wake.

Willie drew his pistol and waved it at Gold-tooth. "Where's my sister?"

The cantina went deathly quiet. Every eye watched the newcomer.

Gold-tooth paused in mid-laugh, a look of recognition on his face. *"You!* Fool *boy* … you should have stayed in Texas. You've ridden to your *death!"* He reached for his pistol.

Nathan launched himself across the table at Gold-tooth. Willie's gun hand quivered as he pulled the trigger, a loud explosion in the small room. The shot punched a hole in the plaster wall just over Gold-tooth's head.

Nathan crashed into Gold-tooth as his gun fired. The shot hit Willie, knocking him down. But Nathan had disrupted Gold-tooth's aim, nudging it off to the right. Nathan prayed it'd been enough.

Gold-tooth tumbled to the floor, Nathan on top. The outlaw's gun skittered away. Their table flipped up on its side, sending coins scattering on the floor and playing cards fluttering up in the air. A whiskey bottle fell with a crash, spewing broken glass and liquid across the floor. The round table had landed on edge and was now rolling like a giant wheel across the room.

The cantina erupted with a deafening chaotic noise—yelling, screaming, and the ear-ringing concussions of multiple gunshots, from various directions.

Nathan and Gold-tooth wrestled on the floor. Gold-tooth was quick, and surprisingly strong for his size. He slipped out from under Nathan and stood above him. Nathan rose and spun to face his enemy. Gold-tooth held a long slender blade in his right fist. It flashed toward Nathan, and he moved his left arm to block the stroke. He lashed out with his right fist, hitting Gold-tooth just below his left eye with a solid thud, staggering him back. Nathan felt a burning, stinging sensation on his left side along his ribcage. Gold-tooth lunged again with the knife, but this time Nathan caught his wrist, preventing the cut. But it had been a feint; Gold-tooth slipped a leg behind Nathan's feet and pushed. He hit the floor with a hard thump on the back of his head, Gold-tooth landing on top. Nathan struggled to clear his head. Gold-tooth pulled his knife hand free and thrust down at Nathan's face. Nathan blocked it inches short of his left eye.

Gold-tooth's face was now right in front of Nathan's. He smiled his gold-toothed smile. Nathan could smell his rotten breath. Gold-tooth leaned all his weight on the hand holding the blade, forcing it down toward Nathan's eye. His head swam from the hard blow on the floor. He felt his strength ebbing as Gold-tooth forced the blade lower and lower.

The noise all around them continued to explode in their ears, the cacophony of gunshots and high-pitched screams. Bullets tearing across the room, a buzzing sound like angry bees, hitting furniture, shattering glass, pounding against the walls. Gun smoke filled the air with an acrid, choking smell that burned the back of the throat.

Gold-tooth laughed and kneed Nathan hard in the groin. Sparks of excruciating pain shot through his body. The sudden, intense pain awakened Nathan's rage.

With a new surge of strength Nathan pushed to his feet, lifting Gold-tooth from the floor. He pushed with all his might, emitting a roar of pain, hurling Gold-tooth up and away. Nathan now held his great Bowie knife in his right fist though he couldn't remember reaching for it. He faced Gold-tooth with a burning fury. For the first time Gold-tooth did not smile, and a look of fear touched his face.

ᏚᎦᎣᏣᏤᏒᏚᎦᎣᏣᏤᏒᏚᎦᎣᏣᏤ

When Willie had burst through the front door, Jim knew the Captain's plan had just come unraveled. His mind had raced, *nothing for it now but to shoot our way out.* He'd done a quick survey of the room. Two of Gold-tooth's gang members had moved from the bar to tables at the other side of the room. This left only the one bandit still at the bar, about ten feet to Jim's left as he'd faced away from the bar. He'd take that one out first when the shooting started. With him gone, he and Tom would control the entire bar side of the room with the outlaws across the room on the other side. He'd reached down and unbuttoned the strap on his holster, suspecting others in the room were doing the same.

Willie had pulled his gun and fired.

Jim pulled his revolver and turned to his left to locate his target, but where he'd expected to see the outlaw he saw the young barmaid instead. In fear she'd backed up to the bar and was now between him and his target. She had her hand over her mouth, eyes wide. He reached out with his left hand, grabbed the

104

collar of her blouse at the back of her neck, and pulled hard. "Down, Missy!" he shouted as he pushed her head down, shoving her back behind him.

In the same movement he pointed his gun at the bandit who'd also drawn his gun. But he wasn't looking at Jim, rather toward where the Captain and Gold-tooth grappled with each other. Jim pulled the trigger, the Colt responding with its satisfying roar, flash of fire, and hard recoil. The bandit slumped to the floor. Jim looked up and saw Tom at the other end of the bar, staring straight at him, his smoking gun now aimed straight at Jim.

"Dammit! Dammit to *hell!*" Jim spat. They'd both shot the same man! Wasting a round, and the initiative in the fight while exposing themselves to their enemies on the other side of the room. Jim dropped to the floor, pulling a wooden table down in front of him. The next instant something hit the bar like a hammer just above his head, scattering wood splinters. *Too damned close,* he thought, and prayed Tom had found cover.

Jim popped his head up over the edge of the table and squeezed off a shot at a figure across the room, another deafening explosion from the big .44 Colt. His shot passed just over the top of the Captain and Gold-tooth where they rolled on the floor, impacting on the edge of an upturned table. He ducked back under his own table as something slammed hard into the opposite side of it. *Good thick wood,* he decided, giving a quick prayer of thanks for that.

He popped his head up again, this time on the other end of the table. The Captain and Gold-tooth were now on their feet, grappling with knives. Jim saw a man stand up, pointing his pistol in Tom's direction. *Fool!* Jim aimed for the center of the man's chest and pulled the trigger. The pistol spoke once again, and the man dropped like a stone. But Jim winced, realizing his shot had passed just inches from where the Captain stood. *Oops, damned fool! Don't hit him!* he scolded himself. Meanwhile the table the Captain had flipped rolled across the room, disrupting Jim's view of his enemies.

He risked a quick glance to his left and saw that Tom had ducked behind the counter of the bar. He was reaching up over the top to fire off his shots. Gun smoke now obscured the view of the other side of the room, but Jim thought he could see Ballantyne behind a table, firing his pistol. There was no sign of the other Ranger Johnson. There was now a whole row of upended tables in the corner furthest from the bar, from behind which the outlaws and their Mexican allies fired into the fray. Innocents who wanted no part in the fight were ducking under any cover they could find. The old barkeep and the two bar maids huddled behind the bar with several other noncombatants. Tom had to step between their huddled forms to fire his pistol.

Gold-tooth and the Captain were now in the middle of the room. They were circling each other, slashing with their knives, oblivious to the gunfight raging all around them, bullets ripping past as they fought, missing them by inches. A candle fallen from a table lit the spilled whiskey on the floor; a low, eerie blue flame snaked around the room, adding to an already surreal scene, before it burned itself out.

Seeing the Captain knife-fighting Gold-tooth in the middle of the gunfight, Jim thought it the oddest fight he'd ever heard of. He continued to squeeze off shot after shot at anything on the far side of the room that presented a target. After emptying the first Colt he was now on the second. Incoming bullets banged against the table, ripped through the wood of the bar, and rattled around the walls above his head.

❦❧❦❧❦❧❦❧❦❧❦❧

Nathan and Gold-tooth had now come to grips in the center of the room. Each man held the other by his knife-hand wrist, and each was trying his best to push his knife into the other through main force. But Nathan was the larger, stronger man, and Gold-tooth was inching back across the room. With a great heave, he stopped Nathan's advance, and for a moment they stood still, perfectly balanced.

Their eyes met, and Gold-tooth smiled a wicked grin, "That *girl* mean something to you, Davis?"

Nathan didn't answer, but it occurred to him Gold-tooth read his reaction like a tell in poker.

"Oh ho! She *does!* Well … don't worry, Davis … she's no longer a *girl* … I've made a proper woman of her … and you should have heard her scream!"

Nathan's face turned dark and his eyes widened.

He'd later be unable to recall how it had happened, but suddenly the two of them hit the wall with a great *thump* that echoed through the room and shook plaster from the ceiling. The gunfire came to a halt, and all eyes were now on the two leaders.

Nathan's chest pressed Gold-tooth's back against the wall and they now stared in each other's eyes, nose to nose. Nathan took a step back. Gold-tooth remained where he was, impaled by Nathan's Bowie knife through the center of his chest. For a moment he still held his own long, slender blade, but then he let it drop. It fell clattering to the floor. He reached up and gripped the handle of the Bowie knife as if to pull it free. But he hadn't enough strength; the blade had buried itself deep into the wooden beam in the wall behind him. He couldn't budge it.

Unnoticed, a man crawled out from underneath a table. He stood up and stepped to the front of the room, pulling a small pistol from his pocket and pointing it at Nathan. Jim aimed his Colt and pulled the trigger … *click*; he was out of bullets.

"Nobody shoots, or the gringo dies!" the man called out. He was an older Mexican and had seemed inconspicuous and unarmed. And he'd taken no part in the gunfight, hiding under a table the entire time.

"This is *my* casa," he said, "I am Señor Rodriquez, the owner, and *you* have come here uninvited, shooting up my furniture and killing my friends. You will leave … *now.*" He pointed at the door just behind him with his free hand.

Nathan turned around and locked eyes with the proprietor. "Not 'til I get what I came for."

Rodriquez's jaw dropped, and a strange look came over his face. *"El Diablo Blanco!"* he said, in a hollow, far away voice. His gun hand drooped as he stared at Nathan.

Nathan stared back, and answered, "You were there, amigo? You saw?"

"Si, Señor. I was there … I saw … I heard those same words then; I will never forget them … *'Not 'til I get what I came for.'* That was after many men had already died." Rodriquez gazed open-mouthed as if lost in a far-off vision. The man shook his head, looked at Nathan again and said, "I was with those who finally made the peace. No, *El Jefe*, if you wish it, I saw *nothing*. I saw nothing *then* … or *now*. Is that what you wish, *Señor León?*"

Nathan paused, looking pensive, then said, "Yes … yes, I think that might be for the best, Amigo."

Just then the door burst open with a loud *BOOM* that cracked the wood, and wrenched the hinges, knocking down the proprietor who'd been standing directly in front. A great, dark hulking shape stood outlined in the doorway, breathing heavily.

Rodriquez, now on the floor, rolled over and pointed his small revolver toward the door. There was a loud concussion, then another. The cantina's owner lay sprawled in a growing pool of blood, the unused pistol dangling limply from his lifeless trigger finger.

A very large man then stepped into the room and aimed the gun at the men on the far side of the room. In a deep booming voice, he said, "Drop guns and stand with hands in air, or by *God's arch-angels* I *will* be sending you straight to *hell!*"

The impaling of Gold-tooth, the sudden appearance of the giant stranger, and his slaying of the cantina's owner were too much for the remaining bandits. They tossed their guns clattering across the floor and rose with their hands above their heads.

Stan leaned down, resting hands on his knees, panting after his long run down the hill. And a moment later Jamie, Georgie, and William all piled into the room in a rush, guns pointed in all directions.

Nathan walked back over to where Gold-tooth still hung from the knife on the wall. "Damn it! I didn't want to do that. I meant to take you alive if I could, but the anger … it's just … *Damn it!*" He shook his head. He felt little remorse for killing the man, who likely deserved it many times over, but once again felt betrayed by his own temper.

Then as he looked at Gold-tooth's face, it surprised him to see he yet lived, and blinked his eyes. But he couldn't speak; blood filled his mouth and oozed down his chin.

"Shall I say a prayer for your soul?" Nathan asked.

But Gold-tooth just shook his head, and spit blood at Nathan. Then he gave one last smile, flashing the gold tooth, now red with blood, before making a coughing, gurgling, choking sound, and closing his eyes for good.

Nathan's men took charge of the prisoners with military efficiency, securing weapons and binding the outlaws who'd robbed the bank back in Texas. The others, along with their Mexican allies would be freed once Nathan and company were ready to leave.

They discovered Willie was only hit with a glancing blow to his left shoulder, thanks to Nathan's timely intervention. But he'd hit his head hard against the wall when he fell and had been unconscious during the whole gunfight—probably a good thing for all concerned, Nathan decided. William bandaged up the wound, placing a sling around Willie's arm.

Ranger Johnson had died in the opening moments of the battle, but he'd also killed his man, one of the original bank robbers from Texas. The two men had drawn on each other at point-blank range, and fired almost simultaneously, both hitting the other dead center in the chest.

Two Mexican gunfighters were also killed in the action, and three others had suffered gunshot wounds, though likely not fatal.

Plus, the proprietor Stan had shot. Jim asked Stan if he felt bad about killing the owner of the establishment, who wasn't even a bandit. "*Nyet!* ... maybe not bandit but *was* great fool for pointing gun at me."

Jim and Tom had come through unscathed, as had Ballantyne, though he still had a smoldering fire in his eyes.

Nathan strode over to the bar and looked straight at the old barmaid, the one who was always listening and reporting back to Gold-tooth. "Where's the girl? *Donde esta la chica?*"

At first, she acted confused, as if she didn't understand him or didn't know what he was talking about. He looked at her another moment, then pulled his Colt from its holster, pointed it straight at her head and pulled back the hammer. "Where … is … the … girl?" he asked again.

Her eyes went wide. "In room back of kitchen, Señor. I show you. Please, no need hurt old Marta … she will show you."

He followed her into the kitchen, Ballantyne coming along behind, bringing the barkeep with him by the arm. "I dinnae trust him, and dinnae want him outta sight while we're back here," he said when Nathan gave him a questioning look. Marta led them to a small wooden door in the back.

"In there, Señor," she said, pointing to the small door. Nathan tried the handle, but found it locked. He thought he heard a muffled squeal from inside. He turned to Marta, "Key? *Llave?*" she shrugged her shoulders and pointed to the bar-keep.

He looked up and said, "Oh si, si Señor! The key … yes, I will fetch it for you … it is back behind the bar… *un momentito.*"

Nathan turned back to the door and said, "Never mind." He stepped forward and kicked the door, waste high. It burst in with a crash. He heard another squeal. He looked in, but the room was dark, lit only by a small candle, high on a shelf. Nathan looked across the kitchen to where an oil lamp sat burning in its sconce. "Hand me that light."

Marta rushed to comply, and when she returned, Nathan stepped into the room.

There was a small bed, and bucket in the corner. From the stench he could guess its purpose. Otherwise the room was empty, lined with bare shelves. He could see there was a figure huddled on the bed, with covers pulled up over its head.

He set the lamp on a shelf, then came over and carefully sat down on the edge of the bed.

"Sue? Is that you, Sue? You needn't be afraid. My name's Chambers. I'm here with your brother Willie. We've come to take you away from this place."

The covers came down, revealing the face of the girl he'd seen back at the campsite in Del Rio. Her hair was all tousled and tears

110

streaked her face. When she looked at him, her eyes widened. "*You?!* You came! Oh … oh my dear *God!*" Then she flung her arms about his neck and held on tightly as heavy sobs racked her whole body.

Nathan lifted her gently from the bed and carried her back out through the kitchen into the cantina to where her brother sat resting, leaning up against the far wall. Jim pulled up a chair for him next to Willie, and Nathan sat in it, the girl in his lap. She refused to let go, still sobbing, her head tucked into the crook of his neck.

Willie looked up. His face was pale as a ghost, and he seemed wobbly from the blow to the head. "Sue? Sue! It's me, Willie. I've come to take you home, Sue."

She snuffled once more and loosened her grip from Nathan's neck. She looked down at Willie. "Oh, Willie! You're hurt!" She jumped off Nathan's lap and knelt in front of Willie on the floor. "Oh, how bad is it? Does it hurt much?"

When Willie didn't answer, she turned and gave William a questioning look.

"He'll be all right, miss. Bullet hit him in the shoulder, but just a glancing blow. No broken bones, but he won't be able to use that arm for a while. Lost a little blood, too. And, he fell and hit his head hard, so I expect he'll have a bad headache for a few days."

"Oh … oh, thank you for taking care of him," she said, smiling up at William as she sat down on the floor next to her brother. William blushed in response.

"Tell me, Sue," Willie said, looking over at her as she clutched at his good, right arm, "did they … did they … *hurt* you?"

"No … they never harmed me, and other than a little rough handling, never laid a hand on me. Several of them wanted to … wanted to … *have me* … you know, like they would a whore or something. But Smith wouldn't let them. He said I would be worth more if they didn't. I don't know what he meant by it. Anyway, he told them he would cut off their … their … *man-parts* … if they touched me. And I think they believed him, so they mostly ignored me after that. But he wasn't kind and always told me the most vile and wicked things. Like he enjoyed my suffering." She shuddered and fell quiet.

"Well, you're safe now, thanks to Captain Chambers, Lieutenant Ballantyne, and their men."

At the mention of his name, she looked back up at Nathan and smiled, though her eyes were still red and swollen with tears. But then she noticed the side of his vest had been slashed and was soaked in blood. It had run down over the top of his trousers, soaking them with a dark stain. "Oh, sir! You are wounded! Has no one tended you?"

Nathan looked down at the gash, noticing it for the first time. "Oh! Gold-tooth gave me a nasty little nick while we were fighting. In the heat of battle … I'd forgotten it.

"Well, let's have a look, sir," William said, coming over and helping Nathan out of his vest and shirt. William removed his glasses and gave them a quick wipe-down, putting them back on before peering at the wound. Gold-tooth's "little nick" was a horizontal gash along Nathan's rib cage on the left side, about halfway between his arm pit and his waist. It was nine or ten inches long and it cut to the bone. When William separated the skin of the cut, he could see several rib bones had been scored by the blade but did not appear to be broken. The cut was still oozing blood whenever Nathan moved.

"It'll need stitching up, sir. Doesn't it … *hurt* much?"

"Well, now that you mention it …" Nathan replied with a grunt. With his adrenaline subsiding, he could now feel a sharp sting, along with a deep aching pain. He also noticed sore places all over his body for the first time. He knew he'd be stiff and sore for several days to come.

Nathan sat in the chair, stripped to the waist, as William went to fetch a bottle of whiskey from the bar.

Sue pulled up a chair and sat facing him, pulling her legs up in front of her. She gazed at him for a long time before speaking. He figured she'd suffered a shocking ordeal, so he didn't press her, letting her choose what she wanted to say, and when.

"At first, back at the river … I thought you and your men were just another gang of outlaws. I'd had my fill of those and had no

112

wish to see more. But then I heard your voice and looked up and we met eyes, and I knew it was *not* so. I don't know how … but it was as if your eyes spoke. They asked if I wanted to be free of those wicked men.

"But I was too frightened to speak. The one you call Gold-tooth, who called himself 'Smith' told me if I spoke to anyone, he would kill them. And he'd force me to watch, knowing I'd caused their death. Then he would make me dig the hole and bury them. After which he'd beat me, just so I wouldn't forget. He was a horrible man …

"When we rode away from your camp, I could feel your eyes on me, like they were burning into the back of my head, but I daren't turn around. In my mind, I begged you, *Please, oh please! Come save me, sir … come save me from these evil men!*

"Then while I lay here, locked in that tiny back room, I kept thinking of your kindly eyes. And I prayed to God *you* would come rescue me. And now … here you are. God has made his answer!"

He shook his head, still thinking about the unintended death of Gold-tooth, "Maybe so … maybe so. But if it is as you say, then it's only because *He* has chosen to use me as an instrument of His grace … for reasons only He can fathom. I'm not a saint; I have no particular gifts regarding these matters, and no special virtues … *God knows.*"

She smiled, though tears still welled in her eyes. "You're too modest I'm sure, Captain Chambers. I expect the saints themselves said much the same thing when they were still alive on the earth." She hopped down off the chair and sat back on the floor when William came back to work on Nathan's wound. He suspected she did not wish to watch the process.

William handed Nathan a bottle, and he uncorked it, taking a big swallow, the familiar warm glow reaching deep down inside him. "Thanks … now get on with it, if you please."

"Yes, sir."

William began stitching the wound.

While William worked, Ballantyne came over and pulled up a chair. "Much pain?"

"None at all, why do you ask?" Nathan winced at William's latest ministrations.

Ballantyne snorted a short chuckle at the show of bravado.

"Chambers … I'm curious. What the proprietor said before ye man Stan shot him. He said *'El Diablo Blanco'*—The White Devil, and he also called you *'Mr. Lion' and 'The Boss.'* I've heard these names before. Rumors, mostly. Concerning a Texan who rode down in tae Mexico and single-handedly took on one of the local bandit gangs tae exact revenge from their leader for some earlier slight. After a time, the Mexicans began tae believe he could nae be killed and started calling him the White Devil. I always thought it just a legend. Why would this Mexican mention that legend, and act as if he knew ye?"

Nathan was quiet for a while and took another swallow from the bottle. Then he looked at Ballantyne, and shrugged, "I expect he *did* know me, though I don't remember him."

"What're you saying, Chambers … you were there?"

Nathan gave him a hard look. "It's not something I'm proud of, nor try to think on much. It was another time … I was almost … *another man*, I think."

Ballantyne's eyes opened wide, "It was *you!?* Then, the legends are true …?"

Nathan sighed and looked down at the floor. "Perhaps it's finally time I told the tale … God knows I've held it inside long enough. While I was still in the Army I … I really couldn't tell a soul. For the men, it'd set a bad example, and as for the officers … well, let's just say there are those who would've been happy to use it against me."

He winced as William poked an especially sensitive spot with his needle.

"Sorry, sir!" William said, but Nathan ignored him.

"Yes, Ballantyne, I think it's time I told the tale. But not here, and not now. Tonight, back in Texas, I'll tell it to you. And to my men. They deserve to know what kind of man they've been following. Maybe they'll think better of it."

Ballantyne scowled, "I very much doubt that, sir. But I will be looking forward to hearing the tale. Tonight then."

Nathan nodded and then stared at the floor, as William continued his stitching. Ballantyne tipped his hat, stood, and walked away.

William finished and looked up at Nathan with a smile, "There you go, sir. Good as new!"

"Thank you, William. I don't know about 'new,' but at least I'm patched back together. I cringe to think what my Momma would say if she knew I'd wandered off into Mexico and gotten myself into a knife fight on my way home! To think … all those years in the Army and I never got a wound half so bad! Less than two weeks into being a civilian and I nearly get myself killed. What's the world coming to, anyway, William?"

"I'm sure I don't know, sir. But my guess is, the same as it's always been."

Nathan started to laugh but cut it short with a wince of pain. "You're probably right about that. Well, at least we'll be safe from this sort of thing once we're back in Virginia!"

ɮᴑꙅᴏᴄᴚᴄᴈɮᴑꙅᴏᴄᴚᴄᴈɮᴑꙅᴏᴄᴚᴄᴈ

The thought of his earlier ill-adventures in Mexico made Nathan more anxious to get back across the border as soon as possible. The men searched the back rooms and gathered together any money or other valuables they found, assuming they were proceeds from the bank robbery, or some other ill-gotten gains. If not? Well, that was just the price of doing business in a place frequented by outlaws. Ballantyne would return the loot to the bank in Bandera. But first he returned Nathan's gambling losses to him, with a smirk causing Nathan to blush. Draw poker was definitely *not* his game!

They also confiscated any guns they could find. No need to make it easy for someone to take up arms and follow.

The men brought horses around to the front of the cantina, including enough to carry the dead strapped to their backs. They'd bring Texas Ranger Johnson back for proper burial by his friends and family, and the bodies of the three dead outlaws for the reward. The bodies were made ready, wrapped tightly in

115

blankets. All except one—Gold-tooth. Nobody seemed eager to approach the place where he still hung, pinned to the wall.

Finally, Stan strode over to him. He stood for a moment looking at the knife handle protruding from the dead man's chest, as if admiring the Captain's handiwork. He reached out and grabbed the handle, giving it a firm tug. But even with Stan's great strength the blade wouldn't budge. By now several of the others had stopped what they were doing to watch.

Stan turned around and looked at his audience. Then he smiled, and shrugged, as if to say, "sorry, but I must do this my way." He gripped the knife handle with both hands, and lifted his left leg, placing his boot on Gold-tooth's chest. Then he heaved. For a moment nothing happened, and Stan's face puffed up and turned red with the effort. With a sudden popping and cracking sound, the knife came free, followed by a great gush of dark, red liquid. Stan hopped back, out of the way of the red torrent that would otherwise have soaked him. The body collapsed in a heap on the floor and a thick red pool began to form around the body. Stan bent down and wiped off the blade on Gold-tooth's shirt. Then he turned and strode over to hand the knife back to the Captain.

But Jim stepped up and knelt over the body. Nathan turned to watch and saw Jim draw his small hunting knife from its sheath. He leaned in over the dead man's face. After a moment, he stood and turned with a smile, holding up a small, bloody object. It glinted with a yellow color—the gold tooth! Nathan scowled at him, but Jim just shrugged and said, "Hey, it's a purty little piece of gold, and he sure don't need it no more!"

ཀྵༀ

Tuesday May 15, 1860 – Greenbrier County, Virginia:

"Miss Abbey ... sorry to disturb you, ma'am, but they's riders in the drive. It's that ... *Mr. Walters*, ma'am!" The maid, Sarah had a sour look that did nothing to hide her disgust. She was a young black woman, good-natured and pleasant, but always a bit shy around the mistress of the house. She was the youngest maid in

116

the Big House and normally didn't watch the front door, but other duties had apparently occupied Megs elsewhere.

"Oh!" Miss Abbey answered, unable to disguise her shock. No member of the *Walters* family had set foot on the Chambers' property for nearly twenty years. Not since the current master, Mr. *Elijah* Walters' father, Percival, and Jacob Chambers had started their long-running feud years earlier. She had seen Elijah Walters, and his father before him, at church every Sunday, and on occasion in town on business. But she had never expected either of them to show up on her doorstep.

"Well ... then I suppose we must ask him to come in. Please do so, Sarah."

"Yes, ma'am," she said, and left the library, heading across the foyer toward the front door.

A few minutes later she returned. "I'm so very sorry, ma'am, but he declines to enter the house. He asks ... no, that ain't quite right, ma'am ... I should say he *demands* you come outside and speak with him, ma'am. I think he's not a proper gentleman, if you'll excuse my being so bold!"

Megs poked her head into the library, "What's all this about, Sarah?"

"Mr. Walters is sitting his horse in the drive, with one of his men. He says he won't come in. He says to me, 'Tell your mistress to come out here straightaway. I have business to discuss with her, and no time to socialize.'"

Megs scowled, "I'll just go tell him you said to *get!* That you said he can just take his sorry hide off'n your land and don't never come back!"

Miss Abbey smiled, but shook her head, "No, Megs, but thank you. Though I agree with the sentiment, we must not lower our own civility on his account. If he wishes to act the cad, it doesn't mean we have to do likewise. I've been sitting in this room reading all morning and it's a lovely day out; not yet too hot. A little fresh air will do me good, no doubt."

"Yes, ma'am. I expect you're right, but it still galls me him treating you that way, after everything else he's done ..."

"Thank you, Megs, but I shall be unharmed by it." She smiled as she stood and looked at the maid in a way meant to be reassuring. But Megs scowled in response. She and Megs had been together so long she assumed Megs saw right through it.

They exited the library and crossed the wide foyer to the large front door, then out onto the veranda. Miss Abbey took the lead, with Megs to one side, and Sarah on the other. They crossed the veranda to the head of the stairs, but here Miss Abbey stopped.

Walters sat his horse out on the drive, still a good fifty feet away. He stared at her with that odd, blank, expressionless look of his, and didn't seem inclined to move. Though under six feet tall, Walters seemed bigger than he was, being thick and muscular looking. In his early forties, he had dark hair slightly graying with a full well-groomed beard.

His foreman, Bob Hill, a taller, leaner man, sat his horse a few paces behind. Bob did not make eye contact with Miss Abbey, and she thought she detected a blush on his face. Embarrassment for his master's bad manners, perhaps? Bob had always been polite to her, and that seemed odd considering the behavior of his employer.

The young groom, Cobb looked up at Miss Abbey with a questioning look. He was out of his reckoning; no guest had ever refused to dismount before. He stood next to the hitching post a short distance from the bottom of the stairs looking uncomfortable.

"Well, Mr. Walters, I've come outside as you asked. But if you think I'm going to walk out onto the drive and stand under your horse, you are sorely mistaken. Will you come over to the veranda, or shall we simply shout at one another?"

Megs couldn't suppress a grin. Though Miss Abbey was kindly, and generally easy going with folks, she could display a backbone when pushed.

Walters said nothing but continued to stare at her without expression. Then he tilted his head, looking up as if thinking on what she had just suggested. He looked back down at her, and without a word, kicked his horse into motion and walked it toward the house. But he didn't stop and dismount at the hitching post as would have been proper. Instead, he ignored Cobb and walked the horse straight up the gravel walking path to the foot of the stairs. There he stopped, looking up at her. His man Bob stayed back by the hitching post, though he also declined to dismount.

Miss Abbey and Walters stared at each other for a few moments before Walters finally spoke, "Miss Abbey."

"Mr. Walters."

"I've come to see if you have considered my offer."

"I have read your letter, if that's what you mean."

"Then you will sell?"

"I didn't say so, did I?"

Walters was quiet for another minute, still no expression touching his face. Miss Abbey thought him the oddest man she'd ever met, and thoroughly unlikeable in every way. She also found she had an instinctive fear of him, though she didn't know why, and had told no one of it, not even Megs.

"It would be for the best if you would sell. With Jacob gone … things could become … very *difficult* for you. A woman … *alone*. With such a large estate … and so many slaves. I wonder what *they* may be plotting now the firm hand of their master has been removed. A mass escape? A violent uprising? Such things have been known to happen without iron hard discipline.

"And … there's no telling what … *predations* might occur from unscrupulous persons."

Miss Abbey, despite her fear of the man, was feeling the heat rising. "Oh … you mean *predations* like cutting timber on my lands without my leave, burning my crops, or convincing my cotton broker to stop doing business with me? Or do you mean *unscrupulous* persons like those threatening and harassing my servants on their way to town for supplies? Or trying to hire away my long-time farmhands!?"

If she thought to provoke a reaction by her thinly veiled accusations, she was quickly disappointed. He continued giving her that odd, bland look she found so chilling.

"I may consider negotiating *somewhat* on the price … for the moment. But don't wait too long. Once things become … *untenable* for you … the price will drop."

Despite her best intentions, Walters' smug confidence fired her temper. The next words she spoke gave her great satisfaction though she immediately regretted them. "I have news for you, *Mr. Walters*. My son, *Army Captain* Nathaniel Chambers, has resigned his commission and is returning home from West Texas where he's been fighting Indians and dealing with … *unscrupulous persons*. He'll soon return and take charge of this farm. I believe you may find my son much more difficult to … *negotiate with* … than a lonely widow!"

It pleased her to see his reaction; for a moment Walters seemed surprised—shocked even, his eyes wide. But he quickly recovered his composure, resuming his bland expression. He turned his horse and slowly rode off down the drive. Bob Hill met eyes with Abbey for a moment longer, a curious expression on his face. Then he tipped his hat politely before turning and following Walters.

Megs turned to Miss Abbey, "You ought not to have said what you did about Mr. Nathan returning, ma'am. If Walters means to do something wicked, he now knows he gotta do it quick."

She met eyes with Megs, "Yes, I know, dear. You're right … *absolutely* right." Then she smiled, "But it sure felt good to say it!"

Megs returned the smile and nodded her head as they turned and headed for the door.

ಐ𝑅ಌ𝑅ಐ𝑅ಌ𝑅ಐ𝑅ಌ𝑅

That evening, back at their camp in Del Rio, Nathan sat on a rock and distractedly stirred the campfire with a stick.

They'd finished their meal, once again provided by their Mexican hosts, who had just ushered their young boys off to bed, whining and complaining the whole way.

Ballantyne stepped up to Nathan and held something out to him. Nathan looked up and saw what appeared to be a whiskey bottle.

"'Tis a Scottish spirit, Chambers. Some folks just call it 'Scotch.' Best liquor there is, though some say it takes a bit gettin' used to if a man's been drinkin' your sweet American whiskey."

Nathan reached out and accepted the bottle with a nod. He pulled the cork and took a swallow. Ballantyne watched his reaction and grinned.

Nathan looked up at him and smiled, "You're right … it will take some getting used to."

"Like us Scotsmen, it's a bit too *complex* for some tastes," Ballantyne said with a wink.

Nathan grinned and took another drink, "Thanks, Ballantyne. By the end of the evening, I may acquire a liking for it."

"Aye … I believe ye shall, sir. But now … I'm thinkin' ye owe me a tall tale of old Mexico."

Nathan sighed, then nodded. "Yes, I did promise it. Though now the time has come, I find I am still reluctant to speak on it." He sighed again and shrugged, "Might as well get it over with. Gather the others, if you would. I'd rather not have to repeat any of it, nor have anyone hear it second-hand."

Ballantyne quickly spread the word, and soon all were seated around the fire, gazing intently at the Captain. Nathan wasn't surprised Billy was absent; he'd be out keeping an eye on things as usual, despite their devastating victory over the outlaws. Nathan thought about how Billy might react to the story and shrugged. He'd probably heard worse from all his years in Texas fighting the Comanche. Likely he would think little of the tale, and it wouldn't change his opinion of his captain one iota.

Nathan was surprised, however, when Sue joined the men. He winced at the thought of telling the story to the innocent young woman. It was not a story for the faint of heart. But then, after what she'd just been through, perhaps she'd earned the right.

"When I graduated from the Military Academy at West Point, they made me a second lieutenant," he began. "I was cocksure … full of confidence and afraid of nothing. So when they told us there was going to be a war with Mexico, I was thrilled. For one, I'd be able to put all my years of military training to use almost immediately."

He looked up and gazed at his audience, locking eyes with Stan, "But more than that … I'd finally have the chance to fight holding nothing back. Always before I'd feared going too far … killing someone in a fight. I'd always had to temper my actions—never completely unleashing the fury of my emotions and full extent of my capabilities."

Stan nodded his understanding, but for once wasn't smiling.

Nathan stared back at the fire, then snorted, "Be careful what you wish for! In Mexico I learned what *real* war was. For the first time, I felt fear. For the first time, I learned what it was like to unleash the fury, holding nothing back. To kill men. Up close, looking them in the eye. Sticking a bayonet into them—hearing them scream in fear and pain. It was …"

He shook his head and was silent for a moment. "At first, we had good success against the Mexican Army, winning our battles easily and driving the enemy from the field in disarray. Though we were almost always outnumbered and cut off from resupply, still we advanced with seeming ease.

"Our young officers, many graduates of West Point like myself, proved well trained and courageous. And our commanding General, Winfield Scott, was unmatched by the enemy's commanders. A veteran of the War of 1812 against the British, he was a master at strategy and tactics. No matter what the enemy threw at us, he always seemed to have a solution, a way to turn the tables on them.

"As for me, my immediate commander, Captain William Montrose Graham, was the very image of what an officer should be—smart, fearless, and resolute. A man who cared about the welfare of his men, but always got the most out of them in battle. We admired him greatly and never wanted to displease him."

He chuckled, "You men think of me as 'the Captain', but to me, *he* will always be 'the Captain.' He was my mentor, and everything I aspired to be.

"But the closer we got to the Mexican capital, the more their defenses stiffened. The battles became larger, more difficult, and more dangerous. Until one day we stood outside the town of Molino del Rey. Rumors said the enemy was manufacturing cannon and other armaments in the town, so General Scott was anxious to capture it.

"The Mexican Army was well dug in behind thick adobe walls. The approach was flat and open, providing no cover for an attack. And we'd heard they had plenty of artillery and ammunition."

He sighed, and for a moment seemed unable to continue. Tears welled in his eyes, and his voice became choked with emotion.

"It was the most horrific day of my life. We marched in lines across an open field under heavy rifle and cannon fire. I will never forget the sounds, smells, and sights of that day. It was … Hell on Earth … truly. Men died in swaths from grapeshot and cannister, cut to pieces, blood splattered on the scorched, dusty ground. The roaring of the cannon was deafening, and the gun smoke was so thick in the hot, still air we could scarcely breathe.

"And yet through the chaos, Captain Graham led us steadily forward atop his horse. Waving his sword, shouting encouragement. Utterly fearless. As long as he was there, we would keep moving ahead; such was our respect and affection for him.

"Then even as it seemed we'd made it through the worst and were approaching the city walls, he fell. I happened to be looking over at him as he toppled from his mount. I rushed to him, but he was already gone, a bullet having pierced his great heart.

"I looked back at our rows of men, tears in my eyes. They stood still, staring in shock at the now riderless horse, prancing nervously."

Nathan paused again and had to wipe his eyes with his sleeve. Tom had to look away; he found it difficult to see the Captain this distraught. It was not something he was used to, and it unsettled him. The other men had sullen looks, and many gazed at their boots or into the fire. Only Sue cried unashamedly, wiping tears from her face with a handkerchief.

Nathan cleared his throat and resumed the narrative, his voice now steadier. "As I surveyed the ranks of our men, I realized for the first time our two first lieutenants were gone, cut down sometime during the long march. I was only nineteen years old, and the man I admired most in life had just been killed before my eyes. I knew if I faltered, all the men in our command would hesitate, and all would die."

He gave a bitter, mirthless chuckle. "I would like to say I did what I did next out of duty, honor, courage, or some other admirable motivation. But the truth is, the senseless death of my beloved commander fired my anger. He should never have ridden into the teeth of the enemy guns atop a horse where he was so exposed, and such an easy target. And the men should never have been ordered to march in straight lines toward almost certain death.

"These thoughts raced through my head and filled me with a burning, mind-numbing rage. I reached down, picked up the Captain's sword, and raised it high. *'Come on men,'* I shouted, *'let us avenge our captain! CHARGE!!!'* I turned and ran toward the enemy walls, now just yards away, holding the Captain's sword above my head, and shouting until my throat was raw. Bullets screamed past me as I ran, but I was never hit. The noise was so deafening I didn't know if my men had heard my yell. And the smoke was so thick I couldn't be sure they'd seen my charge. But I no longer cared and never looked back.

"When I reached the wall, I vaulted on top, then leapt down into the midst of the enemy, fighting with the sword. Mexican soldiers surrounded me, a half-dozen or more, trying their best to impale me with bayonets.

"I fought with ferocity and desperation, venting all my pain, grief, and anger at the enemy. Hacking, thrusting, slashing. One went down, and then another, yet still I was desperately beset on all sides as more came to join the fight. And all the while I never stopped shouting … shouting … mindlessly shouting. I believed these were my final moments on Earth, but I meant to go down fighting to the last heartbeat.

"But then the enemy soldiers turned and fled back into the town, leaving me standing there alone, gasping for breath. I looked over as a flood of blue-coated soldiers poured over the wall, bayonets thrust forward. My men had followed after all. They rushed past me, pursuing the fleeing enemy through the streets of the town.

"But my battle was over. I suddenly felt drained and unsteady on my feet. I thought I might collapse onto the ground. One of our sergeants came over and took me by the arm. I remember his name was Harrigan; he was a proud Irishman, like Jamie. 'That was well done, sir! As brave a thing as I ever hope to see,' he said to me. But when I tried to thank him, and tell him it wasn't bravery at all, I found I had no voice. Nor could I speak a word the rest of that day."

Nathan leaned back and swallowed another shot from Ballantyne's bottle. After a moment he continued, "After that they promoted me to first lieutenant and officially gave me command of what remained of Captain Graham's original company. There were other desperate battles, of course, furious hand to hand combat in the streets of the cities and towns. I led the men into battle again and again, trying my best to preserve the lives of my men while still achieving our objectives. My proudest moment was watching our men raise the Stars and Stripes above the capitol building in Mexico City. Even as the men unfurled the flag, General Scott pinned a gold medal on me, and several others, for 'uncommon valor in the face of the enemy.'

"After the war, most of the commands were disbanded. They sent the enlisted men home and transferred the officers back east to Washington City to serve in the War Department.

"But I balked at the idea of sitting behind a desk after the intense adventure I'd just experienced. I also found my brief taste of life in the West had been to my liking. And ironically, despite the war against their government, I had developed a high regard and great affection for the Mexican people. I had made several good friends among them along the way and was even beginning to pick up the language.

"So when the Army asked for volunteers to stay out in Texas to secure the frontier, I jumped at the chance. I'm sure many of my fellow officers thought I must have been out in the sun too long!"

He chuckled, but then his face turned serious again. "Maybe if I'd known what was coming next, I would never have stayed. If I'd known about ... *El Diablo Blanco*."

He shuddered involuntarily, shook his head, and sighed before taking another shot from the bottle. "This part of the story begins two years later when I was stationed at the Army base on a ranch just north of the border. It was right next to the small town of Franklin, which was within the New Mexico Territory at the time. The station was so new it hadn't been given an official name yet and was simply referred to as 'The Army post opposite El Paso del Norte, Mexico.' The town on the U.S. side is now named El Paso, Texas ..."

Chapter 5. El Diablo Blanco

"Revenge, the sweetest
morsel to the mouth that
ever was cooked in hell."
– Walter Scott

(Eleven Years Earlier ...)

Tuesday May 1, 1849 – U.S. Army post opposite El Paso del Norte, Mexico:

Maria giggled, flashing the dazzling smile that always set Nathan's heart aflutter, handsomely rewarding his latest witty remark. She turned away, continuing to wipe dry the glass she'd just finished washing before setting in on the shelf behind the bar. "Lieutenant Chambers, you are such a wit! How is it you always make me laugh so?"

"I just love to see you smile, *mi amor!*" he answered, returning a bright smile of his own.

With her large, coal-black eyes; long, flowing dark hair; beautiful bronze skin; full lips; and perfect, contrasting white teeth; Nathan thought Maria the most fabulous, exotic woman alive. He never tired of gazing at her and longed to see her whenever they were apart.

But it gratified him to discover she was more than just devastatingly gorgeous; she was also kind, sweet, smart, and talented. Quick to smile and to laugh, she could naturally light up a gloomy day. And she had a lovely singing voice, which she enjoyed using while playing guitar. She sang in the cantina to entertain guests and at home with her family. Or his favorite time, alone with just the two of them out in her parents' garden.

He couldn't imagine a woman he'd rather be with. Best of all, she liked him, too.

Nathan was in love from the first moment he saw Maria, now over two months ago. Whenever he thought of that first meeting, he still felt a thrill. He'd strolled into the cantina, as he'd done dozens of times before, stepping up to the bar for a whiskey. That day he noticed a new barmaid, with her back turned, pouring drinks. When she turned around, and he saw her face for the first time, he thought his heart had stopped. He was immediately smitten. She was the most beautiful young woman he'd ever seen.

But he was curious how it was this seemingly innocent young lady had come to be working in the cantina. And before he considered she might be offended by it, he'd blurted out the question on his mind.

But Maria hadn't seemed put off by it, and explained she'd been bored at home taking care of her younger siblings and had begged her parents to let her take a job singing in the cantina. Her mother was against it and said her late father would never have approved. But her stepfather was more lenient and said they could use the extra money. So after agreeing to be home before dark each day, she'd taken the job. And although she'd been hired to sing, the proprietor put her to work serving drinks whenever she wasn't entertaining.

Ever since that first day, Nathan couldn't get her out of his mind. He visited her every chance he could, either at her workplace or at her family's home. Or if he were lucky, somewhere in between on her way coming or going; then he had the chance to be alone with her in some quiet back alley. And in the past several weeks their playful banter had escalated to holding each other close and kissing passionately whenever they were alone.

He burned to make love with her. But, unlike him, she was still virginal, and he didn't wish to dishonor her or her family. After his war experience, he thought of himself as an "old man" of twenty-one years. Maria, on the other hand, was barely more than a child at eighteen. Besides, he'd been working hard to gain the respect of her mother and father, to convince them to trust a young American soldier. He'd do nothing to risk the progress he'd already made. It was important they liked him and saw him as a proper gentleman. But he regularly dreamed of Maria's beautiful face, sweet lips, and slender, curvaceous body as he lay in his bunk at the Army post. It made for some long, hard, sleepless nights.

She smiled and blushed before turning away from the bar. "You mustn't say such things here," she scolded. But he could see she continued to smile.

"And why not? Who will care? I am proud to be your love. In fact, I am planning on asking your papa for your hand this very evening."

He'd been waiting for the right moment to tell her ever since he'd come to his momentous decision two days earlier. But the moment never came, so he decided to just throw it out in the middle of their playful talk to see what would happen. Her reaction was gratifying in the extreme; her eyes widened, she beamed, and covered her mouth with her hand.

"Nathaniel! You don't mean it?"

"Of course, I do, *mi amor!* I love you with all my heart and wish us to always be together. *Prefiero un minuto contigo a una eternidad sin ti.*"

"Oh, Nathaniel. I … I love you too, *mi amor!*" She glanced around the room to see if anyone was looking before leaning across the bar to give him a quick kiss. It was a slow midafternoon in the cantina with only two other patrons besides Nathan, and they were discretely looking the other way. So with her boss, the proprietor, out for his usual siesta, there was little fear of anyone noticing her indiscretion.

"Do you really mean to ask him tonight?" she said, eyes still wide and smile burning brightly.

"Well … I suppose I should be sure you are in agreement first," he answered coyly.

She rolled her eyes at him, "Is it so difficult to tell, *mi amor?*"

He laughed, "Maybe … maybe not. But in my culture, it's traditional for the man to ask, and the woman to answer." He reached across the bar and grasped her two hands in his. Gazing into her eyes he said, "So, Maria Aguilar Diaz … will you marry me and be mine forever?"

She beamed, and by way of answer leaned in and kissed him again on the lips, this time lingering for several moments before leaning back.

"Does that mean yes?" he asked, grinning brightly.

"Yes … yes! Of course, yes!" she said with a laugh. "A thousand times, yes, Nathaniel, my love!"

ॐ॒ख़ॐख़ॐ॒ख़ॐॐ॒ख़ॐ

The next day when he stepped into the cantina, he immediately knew something was amiss. There was a tension in the air he'd never felt there before. Two surly looking Mexican men, armed with pistols in holsters at their hips, sat drinking at a table facing the door. Nathan instinctively moved his right hand to rest atop the holster at his own hip. The men had been watching him but made no move toward their guns.

Another armed Mexican stood at the bar, talking with Maria. When she saw Nathan enter, she locked eyes with him for a moment, gave him a serious, unreadable look, then turned away.

Very odd, he thought, and his anxiety level increased. But though he was still young by most standards, he was a blooded Army veteran who'd already killed many men in combat. He was strong and bold, and he feared no man.

So he walked past the seated men without another glance. As he approached the bar, the man who'd been standing there talking to Maria turned toward him. He was a strong, hard-looking Mexican with a long dark mustache and dark stubble covering his chin and neck. He appeared to be ten years or more Nathan's senior.

"*Hola, amigo. Buenas tardes,*" Nathan said as he stepped up to the bar. He showed no smile when he said it, though he tipped his hat politely.

"*Hola,*" the man answered flatly, before glancing back across at Maria. She was still looking the other way, as if not wishing to make eye contact with him.

"I am Hernan Ortega," the man said.

"Nathan Chambers. *Mucho gusto, Señor Ortega,*" Nathan responded, extending his hand.

130

"Hmm … but I am *not* so pleased to be meeting you, Señor Chambers," Ortega said with a frown, ignoring the extended hand. Though a head shorter than Nathan he was muscular and looked like he wouldn't shy from a fight.

"Oh? Since we have never met, Señor, I can't imagine why that would be," Nathan said, dropping his hand back to where it'd been resting atop his holster.

Nathan wore his neat, blue officer's uniform and hat, with gold piping and brass insignia, so these men knew he was an American officer. And since they were on the American side of the border, right next to the Army post, they knew better than to start a gunfight with him. Still, he always believed in caution.

"Maria tells me you think to marry her," Ortega answered.

"That's right," Nathan answered, beginning to get his hackles up, wondering where this was headed. He suspected nowhere good.

"But you see, that is not possible, Señor," Ortega said, giving Nathan a hard look.

"Oh? And why would that be, pray tell? And what business is it of yours, I'd also like to know," Nathan said with a scowl of his own.

Out of the corner of his left eye he could see Maria fidgeting nervously, still facing away from the confrontation. Out of his right eye he was surreptitiously keeping track of the two seated men, still facing the door. So far, they hadn't moved or reacted to anything being said.

"For one, you are a *gringo,* and she is *Mexicana,*" he said, emphasizing the word gringo as if it were a curse.

But Nathan continued to meet his gaze and just shrugged, as if to say, *"So what?"*

"And for another … I have not given permission," Ortega said.

Nathan lifted an eyebrow at this, "Oh … I was under the impression her father is Señor Aguilar, who has already blessed the union. Who are *you* that I might need your permission?" Nathan asked. He could feel his temper beginning to rise, but was trying hard to restrain it, knowing what could happen.

"I am *El Jefe de Los Tigres del Norte,*" he answered.

Though he tried not to betray his thoughts, Nathan was now seriously contemplating how quickly he could unholster his pistol. And whether he could shoot all three of them before they got him. To his surprise, this Ortega had just announced he was the notorious boss of the ruthless "Tigers of the North" gang. Reports said they ruled the hills and countryside surrounding El Paso del Norte on the Mexican side. It was even rumored they had an arrangement with the Mexican authorities, a kind of live-and-let-live agreement, from what Nathan understood.

"Ah … *that* Ortega. I've heard of you. But I'd understood you only operate on the *Mexican* side of the border," Nathan said.

Ortega shrugged. "The border is of no matter to me, Señor," he answered with a wicked-looking grin. "This country has always been *Mexicano* … a piece of paper with some ink on it in Mexico City or Washington don't change that."

"Maybe not, but there are a few hundred well-armed men dressed in blue like me who might disagree with you," Nathan answered. He continued resting his hand atop the pistol.

"And … even if this *was* Mexico, which it isn't, I'd still not need permission from …" he was tempted to say "an outlaw" or "a bandit." But he decided to attempt a more civil course for the moment, "… anyone other than her father."

Ortega glared at Nathan, but Nathan wasn't impressed nor intimidated and didn't shy from the outlaw's menacing stare.

But then, incongruously, Ortega grinned and shrugged.

"We shall see, Señor," he said, this time tipping his hat before heading for the door. Nathan noticed the other two men stayed seated at the table.

When he reached the doorway, Ortega paused and turned back. "If I were of a mind to take Maria to wife myself, Señor, what would you say to that?"

"I'd say that's up to the lady and her family … Señor," Nathan answered, tipping his hat toward Ortega. But though the gesture was polite, the look he gave Ortega was anything but.

Ortega grinned, "Perhaps my friends are of a different mind," he said, looking straight at the two seated men who pushed back their chairs and stood as if on cue. Both turned toward Nathan.

To his surprise, they immediately unbuckled their gun belts and laid them on the table.

Ortega chuckled, turned, and walked out the door.

Maria said, "Nathaniel … you should just leave now."

But Nathan unbuckled his own gun belt and laid it on the bar.

"Why?" he asked, never taking his eyes from the two men now walking toward him. They were both tough-looking and strong like Ortega, though younger. The one on the left had a nasty scar across his cheek which ran up under his right eye, giving it a permanent squint, lending him a piratical look. The other one was no better looking, with a nose that appeared to have been severely broken at least once in the past. In his mind Nathan named them "Scar-eye" and "Broken-nose."

"Amigos … we don't want any trouble," Maria said anxiously. "Nathaniel, just go now, please! These men won't try to stop you, will you, amigos?"

The two men paused and looked over at her. Scar-eye shrugged, but Broken-nose answered, "If the gringo agrees to leave you alone, Maria, we are told to let him go. If not …" he shrugged, then grinned. Nathan saw he was missing one of his front teeth. Yep, these two liked to fight, that was certain.

But Nathan turned toward Maria, "No … I don't think so, my lady. It's hot outside and I'm thirsty. I have a mind for a sip of whiskey, if you would. Now, these fellows here can either join me, in a friendly drink … or … *not*. As they wish."

She stared at him openmouthed for a moment, then shrugged, rolled her eyes, and poured him a drink. She slid the glass across the bar to him.

He picked up the drink and raised it toward the men, "What say you, gentlemen? Shall we drink … or *fight?*"

"We'll fight first, and drink later after we kick the shit out of you, gringo," Scar-eye said with a wicked leer.

Broken-nose added, "We'll enjoy our whiskey more watching you bleed."

Nathan shrugged and downed the whiskey in one quick shot, "Suit yourselves, amigos."

"Nathaniel, no. Please don't fight these men. They'll hurt you, *mi amor."*

But Nathan laughed, "These sorry sons-of-bitches? They couldn't beat my grandma, and she's long dead. Look at their ugly faces … seems like they've been the ones getting the worst of it. Just like they're gonna get … *now!"*

At the word *now* Nathan tossed the glass in the air toward the two men and lunged forward. His right fist lashed out, striking the man on his left, Scar-eye. The blow caught the bandit hard just below the eye. He staggered backward as the glass hit the floor and shattered.

Broken-nose swung hard at Nathan's head. But Nathan had anticipated the blow and ducked to the side. He grabbed the man's arm and pulled hard. The bandit's momentum sent him stumbling across the room. He slammed into his fellow and they tumbled to the floor in a heap.

Nathan was immediately on them. Punching one, and then the other in the face. Over and over.

Then he stood over them. The one with the scarred face who was on top, tried to rise, but Nathan punched him again. Scar-eye collapsed back onto his fellow. When Broken-nose on the bottom attempted to squirm out, Nathan kicked him hard in the ribs. After a few more attempts, each met with iron hard resistance, they gave it up and lay on the floor cowering, holding up their hands in supplication.

Nathan reached into the pocket of his tunic and pulled out a cigar and match. He lit the cigar, casually blowing smoke as the bandits glared up at him.

"Sorry about the broken glass, but I believe I'll have another drink now, Maria, if you please."

"What!?" she said, mouth agape.

"A drink … you know, whiskey …?" he said, smiling at her reassuringly.

She shook her head and rolled her eyes but poured him another glass. She came out from behind the bar and handed him the drink.

"Now amigos … I have a mind to test your theory—that I will enjoy my drink more after having kicked the shit out of you, while watching you lie on the floor bleeding." He raised the glass, took a sip, and nodded, "Yep … I have to hand it to you fellows; y'all *do* know how to best enjoy a drink. I find it … *most* satisfying. *Muchas gracias, amigos.*"

He grinned at them for another moment, then took another swallow before slamming the empty glass down on the bar.

"Now … get out! You've worn out your welcome," he said with a scowl.

The men rose painfully, still holding up their hands. But when they started toward the table to retrieve their pistols Nathan said, "Unh, unh! No, you don't! You'll just leave those sidearms right where they are. The price of admission."

The two men exchanged a quick look, then rushed at Nathan.

But he'd been expecting it. He sidestepped to the left, pivoted, and punched with his left fist. The blow hit the closest man, Scar-eye, in the lower back—a painful kidney punch that crumpled him to his knees, groaning in agony.

Broken-nose turned back toward Nathan and took a boot to the chest. He sprawled backward across a table and crashed to the floor. The table tumbled over on top of him.

Nathan turned and knocked Scar-eye to the floor with a punch to the side of his head. He stepped across the room and yanked the table off Broken-nose. The bandit was face down but attempting to rise. Nathan grabbed a fistful of the man's hair and slammed his face into the floor; blood splattered across the wood planks. He lifted Broken-nose's head to repeat the process when a frantic voice stopped him.

"*Nathaniel! No!* You'll kill him! Please … stop."

Nathan looked over at her. The shock and fear on her face gave him pause. He realized she was unused to seeing such violence.

Nathan realized Maria really was very innocent in so many ways. He shrugged and released the man's hair. Broken-nose's face hit the floor hard once again. He grunted but lay still.

"As you wish, *mi amor*," Nathan said, and grinned at her as he stood. She remained wide-eyed and shook her head at him, but the hint of a smile touched the corner of her eyes.

Nathan leaned over, grabbed Broken-nose by the belt and the back of his shirt, dragged him to the door, and tossed him out. The man tumbled down the two front stairs onto the dirt of the road. Nathan turned, snatched the man's hat from the floor and flipped it after him.

He strode across the room toward Scar-eye, who was now sitting up, rubbing the side of his face. The bandit raised his hands, *"No mas, Señor … no mas, por favor.* I am going."

Nathan stopped, made a slight bow, and gestured toward the door, "As you say, Señor." He took another puff on the cigar as he watched the man rise slowly from the floor and shuffle out of the cantina without another look.

"Nathaniel … are you hurt?"

"Me? Of course not, *mi amor.* Those fellows are nothing but big bullies, more used to beating up old men and terrifying women than any *real* fighting. You seem to forget, my dear, I'm a professionally trained warrior. It's my chosen vocation. These scoundrels never really had a chance."

She looked at him with new respect. She'd known he was tall, strong, and brave. That he'd fought in the big war down in Mexico. Not to mention he was handsome, gentle, and kindly. But he was such a gentleman that she had never in her wildest imaginings thought of him as a hard, dangerous man. When the fierce looking bandits had approached, she'd feared for his life. But in the end, it'd been as mere child's play for him.

Still, Ortega was a dangerous man and not one to be taken so lightly.

"Nathaniel, these men may not have been so tough as they looked, but Señor Ortega—he is a hard man. A killer and very dangerous. Do not make an enemy of him, *mi amor,* I beg of you. It will only be trouble."

But now Nathan frowned, "What would you have me do, Maria? Bow down to him? Give him what he wants? Ask him *permission* to marry you? Or even let him have you for his wife?" He growled, "That I will *never* do!"

"I'm not afraid of Ortega nor his band of bullies. I'm not afraid of any man. Besides, I have the entire United States Army on my side! Ortega won't dare cause serious trouble *this* side of the border, and I have no intention of going to the other side unless there's another war."

"I hope you are right, *amor*. But my heart troubles me, and now I am afraid."

"Have no fear, my dear one. I will protect you."

ᏚᎯᎦᏂᏟᏣᏚᎯᎦᏂᏟᏣᏚᎯᎦᏂᏟᏣ

Tuesday May 15, 1860 – Del Rio, Texas:

"But in my youthful pride, I didn't know how wrong I was," Nathan said, slowly shaking his head and tossing another stick on the campfire. Tears welled in his eyes, but he resisted the urge to wipe them away.

"I couldn't protect Maria. I wasn't afraid of Ortega, but I should've been. Not for myself … for *her*.

"That day in the cantina wasn't the end of it. There were more troubles and more fights. Ortega sent others, but I was ready, and always had a couple of soldiers along with me to watch my back. Of course, it didn't always go so smoothly as that first time. Sometimes I took my lumps, but in the end, I always prevailed. It became a kind of game. Ortega would show up himself with several others or just send some of his men by themselves. I would meet them with some of my own men, and we'd have a fight. I took pleasure in humiliating Ortega and his men, and his anger became ever more intense.

"And Maria was becoming exasperated and ever more fearful. She begged me to make peace with Ortega, to ask his permission for our marriage if that would satisfy his pride. After all, if I asked and he said no, then things would be no worse than they were.

"But I refused. In my stubbornness and pride, I saw her suggestion not as a compromise, but as capitulation, bending to his will. Instead, I went to the Captain and convinced him to have

137

Ortega and his men arrested, though they had committed no crimes on the American side, beyond the fighting. But Ortega must've gotten wind of it, as he never showed his face on our side of the border after that, nor did he send any more men.

"Then things seemed to quiet down for a time. I thought all was well and the troubles were behind us. We began planning our wedding and talking about how our lives together would be.

"Then came the terrible day I will never forget …"

ᏩᏒᎯᏋᎠᏒᏩᏒᎯᏋᎠᏒᏩᏒᎯᏋᎠᏒ

Friday June 15, 1849 – U.S. Army post opposite El Paso del Norte, Mexico:

Lieutenant Chambers sat on his bunk, polishing his good riding boots. He'd be off duty in a few hours and wanted to look his best when he met Maria at her parents' house. They lived in a hacienda just outside town. A well-tended farm, gardens, orchards, and various outbuildings surrounded the main house. It was not grand, like the magnificent old estates he had seen near Mexico City, but it was well-built and nicely furnished. It featured whitewashed adobe walls and a stylish, red-tiled roof in the traditional Spanish fashion. Maria's family had lived there for four generations, long before the Treaty of Guadalupe Hidalgo, ending the Mexican-American War, had made it part of the United States.

He knew it didn't matter to Maria what he wore, but he still wanted to make a good impression on her parents. Though they'd recently warmed up to him, he didn't want to risk them changing their minds. Besides, he considered it a sign of respect to her and her family to always dress in his best uniform. Especially when Maria's parents invited him for a formal evening meal, as they had this time.

As he continued working the black polish into his boots and daydreaming of sitting next to Maria at dinner, Sergeant Daniel Young came into the bunkhouse. He was one of Nathan's favorites and often accompanied him on his cantina outings in case there was trouble. Nathan suspected Daniel harbored a secret crush on Maria as he always blushed furiously and became tongue tied whenever she talked to him.

Nathan knew something was wrong. Daniel's face was twisted up in pain, and he looked like he was about to cry. He walked straight toward Nathan, then sat heavily on the bunk opposite him.

They gazed at each other for a long, silent moment, before Nathan said, "What's wrong, Dan? What's happened?"

"I … I …" Daniel started, but then choked up, unable to speak as tears filled his eyes. "She's …" he began again, then buried his face in his hands and sobbed.

Nathan stood, a sudden chill running down his spine.

"What is it, Dan? Is it Maria?" he said forcefully, grabbing Daniel by the shoulders, willing him to speak plainly.

Daniel looked up, tears streaming down his face. "I'm so sorry, sir … I … I didn't believe it when they told me. So I … I had to see for myself before telling you. I went to see … and she was … she was … gone."

"What are you saying? Gone where?"

"They've killed her, Lieutenant! They've murdered Maria, the ruthless fucking bastards. I'm so … sorry … sir …" he choked out between sobs.

Nathan's heart stopped and became hard as stone. He pulled on the boots, grabbed his gun belt and strapped it on. He snatched his hat and headed for the door.

"Come. Show me," he commanded in a cold, hard tone, not looking back.

༄༅།༄༅།༄༅།༄༅།༄༅།

When Nathan arrived at Maria's parents' home, she was laid out on a table in the yard with a blanket covering her. Maria's mother and stepfather sat next to each other in fancifully carved wooden chairs by the table. Maria's two younger sisters, aged ten and twelve, and her little brother, just eight, sat on the ground next to them, clutching at their legs, crying. Señor Aguilar had his arm around his wife, who wept quietly into a handkerchief. A veil partially covered her face. Miguel Aguilar gave Nathan a hard

139

look and slowly shook his head. His eyes were red, but he wasn't crying at the moment.

Nathan stared back at him blankly. Daniel turned away, holding his hand over his eyes. Nathan stepped up to the body and grabbed the blanket above the head.

"No, Señor Nathan! Do not disrespect the dead. Think of the Señora … and the *niños*," Señor Aguilar said.

But Nathan just stared at him. "I … I must see for myself. I must see it for myself …" He snatched off the blanket and sucked in his breath at the horrific scene. Maria's white dress was drenched in blood. Nathan forced himself to examine her body. He was shocked and felt … nothing. Just a cold, hard emptiness. A crushing ache inside where his emotions should be. Then the old familiar, mind-numbing rage simmered and rose inside him. It was like a cancer—a dark, growing thing with a life of its own. A thing he knew he couldn't control …

They'd stabbed her multiple times. He counted the wounds. Nine … ten … eleven. Then he gingerly lifted her skirts …

"No, Señor! It is not proper!" Aguilar scolded, but Nathan ignored him. He had to know … he had to know the full debt to be paid. He saw her undergarments were cut and torn. Blood and other fluids covered her most intimate parts. She'd clearly been raped, likely by multiple men. He shuddered and lowered the dress. Then he gazed one last time upon her lovely face. Thankfully, they had not despoiled that part of her, and as he leaned in close to kiss her, he could almost imagine she was only sleeping.

He carefully replaced the blanket and turned to Señor Aguilar, "I will bury her. Give me a shovel and show me where to dig."

ഽ൝ഽ൙ഽ൝ഽ൙ഽ൝ഽ൝ഽ൝ഽ

The priest and all the family's friends and neighbors had departed or moved inside the house to escape the heat of the sun nearly an hour ago.

But Maria's mother and stepfather had stayed out in the garden while Nathan shoveled earth back into the grave. His muscles ached from digging the hole in the hard, dry earth, and from filling it back in. And the relentless sun had burned the skin of his face and arms throbbing red. The rough handle of the shovel had blistered the palms of his hands. But he took little notice of these things. Within him, a fire consumed all such mortal concerns.

When he'd finished, he stepped up to Señor Aguilar and handed him the shovel. Aguilar gazed up at him, and said, "Señor Nathaniel, I know you wish to go after the men who did this. But it will *not* bring her back. It will only get you killed and perhaps provoke them more. And there are still the *niños* to consider. I would not have the bandits return here in anger."

Nathan glared at him, his face twitched, and Aguilar knew his words weren't welcomed. The older man turned away and took his wife by the arm, but she yanked her sleeve away. He gazed at her for a moment in surprise, then shrugged, glanced back at Nathan one last time, slowly shook his head, and walked to the house.

Teresa Aguilar stepped up to Nathan and lifted her veil. Though years older, it was easy to see where Maria had gotten her lean, good looks. To his surprise, she was no longer tearful; she was clearly angry, and for a moment he thought she meant to chastise him for the earlier offense of uncovering Maria's body.

But she looked hard in his eyes and said, "Don't listen to *him*, Señor Nathaniel. He was not always this way, but he has grown timid. And she was not *his* child like the others, but the child of my late first husband."

She paused for a moment and a look of pain and rage twisted her face, "Kill them, Nathaniel. Kill the dogs who did this. Kill the dogs who took my Maria!"

He returned her hard look and nodded, "Si, Señora. I *will* kill them … I will kill them *all*."

ༀༀༀༀༀༀༀༀༀༀༀ

Tuesday May 15, 1860 – Del Rio, Texas:

Nathan paused his tale to take another swallow from the bottle Ballantyne had given him. He was starting to develop a liking for this Scotch, and it was having the intended effect; the wound on his side had stopped throbbing, and the liquor had helped take the edge off the pain of reliving the past.

But he turned to Ballantyne and handed him back the bottle. "Don't give me any more of this, or I'll pass out and you'll never hear the end of the story," he said. Ballantyne nodded, and took the bottle, but Nathan noticed his face held a severe expression.

Nathan gazed around the group and wasn't surprised to see more of the same. Sue was no longer looking at him, but had her head tucked into her brother's chest, and appeared to be weeping as Willie patted her gently on the back. Georgie had his bowed head in his hands. Nathan met eyes with Tom, who returned a look of sorrow and concern. Everyone had a sober expression, even Stan who scowled fiercely. Nathan imagined Stan wished he could will himself into the story and strangle the bandits.

"I went to see the Captain who confirmed it was Ortega and his men who'd killed her. The Captain had already sent out mounted patrols to scour the countryside north of the border, but he suspected the bandits had already fled to the south. I begged him to let me lead a large, well-armed company into Mexico to hunt down Ortega and his 'Tigers' and put them to the sword. But the Captain refused, saying he couldn't risk starting another war with Mexico over it.

"Of course, I wasn't having any of it, and jumped to my feet saying I would go alone if that's what it took. He begged me to reconsider; not only was it suicidal, but if I left he'd be forced to consider me AWOL. I'd be subject to court martial on my return.

"But I ripped the lieutenant's insignia from my sleeve and slammed it on his desk saying, 'I don't expect to come back alive!' and I stomped out of his office.

"I arrived at the border armed to the teeth. I had four loaded pistols on me—two in holsters at my hips, and two more in holsters tucked up under my arms. I carried two rifles in gun sheaths on my horse, and a large, razor-sharp hunting knife hanging down from my belt in back. And I carried enough powder and lead balls on my spare horse to supply a small army!

"My friend, Sergeant Daniel Young, the same man who'd first told me of Maria's murder, rode with me to the border. But there I refused his desire to come along, not wishing to get him killed. Before we parted I handed him a letter I'd written to my momma. I asked him to mail it after I was confirmed dead or hadn't returned after two months' time.

"Then I crossed over into Mexico to make war for the second time in my life …"

𝕾𝖀𝕾𝕾𝖈𝖘𝕾𝖀𝕾𝕾𝖈𝖘𝖈𝖘𝕾𝖀𝕾𝕾𝖈𝖘

Friday June 22, 1849 – El Paso del Norte, Mexico:

Nathan stopped his horse outside a small adobe farmhouse. He pulled off his hat and wiped the sweat from his brow with his sleeve. He gazed around. The place looked like the half-dozen others he'd seen in the last several days—a poor, dry, subsistence farm of very little means, on sloping, rocky soil. A few skinny orange colored chickens skittered out of his way as he dismounted.

He patted down his sleeves and pantlegs in a vain attempt to remove the thick layer of dust coating him before he moved toward the house. He'd only taken two steps when a small, barefoot boy of about twelve years, appeared in the doorway.

"Hola, Señor," he said.

"Hola, amigo," Nathan answered, tipping his hat, "I wish you and your family no harm. I only want to water my horses and refill my water skins, *por favor.* And I will pay; I have silver."

The boy seemed to relax and smiled as he stepped down from the doorway and approached Nathan. "You may keep your silver, Señor. The water is free from the well, but you will have to pull up the bucket enough times to fill the watering trough for your horses."

"Muchas gracias, amigo," Nathan answered, wrapping the reins of his horse around a well-worn fence post and stepping over to the well.

"I am Pedro," the boy said, *"Mucho gusto, Señor.* What is your name?"

Nathan looked at him a moment, tilted his head and said, "You may call me *El Gringo*. And it is my pleasure to meet you as well, Pedro."

"*El Gringo?* That isn't a name, is it?"

"No. But I have not come to Mexico to give out my name."

The boy gazed at him curiously, as Nathan lowered the bucket down into the well. "Then why *have* you come to this side of the border, *Señor Gringo?*"

Nathan glanced over at him and scowled, "You ask a lot of questions, don't you, Pedro?"

"Si Señor. Momma says I am a great pest to our visitors with all my questions."

"Your momma sounds like a wise lady. Speaking of, where is she? And where is your papa? I have some questions of my own I'd like to ask them."

"Oh, Momma has gone to town for some supplies, and Papa …" the boy was quiet for a moment and lowered his head, gazing at his bare feet.

Nathan nodded, "Your father is dead, isn't he?"

"Si Señor."

"Sorry to hear it. I will answer your question, Pedro, in exchange for you answering some of mine. Deal?"

"Okay, Señor."

"So, I have come here looking for a man named Hernan Ortega. He is boss of a group of … *men* … who call themselves 'Tigers of the North.'"

The boy frowned. "Why are you looking for Señor Ortega and his men, may I ask?"

"I have answered your question already. I will only answer one question at a time, then it's my turn to ask."

"Okay, Señor. What is your question?"

Nathan frowned at him, in mock annoyance, "There you go, asking another question, Pedro."

"Oops, sorry, Señor. Your turn," he grinned.

"I want to know where Ortega lives … where he keeps his men. Do you know where that is, Pedro? If anyone in these hills knows, so far they aren't saying."

Pedro shook his head, "That's not surprising, Señor. Everyone around here either works for the Tigers or is one of them."

"Hmm ... and which one are you, Pedro?"

"Neither. And to answer your first question, 'no,' Señor. I do not know where Señor Ortega and his Tigers live. They won't tell me."

Nathan's initial reaction was disappointment. It was the same answer he'd received everywhere he'd been since crossing the border. But something the boy had said was different from the others and piqued his interest.

"Pedro ... *why* won't they tell you where Ortega lives?"

"Because they know I hate him. He killed my papa, and now he comes and ... *visits* Momma sometimes. She hates him too, but she is afraid."

"She should be."

"Si, Señor. But when I grow up, I will kill him."

"No, you won't."

"Why not?"

"Because he'll already be dead."

"Why will he be dead, Señor? He's not so very old yet."

"Because ... I am going to kill him."

The boy's eyes widened, then he beamed, "And *I* am going to help you!"

"How will you do that, if you don't even know where he lives."

"*I* don't know, but I know where you can find some men who *do*. Some men who are of the Tigers."

For the first time since Maria died, Nathan smiled. But not a nice, friendly smile. More like the smile a crocodile makes before devouring something.

"Good boy. I will pull out my map so you can show me."

"Si, Señor. I like looking at maps, and I know every hill and gully for miles around."

"Good to know."

"And ... now I have thought of a better name for you, Señor."

"Oh, what is it?"

"I will call you Señor Lion."

"Lion? Why Lion?"

"Because … you are the lion who will kill the tigers!"

Five men sat around a rough wood table in the middle of a tile floor. Inside the hacienda it was dark and cool, the thick adobe walls and minimal windows helping to keep the midday heat at bay.

The men were a sullen, hard-looking group of Mexicans. All had scruffy beards and mustaches. Pistols carried in holsters at their hips punctuated the rough look of these men. A meek looking, clean-shaven man was serving out a thick soup in rough, black ceramic bowls along with mugs of *cerveza*.

The talk was subdued, and no one thanked or acknowledged the man serving as they dove into their meal. When he finished attending the others, the server brought his own bowl and sat by himself at the end of the long table and prepared to eat. But he'd just taken a steaming spoonful and was blowing on it when a tremendous noise startled him, and he splattered the soup on the table.

The thick front door had burst open. The silhouette of a large man stood outlined in the doorway. He held a revolver in each fist, and said, "Nobody moves, or all will die."

The seated men stared, openmouthed at the apparition. And all froze in place as they had been, one even holding a spoon halfway to his mouth.

Nathan Chambers stepped in the door and approached the table.

"I am looking for Hernan Ortega. And y'all will tell me where I can find him."

One of the men, with long mustaches and a large scar on his cheek said, "I know you … Señor Chambers!"

Nathan looked at him and nodded, "*Hola*, Scar-eye. It has been a while."

"Not long enough, Señor Chambers. Once again I am not so happy to be seeing you."

"Not surprised. You were not looking well last time I saw you, amigo. I seem to recall you getting the shit kicked out of you in the cantina."

Scar-eye scowled, "You have made a mistake coming here. You will die this time."

"I expect to. But first I will kill Ortega and all the bastards who helped him murder Maria."

"I had nothing to do with *that*, Señor. After … meeting you … in the cantina, I was never sent north again."

"If you didn't murder Maria, then tell me who did."

"Why would I want to do that, amigo?"

"Because then I might let you live."

But Scar-eye grinned, and shrugged, "But Señor, be reasonable. We are five, and you are only one. Though you have the drop on us now … still, you cannot hope to kill us all before one of us shoots you."

"Maybe not, but I can kill *you* for sure," he answered, pointing his left pistol at Scar-eye's forehead for emphasis.

But as he made that movement, a quick motion at the end of the table caught the corner of his eye. He flicked the right pistol in that direction and fired. But even as the man seated there fell backward, dropping his weapon, the others rose from their seats.

Nathan lunged forward, kicking the near edge of the table with the bottom of his boot. The table slid, slamming hard into the men trying to rise.

Multiple gunshots rang out from different directions. But Nathan had ducked under the thick table and fired at his enemies' exposed legs and bellies.

In moments all was quiet again and thick gun smoke wafted lazily in the still air.

Nathan stood cautiously, guns still held out front, as he examined his enemies. All were dead save one, Scar-eye. Nathan kicked the gun from his limp grasp as he lay face up on the floor. He was bleeding heavily from a gunshot to the belly, despite trying to cover it with his left hand.

Nathan leaned over him and said, "You are done, amigo. And it is Ortega who has *really* killed you, as sure as the sun rises. If

147

not for him, I would never have been here to pull the trigger. So why not tell me where he is and have your revenge before you die?"

But Scar-eye spit at him and said, "I will tell you nothing." He coughed, grimacing in agony, then said, "There is nothing more you can do to me."

But Nathan leaned in close and said, "Maybe not, but there is something I can do *for* you. I can give you a swift death and end the pain. I will even pray for your soul. Or I can put more holes in you … the kind that give great pain but don't bring death. Which will it be, amigo? It costs you nothing to help me but may cost you much pain to refuse."

But Scar-eye closed his mouth and just scowled up at him.

"Suit yourself," Nathan said and pulled back the hammer on his right-hand pistol. He pointed it at Scar-eye's groin, then looked him in the eye and raised an eyebrow questioningly.

"Okay, amigo, okay! Don't do it, *por favor*. I will tell you."

"Tell it true, or I swear by God I will find any family you have, and I will kill them. Slowly."

"No amigo, I will tell it true. I have no reason to love Ortega. As you say, he has got me killed. *El Jefe* has taken over a hacienda in a little valley south of town. There he is always surrounded by many Tigers. It is from there he sends them out to do his bidding. Here is how you will find it …"

When he'd finished, Nathan thanked him, and again offered to give him the *coup de grace*. When Scar-eye nodded yes, Nathan asked him his name, which he said was Diego Gonzalez. Then Nathan put him out of his pain with a single shot to the forehead. True to his word, Nathan then said a quick prayer for Diego's soul.

As he turned toward the door, he was startled by the dark silhouette of a person standing in the doorway. He aimed his pistols but paused when he realized the shape was of a woman.

"*Buenas dias, Señora*. You may enter, I will not harm you."

The woman stepped into the room and dropped a burlap sack she'd been carrying as she gazed around the room in shock.

Various fruits and vegetables spilled across the floor from the fallen sack, rolling through pools of blood.

The *señora* moved around to the far side of the table, stepping over the bodies of the dead bandits. When she reached the far end, she gasped and dropped to the floor. She began wailing, "My Francisco! Oh … *noooo* … what have they done? What have they done to you, *mi amor?*"

Nathan made his way around the table from the other direction and looked down at her. She was kneeling over the body of a man. In the heat of battle, and the aftermath, busy interrogating Scar-eye Nathan hadn't really noticed the man before. Now he saw the man was clean shaven and neat looking, not like a bandit at all. With a lump in his throat he realized the man was also unarmed. When Nathan had been under the table, he'd fired at anything moving, unable to distinguish one man from another, and unable to tell that one man among them was unarmed.

"Damn it!" he muttered.

The woman looked up at him, her face twisted in pain, "You have killed him. You have killed my Francisco, you murdering devil!"

"I didn't come here to kill him, only the Tigers. But he was here … helping them …"

"We never wanted them here. They come when they want and take what they will. Francisco did as they said to protect *me*."

But Nathan scowled at her, "That is no way for a man to protect his home and his woman. A man must fight for what's his."

"You dare call my Francisco a coward? You, who have murdered an unarmed man?" The look she gave him had changed from pain to rage. Her face twitched and turned red. "I will kill you, *diablo!* I will kill you," she said, and reached over to pick up a pistol the nearest bandit had dropped when he fell. It was heavy for her, and she had to hold it in both hands.

"Don't do that, Señora. Set it down, *por favor* … you don't want to do that …"

But she ignored him, struggling to pull back the hammer.

"Don't … *Señora, por favor!* Put down the pistol …" he pleaded again as she turned toward him and raised the weapon.

He lunged forward even as she pulled the trigger.

"Ow! Damn it!" he said, jerking the gun from her grasp. As he had reached forward, he'd intentionally grabbed the pistol so his hand was between the hammer and the percussion cap. The result was the hammer slamming painfully down on the meaty part of his hand, puncturing it with the firing pin.

He thought it a small price to pay for preventing the gun from firing. He gingerly pulled the hammer back and extracted his bleeding hand.

The woman collapsed onto her husband and sobbed, never again looking up at Nathan.

"I know it means nothing to you, Señora, but I am sorry. Truly, truly sorry," was all he could think of to say as he stood and headed for the door.

༄༅ༀༀༀༀༀༀༀༀ

Nathan lay prone in the dirt at the edge of a rise. From there he had a clear view of the back porch of Ortega's hacienda, three hundred yards away. Several tough-looking, well-armed men were standing around, or seated in chairs on the patio. He didn't know why they had congregated there in the heat of the day, but he thanked his luck for it. He'd thought he might spend half the day waiting for a target, and then it would be someone walking swiftly to get out of the sun. This … was almost too easy.

Nathan pulled back the hammer on the rifle, retested the seating of the percussion cap, and aligned the sights on a man seated on the porch. Aiming at a spot about two feet above the man's head, he relaxed and slowed his breathing. He squeezed the trigger. The rifle popped loudly, spewing a plume of smoke and flame from the barrel.

He saw the man drop and quickly set the rifle to the side, picking up another, already loaded. He pulled the hammer and aimed at another target. The men on the patio hadn't yet reacted and still milled about.

He squeezed the trigger. *Pop!* Another puff of smoke and another man fallen.

Time to go, Nathan! he told himself. He slid backward down the slope on his belly until he could stand without being seen from the house. He jumped to his feet.

Leaving the rifles where they lay, he ran back down the far side of the slope into a small ravine that followed a dry streambed. It served as a horse trail through the rough country on this side of the hacienda.

He sprinted along the trail toward the hacienda for about fifty yards before turning and scrambling up the far bank. He clambered and scrabbled over the rough, loose, gravelly dirt of the ravine bank to a flat natural alcove roughly six feet above the level of the old streambed. Nathan had chosen the natural platform during his earlier scouting because it was obscured from anyone coming along the trail from the house.

He picked up the four pistols he'd left there and put them back in their holsters. It'd made him anxious leaving them here unattended, but he needed to move swiftly after he fired the rifles; the extra weight of the pistols would've slowed him too much. He'd also left his waterskin, which he now picked up and drank from greedily.

He set the water down and took out a pocket watch to check the time. *Should be any minute now,* he thought. And in a moment, he heard horses galloping, coming from the direction of the house. He stood, pulled the two pistols from under his arms, and pulled back the hammers.

The sound grew louder until a horse passed right in front of him in the ravine. He aimed his right-hand pistol and fired. The rider spilled from the saddle, causing the horse to lose balance and slow. He fired the other pistol at the next rider, and he too fell. The narrow ravine was becoming clogged. More horses and riders came up fast and tried to slow or stop but jammed and jostled together as their riders fought to regain control.

Nathan calmly targeted riders and fired. The range was short, and their heads were at the level of his waist, so nearly every shot was deadly. *Bang, bang, bang!* Men fell from the saddle. Several tried to fight back, struggling to control their mounts, unholster their pistols, and lean back toward him to fire. But he downed most of them before they could get off a shot. Those who did shoot at him fired wildly and missed badly.

It was over as quickly as it had started. The horses milled about or wandered off down the trail, unsure what to do being suddenly riderless. Nathan hopped down and walked over to where the men lay on the ground. He still held two pistols, now the ones from his hips, having emptied the other two.

He made sure all the bandits were dead, finding only one still alive. The man had taken a bullet through the chest. And he had fallen badly, breaking his right leg in a manner that'd likely been more painful than the gunshot. When Nathan looked down at him, he saw he was still conscious.

"*Agua, por favor, Señor,*" he begged, "water … please!"

But Nathan shook his head, "You won't need it where you're going," and shot him in the head.

He counted eight bodies. With the two he'd shot on the patio with the rifles, that made ten today. And the five at the other hacienda two days earlier totaled fifteen. A good start, he decided. That should get Ortega's attention, at least.

He turned to walk back to where he'd left his rifles. But then he heard a sound—more horses coming fast.

"*Damn,*" he muttered and sprinted to where a horse stood, trying to yank a patch of dry grass from the side of the gully. Nathan jumped on, grabbed the reins, and spurred the horse into motion. With a lurch the animal sped down the trail, kicking up dust. Gunshots sounded behinds him, and he felt something zip past his head and instinctively ducked. *Too close,* he thought and urged the horse to more speed.

He knew from earlier scouting, the ravine ended in a long, flat slope. No good going there; he'd make an easy target with no cover in sight. So he pulled his boots from the stirrups, got his feet up under him on the saddle, and leapt off onto a low spot on the bank. He rolled over onto his back, unholstered his pistols and fired at the approaching riders.

Again men fell from the saddle. Two at least, maybe three. That slowed the others and gave him time to scramble up the bank to the top where it leveled off into a narrow plateau. He stood, holstered the pistols, and sprinted across the open ground, looking for any cover that might present itself. But nothing did, and he had to pull up in a desperate, sliding stop in the dry, gravelly dirt as he came to a sharp drop-off. He dangled precariously for a moment above a fall of a hundred feet or more before regaining his balance.

He looked back toward the gully and saw men were coming up over the rise where he had jumped from the horse, only a hundred yards away. Turning to his right, he ran along the edge of the drop-off, looking for a way down or something to hide behind. But rifle shots rang out, and dirt kicked up in front of him causing him to lose balance. He tried to right himself, but his footing gave way and he stumbled and slid. A sickening emptiness lurched in his stomach as the ground went out from under him, and he fell. He hit hard on his side and tumbled, rolling over and over down the hillside, bruising himself on rocks scratching his body on gravel and brush. He came to a stop at the bottom, facing up. Above him was the rim of the canyon from which he'd fallen. After a moment he saw faces looking down at him. But the image was unclear and wavery and he felt disoriented and unable to move. Then someone grabbed him by the shirt near his collar.

ಬಿ‌ಬಿ‌ಬಿ‌ಬಿ‌ಬಿ‌ಬಿ‌ಬಿ‌ಬಿ‌ಬಿ

Ortega had to lead his men a quarter mile from the spot where the gringo fell to find a place where the slope was gentle enough to climb down. Then it was another quarter mile hike back. When they got there, they found marks where the body had ended up. But no body. And there were no footprints leading away. The man had simply disappeared.

"But ... *El Jefe* ... I shot him ... I know I did. It was an easy shot, and I saw him fall," a man said, shaking his head.

Then another man stepped up and said, "You must have missed, Javier ... see, there is no blood."

Javier came over and looked but continued to shake his head. "What kind of man can kill a dozen soldiers, jump from a galloping horse, get shot, fall a hundred feet and then walk away? And leave no boot tracks and no blood?"

Ortega scowled at them, but another man stepped up and answered the question, "A devil. That's what kind of man can do these things. A devil straight from hell."

ℰↄℰↄℭℬℰↄℰↄℭℬℰↄℰↄℭℬ

Tuesday May 15, 1860 – Del Rio, Texas:

Nathan chuckled and tossed another log on the fire. "But there was nothing supernatural about it. As you may have guessed, it was my little friend Pedro who dragged me out of there. And, he had the good sense to scratch out our tracks with a branch off a sagebrush, so they'd not follow us.

"He'd begged me to bring him along when I attacked Ortega's hacienda, and against my better judgment, I had reluctantly agreed. For one, I needed someone to watch the horses while I made my attack, and I thought that would at least keep him well back from any danger. And for another, I'd made him agree if they killed me, he'd get word back to the soldiers in the north telling them what happened. And lastly … well, I figured he deserved to be part of it, given what they'd done to his father, and were continuing to do to his mother.

"Anyway, it was a good thing for me he was there, or I'd not be here today to tell the story. He helped me get on my horse, and we made our way back to his mother, Sofia's house. There I rested and recovered for a few days as Sofia nursed me back to health. At the time it seemed it'd been a good decision to involve him. Later … that decision didn't seem so good.

"It was around that time I first heard the term 'El Diablo Blanco,' the White Devil. The locals had become more cooperative, perhaps emboldened by my success against the Tigers. One of them told me he had heard about it from the Tigers. That there was a gringo from hell wandering around El Paso del Norte, killing Ortega's men. A ghost, or spirit of some kind, who could fly and when shot wouldn't even bleed, and couldn't be killed. The demon was seeking revenge for Ortega killing him when he was a live man, or some other such slight.

"I shook my head and shared a laugh with Pedro when I first heard it. Only he and Sofia knew the truth of my seeming miraculous escape that day at Ortega's hacienda.

"I continued to waylay Tigers, singly or in small groups as opportunities presented themselves. I'd always heard Ortega had somewhere around fifty 'Tigers' in his gang, and I figured by that point I'd killed somewhere near half of them. I was feeling fairly smug about that, though I was sickened by the continuous bloodshed and death. Yet still I had not quenched my rage over Maria's death because I hadn't killed the man most responsible. And though I assumed I must have killed one or two of the others involved in her rape and murder by this time, I couldn't know for sure.

"But when I returned to Sofia and Pedro's home after one particularly dangerous and bloody outing, I discovered their house burned to the ground. When the ruins had cooled enough, I sifted through the ashes, but found no bodies. I searched all around the farm but found nothing. I could envision Ortega taking Sofia, but what of the boy? I was devastated and felt responsible for whatever had happened to them. The nearest neighbors had seen nothing, but had heard gunfire and screaming. I feared the worst.

"I felt despondent. All the killing and fighting had only added to the misery I was feeling, and the blood debt I owed Ortega. And I was no closer to an ending.

"But if Ortega thought to intimidate the residents from helping me by burning the farm, he must've been disappointed. If anything, it stirred the people more, and men began coming to me asking if they could fight too. Though it gratified me greatly, and I felt proud of them, I wanted no more innocent lives on my conscience, so I turned them all away. Besides, I was feeling more and more miserable by the day, and I had no desire to lead other men. But though I fear I treated them unkindly and was

155

unwelcoming, still they continued providing me with information on Ortega and the Tigers.

"And then one day a very odd thing happened, one that I had never expected and could never have imagined. It led to the end of the hunt.

"After Pedro's disappearance, I never stayed in one place for long, and no longer accepted any shelter, fearing I'd get more people killed. So I camped out in the barren places, all alone. One night as I sat next to a small campfire I'd made, eating a pot of beans, I had a sudden, itchy feeling something was amiss. The horses had become fidgety, and I thought I heard noises out in the dark. I stood, pulled my pistols, and faced the darkness. Then men walked into my camp from all sides, holding rifles, but not aiming them at me. There must have been two dozen or more and they had the look of bandits. The Tigers had found me at last, and I knew this was the end. I expected Ortega to walk up gloating ..."

⁑⁑⁑⁑⁑⁑⁑⁑⁑

Tuesday July 17, 1849 – El Paso del Norte, Mexico:

A man Nathan didn't recognize emerged from the darkness and stepped up to face him. The man rested the butt of his rifle on the ground and removed his hat respectfully. To Nathan's astonishment, the other men surrounding the campfire did the same.

"Señor, my name is Jose Garcia," he said.

Nathan stared at him a moment, then holstered his pistols. *"Mucho gusto, Señor Garcia.* Y'all may call me ... Señor Lion, though it is not my real name."

"Mucho gusto, Señor Léon," Garcia answered. "We did not expect you to give your actual name, though a few of us already know it. We men are all of *Los Tigres del Norte.*"

Nathan continued to stare at Garcia blankly. He couldn't imagine where this was headed, nor why they hadn't simply opened fire on him from out of the darkness when they had the chance.

"We have learned somewhat of your *true* story in recent days from one who was there. He was of those who went with *El Jefe*—Ortega—to murder the girl Maria up in the north. He confessed all, and he said he expected that was why *El Diablo Blanco* had come, to avenge the girl.

"Señor, we are hard men and live a hard life. We follow Ortega because he makes it so we don't have to scratch in the hard, dry earth for a living. Nor do we have to fight the Mexican authorities to keep from prison. But we don't follow him to be slaughtered protecting a man who has done such a cowardly and despicable thing to an innocent woman. He has brought this rain of death on us and we want it to end."

Nathan met eyes with him for a long moment before answering, "So … what is it you want of me, Señor*?*"

"We have come here to ask you for peace. To ask you to stop killing us. There are some among us who believe you are not a real man, but rather an avenging ghost who cannot be killed. I don't know about all that, but I do know that a man who was wronged as you were has a right to avenge his honor. So we do not wish to hunt you any longer, nor try to kill you. We wish for you to leave this place in peace."

"No. Not 'til I get what I came for," he answered flatly.

The man's eyes widened for a moment, and then he nodded. "It should not surprise us you say that." He paused, then said, "There is another way that may satisfy all …"

"Another way? What *way*, Señor Garcia?"

"You must come to our camp and fight Ortega. Just the two of you, hand to hand with no weapons, to the death. It is a sacred agreement among the Tigers; if anyone who has proven himself worthy of leading wishes to challenge the leader he may do so if the men all agree. Then *El Jefe* must fight or give up leadership."

"You want me to challenge Ortega to be the leader of your band?"

"It is the way to end this with no more bloodshed, except for whoever loses the fight, of course."

"And what of the other men who helped murder Maria? You said there was one left? What happened to the others, and who is that man? I'll not consider justice done until they are *all* dead."

"You have killed all the others, Señor. They were among the many you have already taken. As for the one who was still alive … after he confessed what he had done, we shot him. He had helped bring this death on us all by defiling the young woman. For that he has paid. But we cannot do the same to *El Jefe*. Only *you* can do that."

"Hmm … and what of the boy Pedro and his mother Sofia? What has become of them? I would know what has been done to them, and who is responsible."

"Ortega holds the woman at his hacienda. As for the boy …" Garcia paused and gave Nathan a hard, unreadable look, "I have been told he was killed when the mother was taken. He ran off into the fields and Ortega sent one of his men after the boy. Gunshots were heard, and when the man returned, he said the boy was dead."

Nathan growled, "I will have that man's head as well!"

Garcia gazed at him another moment, then said, "The man has … fled. He had a falling out with *El Jefe* after the incident and has left the Tigers. I do not know where he has gone. I am sorry, Señor."

ᔔᕐᑫᲪᔔᕐᑫᲪᔔᕐᑫᲪ

Tuesday May 15, 1860 – Del Rio, Texas:

Nathan slowly shook his head as he continued the story, "It was like a strange dream. These men whom I'd been trying my best to kill for nearly a month, led me to their camp, an open space next to a large bunkhouse on Ortega's hacienda. The same hacienda I'd attacked on the day I fell off the ledge. They asked me to set aside my weapons.

"At that point I assumed they would either seize me or just shoot me once I was no longer armed. But I was so sick at heart from all the death and killing I was ready to be done with it one way or the other. So I laid down all my arms, even my knife, and walked into the Tiger's lair with only my bare fists for weapons.

"But the Tigers proved true to their word ..."

ᔥᔍᔑᔥᔍᔑᔥᔍᔑᔥᔍᔑ

Tuesday July 17, 1849 – El Paso del Norte, Mexico:

Nathan strode into the camp, entirely unarmed. The Tigers parted and allowed him to pass. No one threatened him nor tried to bar his way. He made eye contact with the men he passed. Many would not meet his gaze and looked away. But several looked him in the eye and nodded, a clear sign of respect. He nodded back.

From what he understood, none of *these* men had harmed Maria, and it disgusted many of them. Some had even killed one of those responsible.

He stepped into an open space next to a small, hut-like building, and stopped. The Tigers gathered around in a circle. There were at least forty, so he now knew, despite his best efforts and all the carnage, he had not even come close to killing half their number.

He heard voices coming from inside the hut. One he recognized immediately, and a scowl curled his lips—*Ortega!* The other voice he now recognized as well, Jose Garcia, the Tiger who had proposed the idea of challenging Ortega.

Ortega stepped out of the hut, followed by another man Nathan had never seen before. He was taller and leaner than Ortega, but otherwise they looked alike. This must be the brother Nathan had heard mentioned previously. Ortega strode forward and said, "So, who is it thinks they can challenge me to be *El Jefe*, huh? I have killed many challengers over the years, and one more is of little matter."

But when he saw Nathan standing there he stopped, his mouth hanging open. "You ..." he said, eyes widening.

"Yes, it's me, Ortega. I have come to kill you."

159

"You men … seize him and bind him! This is the killer we've been trying to catch all these weeks. Now he is foolish and brazen enough to come into our very camp!" He grinned a wicked grin.

But nobody moved. Nobody obeyed.

Ortega looked around in surprise. "What are you waiting for? I have given an order. Seize the gringo. We'll string him up and skin him alive!"

But again, his orders were met with silent stares. Finally, Garcia stepped up to him and said, "*El Jefe*, this man has proven worthy of leadership. All the men agree on this. And he has challenged you to become *El Jefe* of the Tigers. The sacred code requires you to accept the challenge or step aside as leader. But I must warn you, if you step aside, then he will have the right to order you seized and punished for what you have done."

Ortega stared at him in shock. He gazed around at the men and knew the truth of what Garcia was saying. He had to fight or die.

"Very well, we will follow through with this foolishness. I will kill the gringo, and then we can get back to our business."

"*El Jefe*, you must give up all weapons," Garcia said.

"I have no weapons," he answered.

"Your knife …"

"Ah. I had forgotten." Ortega pulled a long, wicked-looking knife with a curved blade from a sheath at his belt. He turned and handed it to the man who'd come out of the hut with him.

"My brother will hold it for me," he said. But as he handed the blade to his brother, Nathan thought he whispered something to him.

The brother took the knife and stepped aside into the crowd to Nathan's left.

Garcia looked from one man to the other, then said, "In this fight there are no rules. It is over when one or the other is dead." He nodded, then he too moved back into the crowd.

Ortega crouched and circled to Nathan's right. As Nathan moved to face him, he caught a sudden movement behind and to the left out of the corner of his eye. He turned in time to block a knife blade coming at his back. He'd caught the man's wrist with his forearm. The blade had missed, but the man still held it. He stepped back as Nathan maneuvered to put both brothers in his view.

No one else moved or spoke. Apparently, this fell under the "no rules" rule, Nathan decided with a scowl.

He knew he had to move fast. If they caught him between them, he'd be dead. He threw caution to the wind and attacked. He rushed the brother, who thrust the knife at his stomach. But Nathan dodged aside, grabbed the blade arm and twisted it back. With a burst of strength, he shoved the arm up behind the man. There was a strange popping sound. He pushed harder. The man gasped in shock, and then went limp, collapsing on the ground face down. But before Nathan could react, Ortega reached down and pulled out the knife, ignoring the rush of blood from his own brother that followed. He stepped back and glared at Nathan holding out the knife in front of him.

"*El Jefe*, you must drop the blade," Garcia warned.

But Ortega spit, and said, "He has killed my brother ... I will gut him like a pig!"

Garcia frowned, then stepped forward with his hand extended toward Nathan. He offered his own knife, handle first.

Nathan shook his head and scowled, "I don't need it."

Garcia raised an eyebrow in surprise but nodded and stepped back.

Nathan glared at Ortega, "You have killed my Maria. For that you will die, as she did—bloody and dishonored."

They circled each other, Nathan careful to stay clear of Ortega's knife thrusts, and Ortega cautiously avoiding letting Nathan get close enough to grapple with him. They continued to circle for several minutes. Suddenly Nathan's feet tangled with the brother's body. He stumbled. Ortega leapt forward thrusting with the long knife.

But it had been a feint. Nathan had not lost his balance. He'd been ready for the lunge. He leapt to the side, grabbed Ortega's knife arm, and twisted hard. There was a sickening snapping noise. Ortega's arm dangled lifelessly. The blade fell to the ground on top of the dead brother. Ortega stepped back, holding the broken arm. He grimaced in obvious agony. Nathan leaned down and picked up the knife.

He stepped up to Ortega.

"No, Señor! Mercy, I beg you. You can be *El Jefe* … I will leave and never return. Have mercy!"

But Nathan stepped up and grabbed Ortega by the front of his shirt. He looped a foot around the back of the bandit's leg and shoved him hard to the ground on his back. Nathan knelt on top glaring into Ortega's eyes, now wide with fear.

"Mercy …" he whispered.

Nathan said, "This is for Maria," and stabbed the knife into Ortega's groin. Ortega's eyes rolled back in his head and he made a strange, gurgling sound.

"And this is for Pedro," he said, pulling the knife out and stabbing it deep into the man's belly then twisting.

Ortega moaned in pain.

Nathan stood, the dripping knife still in his grasp. He glared at Ortega, watching the bandit writhe on the ground.

"Finally, this one is for me," he said. He knelt and thrust the blade hard up under Ortega's chin. The long knife punched through bone and flesh until the bloody tip protruded from the top of his head. Ortega twitched hard for a moment, and then lay still, eyes staring blankly. Blood oozed from the edges of his closed mouth and gushed down his neck.

Nathan stood and turned to the men surrounding him, still holding the bloody knife in his fist. "I have done what I came to do. Now I wish only to go home. My heart is sick from killing and will go in peace if y'all will let me. If not, I will fight y'all to my last breath."

But Garcia stepped forward and said, "You are now *El Jefe*. We are yours to command, *Señor Léon*."

Nathan looked at him in shock. He'd never believed they would follow through with it, but apparently, they had. He nodded, then said, "Take me to where Sofia is being held."

Garcia led him to where they held Pedro's mother, Sofia, locked in a room of Ortega's hacienda. She embraced Nathan tearfully.

"You are free now, Señora. Ortega and his brother are dead."

"Gracias, *Señor Léon*," she managed to get out between sobs.

"And ... I am so sorry about Pedro. Though I looked, I could not find his body. I will go back with you now and we will search until we find him and can give him proper burial. Then I will hunt down the man who killed him."

Sofia nodded, but could say nothing, wiping her eyes and face with a handkerchief.

He ordered Garcia to give her a good horse, a mule, and a half-dozen cattle from Ortega's stock. After discovering a room filled with contraband, he gave her twice the amount of silver it would take to rebuild her house and buy proper headstones for her husband and son, assuming they could locate Pedro's body.

Then he ordered the Tigers to sell all the Ortega brothers' property and distribute the proceeds among them. After that they were to disband and go their separate ways. He left Garcia in charge to see that it was done as he'd ordered.

He escorted Sofia, with her newfound wealth, toward the house of her cousin, Marta, who lived several miles from Sofia's farm, on the edge of town. Sofia would live there while her house was being rebuilt. Nathan promised in the meantime to scour the hills until he found Pedro's body, after which he'd seek out the killer.

When they arrived at the cousin's home, a modest adobe house on the east end of El Paso del Norte, Marta rushed out to greet Sofia just as Nathan was helping her down from her horse.

"We were so worried about you! And now I am so happy you are free, *mi amor!*" Marta said, kissing Sofia on both cheeks before embracing her fondly. Nathan noted Marta was likely several years older, and clearly many pounds heavier than Sofia. "Oh, this is a most happy, happy day!" Marta said, continuing to beam. Her husband came out from the house and greeted them warmly, shaking hands firmly with Nathan.

But though Sofia was appreciative of the warm greeting, still she could not bring herself to smile, and began to cry.

"Oh ... my dear sweet one ... you grieve for our precious little Pedro, no?"

Sofia nodded, but could say nothing, fighting back the tears.

But Marta stood back and held Sofia at arms' length. "Look at me dear …"

Sofia looked up and met eyes with her cousin. "Sofia, my dearest … when I say this is the very most happy day of all happy days … you *must* believe me!" and she smiled brightly.

Sofia gazed at her with a look of confusion.

"Pedro!" Marta yelled.

A movement in the doorway caught Nathan's eye, and a young boy came running out, "Momma!" he shouted and jumped into Sofia's arms.

Mother and son embraced as tears of joy merged with kisses.

Nathan smiled, taking in the heartwarming sight. He noticed at that moment the tight, aching pain in his chest, which had been his constant companion since Maria's death, slightly eased its grip on him.

Then Pedro stepped back from his mother and looked up at Nathan, grinning. *"Muchas gracias, Señor Leon,* the Tiger killer! Do you now believe I have named you rightly?"

Nathan chuckled, "Si, Pedro. And do you now believe you will never have to kill Ortega?"

Pedro laughed, and nodded, happily returning to his mother's loving embrace.

ಬಿಶಿ)ೞಣೞಬಿಶಿ)ೞಣೞಬಿಶಿ)ೞಣೞ

Friday July 20, 1849 – Franklin, New Mexico Territory:

Teresa Aguilar had just taken a seat in her favorite sitting room, setting down a steaming hot cup of tea, when she heard a knock on the front door. Her husband, Miguel, wasn't at home, so she would have to get up to answer it herself. He'd gone into town early in the morning to replace a broken piece of farm equipment.

Teresa was not expecting guests, though that didn't stop them from coming. Ever since Maria's death, her friends thought she needed "comforting." So they'd come knocking, unannounced, and they'd sit politely and make small talk for hours on end, as if nothing bad had ever happened.

But Teresa didn't want to make small talk. She wanted to scream! They had taken away her sunshine, her *world* … her dear, sweet child … Maria. She could never stop thinking about the evil men who had done this. That they were back in Mexico, safe in their haciendas, gloating about what they had done to her loving daughter. It made her furious, which was a state she preferred over the devastating, heart wrenching sadness she had felt that first day. She knew it was driving a wedge between her and Miguel, but she didn't care. Nothing mattered anymore.

She had prayed Nathaniel would bring her justice, but he had been gone now for weeks, and there had been no word. By now she must assume he was dead. He was a nice young man, and it would be a shame if he too were lost. But still, it had been his *duty* as Maria's betrothed to seek justice for her death, had it not?

Only in the last two days had rumors started circulating. Rumors that Ortega was dead, that Ortega's brother had stabbed him with a knife and taken over the Tigers. Or that someone had killed Ortega *and* his brother and there was a new leader of the Tigers. One said the Mexican authorities had arrested the Tigers. Another, even stranger, said the bandits had all run away for fear of ghosts! And on and on.

She had no idea if any of it was true, but it did sound hopeful. At least there was a recurring theme that something had gone terribly wrong for Ortega.

But what of Nathaniel? What had happened to him?

The knock came again, this time more forceful. That didn't sound like one of her friends … not a woman's knock at all.

"*Ah* … my Maria," she sighed for the thousandth time. She set aside her dark train of thought and stood to answer the door.

When she opened the door, a tall white man stood there. With the darkness inside, and the bright sunlight outside, it was difficult to see his face. But he was dirty and unshaven, and he wore ragged clothes.

"Si? How can I help you, Señor?" she asked.

"Señora … it's me … Nathaniel Chambers … I have returned."

Teresa sucked in her breath in shock and surprise. She gazed up at his face, "It … it *is* you, Nathaniel! Saints be praised! But … what has happened?"

He gazed into her eyes for a long moment, then sighed, "It is done, Señora. Even as you asked."

"*What* is done …? *Oh!* Nathaniel … you have avenged Maria? You have killed the evil dogs who murdered her?"

"Si, Señora. I have killed them. I have killed them *all*. And … *many* others besides."

She gazed up at him in amazement. It was then she noticed the pain, suffering, and sorrow written in his expression, and her heart melted.

"Oh, my dear boy … what have you suffered to do this thing?" she said, and wrapped her arms around him, holding him tight. He stood still a moment, then gently embraced her.

They stood in the doorway for a long time just holding each other. And for the first time since Nathan had buried Maria, Teresa let go of her anger, and embraced her grief. And for the first time since Maria's death, Nathan did the same.

๕ใฦ๏ลใ๛ฮใ๛ๆๆลใ๛ฮใ๛ๆๆลใ

Nathan knelt on the gravesite, now lined with flowers and overhung by a large, proper tombstone. "Maria Aquilar Diaz" it said, "Beloved daughter and sister." He gazed at it a moment, then bowed his head.

"Oh … *mi amor*. I am so sorry," he said as tears streamed down his face. He leaned down and kissed the very earth that covered her. "I have killed you with my arrogance and pride. I should have listened to you.

"If I could live it over again, I would *beg* Ortega for permission to marry. I would humble myself and bury my pride. But now I have lost you, the person I loved best in the world. And I will never see you again. I'm so … so … sorry, *mi amor*."

For a long time, he knelt there and wept, venting his grief and pain.

When he finally stood up, he looked to the sky. "And dear Lord, I have betrayed you as well. I have strayed from the righteous path. I have committed bloody murder and have killed innocents and caused the death of others in my anger and pride. I am no longer a worthy servant.

"But I still wish to be. I beg your forgiveness, though I know I am not deserving. I humbly ask for a sign that you might one day forgive me. A sign to give me strength to carry on and start feeling whole again."

And then as if in answer to his prayers he heard a voice behind him, "Lieutenant Chambers? Is that you?"

Nathan turned and saw it was Sergeant Daniel Young.

"My God, it *is* you, sir! Praise the Lord you've returned. We all feared you dead," Daniel said. "But then today we heard a rumor you were back, so the Captain sent me to look for you. But, sir … you're a frightful sight."

Nathan realized it was true. Besides his eyes, red and swollen from crying, he smelled like a barnyard and was filthy from head to toe. His clothes were practically rags, and he hadn't shaved in a month.

"Yes, I'm back, or what's left of me. It's good to see you too, Daniel. And I suppose I may as well come with you now and face the music. I expect the Captain is going to throw me in the stockade for going AWOL and disobeying his orders, after which he'll doubtless have me court martialed."

"Oh, I don't know about all that, sir," Daniel answered. "He didn't say. He just ordered me to find you and bring you to him."

Nathan sighed, "All right. I'm ready. Lead on."

When Nathan entered the Captain's office, he stood to attention and snapped a salute, despite his disheveled look and lack of uniform. The Captain remained seated but returned the salute. Nathan thought it a bad sign the Captain held a scowl on his face that appeared to be a permanent fixture.

"Have a seat, Chambers. I'll just have the Sergeant clean it off after you've left," he said with a snort.

"Sorry for the appearance, sir. I meant to have a bath and a shave before coming to see you, but Sergeant Young insisted you wanted to see me straight away."

"Yes, Lieutenant. We have some unfinished business to discuss."

"Yes, sir. And I want you to know I won't blame you for any punishment you see fit to mete out. I humbly apologize for my disrespectful manner last time I was here, and I am ready to accept whatever I have coming to me."

The Captain tilted his head and gazed at Nathan for a long moment, and then an odd, twisted smile seemed to light up his face.

"Chambers, a few days ago we heard a strange rumor from across the border. It said some kind of demon crossed over into Mexico, killed Ortega, and annihilated his entire gang. They say the *'Tigres del Norte'* no longer exist on account of a ghost or spirit or something they call *'El Diablo Blanco.'* You know anything about that?"

Nathan fought to suppress a grin of his own. "Oh no, sir. I know nothing about any demons or spirits, sir. Or devils."

The Captain continued to gaze at him another moment, then said, "No ... of course you wouldn't. In any case, seems we owe this ... *White Devil* ... our gratitude for ridding this part of the country of a great nuisance."

"Hmm ... as you say, sir."

"Anyway, Chambers, I brought you in to tell you about the actions the Army has taken in regard to your absence."

"Sir."

"Yes, well ... this is kind of embarrassing, but it seems ... in the usual army fashion ... there's been a mix-up with the official paperwork. You understand ... these things *do* happen from time to time ..."

"Sir?"

"Chambers, after you left, I fully intended to send in paperwork reporting you AWOL and derelict in your duties. Recommending you for court martial."

"Yes, Sir."

Then a grin touched the corners of his eyes. "Instead I seem to have ... *inadvertently* ... submitted the promotion paperwork I had filled out and signed just before ... well, you know ... before the tragedy with Maria."

"You ... did *what*, sir?"

"The sum and substance is ... it looks like the Army has processed your *promotion* paperwork rather than your court martial, Chambers."

The Captain stood and held out his left hand, palm up. Nathan saw there was something in his hand. He leaned down and saw it was the uniform shoulder patch of an Army captain. Nathan gazed at it for a moment then looked up at the Captain in shock and confusion.

The Captain broke into a wide grin, stood to attention, and snapped Nathan a salute.

"Congratulations ... *Captain* Chambers! And ... welcome home!"

Chapter 6. Strangers in a Strange Land

"I have been a stranger in a strange land."
– Moses, Exodus 2:22

Wednesday May 16, 1860 – Del Rio, Texas:

The next morning, as they struck camp in Del Rio preparing for a parting of ways, Tom approached Nathan for a few quiet words.

"Interesting tale last night, sir," he said, smiling only with his eyes.

"Yes … I'd imagine so. Not your typical bedtime story, I suspect," Nathan answered. He gave a Tom a quizzical look, wondering where this was headed.

"No … nothing like my Momma used to read to me, that's for sure," Tom answered. "Still … a good tale, and all the more so for being true."

"As I said before, not something I'm proud of," Nathan said, shaking his head. "I got a lot of people killed, starting with the woman I loved and intended to marry. Not my finest hour, Tom."

"Maybe … but I'd say you did what you had to do and made amends for your mistakes with honor and courage. It was … most *commendable*, sir."

Nathan was surprised by this, "Oh. Thank you for saying so, Tom. But I doubt the others …"

"No … the others are even more effusive in their praise, if anything," Tom cut in, with a grin. "Especially Stan. He can't stop talking about your story and wishing he'd been there to see it himself. And to help kill bandits, no doubt. I believe he now has … a new respect for you, sir."

Nathan snorted a short laugh, "Well, that's something, at least. Though I'm not sure having Stan admire one's bloody handiwork is something one should aspire to."

Tom laughed, "True, true. Still, you needn't worry about the men. If anything, I believe they admire you even more than before. And I think they felt honored you trusted them enough to share a painful memory with them."

"Well … though I was reluctant to talk about it, I do feel better for having spit it out. I haven't thought about some of the more painful aspects in years."

"If I may offer an unsolicited suggestion, sir?"

"Certainly, Tom. Please say what's on your mind."

"Sir, I think … I think it's time you forgave yourself for what happened eleven years ago. I have no doubt whatsoever God already has."

𝕰𝕺𝕮𝕲𝕰𝕺𝕮𝕲𝕰𝕺𝕮𝕲𝕰𝕺𝕮𝕲

Once all was made ready for their departure, they said their goodbyes to their hosts, Fernando, Isabella, and the two boys. Each of the men thanked the family sincerely for all they'd done. After paying Fernando twice the agreed upon amount for the meals, Nathan gave each of the boys a silver dollar which made their eyes open almost as big around as the coins!

Then Nathan and his men stood in a line as Ballantyne, Willie, and Sue prepared to head north, with their train of horses carrying the prisoners and the dead men. They said their cordial farewells to Ballantyne and Willie, who then moved a little off, allowing Sue time alone with her benefactors, as she'd requested.

She stepped in front of them and looked each in the eye. She impressed Nathan; few young women had the courage to stand and face a whole group of men they barely knew. Her boldness and self-confidence had no doubt served her well during her ordeal, he decided.

"I have no proper way to thank you men, except to say I shall never forget *any* of you. You risked your lives to save a young girl you'd never even met. And for no other reason than you are good, God-fearing men. You are my heroes, my saviors. I will *never, ever* forget you to my dying breath."

She then walked down the line, embracing each man and planting a kiss on his cheek. To this joyful, unexpected female attention, each reacted in his own way. William looked stiff and uncomfortable, blushing. Stan beamed, laughing out loud, the others amused he had to bend down almost double for her to reach his cheek. Both Jamie and Georgie smiled shyly and blushed furiously. Jim and Tom smiled and bowed, the only ones capable of a polite, "Thank you, ma'am," to the affectionate attentions of the young woman.

When she came to Billy Creek she paused. He had not been at the cantina and she had only met him when he rejoined the party after they'd crossed the river back into Texas the day before. She knew about his part in the rescue, and all he'd done on her behalf. That he'd been the one to track down the outlaws and find her, making the whole rescue mission possible. But she had never known an Indian before. Growing up in Texas she'd always viewed them with suspicion and had been taught to treat them with caution. The situation forced her to reconcile her lifelong prejudices against the fact an Indian had risked his life, multiple times, to help save hers. She smiled, and asked, "Will an Indian accept a kiss of thanks from a white woman?"

He tilted his head and looked up, as if in thought, then looked in her eyes for a long moment. Then he too smiled. "Ha! When she's as bright and pretty as you he *will!*"

She returned his smile, then leaned in and gave him his kiss.

Then she stepped up in front of Nathan and gazed into his eyes. "I know God sent you to save me. I am only a poor, young girl … I can never repay so great a man! But I promise I will never forget … *never!*" And then she leapt into his arms and once again wrapped her arms around his neck. He could feel her wet tears against his neck. As he held her, he suppressed a groan from the pain in his side. He felt her kiss him on the neck and realized for the first time she was *not* a little girl as he'd been thinking.

When she let loose and stood back, he saw a soft look in her eyes that hadn't been there before, and now tears streamed down her face.

He didn't know what to say. In that moment he knew he'd had an unexpected effect on the young woman. He felt a sadness, realizing this would be a hard parting for her.

"Sue … I've been thinking about what you said … about God and all. And you may have the right of it. It does seem to me God brought us together … there can be no other reasonable explanation. And you needn't thank me … I believe it was something I *had* to do, maybe to make things right with God for the … *other* things I've done in Mexico … things that maybe weren't so righteous.

"But you *can* repay God for his amazing grace … just be the best woman … and one day, wife and mother, you can be. That will be repayment enough. No one can ask more."

She smiled at him, and nodded her appreciation, but seemed choked up and unable to reply.

She mounted her horse, and her party moved off down the trail. But this time she *did* turn back toward Nathan and smiled brightly. He returned the smile with genuine warmth and waved goodbye.

When they were out of sight Sue began to cry and continued to weep long and hard for many miles. Nothing Willie could do or say would console her.

ᏍᎣᏍᎣᏟᎶᏍᎣᏍᎣᏟᎶᏍᎣᏍᎣᏟᎶ

The first two days' ride out from Del Rio on the road to San Antonio were relatively uneventful. But toward the end of the second day Tom noticed the Captain grimacing when the terrain was bumpy. He flinched and looked pained with any sudden movement. When they made camp that evening Tom mentioned it to William, who made the Captain take off his shirt, so he could change the bandage.

When he peeled it back, William had a worried expression, and looked up at the Captain. "A good deal of pain, sir?"

"Well, yes. It does seem to have … *stiffened up* a bit in the last two days."

"Worse than just 'stiff' I think, Captain. It has begun to fester. I'm afraid our friend Gold-tooth did not keep his knife as clean as one could have wished. I very greatly hate to put you through more pain than you're already in, sir. But I'd really like to open it back up and thoroughly clean it out, with a little alcohol this time. I brought along a bottle from the cantina, just in case."

173

"Do you think that's wise, William?" Tom asked. "I've always heard it's best for healing to leave the white pus in a wound."

William looked over at Tom, "Well, yes, that has been the prevailing opinion in medicine for many years. Ever since the ancient Greek physician Galen wrote his theories on 'laudable pus,' in the third century. He observed very deep and deadly wounds rarely exhibited any pus, while less severe, quickly healing surface wounds tended to have more.

"But I believe his logic is flawed; I would argue that deep wounds are by their very nature deadlier. The lack of pus has nothing to do with it. And several scholars through the years have concurred though there has been no definitive agreement in the medical community.

"Anyway, to answer your question, I am of the opinion the pus is *not* good for healing. I base this on simple observations of my own; the surface wounds I have seen that are clean, and show no pus, heal more quickly, cause the person less pain, and leave a smaller scar. They also rarely lead to loss of limbs. It seems reasonable to me, this means little or no pus is a good sign for healing, so cleaning away the pus must also be a good thing."

"Okay … that may be true, but why the alcohol? If you need to clean it why not use water? I'm sure the whiskey will sting like the devil."

"Yes, that's true. I must admit … I am out on a limb on this one. I don't think the whiskey has any real medicinal value, other than if the patient drinks it to ease the pain, but …"

"Yes?"

"Well, you see, I have observed other liquids … water, fruit juice, milk, even wine, will fester after a time, such that you could not drink them without becoming sick. But from what I understand whiskey can sit for a hundred years and still be just as good as the day it was bottled. I don't understand why that is. But it seems to me it is by its nature a very *clean* liquid, and since it won't ever fester, it should help keep a wound from festering. But … it is just my *idea* … and I could be wrong about it and simply causing the Captain additional hardship."

Tom was skeptical. It sounded like a lot of far-fetched nonsense, and he was reluctant to subject the Captain to unnecessary pain and suffering.

"Well, sir. What do you think? Do you want to have William do as he says, or would you rather go with the conventional wisdom, and leave the wound alone?"

Nathan looked at Tom, then at William. They could see beads of sweat on his brow, and his eyes were red and watery. He was clearly in great pain though he hadn't complained all day.

"I'd trust William over some damned ancient Greek," he said. "Never mind the pain; do whatever you think's best, William."

"If you're sure, sir. I'm afraid it's going to hurt much worse than before, and I'll have to re-stitch you when it's done. Best you lie down this time, sir."

William rummaged through his things and brought out a bottle of whiskey he'd stowed there, out of sight lest it become too great a temptation to the others.

"Hey, William! You been holding out on us?" Jim gave him an annoyed look. The Captain had forbid bringing any liquor on their wilderness journey to ensure they kept their wits about them, so they'd not had a taste except in the cantina, and the bottle Ballantyne had shared out around the campfire after.

"Never mind about that, Jim. William's been saving it for medicinal purposes only; and it's a darned good thing, too," Tom answered. He scowled at Jim, who just shrugged, and went back to setting up his tent.

William handed the bottle to Nathan, who took two long swallows, then handed it back. He lay down gingerly on a blanket William and Tom had laid out on the ground for him.

William took out a small, razor-sharp knife he kept for such purposes. He poured a few drops of whiskey on the blade. Then a small amount on the wound. Tom cringed thinking how much that must burn. He could see the edges of the wound were now bright red, and appeared swollen, pushing tightly against the black stitches. There was also a thick, yellow fluid oozing out in places.

William took the knife and quickly cut the stitches, removing them carefully with his fingertips. Then he used the knife to gently pull the edges of the wound apart. Tom could see the exposed ribs underneath and was starting to feel a bit queasy and had to look away. William poured whiskey into the wound, and carefully wiped it out with a clean, white piece of cloth. He repeated this procedure two more times until he appeared satisfied.

While William worked, Nathan laid still, and made no sound. His eyes were shut, and one might almost have thought he was asleep but for the occasional flaring of his nostrils, and sudden heavy breathing from time to time.

Finally, William got out needle and thread, and proceeded to re-stitch the wound. When finished, he poured a little more whiskey over the whole thing, wiped it down once more, and then applied another thick piece of white cloth over the wound. He then carefully wrapped a long, thin strip of cloth around the Captain's midsection and tied it off, to hold the bandage in place.

The Captain didn't stir, and they realized he was now asleep. Whether he'd collapsed from exhaustion, or had passed out from the pain, they couldn't tell.

They covered him up and left him to sleep, walking out of earshot.

"I've been meaning to ask, William—however did you get to know so much about medical practices, and to be so good at patching up wounds?" Tom asked.

"Oh, well it's one of many things I studied when I was at Yale College back in Connecticut. I spent more than two years studying at the medical school there before I decided it wasn't really what I wanted to do with my life. Besides, as you can see, I was ... very *opinionated*, and had strong ideas of my own, which the professors didn't always appreciate. But I've found the knowledge and skills I learned have come in handy out here in the West."

"More than just handy, I'd say. Life-saving is closer to the mark."

"Thank you, sir."

"No! Thank *you*, William. For taking care of the Captain. Do you think he'll be all right?"

"Well, I'd be lying if I said I wasn't concerned about that wound. I hate to see it festering like that … it's worrisome. But … there *are* good things about it. For one, the ribs stopped the blade, and kept it from cutting into his abdomen wall … into his 'guts' as we might say. And … the Captain's a very strong, healthy man. That helps the healing, in my experience. Let's hope now it's been cleaned and re-stitched he'll be back on the mend."

"Yes … amen to that, William."

ಐಖಿಲಿ೧೮ಐಖಿಲಿ೧೮ಐಖಿಲಿ೧೮

The next day the Captain rose just before dawn, as was his habit, and moved about camp as if nothing were bothering him. But Tom noticed he didn't smile as he usually did when greeting the men. Then he ate his morning meal and packed his things in a very businesslike, no-nonsense manner. And when it came time to mount his horse, Tom noted a slight hesitation, a momentary pause he hadn't seen before. But then it seemed to pass, and the Captain swung up into the saddle with seeming ease.

That evening after making camp, Jamie and Georgie took the rifle and went out hunting. An hour after their departure, the men in camp heard a single gunshot in the near distance. The single shot caught everyone's immediate attention, and they stopped what they were doing to listen. But no more shots followed, so they returned to their business. Both men out hunting were armed with pistols, so if there had been any trouble, they'd have heard multiple pistol shots, not just a single rifle shot. A few minutes later the two came back, carrying between them the carcass of a small wild pig, called a *javelina*. They were beaming ear to ear and enjoyed the warm regards of their comrades that evening as they indulged in fresh meat roasted over the campfire.

The next day, their fourth since departing Del Rio, the midday heat intensified, and Tom once again became concerned about the Captain. Though William had changed the bandage again and said the wound looked better, it was clearly still causing him great pain. Occasionally he would wince when his mare hit a bump or

177

would emit a low grunt when she missed a step on the rough ground. He never complained, but Tom could see from his expression it was becoming a difficult slog for him, and the sweat rolled from his brow in beads.

Tom was also becoming concerned about losing their way. With the Captain ailing, he was determined not to become lost in the wilderness. As each mile passed, and the air became steadily heavier with humidity, the surrounding vegetation became ever lusher and thicker. Tall, thorny bushes, too tall to see over, and short deciduous trees, too spindly and brambly to climb, tangled together in ever thicker patches. Adding to that, the terrain was relatively flat—a rolling kind of landscape, making it impossible to see more than a few yards in any direction. And the path had begun to wind around the thickest trees and underbrush, in an ever-twisting fashion, and he had a fear they were moving in circles.

Tom thought it ironic people back east often referred to the "trackless wilderness" of the West. Nothing could be further from the truth; no tracks were *not* the problem. Rather there were *too many* tracks. These trails were made by deer and other wild animals, and later used and occasionally improved or widened by humans. The result was a maze of twisting, branching intersections. Each time the "road" split, Tom would pause and examine the track carefully in both directions to decide which was the more likely course. Usually this was obvious, one fork having clear horse tracks, and the other mostly game animals. But a few times he had to consult with Jim and Billy, and between them they would make their best guess.

More than once Tom wished he had a portable compass so he could tell their exact direction. He'd read Lewis and Clark carried one on their famous expedition to the western sea. But the only compasses he'd ever seen were the large, mounted kind aboard ships. So they had to steer as best they could by the position of the sun. When in doubt, they'd err toward the north, figuring if they missed their mark, they would eventually hit the main westward road out of San Antonio. If they missed San Antonio to the south, they might wander for weeks in the wilderness without finding a major road.

Of course, they would normally have left these decisions to the Captain. But it had become clear to Tom it was all Nathan could do to deal with the pain and keep himself upright in the saddle. Tom decided he would disturb the Captain only in the direst emergency.

What he needs is a distraction, Tom thought. But Jim and Stan were strangely quiet, either lost in their own thoughts, or finally run out of humorous jokes and stories. *Ha, not likely that,* Tom decided.

Everyone seemed dulled by the monotony of the ride, and the relentless heat beating down on them. Only Billy looked up and met Tom's eye. Billy made a motion toward the Captain, and shrugged, as if to ask, *How is he doing?* Tom shook his head, meaning, *Not so good.*

Then Tom had a thought—an interesting story he'd once heard but was pretty sure the Captain had not.

"Hey, Billy. Why is it the Comanche hate the Tonkawa so much?" he called out. The Captain's bowed head looked up, startled by the sudden noise.

"What … the Comanche? Oh, it is a very long, old tale. Would you like to hear it, Sergeant Clark?"

A long tale, Tom thought. *Just the medicine the Captain needs.*

"Yes, Billy, if you please."

The other men started to perk up. Billy rarely spoke much, but when he did his stories tended toward the bizarre and supernatural, with plenty of his own special brand of odd, dry humor thrown in. This typically made for highly entertaining stories.

"There once was a time, very long, and long, ago. Back before the grandfathers of our grandfathers were even conceived by their grandfathers' grandfathers. So long ago, in fact, it is said it was almost the very beginning of time—whenever that was." He shrugged his shoulders and grinned.

"Anyway … in that long-ago time it was different between the Comanche and the *People*, those of us you white men now call

Tonkawa. Back then we did *not* hate each other and fight always, the way we do now. We didn't *love* each other either, of course; there is no amount of time going *that* far back, ha!

"In that time the *People* and the Comanche knew each other, but lived apart, sometimes seeing each other when they shared the hunting grounds. The land was not dry as now. It was filled with a great greenness. It is said the water was abundant, and fell from the sky so often, it flowed carelessly, wandering across the land, heedless of its proper places in rivers and lakes.

"And so, the land was filled with so many animals the *People* did not have to hunt long or hard for their daily meat. And never did they give thought to saving anything for tomorrow. Both the *People* and the Comanche were wasteful in their excess, never having known want.

"But there came a time when the *People* were led by a great and wise man. His name was *Tchezse*—um … *Tchezselkeizl* … well, it would mean nothing in your language, anyway. You would say something like 'Sun-and-Moon-in-Sky-Together-and-Wind-in-Stars,' but that is not quite right either. For my story, I will just be calling him 'Sun-Moon' and you will know who I'm talking about.

"Sun-Moon was very wise, as I have already said. One day he called the *People* together saying, 'I have had a mighty dream of the gods, and they have made my eyes to see many great and terrible things.' And the *People* listened as Sun-Moon told his seeing—of a time to come when water would stop falling from the sky and would no longer flow heedless across the land. It would return to its ancestral home in a few, shallow rivers and lakes or sink deep into the ground. And the land would change from green to brown, and the animals that once provided the *People* with their daily meat would hide away in far-off lands.

"Then the *People* were afraid, and asked Sun-Moon what would become of their children, and their children's children, if there were no greenness and no meat. But Sun-Moon said, 'You needn't worry about your children's children, or even your own children; this *time* the gods have shown me is coming even unto the lives of you who sit before me. If the *People* do not prepare to face the evil time coming, all will perish from the earth.'

"And so, Sun-Moon led the men high into the hills, or deep into caves under the Earth. There the animals were few and fierce, so the men must become great hunters and trackers. And he taught the women and children to cure the extra meat they did not eat daily, with salt and different herbs growing in the earth. In this way their meat might be saved for many months in time of want. And he showed them where to find roots growing under the ground, for water, and food, at greatest need in time of dryness.

"But the Comanche had no great leader like Sun-Moon. They laughed at the *People* for making their hunts so difficult when meat was so plentiful. And they mocked them for digging in the earth for roots when food and water were so easily had on the open earth.

"But Sun-Moon was not angered by the cruel laughter of the Comanche. You see, he was a truly great and wise man—but I think I have already said that. So he went to them and told them also of his dreams, by way of warning they should prepare for the evil days to come. But still they would take no heed and sent him away with great scorn.

"And so, you will not be surprised to hear there came a day when the water stopped falling from the skies. And then the land turned all to brown, even as Sun-Moon had foretold. And though the *People* had been warned, and had prepared as best they could, still the greatness of this evil time was even greater than any had imagined. So although they had practiced hard to become mighty hunters, and great trackers of animals, still, bringing home the meat was hard. Though they ate little, and salted and kept back what they could, still many, and many died. And all suffered great want.

"This story was told me by a wise, old man when I was just a young boy, and he called this terrible time *The Breaking*."

"The Breaking?" Nathan asked, having become absorbed in the tale. "What does *that* mean?"

"He said it was called that because it was a time of such suffering and death, it caused the breaking of all the old ways. Some for the good, and some for the worse. Nothing came through *The Breaking* unchanged, and all that once was, even to the greenness of the earth, was *broken* during that time, and was never again the same.

"Well … it is said while the *People* suffered greatly in *The Breaking*, the Comanche suffered more. They had not heeded the words of Sun-Moon, of course. So they had never learned the skills to hunt the few animals remaining, and to dig the roots from the earth. Their need was great, and they became desperate, and dangerous.

"They saw the *People* still had the meat they had preserved, and a store of the roots they had pulled from the ground. And they became angry the *People* had food, and they had none. So they came to the *People* and demanded they be given the food the *People* had saved.

"But Sun-Moon took pity on them. He said, 'There is not enough of the salted meat and roots for both the *People* and the Comanche, so we cannot give it to you. But we *will* teach you to hunt that you may bring home your own meat. And we will teach you to save your meat by salting, and how to find roots living under the ground that you might dig them up.'

"But the Comanche were hungry and did not want to wait to learn these things. Instead they decided they would take the food from the *People* by war. So they returned to their village, put on their war paint, and collected their hunting spears. By the time they had made ready for war it was becoming dark. They lit torches and carried them to see their way back to the camp of the *People*.

"But Sun-Moon had foreseen this as well and made ready the *People* for the war that was coming. The Comanche came, carrying their torches. They have always been larger, stronger, and more fearsome than the *People*, so they carried their deadly spears with confidence of easy victory. They could already taste the precious food that would soon be theirs.

"But they had forgotten the men of the *People* had become great hunters. Because their prey had been more fierce and cunning, the *People* had learned to use the bow, and shoot arrows with deadly aim. And they had learned to use lightweight throwing spears to hit prey from a distance, rather than short, heavy spears the Comanche used to butcher their easy kills.

"Many Comanche were killed, and the rest fled in fear. But those who fell, and those who fled, all dropped their torches, and the dry earth was set afire. It burned all that night with a great flame that lit the sky.

"When the sun rose in the morning, the *People* found all their food had been destroyed by fire. They were hungry but were also very tired from the fighting and the fire and had no strength left to hunt. Also, all the animals they might have hunted had been driven far away by fear of the flames.

"And so the *People* did the only thing left for them to do. They *ate* the Comanche they had killed."

"They ... *ate* them?" Georgie asked.

"Yes. Sun-Moon told them it was the only sensible thing the *People* could do so they would not all starve and die. And so that is what they did.

"It is said the great flames of the fire sent smoke high into the sky. It climbed so high it mingled with the scant clouds, and caused the water to start falling again, though never so much as before.

"The war with the Comanche, you see, was the end of *The Breaking*, but it was the beginning of the hatred of the Comanche for the *People*."

"Well, I don't see why the Comanche should hate the Tonkawa. Sounds like they lost the war fair and square, and after *they* started it!" Jamie said, and Georgie nodded in agreement.

But Billy shrugged his shoulders and said, "Guess Comanche don't like being eaten. Ha!"

The men chuckled and even the Captain smiled.

"I've heard people say the Tonkawa still eat their enemies," William said.

Billy turned toward him and grinned, "Then best hope I never have to kill *you*, William!"

William shook his head "No," emphatically.

Billy continued, "I have heard of it being done. When the enemy is not of the *People* and is killed in man-to-man battle. Some

183

say it is to honor those who fought the war of *The Breaking.* Others say the fighting spirit of the dead is taken into the living that way. I don't know … seems to me the one left alive had more fighting spirit than the dead one! Ha!"

Though he seemed more alert after Billy's tale, by the time they'd made camp that evening Nathan was already laid down and asleep, as if from utter exhaustion. Tom was still concerned and sat up long into the night watching over his Captain. At first, Nathan tossed in his sleep and seemed to moan as if in pain. But then at some point, it seemed to Tom he began to rest more at ease and sleep more at peace.

ᏏᏋᏁᎬᏣᏋᏏᏋᏁᎬᏣᏋᏏᏋᏁᎬᏣ

In the morning, Nathan was moving around more easily. "Feeling better today, sir?" Tom asked.

"Yes, much. Thanks, Tom. Still, I have to admit I'll be happy to get to San Antonio and sleep in a real bed for a few nights."

"Yes … and walk about on my own two legs for a full day!" Tom agreed. "If my calculations are correct, and we aren't totally off our course, we should be there by late afternoon, sir."

A few hours past midday they crested a small rise in the trail and saw the town spreading out in the distance. Tom's calculations had proven correct, to his relief. But Nathan said he was not at all surprised, and that he had total confidence in Tom's abilities in any given situation.

ᏏᏋᏁᎬᏣᏋᏏᏋᏁᎬᏣᏋᏏᏋᏁᎬᏣ

When Nathan had first seen San Antonio just after the Mexican war back in the late '40s, it was almost a ghost town. It'd been devastated by decades of warfare, and many houses stood empty, their properties abandoned and overrun with weeds.

Originally the domain of the Payaya Indians, a group of Spanish missionaries arrived on June 13, 1691. It happened to be the feast day of Saint Anthony from Italy, so they named the place and the river running through it *San Antonio* in honor of the saint. They established a mission station in the early 1700s. Then in 1718 they built a fortified mission building, originally named the

184

Mission San Antonio de Valero; but it later became known simply as "The Alamo," the Spanish name for the cottonwood trees growing in a grove around it.

The Mexicans wrested San Antonio from the Spanish during their war of independence in the 1820s, followed closely by the Texans, who after several battles took it from the Mexicans in the late '30s. Then a failed peace conference between the Texans and the Comanche Indians led to more warfare in the streets. In the early '40s, the Mexicans once again invaded and attempted to recapture the town. By 1846, only 800 people were left. San Antonio had been one of the most fought-over towns in North America and was showing the depredations of war.

But as Nathan and company arrived in May 1860, San Antonio was booming, with a population well over 10,000. It was now one of the largest cities in Texas, if not *the* largest, along with Houston and Galveston. To Nathan's men, returning from the West Texas wilderness, the city was bursting at the seams. They were wide-eyed with wonder at all the sights they were seeing. San Antonio was filled with people of all different races, costumes, and languages bustling about everywhere.

The buildings varied greatly from one street to the next as if each neighborhood had been settled by different groups of foreigners. Most surprising of all was what they encountered when the Captain led them down a street filled with finely built, well-tended houses. The first man they met, who was neatly dressed in a suit, looked up at them, tipped his hat, and said, *"Guten tag."* And everyone else they met said the same and were just as nicely dressed. The men were shocked; they'd been expecting English, or maybe Spanish—but this?

Nathan smiled knowingly, and the men looked at him in amazement with wondering looks.

"What in name of the archangel's languages are they talking?" Stan finally asked.

"Would you believe … *German?*" Nathan answered and smiled once again.

The others looked at him in disbelief.

"Yes, it's true. After hundreds of years, being fought over by Indians, Spanish, Mexicans, Texans, and us Americans, the most common language in San Antonio, America is ... believe it or not ... *German!*"

He smiled again, knowing he had shocked his men with a fact they had never imagined possible.

"But ... how ... *why?*" Tom finally asked. The others nodded their agreement with his puzzlement.

"Well, Tom, it's one of those fine, odd coincidences. Just when San Antonio was in desperate need of residents, decimated by years of warfare, the German states were in great upheaval with their own wars, revolutions, and whatnot. So, many Germans, most simple farmers but a few well-to-do professionals, packed up their things, boarded ships, and headed to America, their final destination being ... of all places ... *San Antonio, Texas!* This whole neighborhood we are riding through was built by recent immigrants from the German states!"

The men looked around in admiration. This neighborhood was much nicer than any they'd yet ridden through. Houses were well constructed of stone and brick, with small but elegant entries and verandas; lawns were well trimmed, with flowers and gardens neatly tended. Trees lined the street; though not yet tall, they could imagine someday it would make a stately and elegant framework for the neighborhood.

"I've stayed in this neighborhood before. Mrs. Schmidt runs a boarding house not much further on; she is expecting us. She came to San Antonio with her husband and three young children. They built a large house, and re-started her husband's tailoring business, as he'd run back in Germany. They had planned to fill the house with many more children, but he took ill and suddenly passed away. So she sold his business, and has been using her large, mostly empty house for boarding guests to make ends meet. She is ... a *very* special person ... I think y'all will enjoy her home, but please be on your best behavior. She is ... *someone I care about* ..." he finished quietly.

"Certainly, Captain! We will treat Mrs. Schmidt better'n if she was our own Momma!" Jim answered with a grin, an unlit cigar in his teeth. "Ain't that right boys," he said, turning and glaring at the men riding along behind him.

"Oh, yes, sir! Yes, Sergeant. Oh, certainly, sir!" they answered, nodding emphatically.

ঞ৶৹৻৵৶৹৻৵৶৹৻

When they arrived at their destination, Tom decided it would *not* be difficult to treat Mrs. Schmidt as if she were their very own mother; she immediately treated the men as if they were her very own sons! Her overflowing warmth and kindliness quickly won them over. She seemed especially pleased to see the Captain and doted on him with particular warmth.

"Oh, my dear Captain Chambers ... oh! Excuse me! I should now be saying *Mister* Chambers. How quickly a woman forgets. But I am so pleased with the change, my dear. That you will no longer be out in harm's way amongst the savages and uncivilized men. It is so good to be seeing you again, Nathan, dear!"

She embraced him and kissed him on both cheeks, beaming brightly. A slight blush touched his face as he returned her smile. She was still a relatively young woman. And though she could no longer be mistaken for a skinny young schoolgirl ... still, Tom had to admit, she did not exactly have a *motherly* figure either. She had light brown hair tied up behind her head and a pretty face that lit up when she smiled. Tom imagined she had been quite a striking young woman in the flower of her youth. Then it occurred to him she might *not* exactly be thinking of the Captain in the *motherly* way.

She did not wait for Nathan to introduce the men, but immediately turned and embraced each in turn, after greeting them by name. Their stay here in San Antonio at Mrs. Schmidt's boarding house was the one part of the trip the Captain had insisted on arranging personally. Tom assumed he must have written her a letter describing each of his companions in detail.

"Oh, and you must be Sergeant ... oh, I mean *Mister* Clark," she giggled, embracing him, and kissing him on both cheeks. Tom felt his own face flush, just as the Captain's had done.

187

"And *Mister* Wiggins … finally remembered it this time, yes?" and she laughed again.

"Yes, ma'am. Mighty pleased to make your acquaintance. The Captain speaks most highly of you ma'am."

"Oh, does he? *Danke!* How delightful to hear!"

"And *you*, of course, are the great Stan. Oh, my! You *are* a very big one, yes?" She stood on her tip toes to reach his cheeks, and still he had to bend down to meet her.

She greeted the others with the same warmth and familiarity, including Billy whom she treated no differently, without even a hint of hesitance.

Her two young sons, in their early teens judging by their appearance, began unloading the horses. They stowed the traveling gear in a small carriage shed and hauled the personal items into the house.

Her young daughter, Elsa, who appeared to be about ten, came out of the house in a pretty blue dress adorned with a pattern of white and yellow flowers. She curtsied to the men and smiled the same bright smile as her mother. She ushered the men into a room that contained a wash basin. They proceeded to wash the road dust from their hands and faces but hurried to complete the task; they could smell a wonderful aroma of warm food coming from the next room, which was a large dining hall.

"Best hurry up, gents, or I'll be drooling all down the front of my shirt from that lovely smell," Jim said. The others needed no prompting, and soon all were seated around a large table as Mrs. Schmidt and Elsa brought around plates heaped high with steaming hot, home-cooked food. Though it was traditional German fare and unfamiliar to most of the men, it was delicious, and they set to with enthusiasm. The meat was a smoky-flavored sausage their host called *kohlwurst*, which was served with a spicy cooked cabbage, along with various steamed and seasoned vegetables from her garden.

During a pause in his meal, Tom turned to their host, his mind burning with curiosity about the amazing timing of the meal. "Tell me, Mrs. Schmidt; as we had no idea even what day we would arrive, let alone what hour of the day, how did you know when to prepare this wonderful meal? Clearly you would never have prepared so much food just for you and the children?"

She laughed and nodded appreciatively. "So, Mr. Clark, you are as Nathan has described, the ... how do you say it? *Logistics?* Yes? Yes ... the *logistics* officer, so you understand and appreciate how things must be properly prepared and planned, in a boarding house just the same as on a battlefield, yes?"

She turned and called out, "*Comen sie*, Hans!" and the eldest boy came trotting out and stood by his mother.

"My eldest son, Hans here, and several of his friends have been taking turns watching the south road coming into town for the last ... oh, four or five days. This morning one of the boys came riding up, all excited and out of his breath. He described you men perfectly. So knowing that Nathan ... *Mr. Chambers*, that is ... would likely come straight here after such long travels, we were knowing almost exactly what time to expect your arrival."

"Ah, well done, Mrs. Schmidt! Well done, Hans! I approve. Sounds like scouting our friend Billy here would appreciate." Billy looked up from his plate and just nodded in answer; his mouth was stuffed full of food. The boy smiled, said, *"Danke,"* and bowed before turning and trotting back to the kitchen.

And just when they were starting to feel well sated, the young girl Elsa came out bearing a large rectangular tray. A most heavenly smell of bread, with butter, sugar, and cinnamon wafted through the room. *Butterkuchen*, they called it—*butter cake*, in English. Jim once again found himself salivating while Elsa distributed the treat around the table.

And coming along behind his sister, the younger brother laid out a heavy porcelain cup for each of the guests. Their older brother followed behind, quickly filling each cup with steaming-hot black coffee from a large metal pot. Mrs. Schmidt came after, offering cream and sugar from a brightly decorated porcelain tray. Nathan politely declined, preferring his black.

Before Tom dived into his butter cake, he felt compelled to speak. "Mrs. Schmidt, I'm *highly* impressed by the military efficiency and precision of your whole operation. I must congratulate you on it!"

189

She beamed, *"Danke*, Mr. Clark. Thank you so very kindly! And it is high praise indeed, coming from *you*, sir. A man well-versed in such matters, no?"

Tom smiled and nodded in acknowledgment. The children mirrored their mother's gratitude, each nodding to Tom in turn.

ಬುಖಾಲಿ&ುಖಾಲಿ&ುಖಾಲಿ&

When they'd finished the coffee, and the table was being cleared away, Mrs. Schmidt ushered them out the back door. There, several tables and chairs had been arranged around a large, slate rock patio next to the house. Beyond the patio was a sizeable lawn dotted with small fruit trees. The entire sitting area was shaded from the westering sun by an arbor, overgrown with thick, lush vines and leaves filled with green bunches of grapes, small and hard, still months from ripeness. "In autumn, we will harvest enough grapes to vint a few bottles of wine for our guests. Perhaps tomorrow I will send one of the boys down to the cellar to find us a good bottle or two from last year to share out."

Jim felt a twinge of disappointment, forced to wait until the next day for the offered wine. But before he could travel more than a few steps along that dreary path, the boys once again came through; one offered cigars, the other drinking glasses and liquor in a clear bottle, which the boy called *"schnapps."* It reminded Jim of brandy; it was good, though he preferred whiskey if he had his choice. But as he lit the cigar and leaned back contentedly puffing, he decided he could not complain. This was probably the finest treatment he had had since ... well ... *ever!*

"Mrs. Schmidt, your hospitality may go straight to my head ... y'all are treating us old soldier dogs like kings. Soon we'll think we deserve bein' treated this way ever' day. And then the Captain won't know what to do with us!" he laughed, tipping his hat to her.

She smiled, and said, *"Danke*, Mr. Wiggins. I am so pleased you are enjoying yourself. But, please, you must ask Nathan ... uh, *your Captain*, that is ... is this not the way we *always* treat our guests?"

Nathan smiled, nodded emphatically, and then shrugged his shoulders, "Why do you think I always stay here whenever I'm in San Antonio? The Army'd be more than happy to find me a bunk in the barracks, and a chair in the mess hall!"

He chuckled at the thought, and shook his head, taking another sip of the schnapps.

But Mrs. Schmidt put her hand over her mouth in mock reproach, "My dear Mr. Chambers! And here all this time I thought it was just that you loved me so!" and then she giggled.

"Well, yes … of course, there's that too, Alisa," he grinned, blushing slightly.

Then Jamie, who'd been strangely quiet during dinner, turned to their host and asked what'd been on his mind ever since they'd arrived. "Please tell me, my dear missus … how is it so many o' your people have come to this place so far out west in America. And … I'm thinkin' from the looks o' this street, and your lovely house, that ye weren't a comin' here on account o' bein' in poverty?"

"I've often marveled on it myself, why our people were willing to sell their homes and everything they owned to come to the other side of the world to start anew. But several years ago, things were … *uncertain* in various principalities that make up the area you call *Germany*. Though we were not poor, there was great fear we might lose all we had through revolution, war, or political unrest. So, the people became interested in the New World. Some princes even started a … how you say … *company? Organization?* Anyway, they joined together to create something called the *Adelsverein* and arranged to buy large tracts of land here in Texas. It was all to promote the idea of their people coming to America. At that time Texas was its own independent country, and I suppose they thought they might gain some power over the new government. Oh, I don't know, it was all very exciting, but very complicated, and confusing. I know many of their ideas and schemes did not bear fruit as planned, and I think the princes did not entirely get what they wanted out of it. But still, here we are, and here we shall stay. Ourselves and our neighbors on this street, are from the region of Germany called *Niedersachsen*, what you would call *Lower Saxony* in English, near the town of Hannover.

"But what about you, Mr. O'Brien? How did you come to be in America? From Ireland, yes? I understand there are also many people from your country newly arrived in America; is it not so?"

Jamie didn't immediately answer. His face had a faraway look. Then he downed another swallow of liquor and clanked the glass down on the table.

"When I was after bein' a young lad in Ireland the famine was so bad our family had nothin' to eat, and neither did any o' our neighbors. The blight had been getting worse for years, and finally one year it destroyed the entire potato crop in the county, and there was nothin' to harvest. We had eaten all the layin' chickens and geese, and finally the cow that pulled the plow, and now there weren't nothin' left.

"Then my sweet young sister died. It was just a normal sickness, the kind a healthy person might get over in a few days. But she was weak from hunger and hadn't energy to fight. My Dad buried her out back and cried for days; he couldn't seem to stop. We children, you see, were all he had left, our mother havin' died years before … I can't recall now from what.

"Then, he seemed to snap out of it. He got a serious, determined look on him. He ups and sells everything we own, packs me a bag, and takes me down to the waterfront. He says, 'Jamie dear, there's nothin' left for it here in dear old *Éire*. So I'm puttin' you on the boat to America, where you can be alive, and not be dead.'

"'But Dad,' I says, 'surely you're goin' to America with me?' But he shakes his head no, and says, 'There's only enough money for the one ticket. So this is our goodbye. Make yourself a good life in America, Jamie m'dear.'

"'But then, I won't go neither,' I says, tears streaming down my cheeks. I was only ten years old. But he gets stern with me and says, 'You'll do as I say and go, else I will have died for naught.' And he hugged me tight, then turns me around, and shoves me onto the boat. I stumbled into the crowd. When I got up and looked back, he was already gone. I saw him ne'er again."

During the telling of this story Mrs. Schmidt had slowly settled herself into a chair to listen, and now she was wiping tears from her eyes. She reached out and grasped one of Jamie's hands. "Oh, how horrid! Oh, my dear child … how perfectly horrible. I am *so* sorry. No child should ever have to suffer that."

"Oh, well, as for *that* … it wasn't just *me*, missus. The entire boat was packed with children, young men, and young women going to America. They'd all been put on the boat by their parents, so's they'd have a chance to live and not be for starvin' to death. I later learned uncounted thousands of my people, in hundreds of boats, came to America the same way. But I hear the famine has eased somewhat back in old Ireland. So let's hope the worst is over."

There followed a long, awkward silence. It hung like a pall over the group that only moments before had been chatting happily.

Then Stan said, "Now you are making me to thinking my story of hunting seals and fighting drunks is just … much *foolishness*."

Jamie refilled his glass and took another sip of schnapps. Then he looked up and smiled, "I'm sorry, lads … didn't mean to put the old damper lid down on such a lovely evenin', and all. Never you worry; it is all well with me now! I grew up and made my way to Pennsylvania where I got a posh job as an apprentice to a gunsmith. Then met dear old Georgie here and foolishly let him talk me into joinin' the Army. So you see, things couldn't possibly be better!"

But Georgie spluttered after this last statement, nearly choking on his mouthful of schnapps. "What!? You're the one who wanted to join the Army, as I recall … on account of them having lots of guns and such. I'd lived my whole life in that little town in west Pennsylvania with no intention of ever going elsewhere. I was the foolish one, lettin' you fill my head with all that talk of adventure and strange new sights and all."

"Well, you remember it your way, and I'll remember it mine, boyo," Jamie answered with a smile and a wink.

Then he raised his glass to Georgie, who returned the salute with a grin of his own, after which each took another swallow.

"Hey, Georgie … what's the name of the town where you grew up?" William asked. "I traveled across Pennsylvania once; maybe I passed through there."

"I doubt it, William. It's on the road to nowhere, and you can't get nowhere from there! Nobody ever heard of it, and I reckon nobody ever will; it's called Gettysburg."

William thought for a moment. "No … don't recall being there; and you're right, I've never heard of it."

"Told you so."

Then Nathan raised his glass and said, "Well, I for one am delighted that *both* the German and the Irish people decided to come to this country, whatever the reasons. We are all the better for it, I am convinced. In Exodus, Moses said *'I have been a stranger in a strange land.'* Well, I think there can't possibly be a *stranger* land than *Texas*! And yet, here y'all are. But no longer strangers. We are all *Americans* here now. You too, Stan! A toast … to the *Americans!*"

"To the Americans!" they echoed and took another sip.

"And don't forget Billy," Jim said after lowering his glass, "Hell, his people have been here longer'n any of ours. Since *way* before the bad times, the … what was it you called it again, Billy?"

"The Breaking."

"Yes, that was it … since way back before Texas became so hot and dry. I reckon that makes him the most *American* of us all. I've been fightin' Indians since I was old enough to hold a rifle, and believe me, I've hated many of them personally. But as a whole I've got plenty of respect for 'em. Some mighty tough fightin' men, that's for damned sure.

"So … here's to the *first* Americans. Along with all of us that's come after!"

"To the *first* Americans!" they repeated and turned toward Billy, with glasses upheld. He looked up with a puzzled expression, then shrugged his shoulders, smiled, and downed his drink.

ৠ৶৶৶৶৶৶৶৶৶৶৶৶৶

The next morning, they were surprised the breakfast was more of the sort they were used to: eggs, bacon, fried bread with butter, and plenty of hot coffee. Mrs. Schmidt just smiled and shrugged her shoulders, "Since being in Texas I have learned what Texans like to eat for breakfast, yes?" There was, however, still some of the delicious *kohlwurst* left over from dinner. Jim was only too happy to help himself to that, having discovered he liked it even better than bacon.

Tom noticed Nathan had a new spring in his step. "You look very much better today, sir. A night in a real bed did you good?"

"Yes, certainly! You know … after he stitched me up, William said I was 'good as new.' Well, I can tell you for sure I did *not* feel that way at all on the road; *not at all*. But this morning, I *do* finally feel like new."

"Ready to take on another gang of bank robbers?" Tom teased.

"Well, maybe not *that* yet. Anyway, I am feeling so much recovered I think I will risk a short, gentle ride. Will you join me? I wish to pay my respects to Colonel Lee, who is currently headquartered here in town."

"Yes, certainly. It would be an honor."

When Nathan and Tom departed, they left Jim and Stan sitting on the back patio regaling the two young Schmidt boys with tales of the wild West.

"Hopefully they'll not corrupt them too badly."

"I'm sure they'll keep it somewhat in check, sir."

"That's reassuring."

ತುಳೕಣೖೆ೮ಲೕ೮ುಳೕಣೖೆ೮ಲೕ೮ುಳೕಣೖೆ೮ಲ

They arrived at U.S. Army headquarters, Department of Texas, a four-story stone building in downtown San Antonio. It was a testament to the civilized state of the West, that Army headquarters was not in a fort, but rather in a normal looking building in town, with the appearance somewhat of a hotel.

They climbed the short flight of outdoor stairs and entered the coolness of the foyer. They were greeted by a young lieutenant seated behind a desk. It was clearly his task to determine the

195

business of all visitors to the building and distribute them accordingly.

"I am Lieutenant Simmons. How may I assist you gentlemen?" he asked politely, looking up from a pile of papers, but remaining seated.

"My name is Nathaniel Chambers, late commanding officer, 8th Infantry out of Fort Davis. This is Mr. Clark, late sergeant of same. We've come to pay our respects to your commanding officer, Colonel Lee," Nathan answered in the formal manner.

But to their surprise, at the mention of their names the lieutenant's demeanor immediately changed. He lit up and stood, extending his hand to Nathan.

"Oh! Captain Chambers! I had been told to expect you. It is a very great honor, sir. And you too, Sergeant Clark. The Colonel speaks very highly of you, sir. Very highly, indeed! We were all saddened to hear of your resignation, but of course, can understand the pressing need of family and all. Please, come in, come in, sirs. Let me find you a seat. May I fetch you something to drink? It is already a hot one out there today!"

Nathan and Tom were, of course, pleased with the warmth of the reception, which they had not expected.

"So you are saying that Colonel Lee is expecting us?"

"Oh … no, not exactly, sir. You see, he said you very well *might* be passing through San Antonio on your way east. And if you did, I was to extend you all possible courtesy, and give you any assistance you might need. I am ordered to provide you with accommodations, meals, and provisions, if you require them."

"Thank you very kindly, lieutenant, but that will not be necessary. We have already made our arrangements. But tell me, is Colonel Lee not in residence? You make it sound as if he will not be available to meet with us in person? Is there aught amiss with him?"

"Oh, no sir. He is quite well. But alas, you are correct; he is not currently in residence. You have just missed him by a few days. He departed the morning of the 15th May on his way to Brownsville. There he is to take up his new headquarters either at Fort Ringgold or Fort Brown as circumstances warrant. And …"

he smiled, and gave Nathan a curious look, "if I may say so, sir, it is partially your own fault he's gone."

"Oh? How so?"

"Well, sir, the Colonel was so pleased by your report on the success of your recent operations against the Moat Kangly outlaw gang, he decided to use similar tactics himself down along the border. It seems there's a bandit by name of Juan Cortina who's been stirring things up in the area. The Colonel is determined to put a stop to his antics."

Nathan and Tom shared a look and a smile. Though the action against Moat Kangly had looked good on paper, they both knew it had been a close thing. It could very easily have turned out much differently, and not in their favor.

"Well, I'm very sorry to hear we've missed him, though I'm sure if anyone can bring a bandit to ground it will be the Colonel. Oh well, I guess there's nothing for it. Please do extend to him my most heartfelt regards upon his return, and my regrets for missing him."

"Certainly, sir. And if you would like to borrow paper and pen, I would be happy to deliver a letter from you into his hand upon his return."

"That would be very kindly of you, Mr. Simmons. Thank you."

So Lieutenant Simmons led them to a back office and provided Nathan with the writing essentials, on which he wrote:

U.S. Army Headquarters, Department of Texas
San Antonio, May 20, 1860

My Dear Colonel Lee,

I had hoped to see you in person to thank you for your letter dated 22 April and was very sorry to discover your duties have taken you elsewhere. Thank you very kindly for your condolences on my father's passing, and for your very gracious words about my mother. It will be my pleasure to convey to her your regards when I return to Virginia. When time allows it is my intention to visit your

*family home in Arlington and pay my respects to your
wife and family.*

*I hope and trust by the time you read this letter you will
have had great success in your current endeavors. I pray
we shall meet again soon. And, of course, I extend to you
all possible welcome and courtesy of my home should you
ever have reason to be in western Virginia.*

I am, very respectfully, your obedient servant,

Nathaniel Chambers
Late Captain and Commanding Officer
8th U.S. Army Infantry Regiment, Fort Davis, Texas

ɷƦɷƆƸ

They spent two more days enjoying the comforts of Mrs. Schmidt's home, including a much-needed bath and shave. While Nathan mostly rested and recuperated, the men restocked the supplies and enjoyed re-acquainting themselves with the experiences of life in town after so many months on the frontier.

Jim insisted on visiting the Alamo. He wanted to see for himself the place where the famous battle he'd heard about his whole life took place. It was there a few hundred Americans, led by Jim Bowie, William Travis, and Davy Crockett, heroically died fighting General Santa Anna's Mexican Army. The same Santa Anna, Jim reminded himself with satisfaction, that Captain Chambers and the American Army under General Scott later repaid handsomely when they marched into Mexico. Tom accompanied Jim, also curious to see the old church-turned-fort, though now the Alamo just served as a quartermaster's depot for the Army.

While they were out, Mrs. Schmidt arranged for their clothes to be laundered; when they resumed their journey, they would at least look—and smell—much better than when they arrived.

She also arranged for the tailor to come around and measure Nathan for a new suit. "A gentleman must have the proper attire,

Nathan, darling; is it not so?" To Nathan's surprise, the tailor was back the very next day with the suit already completed.

"*Nein*, Mr. Chambers, I am not a *magician*. It just happened I already had a suit made that was nearly the right size and only needed a small adjustment. *Frau* Schmidt said you were leaving soon and couldn't wait, so I made the needed alterations last night. *Comen sie!* Try it on, sir!"

Nathan put on the suit, along with a pure white shirt the tailor also provided. It was black with long, even tails and trousers to match. He added a thin, black, bow-style tie to complete the attire. When he looked in his bedroom mirror he was shocked at the change. He had been so used to wearing an army uniform—or more recently, casual civilian traveling garb—he almost didn't recognize himself.

When he came back downstairs to the reading room, where Alisa Schmidt waited with the tailor, she took one look at him and beamed with pleasure. "Oh *my*, Mr. Chambers! You are such the handsome gentleman now. Oh my … oh my," she repeated, shaking her head, and trying to cover her grin with her hand.

"I'm afraid I'm not quite used to dressing this way. Do you think it suits me?"

"Oh, yes dear. It most certainly does! Don't you agree, Frederick?"

"*Oh ja*, *Frau* Schmidt. It is a perfect fit if I do say so myself. Both in size and in style. You are now the very picture of a fine, southern gentleman, sir."

"Well, then I'll take it! Thank you very kindly, Frederick … *danke*, I should say!"

"*Bitte*, Mr. Chambers. You are most welcome. I am only sorry I did not have time to sew you a fine waistcoat to match. Well, perhaps you can acquire a nice one somewhere on your travels."

Then Alisa jumped up, "*Oh!* I nearly forgot. I have a gift for you, Nathan. One moment, one moment while I run fetch it."

She hurried out of the room, and soon returned carrying a large, round-shaped cardboard box, which she handed to Nathan. "You needn't have done that, Alisa. It is more than enough everything you have already done for me and my men."

"Nonsense, darling. It has been my pleasure ... *all* of it!" and she laughed a mischievous laugh. Nathan gave her a smirk, but again found his checks flushed with red.

"*Open sie* it! Open it, my dear."

He lifted the lid, and found inside a fine, wide, flat-brimmed felt hat. It was black, with a thin silver hat band. "It's beautiful. You really shouldn't have, Alisa, dear. What a fine treat. *Danke!* Guess this'll look a bit nicer with the suit than my dusty old riding hat!"

He put it on. "How do I look?"

"You look like ... like ... oh, I don't know what to say! You are, just ... *beautiful*, Nathan. Just a beautiful, beautiful man." She shook her head slowly, and he saw tears welling up in her eyes.

He laughed. "Well, no one has called me *that* before, but I thank you, dear. *Danke, danke*. For the hat, and for ... *everything*."

ೞഞ൲ Cೞഞൠೞഞൠ൲ Cೞ

Their last night in San Antonio, Tom felt restless and laid in bed staring at the ceiling. A small noise in the hallway outside his door caught his ear, and when he looked over, he could see a dim light shining under the closed door. Curious, he crept from bed, and carefully opened the door a crack, peering out. Candlelight out in the hall dazzled his eyes. It seemed to float of its own volition down the hallway to his right. But when his eyes adjusted, he could make out the form of Mrs. Schmidt, holding a candle in her hand as she moved down the hallway. At first, he assumed she was also restless and was going to check on her children, or some such. But then she paused outside the door to the bedroom Nathan slept in. She glanced back down the hallway, and Tom instinctively ducked back. She quietly opened the door and stepped inside. Tom heard muffled voices from behind the door, and a quiet giggle.

Hmm ... well, they say curiosity killed the cat, and this time it was a Tom cat! he chided himself. Then he chuckled, and closed the door, returning to his bed. *Probably just the thing he needs for his recovery,* he decided. Then a grim, humorous thought struck him. *Oh, God! I hope he don't pop a stitch!*

The next morning, they prepared to depart on the next leg of their journey. They would travel almost due east this time, heading toward Houston, the next largest town in Texas. Fortunately, however, the Houston-Galveston rail line now extended nearly seventy miles west of Houston to the little town of Alleyton. So rather than the full 200 miles, they need only ride 130 of it before boarding the train. And the road between San Antonio and Houston was well traveled and relatively safe, so they did not expect any difficulties or delays. Still, it would be three or more days of hard riding before they reached the rail head.

While the men packed the mule and horses, Nathan sat on the patio talking quietly with Alisa. Tom hadn't said anything about the clandestine meeting he'd witnessed. But still, the men seemed to know, and left the two alone as they said their fond, but sad goodbyes.

Alisa did not know how to broach the painful subject of their parting. So instead she asked him something she'd had on her mind. She'd been curious about it ever since Nathan had sent a letter telling of his return to Virginia. "So tell me, dear … I have heard that farms in Virginia use the black African men for slaves, yes? Surely you do not countenance such?"

"Well, no. Not all farms in Virginia have slaves. Mostly only the *very* large ones …"

"Oh. And your family farm? It is one of the small ones, yes?"

"No … not exactly. It is large … very, *very* large, I'm afraid. And yes, I am ashamed to say it was built with, and continues to prosper, on the backs of slave labor."

"Oh, Nathan! How can you … how can you be a part of such … such an *abomination?* We Germans have seen our share of wicked masters and tyrants in the past, and so can't abide such."

"It is … a *complicated* matter. You see, without that free labor the economics of such a large farm would quickly fail, and it would … force some *uncomfortable* decisions to be made."

They were silent for a moment, and Nathan felt badly. He felt Alisa had always held him in high esteem, and now she was disappointed in him.

"Look … I'm not happy about it either. It's one of the reasons I haven't been back there for almost twenty years. I really can't envision myself a slave master. Likely I'll just sell the place and find Momma a new home, but if I sell off the farm, that implies selling off the slaves with it. Then I'll have been a party to the slave trade, like it or not. And those people will still be … well, whatever I do, in the end they'll still be slaves. So, have I really unburdened myself of the responsibility … and the guilt?"

"Well, couldn't you just … you know … set them free when you sell the farm?"

"I've considered it, believe me. But aside from the loss of a small fortune their sale would net … it's now *illegal* in Virginia."

"*Illegal?* You mean to say a slave owner can't set free his own slaves? Oh, I can't believe it …"

"It's true, I'm sorry to say. Oh, he can free one or two, to be sure. But never a large group together. Certainly not a hundred!

"You see … back in the thirties, there was a small slave rebellion led by a slave named Nat Turner. As you'd expect, it ended badly, and a lot of people got killed, both black and white. And though it was quickly quashed, it caused a panic. So after that, Virginia and the other southern states passed a series of onerous laws intended to prevent that from ever happening again. One of those was a law preventing a master from freeing his slaves en masse. So I'm afraid that's not an option."

They were quiet again and didn't meet eyes again for several minutes.

Then Alisa turned to face him, and he could see tears in her eyes, "Oh, Nathan. I'm sorry for bringing it up. I know you are a good man, and your heart will lead you to the right answer."

Then she smiled, wiping away a tear, "I'd not have any ill feelings between us. Not now … not when …"

She looked down at the ground, no longer meeting his eyes. Finally, she worked up the courage to ask the thing that most troubled her mind, "Are you certain you can't stay a while longer, darling?"

He breathed a heavy sigh. He couldn't explain his ever-growing sense of urgency to get home and deal with whatever was going on back in Virginia, because he didn't understand it himself. But he also knew there was no turning back now, "Would it matter, Alisa? Would it be any easier a week from now? Or a month? No. I think if anything it would be *harder*. But in the end, we both know I *must* go. And you must stay. You would not leave everything you've built here, all your friends and neighbors, uproot your children to travel a thousand miles away just to be with me?"

She didn't answer, but nodded her head, still not meeting his eyes. Tears now streamed down her face, and she wiped them with a small lacy handkerchief.

"And you know I can't stay here. I've already resigned my commission, and am honor bound to return to my family home in Virginia, where ... well, where I am *most* needed. I fear the time has come, dear. I'm very sorry."

But she looked up at him and met his eyes. "No, don't say *that*, Nathan! You have nothing to feel *sorry* about. We have shared ... shared something precious ... beautiful even. And now ... it's over. But don't be sorry ... never *that* ..."

They were quiet again for a moment. Then she said, "It may not matter to you ... but it matters to *me* to tell you, for you to *know*. That ... that ... there has never been another man for me since my husband died. Only *you* ... no one other."

"It matters," he answered softly, "it matters ..."

"I ... I just wanted to be sure you knew that I wouldn't ... that I never ... Well, I didn't want you thinking that I just slept with every *beautiful* man who stayed at my boarding house!"

He smiled. "You know, it never occurred to me to think that. I guess I've never thought of you in *that* way. Maybe you'll be pleased to know ... I've not been with any other woman since we met. Though we've been together but seldom over the last few years, you've been ... *special* to me. I will never forget you, Alisa. *Never*."

"Oh, Nathan! Why is life full of such pain? Why can't people be happy in life without always … the *suffering and loss?*" Tears were again welling in her eyes.

He didn't know how to answer the question, so he just held her close as sobs shook her body.

"But … you're still young, and *beautiful*. Find a good man from around here and marry him. You deserve to be happy."

ও৲ঐেওও৲ঐেওও৲ঐ

They rode slowly away, and Nathan turned to wave back at Alisa, who waved a handkerchief in answer.

He turned toward Tom and their eyes met. They exchanged a serious look and Nathan gave a heavy sigh.

"Regrets, sir?"

"Of course. Believe me … I nearly begged her to come along. But it would've only made it harder for her; in the end her home is here with her children, and her neighbors from the 'fatherland' … and mine is now back in Virginia."

"I'm sorry, sir."

He sighed again. "The world has turned a page. But maybe … after a time … it will be enough to know she's well and happy. Though we may never meet again."

"Well, I for one feel privileged to have met her, sir … but still, it's a sad parting."

"Yes … it is that. A *very* sad parting."

And then he was quiet, and his eyes became watery, so Tom left him alone with his thoughts.

ও৲ঐেওও৲ঐেওও৲ঐ

Tuesday May 22, 1860 – Greenbrier County, Virginia:

Walters paced the floor of the study, his face a dark storm cloud. Bob had rarely seen him so agitated, and it frightened him. He'd seen what Walters could do when angry; he'd never wanted that anger directed at him. Not *ever*.

"Sir, Jacob Chambers died around the last week in March, as I recall. If we assume she asked young Chambers to come home

204

shortly after, it'd take … something like a month of travel. Plus, time to prepare, so … make it six weeks. And about a week for the original telegram to reach him. So that'd make it … the first week of June at the very earliest. Still plenty of time …"

"No! She'll *never* sell with her son coming home! The *bitch!* Who does she think she is, anyway? Playing the queen up on that hill. *Pah!* What'd she ever do to deserve that farm? Slept in Jacob Chambers' bed is what, the *whore!*"

He was quiet for a moment, his face twisted up in anger. He continued to pace, then suddenly stopped and turned back toward Bob. His face had switched from seething anger to that odd bland expression everyone found so disconcerting, and which usually meant bad trouble for someone.

His voice was now quiet and controlled, in stark contrast to only a few moments earlier. "Did you see the smug look on her face when she bragged about her great son the Army Captain? Makes me want to stick a knife in her guts and twist … then we'll see how smug she looks. In fact, that's exactly what I mean to do …"

This statement so shocked Bob he didn't know what to say, but a gasp came from the study doorway.

"*Mr. Walters!* Who are you speaking of? And how can you *say* such a thing?!"

Bob turned to see young *Mrs.* Walters standing in the doorway, her hand over her mouth and a look of shock on her face. Margaret Walters was only half Elijah's age—willowy thin and somewhat plain looking, to Bob's thinking, with straight brown hair cut to shoulder length. Walters had met and married her on a trip to Richmond the previous fall and brought her back to the farm to the surprise of everyone there. But Bob thought it an odd match; he rarely saw them conversing and never saw anything approaching affection. And though quiet and introverted, she had a kind smile and was always polite. Quite different from Walters, he decided.

Walters was unabashed, "It's none of your business who it is. And I'll do as I wish concerning the matter. The bitch is nothing to me and keeps me from what I want. All my life I've listened to

Daddy whine and complain about the feud, but never did he *do* anything about it!

"I'll not waste my breath whining and complaining like he did. I mean to put an end to this nonsense for good and all. And if I have to bury a few bodies to do it, so much the better. That smart-mouthed widow ... if the son comes home and finds her already dead, he'll sell out and go straight back where he came from."

"I can't believe what I'm hearing! That the man I married could ..." she suddenly choked up, unable to finish speaking, tears welling in her eyes.

"You married me, *my dear*, because you're a nobody slut from a nobody family. They couldn't wait to stop paying your upkeep and were only too happy to be rid of their last, useless daughter. I brought you from Richmond to satisfy my carnal needs, nothing more! There, now I've said it ... are you satisfied? Now shut your mouth, go to your room and stay there until I send for you ... if I ever do!"

Her eyes widened, and her face turned pale. She turned and fled from the room.

"Josiah!" Walters shouted, calling for his butler.

"Yes, master?" A black man, neatly dressed in a white coat suddenly stood in the doorway, as if conjured by a magician.

"See to it Mrs. Walters goes to her room, and nowhere else. Put a watch on her door and don't let her out until I say so. Do you understand me?"

"Yes, master." He turned and went to carry out his orders.

Bob stood where he was, feeling awkward and embarrassed. He felt sorry for the woman. But he knew there was nothing he could do her. It was easier not think about it too much, and to mind his own business. But it bothered him and nagged at his conscience.

"Fucking bitch ... thinks because I married her, she can run my house! Think again, little whore! You're mine now, bought and paid for! I'll be Goddamned if you're going to tell me what I can or can't do in my own house!"

Bob said nothing, deciding it was the safest course of action, but a growing knot in his stomach seemed to disagree.

"Now … I believe we were discussing the impending demise of one Abigail Chambers …"

Friday May 25, 1860 – Greenbrier County, Virginia:

"Yes, you have it right. I'll pay you fifty dollars to commit two or three armed robberies out along the road to the west of Lewisburg. And … you can pocket any money you collect."

"All right … what else?" the man asked. He was large and burly, with long black hair and ill-kempt beard. He'd spent time in prison and had a reputation for trouble. Bob reckoned he might be just the right man for the job.

"You should hire two or three others to ride with you, so it looks like a gang. And, be sure to threaten bloody murder, and give out a few beatings. Nothing serious, mind, and no killings; that'd stir up too much trouble with the law."

"Hmm … can't disagree with that."

"And finally, wear bandanas to cover your faces so you can't be identified. Most importantly, you will wear an eye patch," Bob said.

"You mean, like a pirate or something? What for? There's nothing wrong with my eyes, either one!"

"Yes, yes, of course … the point is, if you're wearing an eye patch, that's all folks will remember; like from an old adventure book … *you understand?* Once you take it off, you could walk right past those same folks on the street, and they'd not even know it was you. It's all they'll remember when they talk to the law. So they'll spend all their time looking for a one-eyed bandit."

"Oh! Now I see … very clever … yes … very, very clever. But … what're *you* getting out of it? Why you payin' me to rob people and you don't even want the money?"

"It's all on account of what comes next. You agree to the whole job, or there's no deal. I'll pay you half now. You must commit all the robberies in a week's time. Then meet me back here at this same time next week, and I'll pay you the second half."

"All right. So what I gotta do for the rest?"

"Then … the next part is worth a hundred dollars, but this time you're not just committing robbery … this time you'll have to kill someone."

"Whewww …" he whistled, leaning back in his chair. They sat at an old, stained table in the private back room of a roadside inn on the south side of Lewisburg. Bob had slipped the innkeeper two dollars to ensure a private meeting with no one eavesdropping on their dark business. "Now I'm getting the picture. Whoever you's fixing to kill … the law'll reckon it for another robbery by the mysterious one-eyed bandit and his gang. Only this time he lost his temper and killed someone. Yep … very clever, mister. Only it'll cost you more than a hundred bucks!" he smiled, an evil gleam in his eye.

Bob scowled and acted put out. But he'd been expecting it, and it was still well under what Mr. Walters was willing to pay. If he played his cards right, he'd pocket the difference, and no one would be the wiser.

Then he grimaced as he felt that familiar knot in his stomach. The nagging pain that seemed to remind him he had a conscience … a conscience trying to chastise him for arranging the murder of an innocent woman.

Chapter 7. Water, Water, Everywhere

"Water, water, everywhere,
And all the boards did shrink;
Water, water, everywhere,
Nor any drop to drink."
— Samuel Taylor Coleridge
(The Rime of the Ancient Mariner)

Thursday May 24, 1860 – Road from San Antonio to Houston, Texas:

It had been hot and dry as they left San Antonio, dust kicking up from their horses' hooves even at a slow walk. But when they made camp at the end of the first day, they could feel a change in the air; the humidity had increased dramatically, making sleeping uncomfortably hot.

The next day there was no wind, and the heat with its added humidity was stifling. Sweat rolled down them in beads, saturating their clothing.

"Damn it all to hell! I feel like I'm a-having a hot bath with my clothes on!" Jim grumbled.

But it soon got worse. Come mid-afternoon, dark, low-hanging clouds moved across the sky. For a few moments, they enjoyed a respite from the heat of the sun. But what pleasure they might have enjoyed from the unexpected shade was quickly nullified by a sudden deluge that soaked men, horses, and baggage to the bone. The area they were passing through was a gently rolling plain of tall grass several miles across, devoid of any tree or structure that could have provided shelter. So they had no choice but to lower their heads and endure the sodden pounding.

After less than half an hour the rain stopped, the clouds rolled by, and the sun came out. The ground steamed from the intense heat and heavy moisture. If the humidity had been bad before, it was now almost unbearable. And the rain had turned the road to a sticky brown paste that caked the horses' hooves and forced them to a plodding crawl. Any time they could, they moved off into the tall grass. It avoided the sticky mud of the road, but still impeded their progress; the roadbed leveled out the normal ups and downs of small ravines and gullies. When the day was over, they pitched their tents and collapsed in a steaming-hot exhaustion.

The next day was almost an exact repeat of the day before. High heat and humidity in the morning, followed by a torrential downpour in the afternoon that didn't decrease the heat but added to the humidity. This time, however, they took heed of the rolling clouds and broke out their oiled overcoats, and so averted another total drenching.

And the next day was the same. And the next.

Toward the end of the fourth day, Tom estimated they were no further than they originally expected to be at the end of the second day.

"Damn it, sir!" Jim said as they plodded along through the steaming, sticky, hot muck. "Back at Mrs. Schmidt's house, when you said Texas was the strangest land one could imagine, I never thought your words would prove so true!"

"For once I'm sorry to be right," Nathan grumbled. Their lack of progress fueled his growing frustration and anxiety.

"It seems like the closer we get to Houston the harder it is to get there," Tom added.

"Seems like the weather gods are again' us," Jim agreed.

"Let's not blaspheme, Mr. Wiggins. There is only *one* God. But I *will* believe Satan has had a hand in this inexplicably bad weather, as if intentionally delaying our journey."

"As you say, sir; as you say. All's I know is this is a nasty, hot, devilish business. I can't ever recall being so insufferably hot and wet at the same time!"

"Amen to that, Mr. Wiggins."

ༀ༒ༀ༒ༀ༒ༀ༒ༀ༒ༀ༒ༀ༒ༀ༒

They reached Alleyton on the evening of the sixth day out from San Antonio. The rain had stopped before the previous day. The intense heat from the sun had dried out the road so quickly they were once again kicking up dust from their horses' hooves. They looked at each other and shook their heads in disbelief. Weather gods, *indeed!*

At the end of the day they made camp in an open field next to the new Alleyton rail station. If they'd started their journey a half year earlier there would have been no railhead at Alleyton, forcing them to ride all the way into Houston. But they'd recently completed the rail line extension.

Even before the men were out of their bedrolls in the morning, the small town was a beehive of activity surrounding the rail station. The smell of freshly cut lumber filled the air, along with the sound of many saws and hammers. The train depot building was a framework of boards with no walls. Across the way another building was rising from the ground. It would soon be a roundhouse for train engines, but now it was nothing more than a swarm of workers putting up beams.

Nathan watched as railroad workers uncoupled the engine from the waiting train. They then drove it down the tracks to a Y-shaped section of track, which allowed the engine to turn around. He had seen train turntables back east—impressive, permanent facilities built at the end of the line. But anywhere in the West, it was safe to assume the railhead was only temporary; next year it would extend even further west. And the year after, yet further.

They were already talking about extending the railroad all the way to the West Coast. The skeptics were saying the project was too monumental to ever be accomplished. But when Nathan thought about it, he couldn't imagine a scenario where that wouldn't eventually happen. In his mind, it was only a matter of time.

So in the West they resorted to simpler, more expedient methods to reverse direction; the engine was de-coupled from its cars and sent down to the Y-shaped track that served as a turntable. Then, using a three-point turn, it ended up on a sidetrack going in the opposite direction from which it had come. Finally, they switched it onto the main line and backed it until reconnected with the opposite end of the train to resume the journey in the other direction.

The backing steam engine pulled to a stop, banging loudly against the passenger cars. The platform swirled with a choking dust that coated Nathan's skin with an itchy gray film in the sweltering heat. No one else stood on the wooden platform; but seven other men, grim faced in the heat, stood holding the reins of a group of horses and a mule in the bare dirt just past the platform. They would board the horses before taking their seats in one of the passenger cars.

These were good men, he thought proudly, though they were no longer obliged to serve him as they had in the Army where his word had been law. He strolled toward the train, only vaguely aware of them moving the horses. He knew they would handle this job as competently as they did all the tasks set before them. These were the best men he'd ever served with. He felt a little guilty for taking them from the service that'd molded and made men of them.

Once they had gotten moving, the advantages of train travel became immediately clear. Aside from being sheltered from the vagaries of the weather, their travel time should dramatically decrease. Not counting any whistle stops along the way, they should arrive in the town of Harrisburg, just south of Houston, in about five hours. Based on their previous week of travel, that might have taken them another three or four days riding horseback.

Nathan sat in a seat by himself at the back of the car, smoking a cigar and blowing the smoke out the open window. He and his men occupied most of the seats in one passenger car—one of a total of six on the train, all of which were filled with passengers.

He wore his black suit, white shirt, thin black bow tie, and wide, flat-brimmed black hat he'd acquired in San Antonio. He realized a stranger would never assume the well-dressed gentleman was in any way associated with the rough-looking men sharing the car with him. The men wore their old travel attire, same as they'd worn since Fort Davis.

Frequent stops made the ride longer, but easier to endure. Every small town and junction along the rail line was a potential stop, depending on whether there were passengers waiting to board or wanting to depart. These were welcome opportunities for the men to get out and stretch their legs.

It was after one such stopover that something unusual caught Nathan's eye. He was sitting in his typical seat in the back of the passenger car, gazing out the window when he noticed three men conversing together on the platform. These men interacted like they knew one another well, but when it came time for them to board, they each went to a different passenger car. This odd behavior piqued Nathan's interest, so he continued watching as one member of the trio entered their own car. Although he was a small man, young and lean, the traveler had a tough look. He carried a pistol in a holster and wore crude, travel-worn clothing, much like Nathan's men. The man quickly settled into a seat by himself, pulled his hat down over his eyes, and appeared to fall asleep. Nathan mulled over this interesting development as he lit another cigar.

Two more whistle-stops came and went—nothing out of the ordinary, and Nathan was thinking he may have been overly suspicious of his new fellow passenger.

The third stop was a remote platform with only a small, new-looking, hut-like station. Here, once again, Nathan saw something to make him sit up and take notice: two men, rough-looking like the earlier ones, standing on the platform, holding *five* horses. Maybe, Nathan told himself, perfectly innocent … maybe *not*. It could be these were just local farmhands waiting to meet the new hires, bringing them horses for the ride back.

Or … it could mean something *else*. When they were out in West Texas, the Army was typically the only law enforcement. So recognizing and dealing with all types of scoundrels and outlaws was a regular part of their duties. He reflexively felt the hard outline of the small Colt in his vest pocket. A quick glance confirmed another interesting piece of information; there were no telltale wires leading to the station, meaning there was no telegraph service here. Their rough-looking fellow passenger stood up, seeming to make a great show of yawning and stretching. Nathan leaned back into his seat, pulled the brim of his hat down low, and pretended to sleep. But, despite his relaxed appearance, he anxiously awaited what would happen next.

He didn't have long to wait. The moment the train came to a complete stop, the suspicious young passenger pulled his pistol and waved it from side to side, covering the men in the car. He shouted "Nobody moves. This is a hold-up!"

A silence fell over the car. Nathan knew his men had been taken completely by surprise. He felt a twinge of guilt he'd not found some way to at least warn Tom about his suspicions. But he'd never been entirely sure it wasn't just fanciful imagination on his part, making something of nothing to relieve the boredom of the long train ride.

Nobody moved, nobody spoke. Outside they heard shouting, and a woman's scream.

The gunman had positioned himself between Nathan and his men. Nathan thought this a foolish move. The man had to turn from side to side to keep an eye on all them at the same time. After a brief awkward silence, the man again spoke. His nervousness and agitation clear in his speech.

"Look, there don't need to be no trouble … you fellas, no need for any trouble." he repeated, waving the gun in the general direction of Nathan's men. "I can see you're working men, like myself. I don't expect you have nothing worth the taking. I'll just be having whatever the rich gentleman holds and be on my way."

The men remained silent, waiting for their captain to take the lead, not wanting to make a wrong move that might turn deadly. Only Billy Creek appeared unconcerned. He sat with his arms folded and a smirk on his face.

The stony silence from these strangers seemed to unnerve the robber.

He turned the gun toward Nathan. "Well mister, let's have it … your watch, jewelry, coins, paper money … anything you got of value." He extended his left arm, in which he now held a small cloth sack. He waved it at Nathan, as if expecting him to take the bag and fill it with loot.

Nathan stared at the young man for a long moment. Then he shook his head, said, "No," and leaned back in his seat.

This response shocked and baffled the gunman. This was *not* the way he'd planned it. He had never, in his wildest imaginings, considered someone would flat refuse him at gunpoint. He tried again, "I don't think you heard me rightly mister, I said give me your valuables."

Nathan leaned back casually in his seat. He slowly and deliberately peeled back the right-side of his jacket exposing the inner pocket. The pocket contained a brace of cigars in a silver holder. If the robber thought he might finally receive the demanded loot, he was quickly disappointed; Nathan drew out a single cigar, put it in his mouth, struck a match and puffed. After a moment, he took the cigar from his mouth and repeated, "I said 'No.'"

"Look here, mister ... I got a loaded gun pointed straight at ya. I don't expect I'd miss from this distance, so you'd better do as I say."

Nathan continued to calmly puff on the cigar. He took it from his mouth and pointed it at the young man. "Let me ask you something, boy ... are you a *murderer*, or simply a thief?"

The man sputtered, "Well, I ain't *neither*; me and the boys is down on our luck is all. Thinking takin' some goods off a few folks better off'n us would turn things our way for a spell."

"Ah, well, you see there, *that's* your problem. When I looked you in the eye just now, I knew you were no killer. And now you've confirmed it for me. I'm sure you've never killed a man in your life. And you're not about to start now, just for a pocket watch, or a few gold coins, assuming I have any."

The gunman apparently could think of no answer to this, so Nathan continued.

"Now we've established you won't shoot me, your gun becomes useless. I now have no reason to give you any of my hard-earned valuables. And clearly you've done nothing to earn them."

He casually took a few more puffs as if discussing nothing more urgent than the weather at Sunday dinner. "And now we've concluded you can't use the gun that leaves only taking my valuables by main force. But there again, I believe you have a problem. I appear to be bigger and stronger than you, and I suspect, on account of my years out West among the Indians, I'm likely a more experienced fighter. And, unlike you, I *have* killed *many* men in my time."

This last statement seemed to shock the gunman. He became red in the face and waved his gun at Nathan. "Well, mister, what if I *do* shoot you, and take what I want off of yer dead corpse?!"

"Well … I'm sure you know … if you rob me and they arrest you later, you'll likely go to prison for a few years. But if you *murder* me … they will surely hang you!"

He paused a moment, then said, "Now, you may think they might never catch you. That's possible, I must admit. But … I noticed these other gentlemen in the car are also armed. What if they don't *approve* you shooting me down in cold blood to rob me? They may intervene on my behalf, which could prove unfortunate for you."

His men continued to sit silently, listening with breathless anticipation, to this odd conversation. Tom decided it was the strangest discussion he'd ever seen, the unarmed man threatened at gunpoint firmly in control of the exchange.

The gunman again turned to the men and said, "Look, like I said before, I got no beef with any of you boys; don't mean you no trouble …"

"Well, perhaps we should *ask* these gentlemen what they think of you shooting me and taking my valuables. Gentlemen … since you seem to be a rather untalkative lot, perhaps you should just *show* this young fellow what you think of his idea …" He gave Tom a wink.

There was a sudden flurry of movement, and before he could think or react, the young gunman stared down the barrels of six fully loaded Colt revolvers. Only Billy Creek hadn't pulled his, continuing to watch with an amused expression on his face. The young man appeared to wilt in the face of this unexpected opposition. His raised his hands and let the pistol dangle from his index finger by the trigger guard. Nathan stood, grabbed the pistol and shoved the man down into the seat opposite him.

"What's the situation outside, Tom?"

"One man outside, holding the horses, and looking nervous. I don't see the others, and don't hear any more shouting or screams, so I expect they're in the other passenger cars collecting loot."

"Hmm … yes, and probably one is down at the engine making sure the train doesn't go anywhere until they've finished their business. So the question is, what to do with our young guest and his associates …" He leaned back once more and puffed on the cigar.

Stan said, "He not much of outlaw, Captain; skinny little thing … you want me throw him from train? Or better we wait 'til train moves … more fun this way!" He leered at the young outlaw, displaying his large, toothsome smile.

"Thank you, Stan … but *no*. I think … we will use this young fellow as our ambassador, though I doubt he knows what that means."

Nathan again turned to the outlaw. He gave the young man a hard glare. "Now listen here … *what was your name?*"

"Samuel Henderson, sir. But folks call me Sammy," he answered, before remembering it wasn't a good idea for an outlaw to give out his real name.

"All right, Sammy. Here's what we're gonna do … You'll walk out of this car, slowly with your hands down at your sides, where I can see them."

The man nodded agreeably; he seemed relieved he might get out of this without being killed or sent to prison.

Nathan continued, "You will walk calmly over to the man holding the horses."

"They's now three of them back at the horses, Captain," Jim called out from his seat looking out the forward-most window.

"*Men* at the horses," Nathan corrected himself, "and you will tell them exactly what happened here."

"*Exactly*, sir?" Sammy asked, clearly not proud of how he'd played his part.

"You can tell them you were brave and stalwart before we got the jump on you, for all I care …"

"Okay, thank you, sir."

"You'll tell them Captain Nathaniel Chambers, late U.S. Army commander returning from West Texas, and a heavily armed troop of his ex-soldiers, is riding in this car. And he does *not* wish to be disturbed by the likes of you, or your partners. You will tell them I said they must ride off at once, with no further molesting of passengers nor crew of this train. There will be no discharging of firearms, nor damaging of the train, nor its facilities. They may take with them whatever loot they've already grabbed, but *no more.*"

The soldiers looked at their captain with surprise. He'd never been soft on outlaws before. "But Captain," Jamie said, "these lads're outlaws … after robbin' the train! Ain't we gonna shoot 'em, or at least arrest and take 'em in?"

"Nope. For one, it's no longer our duty; it'd be a great deal of bother for us and would greatly inconvenience us on our journey. I'm already feeling anxious about all the delays we've suffered.

"And for two—though I seriously doubt these fellows could hit the larger side of a barn with a pistol even from spitting distance, unless they were to throw it—it *is* possible one of us could be hit on accident by a stray bullet. That would be *most* inconvenient."

Billy Creek snorted a laugh. The outlaw looked offended but didn't offer a disagreement.

"And for three, this train carries nothing of value beyond our horses which we won't let them take, and various small items carried by the passengers. And such is not worth killing over, nor dying for. If our fellow travelers aren't prepared to defend their own property, I see no reason *we* should risk life and limb doing it for them.

"Finally, I can tell Sammy here is no outlaw. Just a foolish young man, as are the others, I suspect. If we were to arrest them, I fear the law would be less understanding. Likely they would waste away the better part of their youth behind bars, perhaps even being warped into real criminals in the process. Given there's been no great harm done here, that seems … a bit of overkill. Perhaps even an undeserved bondage one might say."

He met eyes with Tom, and the two exchanged a meaningful look. Tom nodded. If any of the others disagreed with the Captain's reasoning, they kept it to themselves. So there was no further discussion.

"All that being said …" Nathan leaned over and stared hard into Sammy's eyes once again. "Don't waste the chance I'm giving you by doing something stupid. You tell your comrades … if they don't do *exactly* as I say, I *will* set my men on them, and they *will* shoot down every last man, no quarter given. Do you understand me?"

"Yes, sir! Me and the others'll do just as you say. There'll be no more trouble, I promise you. No hotheads amongst us … nobody came here to kill, or get kilt, that's for sure …"

"Good. And take this as a chance to straighten up and behave properly, as your Momma no doubt taught you."

Sammy looked down, and nodded, unable to meet the Captain's stern gaze, "Yes, sir."

"Up and at 'em, then," Nathan said, "I'll just keep your pistol; compensation for the trouble you've caused us. Otherwise you're free to go."

The young man stood and exited the car. Nathan held Sammy's pistol in his right hand, a dirty looking and well-worn Remington revolver of dubious functionality. He immediately shifted it to his left hand and pulled the small Colt from his vest pocket with his right. Better to have a weapon in hand he knew was reliable if things turned sour.

They watched as Sammy walked deliberately toward the gathering group of men. They could see he was following Nathan's instructions to the letter: slow steady movements, hands held stiffly out at his sides (not over his head) where they could easily see them. Once he joined the group of men, they saw him talking rapidly, and gesturing wildly. There were now four men by the horses, and these glanced nervously toward the car where Nathan and his men were waiting. One robber shouted something Nathan could not quite make out. Then the last of their party came out from the engine at a trot, holstering his pistol as he moved. After a brief discussion, the group slowly mounted, apparently trying to be deliberate, taking care to make no sudden movements Nathan and company might misinterpret.

The group moved off at a slow trot, never looking back. The not-so-great train robbery was over.

When they reached Harrisburg, just south of Houston, they stopped to take on more passengers. Thankfully, there were no goods to be loaded this time, or it might have delayed them for several hours. Later in the year, after the cotton harvest, the outbound train to Galveston would be full to the brim. But this time of year, most of the goods were being brought *into* Texas. So the train headed for Galveston was nearly empty, save the passengers.

The train started out again and now turned south toward Galveston on the Gulf Coast. They had settled comfortably into their seats by mid-afternoon, several of them dozing, when the clouds once again opened up. Hard rain pelted the metal roof of the rail car with a loud rattling sound.

Nathan looked over at Jim and smiled.

Jim returned the smile and said, "The devil can storm all he wants now, far as I'm concerned. Won't stop this train, I reckon!" They shared a laugh.

After three more hours, they crossed over a long wooden railroad bridge, arriving in the island city of Galveston. The train let them off at the depot, right in the waterfront wharf area. This suited Nathan perfectly, as his first task was to secure passage on the next ship bound for New Orleans. He took Tom, leaving the others to secure the horses and find a place to corral them while awaiting the next stage of their journey. The Galveston depot couldn't have been more different from the one in Alleyton where they'd started out the day. The port was swarming with men unloading goods from dozens of ships all along the wharf, moving them to the waiting trains in the rail yard. Nathan could see now why the train conductor had been eager to unload his passengers and their horses; the train would have to queue up and wait its turn to be loaded for the return trip.

Once again, they were traveling in the right direction at the right time of year. They quickly secured passage on a steam ship heading to New Orleans, at a ridiculously low fare. These ships expected to return empty this time of year, so any fare was a win for them. The *SS Abigail Adams*, out of Boston, would depart at first light, so they'd have to load and secure the horses before sundown, which suited Nathan just fine. He and Tom hurried back to round up the others.

When they returned to the train depot, they found Georgie waiting for them.

"We found a corral where we could stow the horses and gear a few blocks over. Sergeant Jim sent me back to wait for you. Follow me, sirs!"

ᔎᔎᑤᑯᔎᔎᑤᑯᔎᔎᑤᑯ

They rounded up the horses, paid the proprietor a small gratuity, and prepared to leave for the ship. But Jim pulled Nathan aside for a quick, quiet conversation.

"It's Billy, sir. I reckon he may be sick. The whole time we was here he sat huddled in a corner by himself and wouldn't talk to no one."

"Has William had a look at him? Is it a fever do you think? Is he in a cold sweat?"

"Well hell, sir! We're all sweating like pigs from this damned heat. I'm soaked to the bone myself. So yes, he's sweating, but nothing unusual given the circumstances. And yes, William tried looking him over, but Billy shrugged him off. Now he's just sitting there muttering to himself and won't talk to no one … not even me."

"Hmm …"

"You have a thought, sir?"

"*Maybe* … you go ahead with Tom and the others. Take the horses down to the ship and get them stowed. Billy and I will be along shortly."

"Well … if you say so … Yes, sir!"

221

"Thanks, Jim."

"No, *sir!* You don't never have to thank me for doing what you say. Not *you*, sir. Not now, not *never*."

"Okay, *Mr. Wiggins*. We'll see you down at the boat, then."

Nathan walked over to where Billy sat, huddled against the stable wall at the edge of the corral. His head was in his hands and he didn't look up as Nathan sat down next to him.

"I can't wait to get out of this town. Do you know why?"

"No, Captain." Billy continued to stare at the ground between his feet.

"Billy, you're the scout … what's interesting about this island? About the land itself."

"Flat. Flat as Sergeant Jim's griddle. No hills, no valleys …"

"Yep … that's right. Wherever you look, this damned island is as flat as a too-young girl's chest. All's it'll take is one big wave from out yonder sea … and this whole thing'll be under water. I for one would rather be on a boat when that happens. What say *you?*"

Billy did not immediately answer. Finally, he looked up, with eyes puffy and red.

"Captain … I am 'shamed. Ain't never seen water too wide to swim. The soldiers told me about it before, but I never believed them. Now I've seen it and … I'm …"

He became quiet again and covered his face with his hands.

"Billy. How many times in the Army have you had to choose between your natural-born fear of getting yourself killed, and your loyalty to your fellow soldiers, and your officers?"

Billy looked up and met his eye, then shrugged. "Hundred times … more, maybe."

"Me, too, I reckon."

"*You*, Captain? You never fear nothing."

"Of course, I have fears, Billy. Every man has them; and it's a damned good thing too! That's what keeps a man's mind sharp and his eyes focused when there's danger to life and limb. The trick is to master your fears and *use* them for the Lord's good, intended purpose, and not to let *them* master *you*.

"Take this island; when I stepped off the train, I noticed the terrible flatness of it. Nothing but a few feet of dirt between us and a vast, endless sea from which come storms of unfathomable power. And a great fear came over me.

"But you did not see me shrink and cower, nor tremble. Rather it made my mind keen, thinking on all the ways to avoid the danger, and my eyes sharp to figure how to escape the worst should it come. That's why a man has fear in him—not so he'll be a coward, but so he'll be a better, stronger fighter!

"In the Bible it says, *'God hath not given us the spirit of fear; but of power, and of love, and of a sound mind.'*

"And … to tell the truth, I don't much fancy getting on a boat and sailing out into the middle of the sea, either. A captain I may be, or rather *was* … but not a *ship's* captain! That I would *never* be! I will keep to the land, thank you. But this is the road I *must* travel, so travel it I *will*. We're all getting on that boat together. And either you stay here, and go back to Texas, or you master your fear of the water and come along with us."

Billy gazed at the Captain a long time before speaking.

"Captain, you shame me … *and* give me courage … I will do this thing I fear most."

"Good man! Then I reckon this'll make one hundred *and one* times you've overcome your fears!"

He laughed, "Hell, Billy. The good news is … if the boat sinks, we'll all die together; as it *should be* for comrades in arms, don't you think?"

Billy was quiet for another long moment. Finally, he said, "Yes, it is so. If one dies, we all die. My shade will have good comrades for the fighting in hell."

They shared a quiet laugh, then rose, and the Captain gave Billy a firm pat on the back as they strode out of the corral, heading to the boat.

☙❧☙❧☙❧☙❧☙❧

By mid-afternoon on their first day out from Galveston, the land finally slipped over the horizon to the north, leaving them a view of water in all directions. The powerful steam engine

223

rumbled noisily, belching black coal smoke from its single large smokestack amidships. On both port and starboard sides, a large paddlewheel churned the water, sending up a steady spray.

There had been a slight breeze in the morning, so the ship had initially left Galveston Bay under sails. The ship's captain, a large, genial, full-bearded man by the name of McMasters, explained to Nathan they used wind power any time they could to save fuel.

But by mid-morning the wind had completely died out, leaving the sails luffing ineffectually from the three tall masts. In earlier days, a becalming of this kind would have left the ship in the doldrums. They'd have had to either wait it out or launch the tender and tow the ship by oar power.

But thankfully, these were modern times, so Captain McMasters simply ordered the sails brought in, and the steam engine fired. Soon they could hear the machine rumbling to life and could see black smoke mixed with white steam streaming high into the clear sky. In short order they were moving again.

The land had now slipped out of sight. Nathan moved over next to Billy who was leaning against the rail, looking out toward the north.

"How're you doing, Billy?" he asked quietly.

"I am *well*, Captain. It is a *sight!* Nothing for the eye to see but water. It is … beyond the dreams of a man from the West. But … now, I am ashamed for my fears. It is smooth like a pane of glass. Not even a ripple. It does not look like a thing to be feared."

"I'm glad you're feeling more confident, Billy. But don't be fooled by its calmness. Even a lion must sleep sometimes. But best not to wake him and stir his wrath. Remember, he still has teeth!"

"Yes, Captain. I will remember."

It seemed but a tiny distance from Galveston to New Orleans on a map, the two being the closest major ports in the western Gulf. But it was a sea journey of around 450 miles, or 390 nautical miles. The last hundred miles were from the mouth of the Mississippi River upstream to New Orleans. Assuming an average speed of five knots, maintained for twenty-four hours a day, they could make the trip in a little over three days. Captain McMasters, however, planned on allowing four days. He liked to

224

time the last and most dangerous leg upriver to be in daylight as much as possible. That would mean wasting one night anchored outside the river mouth waiting for the dawn.

Just as the sun was setting, the wind kicked up again, so the crew ran up the sails, and powered down the steam engine. The soldiers watched the efficiency and skill of the sailors with admiration, careful to stay out of the way when they were working the sails and rigging.

❧❧☙☙❧❧☙☙❧❧☙☙❧❧

That night, they bedded down on the deck, in a place that wouldn't be in the crew's way. Captain McMasters had offered Nathan a nice cabin on the main deck, but there were no other cabins available for his men. He also offered them shelter below decks in the spaces usually used for freight. But Nathan declined the ship captain's offering, choosing to stay with his men. And since it was a warm, pleasant evening, they opted for the fresh air above decks. Besides, they were well used to sleeping out of doors, and were well prepared for it.

The second day was nearly a repeat of the first. Breeze in the early morning—sails; calm by mid-morning—engine; and breeze again as the sun was setting—back to sails, lasting all night.

After the breeze repeated its disappearing act right before noon on the third day out, Nathan stepped up onto the quarterdeck to speak with Captain McMasters. He entered the ship's control room, and McMasters looked over, grinning at him.

"Mr. Chambers. What do you think of our weather?"

"Seems a little … repetitive? Reminds me of the weather around Houston in that regard, only a whole lot more pleasant."

McMasters laughed. "Yes, this time of year the weather in these parts is almost like clockwork … except when it isn't; then *watch out!* Mostly it seems like once the sun hits the water from straight overhead, it calms the breezes and waves down to almost nothing. Like as if they was too hot to move!"

"Yes, so I've noticed. Nice you have that little engine back there."

"Yep … not quite like the old days when you'd spend half the day in the doldrums. Oh … Chambers, have you met my first mate? This is Albert Harvey. Mr. Harvey, meet Mr. Chambers."

Nathan found himself taken aback by this pronouncement; the person standing beside the ship's captain was a black man. Nathan had initially taken him for one of the common sailors. He'd seen him at various times around the deck performing different tasks. He had also seen two other black men among the sailors.

His surprise must have shown, as the first mate gave him a sideways look. "Mr. Chambers … I hear you are a gentleman from Virginia. As such, I expect the idea of a free black man being a first mate over a bunch of white sailors is offensive to you. In fact, I hear the very idea of a black man being free is offensive in that part of the country."

Nathan smiled, and shook his head before extending his hand, "I'm sorry, Mr. Harvey, but you have taken me by surprise. But the shame is on me for making false assumptions. And no, I am most definitely *not* offended by your position, nor that you are a free man! Quite the contrary, in fact."

And with that Harvey reached out and took Nathan's offered hand in a firm handshake.

"A pleasure to make your acquaintance, Mr. Harvey!"

"Likewise, Mr. Chambers."

"Mr. Harvey has been working my ships since … oh, I don't know how long … since he was just a young rascal, anyhow. He knows every inch of this ship, and several others owned by the Mayfield Shipping Company, our employer out of Boston. He's been riding herd on the *Abbies* for … well, almost three years now."

"Abbies?"

"Oh, sorry, Mr. Chambers. It's an old tradition among sailors to refer to themselves collectively by the name of their ship … in our case, the *SS Abigail Adams*; you know, wife of the second president, and mother of the sixth, and probably the most well-known and beloved woman in the history of Boston. So our men are the 'Abbies,' you see?"

"Oh … yes, I see. And I am very familiar with the story of Mrs. Adams. The name of your ship would please my mother; her name is Abigail, also named after *your* great lady. She goes by Miss Abbey."

"Well, quite a fine coincidence! Please do give her my best regards, on behalf of her namesake ship, when you finally see her."

"That I will, Mr. McMasters; that I will. Thank you kindly."

"But … tell me, Mr. Harvey, if you don't mind satisfying my curiosity … have you *always* been a free man?"

"Oh, yes, sir. Born and raised up in Boston. My parents escaped out of a farm in Maryland when they were teens and made their way up to Boston. There they ended up working in a warehouse at the Mayfield Company. But since I was big enough to walk, and maybe even before that, I wanted to go out on the big ships. So as soon as I was old enough, off I went. And I've been sailing ever since. But … surely, sir, what I hear about gentlemen from the South can't be all lies."

"No … I'd say I am probably unusual in that regard. I've spent most of my life away in the Army, and only now am returning to Virginia. And, I am very pleased to see a man so thoroughly put a lie to all the talk of black men being inferior, or even something less-than-human. I have never believed it myself. But growing up surrounded by black men held in slavery I've had little enough chance to disprove it."

"Well, I may not be a genius, but I *do* know how to run a steam ship! That one thing I know for sure! And those other two Negro fellas you saw out on deck are also free men, born and raised."

"I'm very happy to hear it, Mr. Harvey. It gives me great hope for the world, after all."

"Amen to that, Mr. Chambers. Amen to that!"

ᔕᗞᘔᐺᘓᗞᔕᗞᘔᐺᘓᗞᔕᗞᘔᐺᘓ

Shortly before 6:00 that evening they arrived at their first destination, the mouth of the Mississippi River. Aside from a fine-looking flight of brown pelicans cruising past the ship, their wingtips just inches off the water, the place could not have been drearier and more hellish. All along the last miles of the river were mud banks, slimy green and black, speckled white with the droppings of thousands of sea birds. Low, scraggly looking bushes dotted the mud banks, apparently the only plants able to grow under these severe conditions. These "arms" stretched far out to sea like two tremendous jetties, with the muddy brown river oozing along between them. Where it finally met the sea the water slowly boiled in a murky brown and blue bubbling mass.

Though hellish it might be, it was certainly not devoid of life; Nathan counted more than forty ships anchored off the mouth. Once again, he stood on the quarterdeck with McMasters.

"What are they all waiting for?" Nathan asked, peering out through his collapsible spyglass.

"Same thing we'll be waiting for—a river pilot."

"River pilot?"

"Yes, no ships of any size dare go upriver without one. First you have to navigate the sandbar at the mouth. Further upstream the banks and underwater shoals are constantly changing. Not to mention various snags floating down the river. Very dangerous business; plenty of ships went down in the early days, so they made a law requiring a river pilot to guide every ship."

"So … where do we get a pilot?"

"Oh, they'll come to us, never fear. It's too late tonight to start upriver, but first light tomorrow this place will be crawling with pilot boats trying to get our business. But Mr. Harvey has a sense for getting the ones that know what they're about and leaving off the ones that just come to take our money. For tonight, we'll have to drop anchor and wait like the rest."

೨ಲ೧೮ಬ೨ಲ೧೮ಬ೨ಲ೧೮

That evening they maneuvered the ship into a favorable spot to drop anchor. They powered down the engine and the cooks served out the evening meal. After the meal, most of the sailors had no duties for the first time since several days before sailing from Galveston.

So Nathan and his men gathered about the soldiers on the deck, and the two groups exchanged friendly banter. One sailor

228

brought out an instrument that appeared to be handmade—something like a flute carved from a stick of wood. Another pulled out a small handmade drum, and they started a lively tune. With light duties and fair weather, the Captain had ordered an extra ration of rum this evening for the crew, so they were in a jolly mood. Several of the sailors danced to the tune.

Nathan enjoyed the evening. It made him think back on their first night at the camp in Del Rio, and the warm hospitality of their Mexican hosts. Stars appeared in the sky above. That and the good humor of the crew helped counter the mucky desolation of the place their ship now sat at anchor.

He saw Stan lean over and whisper something to William. William smiled, shrugged his shoulders, and walked over to the place where they'd piled their belongings, up against a bulkhead. He came back holding a small, travel-worn, wooden box. Nathan recalled seeing it amongst their things but didn't know what it contained. William opened it and reached inside. The soldiers smiled at each other knowingly, and the sailors watched with curiosity. He pulled out a well-worn but elegantly carved violin and bow! This impressed the sailors—an authentic, fancy-looking instrument. A hush fell over the gathering as William plucked at the strings, listening intently to the sound and making small adjustments to the tautness.

Once satisfied, he sat up straight, stuck the back end of the violin under his chin, and stroked the bow slowly across the strings. The tune he played was both beautiful and haunting, rich and sweet in the still evening air. The men of both stripes, sailor and soldier, stood still and quiet as if mesmerized. It was a wonderful sound, the likes of which most had never heard. Nathan thought it a familiar tune but couldn't quite place where he'd heard it before. He looked around at the faces of the men gathered there listening and saw smiles, faraway looks, and more than one set of watery eyes.

When it ended there was an awed silence. Nobody spoke or reacted. Nathan, wanting to rescue William from the uncomfortable silence said, "That was quite exceptional, William. What tune is it?"

"It is a tune written by the Austrian, Franz Schubert. It was part of a seven-song cycle he wrote based on a long poem by Englishman Walter Scott called *'Lady of the Lake.'* The song was originally called *'Ellen's Gesang Dritte,'* in German; 'Ellen's Third Song,' we would say. It is also known as the 'Hymn to the Virgin,' although most people refer to it by its opening line, *'Ave Maria'*; that is, 'Hail Mary' in English."

"Well, whichever name you call it, there's no doubt it's a splendid song. And you play the violin superbly! One day you must tell me how it is you learned to play so well. Thank you, William. Thank you very kindly!"

William bowed, but Stan stood up, "Yes, yes … *very* pretty William, very pretty. But if you keep playing this type song, soon we are all crying like babies for our Mommas! These sailors want drink rum and dance. You must play *livelier* tune, William!"

William looked at him a moment then tilted his head as if in thought. He gazed upward, scratching the back of his head with the base of the bow. Suddenly he raised the bow, as if struck by a thought. He stood up, tapped his boot on the wooden planking of the deck, and launched into a jaunty tune. The sailors smiled and laughed; it was a song they all immediately recognized. Of course, a soldier would think to play it on a ship amid a bunch of sailors; it was the "Sailor's Hornpipe," the traditional, almost cliché dance song of sailors. After less than a moment's hesitation, the flute player and the drummer joined in with enthusiasm, and several of the sailors danced again. Soon more joined them. Then suddenly Stan was in their midst, dancing and twirling wildly, men moving to stay out of his way for fear of being trodden by the giant man. The other soldiers joined in the fun, though they were not especially good at it.

When the song ended there was loud and enthusiastic applause for both William's playing, and Stan's dancing. The flute player launched into another song. It had a simple melody, and though not as familiar as the Hornpipe, after a few moments of listening, William picked up the tune and played along. Adding the "fiddle" to the music gave it a life and a depth well beyond what the sailors were used to. Many continued to smile and nod at William in appreciation.

It was very late, and the ship was now quiet again, the men having dispersed either to bed or to their evening duties. Nathan pulled his blanket up under his chin to counter a chill in the air. He noticed the stars were no longer visible overhead. Clouds had rolled in, and the breeze was once again picking up; but this time there was a cold bite to it. He remembered McMasters saying when the weather changed, "watch out!" *Watch out for what?* he wondered, as he faded off to sleep.

Around midnight a man holding a lantern shook him awake. "Sorry to bother you, sir. Captain sends his respects and suggests you and your men move below decks for the rest of the night. Appears to be a squall coming on, and you're likely to get a good soaking if you stays up here."

"Thank you kindly, mister. We'll do that."

Shortly after, they were once again settling back to sleep, this time in a musty smelling hold, a place typically filled with cargo of one sort or another. Several sailors had also helped move their stack of belongings down with them.

As he settled back into his bedroll, he heard a loud wailing, and the ship leaned hard over. Then he heard rain lashing the deck, and voices calling out up above, as the ship rocked side to side and heaved hard, end to end. He suddenly felt very thankful for the wooden walls surrounding them, and the decking over their heads.

Then, just as he was about to fall back asleep, a voice in the back of his mind spoke to him. It asked, *But, what about the horses?* He sat bolt upright, and turned to Tom, reaching out and shaking him awake.

"Tom … we must see to the horses. We can't leave them alone in this storm."

"What? The horses? Oh … oh, yes … yes, of course." He sat up, rubbed his eyes, and reached over to poke Georgie, who was the man lying closest to him.

231

Soon they were all roused, heading out the hatch of their compartment, and down the passageway to where they'd quartered the horses. The ship continued to pitch and roll in the heaving seas, the men having a hard time keeping their balance and moving in a straight line without stumbling, bumping into each other or against the bulkheads.

When they finally reached the horses' compartment, they were pleasantly surprised to find the horses upright and steady on their feet. As the ship moved, the animals instinctively moved with it, much better so than their human counterparts. But Nathan could see a wild, panicked look in their eyes, and he could sense their growing fear. Several pulled frantically at their ropes, thrashing their heads from side to side in a vain attempt to free themselves from the ropes securing them.

"Quickly, each man take a horse, or two! Put your face up next to theirs and speak to them softly … they will weather the storm better than we, if we give them a little reassurance."

They distributed themselves about the pen, each to his own favorite horse, and those closest also taking turns comforting one of the two spare horses or the mule. The sailors had secured each animal to the deck with a soft canvas collar about the neck attached to a rope on either side. This prevented them from moving about and jostling each other. Nathan pulled Millie's head down and stroked it, speaking soothingly into her ears, "That's a good girl, now. Nothing to fear … I'm with you … good girl, Millie …" and on and on until the tension drained out of her muscles. She began to relax, while continuing to roll with the movement of the ship.

When they'd first boarded the ship, Nathan had asked McMasters about slings for the horses, such as he remembered they'd used on the long voyage to Mexico years ago. But the ship's captain assured him it wasn't necessary for a voyage of under a week; they'd found horses fared better without any such support on a short journey. As long as they secured them well, fresh air and clean stables were the most important thing, along with plenty of water. Since the ship was empty of cargo, there was plenty of room to spread the horses out. This also made it unnecessary to remove their shoes, lest they kick each other. And Nathan could see the crew was doing a good job of keeping the area clean and ventilated.

Within about a half-hour the horses had settled down and were much calmer, even though the ship's movement had increased. Nathan decided they could watch the horses in shifts, now that they were no longer panicked. He told the sergeants to assign two-man shifts for the rest of the night, and the following day as needed, including himself. Then he headed back to bed.

☙﷽☙﷽☙﷽﷽☙﷽

If the scene at the mouth of the Mississippi had been hellish before, by morning it was thoroughly nightmarish. Great rolling waves pounded and rocked the ship, spraying sheets of water onto the deck. The great rollers pounded the narrow, muddy spit of land separating the gulf from the river, riding high up over the land, and in places all the way over onto the river side. Low, scudding clouds blocked out the sun, making it difficult to tell the time of day. Rain came down in sheets seemingly from every direction, blown sideways by the blustering wind.

After taking in the sight, Nathan joined his men, who were huddled up on the deck. They'd broken out their oiled overcoats in a vain attempt to stay dry, but Nathan decided they looked even more miserable than on the ride to Houston. Georgie in particular looked unwell. Sure enough, a few moments after Nathan's arrival he walked over to the railing and heaved over the side into the pitching sea.

But Nathan was more concerned about how Billy was doing, so he leaned in close and looked him in the eye, the obvious question unspoken.

"It seems the lion has teeth after all," Billy said and smiled. "But I find I am no longer afraid."

"Glad to hear it. I'm proud of you, Billy. Good man."

"Thank you, Captain."

Nathan's next stop was up on the quarterdeck to speak with McMasters.

"Hello, Mr. Chambers! What do you think of our weather now?"

The greeting was friendly, but there was an undertone of concern. And the speaker was *not* McMasters, but the first mate, Mr. Harvey. He stood, looking out to sea, another sailor Nathan did not know was manning the wheel.

"Good morning, Mr. Harvey. I believe I'd prefer the weather of yesterday and before, if it's all the same to you!"

"You'll get no argument from me there, sir. We've had a long night of it up here on the quarterdeck, and it's not over yet, I'm afraid. Captain has gone below to get a little shut eye, but not sure how long he'll be able to stay away. He gets a bit ... *twitchy* ... when there's rough weather."

"Tell me, Mr. Harvey ... am I misremembering, or ... were we pointed in the other direction last night?"

"You are not mistaken, sir. You see, we always play out the anchor from the bow, that is, the front of the ship. That way the "pointy end" of the ship is always directed into the current. Or into the wind, if the wind is stronger than the current. This keeps the ship more stable, and less vulnerable to any large waves that may strike. Close in to shore here by the river mouth, the current is normally out of the northeast, so yesterday with little wind the current pointed the ship in that direction. But this storm blew in from south by southwest, so it swung us around as the wind and waves pushed against the ship. You probably felt a lot of rocking and whatnot before she settled into her new position a bit after the storm hit."

"I still feel a lot rocking and such, to tell the truth."

"Yes, well, now you are experiencing the bad part of riding out a storm at anchor; the anchor tends to pull the bow down into the waves, rather than letting her ride up over as she would in open seas."

A huge wave crashed against the front of the ship, as if to punctuate the first mate's point, sending a sheet of spray up onto the deck. A half-foot wave of water rolled down the deck, soaking everything in its path before spewing out the scuppers on the sides like water through a fire hose.

234

"Like *that!*"

"Yes, I see what you mean."

They were quiet for a few moments. Nathan felt mesmerized by the view of the waves rolling in, smashing against the bow of the ship, sending spray flying, and flowing down the deck in a rush. The pattern repeated itself over and over.

Then something changed.

"What *the!?*" Harvey shouted.

"What is it?"

"Didn't you feel that? The anchor slid!"

"To be honest, with the rocking and the pounding of the waves, I really didn't feel anything else …"

"Oh! Damn! There it is again. The anchor is slipping. That's *not* good … no, sir! Not good at all! Maybe it'll catch hold again."

Nathan had felt nothing different at all, but now he watched Mr. Harvey in tense expectation.

For a few moments, nothing more happened; the waves continued to pound against the bow of the ship, but the first mate stood motionless, an odd, expectant look on his face.

"There … *there!* Surely you felt *that?* A shudder … a sudden vibration right up the spine of the ship. The anchor is dragging again. *Damn it!* Not what we need now. If we hadn't already fired the engine to run the bilge pumps, I'd start her up now. Good news is … we're still a ways out from shore, but we can't risk getting in much closer.

Nathan looked back, and it did seem they were closer to the muddy spit than they'd been before. Or was he just seeing what he feared to see?

Harvey walked over and opened the control room door. Rain poured in and swirled around the room. He leaned out and shouted, "Mr. Cauley … please go rouse the Captain … give him my compliments and ask him to return to the bridge as soon as may be!"

Nathan heard a voice shout out in answer through the howling wind, "Aye, sir! On my way!"

But Harvey had only just pulled the door closed and returned to stand next to the man at the ship's wheel when the door burst open. In strode Captain McMasters, water streaming from his oiled overcoat.

"Harvey … the damned anchor's dragging!" he said without prelude.

"Yes, sir. I know. I just sent for you."

"It woke me right out of a dead sleep. Felt it right down the keel of the ship. Damn it! Damn it to hell! Shall we pull the anchor, do you think?"

"Well … we'll likely hit harder ground again and catch hold before we flounder on the spit. But even before the anchor slipped, I wasn't liking the way the bow was diving. We've been taking on a lot of water, the bilge pumps barely keeping up. So I was already thinking we should weigh anchor, head out to deeper water and ride out the squall."

Nathan winced. To him the instinct was to head in to shore in foul weather, not further out to sea.

"Yes … yes, you may be right." McMasters stared out at the waves pounding against the bow. He extended his gaze out beyond to the open sea.

After a few moments, he turned back to Harvey and said, "Yes. Yes, please give the orders to weigh and make for open water."

"Aye, Captain."

Albert Harvey stepped over to the metal speaking tube and shouted, "Mr. Stenson, do you hear me?"

He leaned his ear to the tube and listened.

"Aye, aye, sir! Stenson, hearing you, sir!"

"Mr. Stenson stoke the engine, if you please. We are preparing to weigh anchor and head to sea."

"Aye, aye, sir. Stoke the engine and prepare for heading to sea!"

Harvey stepped over to the door, opened it, wiped the spray from his face, and shouted, "Mr. Cauley! Pass the word; prepare to weigh anchor!"

"Aye, aye, sir. Prepare to weigh it is!"

About five minutes passed, during which Nathan detected a noticeable increase in the noise and vibrations put out by the engine. He made a silent prayer thanking God he lived in the age of such modern wonders. The thought of an old-style sailing ship moving out in this weather was truly frightening.

The door suddenly flew open, with its requisite spray.

"Prepared to weigh anchor, sir!"

"Thank you, Mr. Cauley. Weigh anchor, if you please!"

"Aye, sir. Weighing anchor!"

He slammed the door, and Mr. Harvey returned to the speaking tube and called out, "Mr. Stenson, prepare for half-ahead!"

"Aye, aye, sir! Prepare for half-speed-ahead."

Harvey stared out the front window to the bow area, where six men gathered around the capstan. He could see them turning it, pushing the bars while walking in a circle, slowly raising the anchor.

"Half-ahead, Mr. Stenson."

"Aye, sir! Half-speed-ahead."

At first Nathan couldn't tell any difference. But then he felt it without a doubt, a definite change in the ship's motion. A forward movement, pushing ahead, and the bow riding slightly up the incoming waves rather than diving into them. He had to admit it was reassuring; they were no longer helpless under the force of the waves.

It was a tricky maneuver in high seas, and Nathan could sense a nervous tension among the mariners. Normally, in calm seas, they'd bring the anchor all the way up before moving forward, but they couldn't risk it in this heavy weather. Once the anchor no longer gripped the bottom, if the ship had no forward momentum it would be entirely at the mercy of the waves and wind. There was a very real possibility of floundering or capsizing. But moving forward with the anchor on its way up might also be a hazard; too much speed and the anchor cable might come up under the ship and foul the paddles or the rudder, which would spell disaster.

"Slow a quarter, Mr. Stenson!" Harvey shouted into the tube.

"Aye, sir! Slowing a quarter!"

Harvey and McMasters stared out at the men turning the capstan, as if waiting for some sign with anxious anticipation.

Finally, the men stopped moving, and one of them turned and gave a thumbs-up signal.

"Full ahead, Mr. Stenson, if you please!"

"Aye, aye, Mr. Harvey! Full steam ahead! And, yes sir, it *does* please me ... *greatly!*"

This last comment from the engineer brought a smile to McMasters' face. Nathan could feel the tension leaking from the room.

The door suddenly burst open, splashing them again with sea spray. It was immediately pushed closed.

"Oh! Sorry, sorry! Didn't mean to douse you!"

It was Tom Clark. "My apologies for bothering you gentlemen, but us 'land lovers' were getting a little concerned, what with all the shouting and running about. And it seemed like we were moving out away from the land. Has something happened?"

McMasters answered him, "Nothing of concern, Mr. Clark. Us sailors were just tired of viewing land and decided we'd prefer the view further out to sea!"

This elicited a puzzled look from Tom, until McMasters and Harvey laughed, and Tom knew he was being kidded.

"No, Mr. Clark ... nothing serious, but we weren't liking the way the ship was riding at anchor. Decided it'd be best to take her out into deeper water," Albert answered.

"Excuse me my ignorance, but is that wise in such a strong storm?"

"Oh, no, Mr. Clark; this isn't any kind of storm to worry over; just a gentle spring squall. It's the storms that come in the fall you'd best avoid. Those great monstrous, ship eating, port destroying storms they call 'hurricanes!' A mariner's worst nightmare, that is. No sir, we'll be safely back in Boston harbor long before it's the season for those, thank you very much!" McMasters answered, then looked up and made the sign of the cross on his chest.

"For a ship like ours, it's safer to stay out away from the land, in deep water. So long as we have engine power, there's nothing to fear," Harvey explained, with a reassuring smile.

Nothing to fear, Nathan had to remind himself several times throughout that day, as the wind howled in the rigging, and the waves continued to hammer against the ship's bow. But the *SS Abigail Adams* forged ahead gamely, spewing smoke and steam from her stack, as if no amount of wind and waves could stop her.

He and the men spent most of that day below decks in their makeshift sleeping quarters. It was musty and stale smelling, but relatively dry, and out of the wind. Still, it was an anxious day, and a long night for the landsmen. They continued taking shifts comforting the horses.

In the early morning, long before daylight, Nathan woke from a fitful sleep. He'd served his horse-shift earlier in the night and was still sleepy headed. For a moment he had trouble getting his bearings. He lay still, listening for the noise that must have awakened him. Then he chuckled softly to himself; it wasn't a noise, but rather a *lack* of noise that had awakened him. The wind was no longer howling, and the bouncing of the ship had slackened considerably. He pulled the blanket back under his chin, rolled over, and went back to sleep. He slept a deep, sound sleep. And for once he was *not* out of bed before first light.

In the morning he awoke from sleep and looked up to find someone he didn't recognize standing over him. His instinctive reaction was to strike out; but then he remembered where he was and relaxed.

"Sorry to wake you, sir. Captain sends his compliments and invites you to the bridge. He says to tell you … he says, 'tell him he may enjoy the view better this morning' … yes, sir. That's exactly what he told me to tell you, begging your pardon, sir."

"Thank you, mister …?"

"Tellers, sir."

"Thank you, Mr. Tellers. Please give your captain my regards and say I will be along shortly."

When he came up on deck, he could see the waters had indeed calmed down, as he'd felt during the night. The sea was still choppy, and the ship rode up over great rolling waves with barely a splash. He had to agree; he much preferred the view today from the one yesterday. The clouds were breaking up, with blue patches here and there letting the sun shine down in great sparkling streaks at various points out across the water. It was a truly beautiful, awe-inspiring sight, such as he had never seen.

When he arrived on the quarterdeck, McMasters was there, and greeted him warmly with a bright smile.

"Weather more to your liking today, Chambers?"

"Yes, I'd say so. And what a beautiful sight! Not a view you'd ever have on land."

"Yes, it's a pretty day for sure. But that's not what I brought you up here to see. After we reach the crest of this roller and start down the other side, kindly look straight out ahead of the bow."

Nathan watched straight ahead as the ship rode up over the roller, the bow tipped up toward the sky. Then as it crested the top, the bow tipped back down, granting a view of the horizon ahead. Nathan strained his eyes into the far distance and saw ... two green humps ... land of some sort.

"Land?"

"Yes, of course, *land*. But not just *any* land; that's the two spits lining the mouth of the Mississippi! Can you believe it, sir? All night heading south by southwest in the teeth of the storm, pitch black, and then at three bells the storm finally plays out. So, I heads for the sack and leaves the ship to Mr. Harvey.

"Damned if he don't turn the ship about and bring her right back in to where we started! There ain't one sailor in ten thousand that could do such a thing! And from nothing more than keeping a keen eye on that old compass and a steady bearing in heavy seas. Our Mr. Harvey is truly some kind of seaman; I've rarely before seen the like! I figured we would spend half a day cruising along the coast just to figure out where we were, not even knowing if we sailed in the right direction or wrong. And yet ... here we are, as smartly as you please!"

"Yes, that's an amazing piece of navigation, I can see. I assume you have sent him to a well-deserved rest?"

"Yes, there won't be much more to do for a while. We'll anchor up again by the mouth and wait for a pilot to arrive. Since we missed the rush at first light, it may take a little longer before one comes for us. Then we'll get going on up the river."

Nathan was quiet and thoughtful for a moment, slowly shaking his head.

"What are you thinking, Chambers?"

"I'm thinking your impressive first mate is serving to put an exclamation point on my thinking about black men in general, and the reprehensible institution of slavery in particular."

"And I say, amen to that, Mr. Chambers. Amen to that," McMasters said, nodding his agreement.

ಬುಞಾರುಞಬುಞಾರುಞಬುಞಾರುಞ

As McMasters had predicted, it took several hours after they anchored at the mouth for a river pilot to arrive. By then there were a half-dozen other ships also waiting at anchor. Soon they could see several row boats cut across the water from the river mouth, one to each of the ships.

Although the waves were nothing like they'd been at the height of the storm, still they were vigorous. The ship continued to roll up and down, and rock side to side. Nathan watched the pilot's arrival with curiosity, wondering how he would get aboard the much taller ship with all that motion.

He watched in admiration as the pilot, his oarsman, and the ship's crew pulled off the minor miracle with much grace and seeming ease. The small pilot boat approached the ship, and the crew threw down a rope ladder. Some thirty feet long, it was just the right length for the pilot to reach without the end dragging in the water. The pilot boat carefully pulled up next to the ship adjacent to where the ladder hung down. The pilot stood in the bow while the oarsman maneuvered the boat up close to the ladder. They were careful to keep back from the large, rocking ship, which could crush the small boat in an instant.

At the height of a bouncing wave the ship rocked toward the small boat, so the ladder hung out away from the ship. The pilot reached up and grabbed the third rung of the ladder. He sprung neatly up onto it. Then, he paused in his climbing as the ship rocked the other way, causing the ladder to swing toward the hull.

Nathan cringed as it seemed to him the pilot would be smashed against the hard side of the ship. But at the last second, the man extended his right leg, and absorbed the shock by placing the bottom of his shoe against the hull and bending at the knee. As soon as he'd stopped his momentum, he scrambled quickly up the rest of the way, grabbed by several helping hands as he reached the top. It was as neat a maneuver in a dangerous situation as he had ever witnessed.

With the pilot's guidance they arrived four hours later at the small town of La Balize, the original name given it by the Frenchmen who'd founded it. But the sailors simply called it "Pilotsville." Its only purpose was to serve as the headquarters and exchange point for the two groups of river pilots that worked this part of the Mississippi. One group, the Crescent Pilots, worked the river north to New Orleans. The other group, the Bar Pilots, plied their trade from the mouth to Pilotsville. This required maneuvering over the ever-shifting sandbar formed where the river spilled into the gulf and fought against the tides.

To call the rag-tag cluster of huts a "town" was a good stretch, Nathan decided. Built entirely on stilts, hot and humid, it was surrounded by swampy, noisome, half-land-half-water; swarming with mosquitos, and alligators. He couldn't imagine a more miserable place to live, but McMasters told him many families of pilots and fishermen stayed there. It seemed to be half derelict, or in a constant state of repair because of the frequent storms that lashed it.

They anchored the ship. He could see two men repairing a wooden "sidewalk" connecting the various buildings and built entirely on stilts. A section about ten feet long appeared to have collapsed, and the men were laying on new boards to bridge the gap.

It was getting on to evening, so McMasters had decided to wait until first light to bring on the Crescent pilot for the trip to New Orleans. It would take another fifteen hours or more to reach the city, and he preferred to make most of that hazardous run during daylight hours.

At first light the next morning, the new river pilot joined them, and this time the on-boarding wasn't nearly as dramatic; the river was as smooth as glass. The only challenge was the steady southward flow of the great river. They were soon moving again at full steam. All that day they made their way upriver, and the farther north they went, the drier the land became, and the more civilized. They went to bed that night knowing that when they awoke in the morning, the *SS Abigail Adams* would be safely docked in New Orleans.

Chapter 8. A Place Like No Other

"New Orleans is noisy,
bustling, gossiping,
and a thousand leagues
from the United States."
– Alexis de Tocqueville

Friday June 1, 1860 – New Orleans, Louisiana:

They said their fond farewells to McMasters, Harvey, and the other sailors, and promised to visit should they ever find themselves in Boston. Nathan offered all possible hospitality should the sailors have reason to be in western Virginia.

They led their horses down the gangplank and away from the docks, saddled up, and rode slowly through the cobbled streets of New Orleans.

Nathan, having been here before, watched his young companions' reactions with amusement. New Orleans was a place like no other in the world. It was the country's most prosperous and vibrant city, in the world's most prosperous and vibrant nation. That meant architecture unrivaled outside of New York City, culture and language imported straight from Paris, and commerce unmatched outside of London.

As they rode along one street, brightly dressed women leaned over from second-story balconies, revealing generous amounts of cleavage. They called out to the men as they rode by, "Hey handsome, come and see me later. You'll have the time of your life," *"Bon jour, mon cherie! Entrez s'il vous plaît,"* "Stop and come up to visit me, lover. Don't keep riding, my darling," "Stay and rest; you'll not be sorry, handsome," "Come, my lover, come stay with me," "I'm waiting for you, come up and see me … ," and so on, and so on.

Stan seemed to attract the most attention from these women. At first, he blushed, and shrugged his shoulders. But soon he got into the spirit, and shouted back, "Yes, my sweetheart, as soon as

I tuck my little children here into bed, I will return. After I've had my lunch, I will return, dear one. I must put up my horse and then I shall be back, my love," and on and on. Jim was soon laughing out loud and slapping his thighs with his hat. The others blushed and ducked their heads whenever the women addressed them. Nathan just smiled and shook his head in amusement, tipping his hat politely toward the women, puffing on a cigar.

They also rode through neighborhoods of the most elegant houses they'd ever seen—magnificent, multi-storied, beautifully trimmed and painted, with gardens that would put those they had admired in San Antonio to shame. Huge trees overhung the streets, strung with Spanish moss hanging down in great, gray "beards."

They finally arrived at their destination: the St. Charles Hotel. Built in the traditional Greek style, elegant in its white marble facade with formal columns, the St. Charles looked much like the Acropolis in Athens might have in its heyday. Four stories high, it occupied an entire city block. It was by far the most impressive and magnificent structure any of the men had ever seen.

And it was not only the finest hotel in New Orleans, but very likely the finest in North America. Nathan again enjoyed with great satisfaction the jaw-dropping reaction of the young men. At a time when travelers typically stayed in ordinary inns, boarding houses, or with private individuals, the St. Charles was the first *great* American hotel.

And like the hub of a giant wheel, businesses and dwellings spread out from it in every direction. St. Charles Street was the most vibrant street in the United States, and possibly the world; between Lafayette and Canal Streets was an almost non-stop line of barrooms and restaurants, fifty or more. And the hotel had its own dining facilities; besides the guests it housed, hundreds of outsiders dined every day at the St. Charles.

Nathan, having stayed here several times before, wouldn't consider staying anywhere else in New Orleans. It was a place so grand, and so superior to anything else, it drew in the well-to-do like moths to a flame. In a city like no other, it was a hotel like no other.

They dismounted in front of the hotel, and four black men, dressed neatly in white, came rushing out to greet them and take their horses and baggage. The entrance to the hotel passed between massive columns before mounting a broad set of stone stairs leading up to the second story. At the top of the stairs were two more black men, these in matching black suits with purple, shimmering waistcoats. They held the large, ornate, gilded doors open for the new arrivals with white-gloved hands, politely bowing them in. The men stepped into a world none but Nathan had ever seen.

The foyer was a full stones-throw wide and deep. It reached three stories up, from the second story landing all the way to the very top of the four-story hotel. Guests on the top floor could look down on the foyer from a balcony wrapping around the room on three sides.

As impressive as was the size, the elegance of the room was almost beyond description. The broad floor was tiled in marble polished to a mirror-like sheen. Dozens of massive, Corinthian-style fluted marble columns encircled the room, each with its intricately carved capital atop. A great, multileveled chandelier hung down from the ceiling, a full two stories high. It lit the center of the large room with a multifaceted, sparkling glow of glass and shining brass. Tom felt sorry for the poor fellows who had to keep that massive thing lit all day.

A small team of hotel clerks assisted guests from a large, ornately decorated window to one side, while further back a semi-circular room lined one wall. Between its smaller Corinthian columns, bartenders served out liquid refreshments to the guests.

Every square inch of walls and ceiling was covered with paneling, gilding, and sculpture. A clock on a mantle above the clerks' desk was circled in intricately styled gold, with a gold life-sized eagle, wings outspread, perched on the top. A great marble-column-framed fireplace occupied the greater part of one wall. Its elegantly carved mantle practically overflowed with bronze statuary of angels, demons, and animals of all description, both real and imagined. And mixed among them were huge bouquets, bursting with every imaginable variety of flower in all the colors of the rainbow. These were set in exquisitely decorated ceramic vases that had a foreign look to them—Chinese, maybe?

Various side rooms surrounded the great room: a large, cafeteria-style restaurant, a smaller bar, a library, a gentlemen's lounge, and even a barber shop. A broad curving stairway lined the back of the foyer. One flight ran up to the third and fourth floors, another ran down to the first-floor rooms. There were no guest rooms on the second floor; the foyer and all the other common rooms filled that level.

A crowd of forty or fifty milled about the foyer, mostly men, generally well-dressed, but a few like Nathan's party in drab traveling garb. One group comprised a half-dozen or so army officers in their dress blues. Nathan looked them over carefully for a few minutes before deciding he recognized none of them.

Multiple groups of men were engaging in various conversations. Several were loud and animated, with occasional bursts of raucous laughter. The barkeeps had apparently been doing their job!

But despite all the people standing about, Nathan and his men could walk across the grand room with no one having to step aside. The group of young men, fresh from army duty in West Texas, strolled through the room, wide-eyed, staring about, trying to take it all in.

Georgie elbowed Jamie, "Hey ... you ever seen anything the like of this?"

"No, boyo ... never in life. Captain payin' for us-all to stay in this place?"

"Yep, I reckon so. I heard his family had money, but ... *this?*"

They shared a look, rolled their eyes, and grinned.

Jim leaned over to Tom and whispered, "Didn't know the Captain liked us *this* much!" Tom smiled at him and shrugged.

Once again Nathan watched out of the corner of his eye and smiled.

ᏚᎯᏋᏣᏋᏚᎯᏋᏣᏋᏚᎯᏋᏣᏋ

Nathan and Tom took rooms on the fourth floor, while Jim and the others ended up on the first floor. After settling in, they held

247

a brief meeting back in the foyer. They sat on a set of beautifully carved hardwood benches, padded and covered in red velvet, off to one side of the room. It was only about noon, so they decided to split up and go their separate ways for the afternoon, and possibly the rest of the day.

Nathan needed to visit the bank. For years, the Army had been depositing his officer's pay in a bank here in the city, per his request. As he had withdrawn but little over the years, it was now a sizable fund. He intended to draw out enough for the trip home. The remainder he'd have transferred (for a small fee) to a bank in New York he'd used back when he was a cadet at West Point. He planned to leave nothing behind on deposit; now that he was out of the Army, he couldn't envision any reason for ever returning to New Orleans.

Tom decided he wanted to see if he could buy more suitable attire for the St. Charles, and for civilization in general. All he'd brought on the trip were his rough, travel-stained traveling clothes, plus his master sergeant's dress uniform, neatly packed away in the luggage.

Jim decided to find a good card game; ever since watching the Captain's misadventure at the cantina, he'd had the itch to try his luck at gambling.

The others had no specific agenda. They decided to just go out and see what there was to see in the city. Billy, having no interest in banks, clothing stores, or card games, followed along to see what kind of mischief the rest of the men would get into.

ᔑᓭᘔᓕᔑᓭᘔᓕᔑᓭᘔᓕ

"Well, what next, do you think? Shall we go out on the lash?" Jamie asked, after the group had finished up their midday meal and pushed back from the table.

There was a brief silence, then Stan said, "Well … I *did* promise women I would return …"

For a moment, the others couldn't think of what he meant. Then William said, "*Not* those disreputable, scantily clad women, hanging from the upper-story balconies? The ones showing all

248

measure of bosom, and shouting obscenities at passing men with no shame?"

Stan laughed, and slapped William on the back, "*Of course, those women! What other kind would they be?*"

Jamie and Georgie laughed, Billy shook his head, and William rolled his eyes.

"Come … let us go find them again. Is anyone remembering twisty road Captain brought us in on?"

Billy remembered, naturally, but wasn't about to volunteer his services to help the men find these shameless women, who were likely nothing but trouble.

Since nobody answered, Stan waved down the waiter. "Hey … if young men … such as us here, who are new to city, want to find women … hmm … how you say … *not-too-particular?* Yes, maybe that is right … *women not-too-particular* … where they be going in city?"

The waiter smiled at the question. "Well, when I was younger, and *much* more foolish … I used to go down to Gallatin Street sometimes. There are plenty of girls down there who are … *not-too-particular.*"

ജ഻൜ൠൟജ഻൜ൠൟജ഻൜ൠൟ

At about the same time the others were finishing their lunch, Jim took a seat at a table of six. The men at the table had been gambling on various card games. Jim had been watching and waiting for a seat to open up. He'd been carefully studying each of the men, memorizing their actions and expressions as they handled their cards and made their bets.

They prepared to start the next round, and each man was dealt a card. Jim drew high card, so got to choose the game. Before calling it, he reached into his vest pocket, pulled out a cigar and lit it. Then he looked around the table, thinking about what game to call, as the dealer shuffled the cards. His left hand was unconsciously fiddling with something in his pocket. When he realized what it was, he smiled—the gold tooth.

"Draw poker," he said, and chuckled.

Tom passed beneath the great columns heading back into the St. Charles. He took the broad stairs two at a time. He was pleased with his outing. For one, it had been an enjoyable and entertaining walk—and it felt *very* nice to be on dry, solid ground again, he had to admit! And best of all, he'd accomplished the goal of his mission to his complete satisfaction.

Before setting out he'd decided to see if he could find a ready-made suit of the proper fit. Though a tailor normally sewed suits to order after carefully taking one's measurements, Tom thought his chances good. He was of medium height and build, and it was likely that if a tailor had a suit made for display it would fit him. Big Stan, on the other hand, would be completely out of luck in that regard!

Tom couldn't wait the day or two it usually required; the Captain had said they'd probably only stay in the city two or three days at the most before continuing their journey. Besides, he felt ill at ease in the grand hotel dressed the way he'd been; he was ashamed to be seen next to the Captain in his fine new suit.

The first three tailor shops he visited turned him down cold, after looking at him as if he'd asked for a suit with three sleeves! But at the fourth shop the tailor did not immediately answer. Instead he tilted his head and looked Tom over. He stepped back, circled around Tom eyeing him closely, then pulled out a tape for a few quick measurements.

Finally, the man answered, in a thick French accent, "*Oui* ... is possible, monsieur. You are of the exact right size. So it may be I will be having the suit that will suffice. Come, *s'il vous plaît*."

He led Tom back through the shop to where he had several suits on display. They were hung on male dress forms—a mannequin with only a trunk, no head or arms; the "legs," a mere wooden stand, like a coat rack.

The tailor walked over to a fine-looking black suit, took out his tape measure and checked various measurements, then made the same measurements on Tom. Tom looked around at the other suits. "What about that one?" he asked, pointing to a gray suit over to his left.

"The gray one? *Oui, oui,* could be. Is not as … how you say … *elegant,* as the black one."

"That's okay. I like the looks of that gray suit. Can you check the fit?"

"*Oui* … come."

He agreed the black suit had looked magnificent, but Tom liked the idea of the gray one for a couple of reasons: first, the black one appeared to be the most expensive suit in the store. He didn't necessarily want to spend *all* his money on a suit. Second, the black suit was at least as fine as the one the Captain had acquired in San Antonio, if not nicer. Tom was uncomfortable thinking about showing up in a nicer suit than the Captain's. That would seem as if he were trying to one-up him. He shuddered at the thought; that he would *never* do. He didn't want the Captain to even *think* it. Though he knew the Captain would say nothing, too much the gentleman for that. No, the gray one was nice, but not as elegant as the black one. Exactly what he'd been looking for.

And he was in luck, the fit was almost perfect. The changes the tailor had to make were minor, and he promised to finish them in a few hours (for an extra fee). So Tom could pick up the suit later after having lunch and seeing if he could find a hat and shoes to match.

He sprang up the steps of the St. Charles in fine spirits, dressed in his new gray suit, shiny new black shoes, and new hat in the popular round "bowler" style. His old clothes and boots he carried tucked under his left arm, wrapped in a scrap piece of cloth the tailor had given him.

He reached the landing and approached the entrance. There he could see a couple standing in front of one of the gilded doors, as if waiting for it to open. Tom guessed some other duty had distracted the doorman, so he sprang forward, grabbed the great brass handle, and pulled it open. He turned toward the waiting couple, and bowed slightly, holding the door for them, "Please … won't you enter, with my compliments?" he said.

From behind he'd assumed they were a husband and wife, neatly dressed, either returning to the hotel after an outing or coming in for dinner. But now he noticed, to his surprise, the lady was *very* young—close to his own age, while the gentleman was much older—gray-haired and mustached.

Though he was old enough to be her father, Tom didn't want to make assumptions. So after they thanked him kindly, Tom asked the gentleman, "Are you and your wife guests of the hotel, or just coming in for dinner?"

"Wife?" The man seemed puzzled by the question, but then chuckled. "Oh *no*, my good fellow. She is *not* my wife. This is my beloved *niece*, Adilida. Miss Adilida Boudreau, I should say ... and I am her uncle, Edouard Boudreau." He was a handsome man and spoke with a French accent. Edouard smiled brightly at Tom; he was apparently either in fine good humor or was one of those people who always appeared jolly.

"Very pleased to make your acquaintance, Mr. Boudreau, Miss Boudreau. My name is Tom Clark, from Connecticut," and this time, no longer holding open the door, he could remove his hat and make a more proper, formal bow.

The man returned the bow, and the woman curtseyed and smiled prettily. She wore a dark red, silk dress, neatly trimmed in black and beige. It featured the interesting contradiction of a high collar around the sides and back of the neck, offset by a plunging "V" in front. It ran down far enough to reveal a cleavage Tom found difficult to keep his eyes from. He thought her dark auburn hair was a perfect contrast to her pale white skin, and bright green eyes. He decided she was a distinct pleasure to look at.

Mr. Boudreau extended his hand, "The pleasure is all mine, Mr. Clark."

"Oh, *no*, Uncle! The pleasure is most certainly all *mine!*" the young woman said with a giggle and flashed Tom a smile that made his heart skip a beat.

"Well, yes, I can see that Adilida, now you are mentioning it. He *is* quite the handsome young fellow."

"Oh ... uh, thank you sir," Tom answered, though it was a bit awkward being talked about to his face in that manner. Besides, he'd never thought of himself as especially handsome, though he imagined he looked rather dashing in his new garments. And he knew his time in the Army had instilled in him a confidence and self-assurance that was, he assumed, above the norm.

It had not always been the case. When he was a young man back east, he'd taken a job working for his uncle in the family freight-hauling business. But despite taking to the job easily, his uncle was constantly critical of his work, making Tom feel anxious and inadequate.

Over time, Tom began to suspect his uncle was putting him down in order to play favorites with his own two sons, Tom's cousins, cousins who were less capable and competent, by Tom's way of thinking. But Tom's own father was unable or unwilling to accept criticism of his older brother, Tom's uncle. So Tom had to just suffer and endure the humiliation, day after day.

Then one day while walking to work, Tom stopped to listen to an Army recruiter who was standing on top of a table set up on the street, shouting out to the passersby. He told of the adventures one might have out West, and how the Army would make men out of boys.

Tom thought about it all day at work. On the way home the Army officer was still there, so Tom signed up on the spot. And next thing he knew, he was out in Texas.

And though it was nothing like he'd imagined, in the end he had to admit, the Army *had* come through as promised. He *did* feel like a man now, mostly thanks to the Captain. His confidence in Tom had been the boost he'd needed to live up to the potential he'd always felt inside.

"So ... Monsieur Clark, *from Connecticut* ... what brings you to our lovely city of New Orleans?" Adilida asked, still smiling brightly, gazing into Tom's eyes in a most distracting manner.

"Oh, just passing through on my way from West Texas back east to Virginia."

"Oh, *my!* This is not a journey to be undertaken lightly, Monsieur Clark; there must be quiet a tale behind it!"

"Well ... yes, I suppose there is ... it has been ... *interesting*, so far. You see, I am recently come from service in the Army, fighting

Indians out on the far edge of Texas. I'm now accompanying my former commanding officer returning to his home in Virginia …"

"Oh … *oh!* Surely it is not so? Truly, fighting the wild, savage Indians in the far west lands? Oh, *my* … you must be so *very* brave!"

Tom blushed, "Oh, well, at the time it didn't seem so … just … doing my duty, you know."

"Oh, Uncle! May we invite Monsieur Clark to join us for dinner? Now I simply *must* hear all his adventures from out West, or I will not be able to sleep tonight!"

"Yes, certainly, my dear. Monsieur Clark, would you possibly be available, to bless us with your presence as we dine?"

Tom thought about the Captain for half a moment; he'd be expecting they'd dine together. He felt a twinge of guilt, and yet … they'd made no specific plans. Still, he surprised himself by answering, "It would be my honor, sir."

Adilida giggled with pleasure and clapped her hands together in apparent delight. She wore long white gloves, so her clapping made almost no noise.

"Oh, thank you, Monsieur Clark! May I call you Tom? Or is it *Thomas*, truly?"

Tom blushed again, "It *is* Thomas, actually; but everyone calls me Tom. But you may call me by whichever pleases you."

"*Merci! Thomas*, then! It is a much nicer name, and fits you better, I believe." She reached over and took his arm, flashed him another dazzling smile, then turned to walk with him. As if it were perfectly natural for him to escort her to dinner.

Tom had never liked it when anyone called him "Thomas." Back home, it usually meant he was in trouble for some misbehavior; and in the Army, it meant a formal summons, which was almost always uncomfortable. But he found he liked the way *she* said it; with her lovely French accent it sounded like "toe-MOSS."

They strolled across the foyer toward the dining hall. Edouard said, "Oh … *excusez moi*, Monsieur Clark … er … *Thomas* … but you so took me aback when you called Adilida my *wife* earlier … I failed to answer your question. We are, in fact, guests at the

254

hotel, as I suspect are you? *Oui?* Ah, *oui*. I am here on business, a tedious process of negotiating shipping terms for my dry goods store and making other arrangements. We live in the small town of Thibodeaux, about … hmm … sixty miles or so to the west. It is mostly sugar plantations there—my main customers.

"And dear Adilida has been gracious enough to accompany me. A little holiday in the big city for her, and the pleasure of her lovely company to counter any loneliness for me."

"Oh, but it is always a pleasure to travel with you, Uncle! You are the kindest, most jolly man I know, and a very happy traveling companion."

"*Merci beaucoup*, dear one. Sweet of you to say."

സുഭുരുഭുസുഭുരുഭുസുഭുരുഭ

Tom couldn't remember a more pleasurable dinner. For starters, the waiters treated him like royalty, with plenty of bowing and scraping, and lots of "Yes, Mr. Clark," and "No, Mr. Clark." But even more to his satisfaction, both Adilida and Edouard listened intently as he spoke, hanging onto his every word. He greatly enjoyed their reactions to his stories of adventures out in Texas. They "oohed" and "aahed" appropriately with every twist and turn, of which there were plenty. Most popular were his narratives of the two recent battles: the ambush by Moat Kangly, and the gunfight in the cantina against Gold-tooth and his gang. Tom had played a key, even heroic role in both incidents, and Adilida was not shy about telling him so!

In between Tom's stories, Edouard told his own tales—always humorous, with an interesting and surprising twist at the end, typically evoking a startled laugh of surprise from his audience. Tom wondered if these stories were true, or simply made up for entertainment, but decided it really didn't matter either way.

When it was Adilida's turn to tell her story, the mood turned more serious. She described the tragic loss of her parents when she was just a young child. They'd drowned, along with many other passengers, when the boiler had exploded on a steamer traveling the Mississippi. Uncle Edouard, who'd earlier lost his wife in childbirth, immediately adopted her into his family, and raised her as one of his own.

Then she informed Tom she was in fact already a widow at the young age of twenty-two. Her husband had been much older, a kindly man who did business with Edouard and was a regular around his store and in their home. They'd only been married a little more than a year when he took ill and died after months of slowly wasting away. Tom noticed she spoke of her late husband as a good man, who treated her well, but there was little passion or enthusiasm in her narrative of their life together.

Tom was amazed at Adilida's happy, positive demeanor, despite a life that'd seen more than its fair share of tragedies and losses, and he told her so.

"Oh, Thomas, it is so sweet of you to say. But … why should I not be happy? Though I lost my parents, I was so very fortunate to have Uncle to take me in and give me the best possible upbringing. And though my late husband has sadly passed, I am still alive and in good health. And I still have Uncle with me!" She beamed at him and gave his arm an affectionate squeeze.

Edouard returned her smile brightly, "Thank you, my dear. It has been the great pleasure of my life having you for a child. I have been truly blessed."

They enjoyed a delicious steak dinner and were about to order dessert when Edouard announced he was departing for the gentleman's lounge for a smoke and a drink before bed. They said their goodbyes, and Tom concluded they *definitely* did things differently in New Orleans. Back east an elder relative would never leave a young, unmarried couple alone and unchaperoned in the evening hours. *Oh well,* Tom thought, *when in Rome …*

Tom and Adilida shared a delicious pastry for dessert, then pushed their chairs back, feeling quite satisfied with their meal. Tom felt a flush on his face—probably the effects of the wine they'd had for dinner, or else it could be the proximity to such a beautiful and charming young lady. At any rate, he decided a stroll out in the evening air would be just the thing, so he invited Adilida to join him.

"Oh, but do you think it is safe, Thomas? Uncle has warned me not to go out at night in the city. There are … *dangerous* men about after dark, I am told."

Tom laughed, "Adilida, I've been out West fighting men who would freeze your heart with fear … I can't imagine any man in New Orleans who would frighten me."

Adilida gazed into his eyes for a long moment, before saying, "I believe that is true, Thomas. I will go with you," and flashed him another of her pulse-pounding smiles, her bright green eyes sparkling.

As they strolled along the street, she held tight to his arm, occasionally leaning her head against his shoulder. He liked the feeling. The street was alive with throngs of people, such as Tom had never imagined possible. It seemed like more people came out at night in New Orleans than were around during the day. Many were drunk and staggering about, but Tom led Adilida with a self-confidence that left her in no fear of the revelers.

They stopped on a rise at the edge of a park. A full moon glowed in the sky above so they could see clearly, though there were few lights shining from any of the surrounding buildings.

"Oh, Thomas … the night is so beautiful. Thank you for bringing me out here; *merci beaucoup*. This evening has been … *most* lovely."

"Not nearly as lovely as you, Adilida," Tom said, then remembering the French he'd learned back in school added, *"Tu es encore plus belle que le clair de lune."* He felt a growing affection for her and surprised himself he'd expressed it so directly. *Must be the wine,* he decided.

"Oh, Thomas! You are so sweet, and your French is most excellent!"

She was quiet and seemed to become thoughtful for a moment, gazing out at the scene. Then she turned to him and said, "I … I have never known a *real* bold man like you before. My late husband was much older and … well, let's just say he was not too adventurous or romantic. He would never have ventured out at night in the city. And he would never have spoken the words you have just spoken to me.

257

"Now that I have been married … the men my age back in Thibodeaux seem as silly boys. But you … you are a truly heroic and gentlemanly man, like in the old tales."

She reached up and gave him a quick kiss on the cheek. It surprised him, and when he looked down at her, he could see her eyes shining in the moonlight. He thought he'd never seen anything so beautiful. So he bent down and kissed her softly on the lips. She did not pull away but leaned in close and reached up on her tiptoes to meet him. After a moment they separated, but rather than moving back, she leaned against him, the side of her head resting against his chest. He put his arms around her and held her gently.

Then she looked up and said, "Thomas … I know we have only just met … but I feel so … so … *comfortable* with you. Like we have known each other … *always*."

He laughed but held her closer. Never could he recall reacting to a woman this way. But he'd never been with a real *lady* before. Oh, he'd paid for whores occasionally, but had always felt ashamed afterward. This was an entirely *different* thing. He was feeling a burning desire for Adilida, the likes of which he'd never felt.

But he was also still nervous. He feared doing or saying anything to spoil the mood.

They returned to the hotel and walked across the foyer. He struggled with what to do next. It'd be awkward to just say goodnight, and head off to his room, but … what else could he do?

But Adilida resolved his dilemma for him. As they walked, she leaned close and whispered in his ear, "Come, Thomas. I wish to show you something …"

By this time, he'd decided he would follow her anywhere she wanted to go. So it never occurred to him to ask what she wanted to show him.

He walked her across the foyer, stopping briefly to retrieve his bundle of old clothes, deposited earlier with the hotel clerk. They headed for the great staircase, arm in arm, walked up to the third floor, and down the hall. They stopped in front of a door, and she produced a key—from exactly where, he wasn't sure; she'd not been carrying a bag. She unlocked the door and led him inside, closing the door behind them. To his surprise, she turned toward him, wrapped her arms around his neck and gazed up into his eyes.

"Thomas … I have never imagined myself being so … *forward*. But I have never met a man like you. So handsome, so brave, so *heroic*. I am … *burning* inside for you." She placed her lips on his, and kissed him, sweetly at first, but soon becoming more vigorous.

He sensed his body responding in the most natural way a man can respond to the affectionate attentions of a lovely young woman. But he was self-conscious about it and feared she would take offense. So he tried to back slightly away, so as not to embarrass himself, or upset her.

But she did *not* back away and continued to press forward. She pushed him up against the closed door until there could be no doubt; she could feel his arousal, pressed hard up against her, but she was *not* offended. In fact, her kisses had become more intense and urgent. He could feel her firm breasts pushed up tightly against his chest, increasing his arousal.

Tom's heart beat wildly; with Adilida's lips covering his mouth he could scarcely breathe. Then she pulled away suddenly, giggled, and took his hand. She led him over to the bed and pulled him down onto it with her.

"What about your uncle?" Tom thought to ask, before things went too far.

"Uncle has a room down the hall. He will turn in later, after drinking whiskey all evening. He will not remember to call on me until morning. There is nothing to fear, *mon cherie* … Thomas, *my love*."

No one had ever called Tom *that* before. It was a heady feeling. He was young and strong, and intensely alive. He was alone with the most beautiful, desirable woman he could imagine, and she clearly *wanted* him. Life could not possibly get any better than this.

And then … *it did* …

It was sometime in the very early pre-dawn hours; the street outside was still as black as coal. Stan and the other former soldiers sat at a table in the downstairs tavern area of the building in which they'd spent the better part of the evening. Having finally worn out their welcome upstairs and used up most of their spare money (those things tending to go together) they'd been politely ushered out.

There'd been a steady flow of drunken sailors and other rough-looking characters through the tavern area all evening. At one point, even from upstairs they could hear loud music, boisterous dancing, and raucous laughter shaking the building.

But now the action had died down. Two old sailors sat at a corner table. One of them appeared to be passed out, his head on his hands. The small room was otherwise empty, except for the four ex-soldiers.

"Damn it, Stan! I really wanted time with that *dotey* red-headed lass, but you never were letting her up for air," Jamie grumbled.

"What? Why so angry, Irish? Plenty of pretty little girls up there. Why you care about one red-haired one?"

"Cause the red hair means she's likely Irish like me. I ain't never been with an Irish lass afore. When I left Ireland, I was too young, you see … and I've been after only out amongst the English!"

"Oh, well … if that is all … next time I meet Russian missy I give her to you. Then we are even!"

"That ain't the point, Stanny boy. I don't want no damned Russian lassie … I wanted that red-headed Irish lass, you see?"

But Stan looked tired and seemed annoyed with the whole matter, so he shrugged his shoulders, and didn't bother responding.

William stared at the two in disbelief. All he wanted was to find a bed, crawl in and get some sleep. He couldn't believe he'd allowed the others to talk him into all the drinking, and the whoring. He knew he'd feel badly about the whole thing later, once he was no longer too tired to think.

"Well, who's got any money left, mates? Come on, put it out on the table and let's see if we have enough to buy us a drink."

They all dug in their pockets and pulled out whatever coins they found, making a small pile in the center of the table.

"Well … it ain't enough for gettin' us *langered*, but could be it'll buy a bottle of somethin' nasty, eh?"

"I don't know, Jamie … I already got a pounding headache from all the whiskey we drunk earlier," Georgie said, holding his head in his hands to emphasize the point.

"Nonsense, Georgie-boy. Ain't you never heard o' 'hair of the dog' for curing a hammered head from too much liquor?"

"I heard it … it just never made no sense to me."

"Well, me neither, truth to tell. But let's be givin' it a try, shall we?" Jamie said as he scooped up the coins and headed for the bar.

As Jamie stepped toward the bar, a group of six men walked in the door. Jamie thought them an especially unfriendly looking crew. In fact, they looked downright disreputable. But then Jamie glanced down at himself—*travel-stained shirt, with … hmm … wonder what the dark, wet spot is? Oh, well …*

The newcomers walked right over to the bar and talked with the bartender in low tones. Jamie thought the bartender looked nervous, and seemed to be answering their questions with short, mono-syllable answers, interspersed with shoulder shrugs.

None o' my business, he decided, stepping up to the bar. He peered up over the edge, hoping to spot a loose bottle he could procure while the barkeep was otherwise occupied. But having no luck, he stepped over to where the newcomers were standing with the barkeep.

"You're late, ya sorry *gom*. This is after the second time this month. We ain't running no nursery here, you know. We're expecting to be paid when it's time. If we ain't gettin' paid, we'll be for takin' our payment from your sorry *mog* hide," one of them said, as Jamie walked up. He noticed the man was Irish, like himself, from the strong accent and slang.

Hmm … some kinda shake down, he thought. *Still … none o' my concern,* he decided; in *this* neighborhood such doings were likely commonplace.

"Excuse me, fellas … not meanin' to interrupt your business or nothin', but me and the boys is *out on the lash* and gettin' a bit thirsty. Mind if the barkeep grabs us a bottle, quick like?"

Despite the lateness of the hour, and his own pounding head, plus his irritation at Stan, Jamie did his best to put on a friendly demeanor. He hoped to avoid stirring up any trouble.

But his efforts proved for naught; the one who'd been doing the talking looked over, gave him a disgusted look, and spat at his feet. "Bugger off!" he said.

It was just the wrong thing to say at the wrong time, and Jamie replied immediately without thinking, "Bugger off, yourself! All's I want is a drink for me and me pals. No need to go acting the maggot."

The reaction was swift; two of the men grabbed Jamie by the arms, and the surly one stepped up and slugged him hard in the stomach.

Georgie had been watching the whole thing develop from his seat at the table. He shouted, "Hey!" jumped up, ran over, and leaped on the back of one of the men holding Jamie.

William was also up on his feet, suddenly wide awake. He started toward the fight when he realized Stan wasn't moving.

"What're you doing, Stan? Can't you see there's a fight?"

"Nyet. Not *real* fight. Am tired. Not worth bother."

"What do you mean, there's … well … six of them, I think."

"You go have fun, William. I will stay and watch."

William could hardly believe what he was hearing but had a strong sense of urgency for his companions. He glanced back toward the bar and took in a scene of utter chaos—arms flailing, bodies rolling around, men kicking and cursing. He ran over, punching the first man he saw who wasn't one of his own. The man looked shocked, staggering back. Despite his meek appearance, William had been formally trained in boxing, and knew how to land a solid punch. He traded blows with the stranger as they circled each other. Jamie and Georgie were both now fighting two or three men each. But they'd apparently surprised their opponents with their ferocity, and seemed to be holding their own, despite the uneven odds.

William deflected another blow from his opponent, landing a well-timed counter punch. He heard Stan call out, "You are doing well, William! You will make fine fighter one day!"

Thanks a lot … for no help! William thought bitterly, as he ducked another swing from his opponent.

Just then Jamie extricated himself from a pile on the floor. He stood and landed a perfect kick to the face of one of his opponents who was rising to continue the fight. But someone grabbed him by his collar and dragged him back to the floor. There two men held him while another punched him.

"Stan! For God's sake, help Jamie … before they take his head clean off!" William shouted.

"Oh, all right! I was sure *our* Irish could beat *theirs* … but maybe he is needing more practice," Stan said with a laugh.

Before anyone saw him move, Stan was standing over the man pounding his fist into Jamie. Jamie wasn't passively taking his punishment; he was squirming from side to side to avoid taking solid blows. Stan reached down, grabbed the man's shirt in the middle of his back with one hand, and heaved. The man hurtled backward across the room, slamming hard into the bar, before crumpling to the ground in a heap. Taking advantage of the respite, Jamie rolled to his left and punched the one holding him on that side, driving him off. Stan kicked the other in the face, sending him careening across the floor.

Stan reached down and offered Jamie a hand up. "Not too bad, Jamie. You fight pretty good, for thick-headed Irishman."

"Thanks, Stanny boy, but I was after gettin' myself kicked and booted when you lent a hand. And next time, you can have all the bonny redheads you want, and I'll not complain a whit!"

Stan laughed.

They looked up in time to see William give his man the *coup de grace*, a neat right-hook that sent him sprawling on his back. But Georgie was taking a beating from his two assailants. He was curled up against the wall over to one side of the bar, his arms covering his head to block the blows raining down on him. The bigger of the two saw Stan approaching and stood up to face him.

He stepped up to Stan and threw a punch with his left hand. It was a sucker punch, intended to surprise an opponent who'd be expecting the blow to come from the right. But Stan caught the fist in mid stroke in his huge right hand. He held it fast for a moment, then grinned and gave a quick hard twist to the right. The man called out in sudden pain and fell to the floor, grasping his left arm and writhing in great agony.

The second man now grabbed an empty bottle from a table and smashed it. He held the shattered bottle up, waving it at Stan.

Stan glared at the man and said, "You cut me with bottle, I get angry ... and when *this* happens ... I hit you *hard.* By tomorrow ... even your own momma will not be knowing you."

Then he grinned. Not a nice, friendly grin, but one filled with menace. "But ...," he shrugged, "you already plenty ugly. Could be I *improve* your looks, no?"

The man's eyes widened. He dropped the bottle and ran out the door. The fight was over.

The other bullies helped each other up and staggered out after him, one gingerly supporting an injured arm as if it were lifeless.

"Did you break it?" William asked.

"*Nyet* ... not broken. But it hurt like *fucker!* No use for couple of days. Is good trick! Old China man in Port Land taught me, long time ago."

"Well, yes, it *is* a good trick. But I'm afraid few men could pull it off with as much ... *style* as you."

Stan grinned.

Jamie helped Georgie up, and William lent a hand as they half-carried him over to the table where he sat down hard. He had a bloody, swelling lip, and one eye was looking a bit purplish and would likely turn into a shiner by the next day. "It's okay ... I'm all right ... just give me a minute to catch my breath. Jamie where's that bottle you went to get?"

Jamie slapped himself on the forehead. "Well, if I ain't the *stuttles!* I done forgot all about it in the commotion!"

He walked around to the back side of the bar and grabbed a bottle himself. The bartender had gone missing during the fray.

They didn't bother with glasses but passed the bottle around until they'd all had a good swig. When it came Georgie's turn, he took several long swallows.

"Hey, Jamie … I think there may be something to that 'dog-hair' thing. I feel better already," he said.

"Hair of the dog," Jamie corrected, then added, "and you're welcome. But sorry you had to take a batterin' on account o' me acting the *whanker*. Never could be learnin' to keep me big mouth shut."

"Oh, never mind about that," Georgie said, "them fellers was itching for a fight whatever you'd have said. I think they was already liquored up and meaning to provoke us the minute they came in the door."

"Well, that's nice of you to say, *boyo*, but I'm still *scundered* for making you take a poundin' helping me out."

"Don't mention it … you'd have done the same for me."

"True enough, lad … true enough."

But they'd barely passed the bottle for a second round when a man entered the bar. He carried a short, double-barreled shotgun, leveled at them. Another man came in behind him. This man had a revolver, also pointed their direction.

"Good evening, monsieurs. My name is LeBlanc. I am the *gendarme* of this parish. I am understanding there has been trouble here tonight, no?"

He spoke with a heavy French accent, but the leveled shotgun had the men's attention, and eliminated any possible misunderstanding from a language barrier. He wore a bright, tin star in a circle on his vest, in case the men were unfamiliar with the term *gendarme*.

"Lookie here, my good officer," Jamie said, "we was just out for a *craic* when this bunch o' dodgy hoodlums came in pickin' a fight with us. All we done is defend our honor … and our dear bodies …"

"Well, gentlemen … I am sure you speak truly … but …" he shrugged his shoulders, "it is not for me to determine such things. It is only my duty to bring you to the judge to decide."

"Judge is it?" Jamie said, in disbelief, "Judging us for what, pray?"

"Well … for drunk and disorderly, for fighting in a public place, and for … hmm … property damage …" he pointed over at a chair that sat crookedly on three legs. No one could remember how it'd been broken, but they'd not been too concerned about "property damage" in the midst of the fight.

"Come along nicely, and peacefully, gentlemen. I am not wishing to disturb the slumber of the residents with gunfire. And I do not want to burden the parish by paying the undertaker for disposing of your remains."

His point taken, they stood from the table, and shuffled out the door, the gendarme walking several paces behind, shotgun still pointed in their direction.

As they moved through the dark alley outside the tavern, they had to weave their way between bodies lying about on the ground or leaned up against the sides; either dead drunk, or just plain dead, they couldn't tell. They walked down through the adjoining street. No one noticed a figure get up off the sidewalk where he'd been sitting, leaning against a brick wall in the dark. The figure followed at a discrete distance until they reached their destination, then turned and disappeared into the darkness.

ɤɤɤɤɤɤɤ

A light tapping on his door awakened Jim. He was instantly awake, despite the large quantity of whiskey he'd consumed over the course of the evening.

He thought he recognized that quiet knock, so he wasn't surprised when he opened the door to find Billy standing in the hallway outside.

"Come on in, Billy. What the hell time is it, anyway?" he asked. Scratching his backside, he walked over to the side table and turned up the wick on the oil lamp that'd been on a low burn.

"The clock downstairs said three and a half o'clock," Billy answered, as if expecting the question.

"All right, then, I'm assuming this ain't no social call."

Billy looked puzzled. He didn't know what a "social call" was, so didn't answer.

"Sorry … what I mean is … it must be something important for you to wake your *officer* at such an … ungodly hour, scout …"

"Yes, Sergeant Jim. You are correct. I would not awaken you at this hour if not for a good reason. I understand how … white men … like to have their correct amount of sleep. There has been trouble with the men."

"Oh? What kind of trouble?"

"There was a fight."

"Well, there's nothing unusual about that. They *are* soldiers, after all."

"Yes, Sergeant Jim. The fight was *not* the trouble. They had a … *successful engagement*. The trouble came after."

"After? What trouble came *after* the fight?"

"Men came with guns. They had shiny stars on their shirts."

"Lawmen?"

"Yes … I suppose … except…"

"Except?"

"Well … the Captain has always told me lawmen are on *our* side and help us with outlaws. The men in the fight were *outlaws*, it seemed to me. But the lawmen spoke with them outside in a friendly way, then came and took *our* men away. This did not seem right."

"Hmm … that *is* interesting, Billy. You're right … lawmen *shouldn't* behave like that. Well, maybe it's all a misunderstanding. Such things have happened before. Then what happened?"

"They led our men away with guns. Took them to a building … a jail, I guess, though I did not go inside."

"Yes … I expect not. So … let me ask you this, Billy … what were *you* doing while our boys were having a fight with these outlaws?"

"Watching."

"Only watching? Not inclined to help?"

"No, Sergeant Jim. Being smaller than you white men I like *watching* this kind of fight better'n being in it. Besides …"

"Yes?"

"Big Stan was there. They had no need of me."

Jim laughed. "True enough. With Stan there, they'd have no trouble in a bar fight."

"Yes, he is … a fighter like I have never seen."

"Yep, I agree, Billy. I ain't never seen the like, neither. You'd think a big man like him would be slow and clumsy. But he's as quick on his feet as a cat, and his hands move like a biting rattler."

Jim finished pulling on his second boot, then stood and stretched his suspenders up over his shoulders.

Billy asked, "Shall we wake the Captain, do you think? It is a very *bad* area … very dirty, stinking like a latrine. Plenty of wicked looking, drunken fellows wandering around, or laying on the ground."

Jim paused for a moment, then said, "No … no, let's see if we can straighten this thing out without waking him. He's already like to pitch a fit over the trouble they've gotten into, without adding bein' woke up in the middle of the night to the bill. Let's go fetch Sergeant Clark instead. Best if we can all be back here in good order, before ever the Captain wakes up in the morning."

☬☬☬☬☬☬☬☬☬☬☬

As Jim stepped over a man lying on the boardwalk, Billy said, "This is the place of the fight. The jail is a little further."

Jim looked over at the door for a moment. Then he said, "I'm fixin' to step in and see if anybody in there saw what happened with these so-called lawmen earlier. You stay here … if somethin' happens to me, you *will* have to go fetch the Captain this time."

Billy nodded and moved over into the shadows of the alley. He sat in the same spot where he'd been earlier in the evening. It was dark, and inconspicuous, yet afforded him a good view of the entrance, and on into the room. The door was never closed, from what he could tell, if it even worked at all.

Tom had *not* come with them, after all. They'd found his hotel room empty. When he hadn't answered Billy's soft knock, and Jim's more insistent one, they tried the doorknob which was unlocked. When they entered, they found he wasn't home, and his bed hadn't been slept in.

"Well, that's odd," Jim said, "not like him. Maybe he and the Captain went out somewhere and found themselves a good card game …"

Billy just shrugged. There being nothing else to do, they'd set out for Gallatin Street without him.

When Jim entered the tavern, he immediately sized up everyone and everything in the small room. Three round tables and two square ones, of various sizes and styles, all scratched and stained. Two older, sleepy looking sailors sat at one of the smaller square tables. And three surly looking younger fellows sat toward the middle of the room at a larger round table. And if he wasn't mistaken, one of them was nursing a shiner.

He walked up to the barkeep, and said, "I hear some friends of mine were in here earlier; four men, regular looking fellows, except one is big as a bear. I heard there was a fight. I want to talk with anyone that saw what happened, especially *after* with some … *supposed* lawmen."

The barkeep didn't look pleased with this question and continued to stare down at the glass he was wiping with a towel. He never answered. But after a moment he glanced quickly up at Jim. He tilted his head and rolled his eyes toward the men seated at the table in the center of the room. Jim took his meaning, nodded, flipped a coin out onto the bar, and started over toward the table. He pulled out a chair and sat on the side opposite the three men. The men seemed startled by his sudden appearance but looked at him saying nothing.

"Mornin' gents … name's Wiggins. I'm lookin' for some friends of mine, and I believe y'all might know something about what happened here a few hours ago. I heard they's a fight … and from the looks of you fellas, I'd guess y'all were in it. I want to know about *after* … who took them away at gunpoint, and why…"

For a moment, the three stared at him, bleary-eyed, as if he were speaking in a foreign tongue. Then the man on Jim's left, the biggest of the three and the one sporting a fresh shiner, finally answered. He had a thick Irish accent, "Go bugger off and fuck your momma, asshole. Or we'll do for you like we done for your friends! Ain't that right fellas?"

The others nodded but said nothing. They did *not* look especially enthusiastic about the idea, however.

Jim laughed, "Well, from the look of you bully-boys, I'd say y'all *got* better'n you *gave* in that fight, unless I'm sorely mistaken. And knowin' my men, it'd take a whole lot more'n the likes of y'all sorry sons-of-bitches to whup 'em." He sat back in his chair, stuck an unlit cigar between his teeth, folded his arms across his chest, and grinned.

But he'd not impressed the big one on the left, "Look *culchie* ... like I says before, go *bugger off* before I hurts you. I ain't in the mood for no more fucking nonsense."

Jim leaned forward in his chair as if he intended to say something more. But instead he reached out suddenly with his left hand. He grasped a handful of the man's hair and slammed his face onto the table. The man grunted and came up spewing blood from his nose.

Jim twisted quickly to the right. Leaning back, he planted his boot mid-chest on the man to his right. The blow knocked the breath from the man and sent the chair spilling backward. The back of the man's head slammed into the floor, and for several minutes he didn't move.

Jim was on his feet. The man across from him rose from his chair but his face met Jim's fist coming hard downward. The blow knocked him back into his seat. He immediately covered his head with his hands and moaned.

No one moved or spoke.

Jim sat back down and slid his chair closer to the big man on the left, who was now holding a dirty rag over his nose. Blood covered the front of the man's shirt.

"Now, fellas ... I'm wantin' to know what happened here earlier. Who the men were that came with guns, and why they took my friends away ... before I lose my temper ..."

ᏕᎤᏋᎣᏣᏨᎿᏕᎤᏋᎣᏣᏨᎿᏕᎤᏋᎣᏣᏨ

Jim learned plenty after that—more than he needed to know. The three men became very talkative once they'd experienced Jim's very particular means of persuasion. They told him all about LeBlanc and his cronies, including the local judge who was a cousin or something of LeBlanc's. These bully boys were in the shake-down business (when sober), but they, in turn, got the shake down from LeBlanc, who was backed by the judge. His side business was arresting anyone he thought might have money (or friends and relations who did) on trumped-up charges and basically extorting money from them for their release. In New Orleans, it was a very lucrative business. And because they could easily buy LeBlanc off, the local politicians and city officials, who all had their own schemes going, were very happy to accommodate him.

Disgusting, Jim thought, *and they call this place civilized. Better out in Texas amongst the Comanche, and good, honest criminals like Gold-tooth and his ilk.*

But there was nothing to do but go bluff or badger the so-called lawman into letting his men go; he was fairly certain he didn't have enough money on him to *buy* their way out. He had Billy point out the place to him from a safe distance, then they parted company. Jim didn't trust this LeBlanc and couldn't predict what would happen. So he told Billy to wait a half-hour, and if he hadn't returned, to go get the Captain.

He entered the jailhouse, a dirty, moldy-smelling brick building, and walked through a bare, dirty foyer to an open door. Inside was a large desk. Behind it sat a man leaned back in a chair with his boots up on the surface of the desk. He glanced up with a disinterested look as Jim approached.

"You LeBlanc?"

"Yes, I am *Gendarme* LeBlanc," he answered, lowering his feet to the floor and sitting up in the chair.

271

"What may I do to be of assistance, monsieur?"

"The name's Wiggins. I understand you are entertaining some of my men in here, and I've come to fetch them out."

"Well … let me see …" he reached up on the desk and picked up a large book that lay open in front of him. "We presently have several … *guests* … in our little hostel. What did you say your friends' names were?"

"I didn't. But I'm sure you know the ones I'm talking about. Three normal looking fellows, and a *huge* one … brought in a couple of hours ago from a place down the street?"

"Ah, yes. The 'drunk and disorderly' ones. Yes, they are here. And you say you wish to arrange for their release? There will, of course, be a charge for their … *bail*. Do you have the funds about you?"

"Look here, LeBlanc … I'm well aware of your little game, and I don't intend to play along. You and I both know they ain't done a thing other'n be stupid enough to fall into your spiderweb. My boss is well-connected at the highest levels of the U.S. government. And if'n I don't return with these men in tow in a soldierly, punctual fashion … well, I fear there'll be hell to pay!"

It wasn't a complete lie. After all, he'd been made to understand the Captain was friends with Colonel Robert E. Lee. And Colonel Lee was certainly a high-ranking officer in the Army, seeing as how he was commander over all of Texas. And the Army was *definitely* part of the U.S. government!

LeBlanc raised an eyebrow at this. He said, "Well, of course … there must sometimes be … the *exceptions*, no? Perhaps … just this once, since it is but a minor offense, we can let these fellows go on their way with but a … *stern warning*, shall we say?"

"Yes, a stern warning seems the proper punishment to me."

"Come … I will show you where they are, and then we may see to their release."

"Much obliged, sir."

"Think nothing of it, monsieur. Come …" he extended his arm toward the back of the room where a door of iron bars stood closed fast.

LeBlanc picked up a ring of keys from a hook on the wall and unlocked the door.

"Sorry, monsieur, but it is the rules I must check you for weapons before we may enter the lockup. You understand, no?"

"Yes, yes, certainly … check away."

Jim had brought no weapons, anticipating this happening, so he had nothing to hide. He held his hands above his head as LeBlanc gave him a quick pat-down. Jim had to admit LeBlanc knew his business, as he quickly discovered everything Jim had on his person other than clothes: three cigars in a vest pocket, an old dented and scratched pocket watch his Daddy had given him, and a small leather pouch containing a handful of coins. Also, one tiny, oddly shaped hunk of gold. When LeBlanc held this up and looked at it closely, he turned to Jim with a raised eyebrow.

Jim laughed and shrugged his shoulders, "A little souvenir … from an old friend of mine."

"Remind me to never become your friend!" LeBlanc said with a smile. He quickly put everything back where he had found it until he got to the cigars. He withheld one, saying, "A small fee … let us call it … *the charge for admittance*, no?"

"All right, you can have it. Small enough price to pay to get this business over with."

"*Oui*, monsieur. Your cooperation with this officer of the law is *most* appreciated." He bowed and waved Jim forward with an outstretched arm.

They walked down a short hallway, with cells on each side. These were tiny, only big enough for one or two bunks. Each room had a locked door of iron bars. The lockup had a nasty, outhouse kind of smell, if the outhouse had been vomited in regularly. Several of the cells contained men passed out on their bunks. Dead drunk, Jim assumed. There was a larger iron-barred door at the end of the hallway. This room was much larger than the others. They used it as a temporary holding cell where they could dump large groups of "guests," before being either "bailed out" or moved off into the smaller rooms. When Jim approached the door, he could see his men inside, along with a few other, sorrier looking fellows.

Georgie was the first to see him, and was about to say something, when Jim gave him the "shush" sign with a finger to his mouth. He wanted to continue his bluff, but if the men said too much, it might ruin the whole thing. Georgie seemed to take his meaning, and said, "Hello there, Mr. Wiggins. We men are certainly happy to see you here, ain't we fellas?" He turned his back on LeBlanc and gave the others a wink and repeated the "shushing" sign with his finger to his lips.

"Yes … cheers, Mr. Wiggins, sir," Jamie said, with William and Stan nodding their agreement but keeping their mouths shut. Since they didn't know exactly what it was they *weren't* supposed to say, they waited for Jim to make the next move.

"Well, it sounds like you boys've had a time of it. I'm fixin' to take you outta here. Our employer would *not* be pleased to see you in this place, so the sooner we're gone the better. Mr. LeBlanc … if you don't mind …" he waved LeBlanc toward the door so he could unlock it.

"But of course, monsieur. It will take but a moment." He stepped forward, selected a key on the ring, inserted it into the lock, and turned it with a *click*. He stepped back with a bow, ushering Jim forward. Jim grabbed the door, pulled it open, and stepped into the doorway of the cage.

He felt a hard shove from behind and stumbled forward into the room. If Georgie hadn't been there to catch him, he'd have landed face first on the floor. He came up cursing, but the door was already closed behind him, and LeBlanc was turning the lock with the key.

He laughed, then whistled as he strolled back down the hall, twirling the ring of keys on his finger.

Jim decided he needed to acquaint that fellow with his fists, in the worst sort of way.

Chapter 9. The Law and the Outlaw

*"There is no more dangerous
menace to civilization
than a government of
incompetent, corrupt,
or vile men."*
– Ludwig von Mises

Friday June 1, 1860 – New Orleans, Louisiana:

"Well no, Tom; you don't owe me an apology. We hadn't made specific plans, so what you did with your evening was your own business. And no need to worry about me. I spent a thoroughly enjoyable evening in the men's club smoking cigars and sipping whiskey with a group of army officers passing through on their way west. Gave me a chance to spin all my tales of Texas—several of which were actually true!

"I will admit, however, to a minor bout of curiosity about how you spent your evening, if you will indulge me."

"Of course, sir. I was about to do just that. In fact, I really need your advice, as I seem to have *'put my foot into it,'* as they say."

"Oh … in what way?"

"Well, the afternoon started out innocently enough. As you can see from my attire, I had a highly successful expedition."

"Yes, my compliments on that. *Suits* you nicely, if you'll pardon the pun!"

Tom smiled and rolled his eyes. "Thank you, sir. Anyway, I was just arriving back at the hotel, hopping up the stairs feeling very pleased with myself when I bumped into this couple coming in at the door. They seemed an unlikely pair, as the young woman was somewhere around my age, but the gentleman looked older than my father. Well, I struck up a quick conversation with them. It turns out the gentleman is her uncle. He's in New Orleans on business from a small town a little way to the west, and she's accompanying him for a holiday. They asked me my business, which I told them, and … well, we three seemed to hit it off, and next thing you know I was having dinner with them."

"Ah … I'm getting the picture here. Don't tell me … at some point the old man got tired and wandered off to bed. This left you … being a proper gentleman, of course … to keep watch over the … well, you didn't exactly say it, but I am assuming here … the *lovely* young lady."

Tom's mouth dropped open for a minute, and he gave Nathan a blank look. "Well … yes, that's exactly right, sir. Were you actually watching me the whole time?"

Nathan laughed, shaking his head. "No, of course not. But you must admit this little tale has a fairly predictable plot. Sorry … please *do* go on with your story."

"Well, yes, as you've surmised … the young lady is just about as nice to look at as … well, as one could possibly ask a young lady to be!

"And, as you say, we had a thoroughly enjoyable dinner. Then the uncle, Edouard Boudreau, dismissed himself and headed off to the men's lounge for a smoke and some whiskey. Since you were also there, you probably saw him. Distinguished-looking gentleman, gray hair and neat looking mustaches, slightly curled up at the ends. Has a friendly smile which he uses quite often."

"Oh yes, certainly! I remember the fellow, introduced himself to our little group sometime during the evening, though I hadn't made the connection until you mentioned it just now. *Edouard* … yes that was it. Very likeable fellow."

"Yes, I like him very much. So much so I was actually a bit disappointed at first, when he departed our company. But, of course, the young lady … Adilida Boudreau, that is, soon caused me to change my mind on that matter."

"Yes … I can imagine so. Pretty young ladies have a way of doing that to young men." He smiled, as if speaking from experience on the subject.

"I'm assuming from the name and the uncle's accent they are of the French persuasion. Cajun … or Creole?"

"Cajun, I think they said. Though I'm not sure I know the difference."

"Oh … well, it's really quite simple. The Cajuns, sometimes referred to as Acadians, are people whose French ancestors were living in Canada, along the east coast, in the region the French call Acadia. As you'll recall, the British, with help from us Americans, fought and won what we now call the 'French and Indian War' in that area. So they forced out the French who'd been living there. Most returned to France, as one might expect. But the others stayed in the Americas, so came to the other major French colony in North America: Louisiana."

"Oh … that makes sense. And what about the Creoles?"

"Well, it basically just means people born in Louisiana, but whose ancestors came over from France, or from one of her other colonies not Acadia. The easiest way to think of it is … anyone born here who is French speaking, but not Cajun, is *Creole*."

"Oh, okay. Thank you for explaining that … I was curious but didn't want to sound foolish asking someone who lives here.

"So to continue my story … Adilida seemed attracted to me and was thoroughly taken with my wild tales of adventure in the West. In fact, I expect while you were telling tales to the officers in the men's lounge, I was telling the very same stories to Adilida and Edouard!"

"Likely so! What a funny coincidence."

"Yes, isn't it? Anyway, the room was getting a bit stuffy. So, we took a little stroll in the moonlight before returning to the hotel. And then … well … one thing led to another … *you know?*"

"Yes … I think I do. I've walked that same road myself … once or twice. And I have a fairly good notion which *'one thing'* it was that led to the *'other thing'!*"

Tom blushed, but they shared a quiet laugh.

"So that explains your absence during the evening. And I'm pleased to hear you were AWOL for a very happy and enjoyable reason. Not out whoring and carousing, spending the night sleeping it off in some filthy jailhouse.

"But … a moment ago you said you wanted my advice on something?"

"Yes, sir. You've probably already guessed by now … it's about this girl."

"Adilida?"

"Yes, sir. Well … the trouble is … we're headed for Virginia in a few days and … she … well, she *isn't.*"

"Oh. Oh, yes … I see. Well, what are you thinking about it?"

"Well … she is a perfectly lovely person … beautiful, charming, intelligent and … well, and everything else a man would want in a woman. And she seems to have true feelings for me."

"And you? Do you have 'true feelings' for her as well?"

"I don't know, sir. I'm … I'm not like that, you know. Oh, I *like* her all right. As I said, she is a thoroughly likable person, in every possible way … but I take a while to have … *those* kinds of feelings. I'm not ready to marry her today, if that makes it plain. But that doesn't mean I might not want to marry her *someday*. Am I making sense, sir?"

"Well, yes … I understand what you're saying. So if you've decided you aren't ready to marry her, which I think is wise, having just met … then what is it you want my advice on?"

"Well, it's just that … having …"

"Slept with her?"

"Yes, sir. After having done *that* … a proper gentleman, with a proper lady … well, he can't just ride off a thousand miles and never look back. It … it doesn't seem proper, if you know what I mean. I feel like … I'll be a complete cad if I do that. And worse, she may think I see her as nothing better than a common whore. It makes me sick to think of giving her that impression. She's so sweet and kind, and she has these *eyes* … well, you understand."

"Ah … now I see your dilemma. But didn't the young lady *know* you were leaving in a few days?"

"Well, I told her I was on my way to Virginia. But … I guess with everything else that happened, the subject of *when* never really came up."

"Oh … I see. Well, I guess you'll just have to tell her the bad news. Or …"

"Or?"

"Tom … you're no longer enlisted in the Army, so you can come and go as you please. You aren't obligated to travel to Virginia with me. Feel free to stay here and see where your feelings toward Adilida lead you."

"Oh *no*, sir! I would *never* do that! I promised to go with you to help run your business affairs, and that is exactly what I intend to do. Not a hundred Adilidas would stop me from doing *that!* No, sir. Don't even suggest it … that I will *never* do!"

"All right, all right … I appreciate the loyalty. But, in that case, I see only one option."

"What's that, sir?"

"You must invite her to come with us. Or at the very least, ask her to come for a visit as soon as possible after we return. She may enjoy the journey by steamship better than going with us cross-country by train. Her uncle too, of course, though he may not be able to leave his business for so long. And if she says no, you have at least proved yourself a proper gentleman, with proper feelings for her."

"Oh … thank you, sir! Are you sure? It's not too great an imposition?"

"Certainly not! Not for *me*, anyway, Tom. Though you may have to fight off the others, once they lay eyes on your beautiful young lady—especially Stan. He seems to have a special … *rapport* with the women!"

Tom laughed, "Well, sir … I'll tell you, she's pretty enough I'd even fight Big Stan for her!"

"Well, that's high praise indeed! There *is* one condition, however …"

Tom raised an eyebrow.

"That you must first introduce me to her!"

"Oh! Oh, of course … how rude of me! I meant to invite you to do just that. We're supposed to be meeting up in the dining room for our midday meal. Won't you please join us so I can make the proper introductions?"

"It would be my pleasure, Tom."

ℰℐℭℭℰℐℭℭℰℐℭℭ

They were finishing up their breakfast, when one of the hotel clerks approached their table. "Mr. Chambers?"

"Yes."

"I am sorry to disturb your meal, sir. But there is a … *man* … here to see you."

"Well, we've not yet finished breaking the fast. Please just bring him in and he can join us at table."

"Well … yes, sir. Normally I would do that, sir. But … in this case I believe it would be best if you were to meet this man out in the foyer. If you don't mind."

Nathan found this answer very odd. He couldn't think of any reason the clerk wouldn't bring this "man" into the room. Also, odd he didn't say "gentleman," as would have been normal under the circumstances. Nathan pulled out a cigar but didn't yet put it to his mouth, leaning back in his chair.

"What exactly is it about this … *man* … that makes you hesitant to bring him in here?"

"Oh … sir … I'd rather not say, in front of these other gentlemen."

Now Nathan was becoming annoyed. He'd rather not jump up from his unfinished meal and walk to the foyer simply because the clerk was uncomfortable talking about this man.

"Well, mister …?"

"Wilburn, sir."

"Well, Mr. Wilburn, you have my permission to speak before all these gentlemen. I wish to clear this matter up and determine what this *'man'* in the foyer wants with me."

"Well, if you insist, sir. The man says he is in your employ, and he has an urgent matter to discuss with you."

"*What!?* He's one of *my* men? Well, what are you waiting for? Bring him in at once!"

"Well, sir … it's just that … he's not a *proper* gentleman. He does not *belong* in this gentleman's club."

This statement confused Tom; he couldn't think what the man meant by it. So he turned to Nathan with a puzzled look. But he could see a sudden change in the Captain's expression. He had a dark frown, like a thunderhead about to burst forth in storm.

"What exactly do you mean by that, *sir*?" Nathan sounded highly offended. Tom still did not understand.

"It's just ... he's ... he's an *Indian!*" the man stammered.

Nathan sat back in his chair, took out a match, and lit the cigar. The clerk stood still where he was, not knowing what to do, a fearful expression on his face.

Nathan took a long drag on the cigar and blew it out slowly up toward the ceiling. Then he suddenly leaned forward and pointed at the clerk with the lit cigar, a dark storm brewing in his eyes.

"Let me ask you something, Mr. Wilburn. Have you ever served in the Army, or been a lawman, or done anything dangerous for the benefit of others? In fact, anything at all besides working in this grand, fancy hotel in the midst of this great, sparkling city?"

"Uh ... no sir. I have never done any of those things."

"Well then, let me tell you something, *sir!* While you've been here wiping up spilled whiskey, and cleaning out dirty ashtrays, that ... 'Indian' has been risking his life fighting for the United States Army in Texas. Fighting against the enemies of our civilization. Serving this country so people like you can live in a nice, comfortable, safe place with no fear of ravaging Comanches, bandits, or foreign armies. And he has never asked for anything in return, not even a thank you. He is respectful, literate, polite, and clean—cleaner than most white men I've known, for that matter."

Tom could see a Nathan was battling mightily to contain his anger and to resist lashing out as he might have done out West. The effort turned his face red, and Tom noticed a barely perceptible quiver.

"Now ... Mr. Wilburn ... while I still have a reasonable control over my temper, will you *please*, go fetch Mr. Creek from the foyer and escort him in here, in the respectful and gentlemanly manner he so richly deserves?"

But despite Nathan's logical reasoning, thoroughly intimidating manner, and barely restrained anger, the clerk continued to resist. "Well, yes ... of course, I understand, Mr.

Chambers, and I agree with you. Except ... well, the *other* gentleman ..." he waved his hand toward where a dozen or so men sat. Every one of them was now watching and listening intently to the odd scene unfolding in the typically quiet and stoic atmosphere of the men's lounge.

Nathan took a quick glance around the room, pushed back his chair and stood, facing the other gentlemen.

"If any man in this room believes I'm in the wrong, let him speak now, that I may seek my satisfaction from him!"

He stuck the cigar back in his mouth and glared about the room, arms folded across his chest.

Tom sat back and smiled, thoroughly enjoying the show. As he expected, no one said a word. And several men turned around to mind their own business. The clerk made a short bow, and fairly sprinted from the lounge.

In a moment he returned, Billy in tow. He pulled back a chair, and gestured for Billy to sit, with a polite, "Sir ... if you please."

But as the clerk turned to leave, Nathan said, "One moment, Mr. Wilburn. Before you depart, I will have you apologize to Mr. Creek for making him wait in the foyer, and for treating him in a less than respectful manner. Further, you will assure him he, as a paying guest of this hotel, may come and go throughout any of the common rooms as he pleases. And that you will pass the word amongst the other clerks to make sure they also abide by this. Am I understood, Mr. Wilburn?"

"Yes ... certainly, Mr. Chambers. *Very* well understood. Mr. Creek, please accept my humble apologies for my earlier treatment of you, and my inexcusable lack of manners. And please be assured you will be afforded free rein of the hotel and all its common spaces. I will be sure the other clerks respect this as well." Then he made a deep bow.

Billy looked totally perplexed. Not knowing how else to respond he said, "Okay," and shrugged his shoulders.

Tom had to suppress a laugh. But Nathan was still smoldering, and in no mood for humor.

"Sorry about that, Billy," he said, "I will *not* have my men treated in such manner."

Billy shrugged his shoulders again, "I've been treated worse by men I've liked better."

Nathan continued to scowl. Then he remembered the purpose for Billy's visit, "The clerk said you had something *urgent* to report?"

"Yes, Captain ... Sergeant Clark ... your scout has come to report on the current dire and misfortunate disposition of your troops, including the Officer of Scouts ..."

ʚ୨ꞓ୨ꞓʚ୨ꞓʚ୨ꞓʚ୨ꞓ

Billy explained everything that had happened while they walked. It was about a half-hour by foot between the hotel and the jailhouse near Gallatin Street. By the time they got there Billy had given them a thorough briefing, so Nathan had a pretty good idea what to expect from Gendarme LeBlanc. The incident with the hotel clerk had already fired him up, so he was in no mood for any nonsense from the crooked lawman. He had, however, taken the time to stop by his room before they left, and he'd put the small Colt in his pocket. Just in case ...

When they approached the dilapidated brick building that housed the jail, Billy paused, as if planning to hang back and observe once again. But Nathan stopped and turned to him, "No ... this time I think you will come along, Billy. There's no one to go fetch if things go awry. So we may as well be in this all together."

Billy smiled, thinking of the words the Captain had used to get him on the boat. *"We're all in this together."*

"Yes, Captain!"

When they entered the office of the jailhouse, they could see LeBlanc seated behind the desk with his feet propped on it.

Nathan walked right up to the desk, reached out and slapped the man's feet off the furniture. This caused him to sit up involuntarily, his boots hitting the floor with a thump.

"You will stand and show proper respect when gentlemen enter a room!" Nathan growled.

LeBlanc jumped to his feet, "My apologies, monsieur! I must have dozed off!"

283

"You are an officer on duty; you have no excuse for sleeping at your post. Disgraceful! The taxpaying citizens of this parish are providing your wages, are they not? How do you think they would appreciate their largesse being repaid in such slovenly manner?"

"Uh … uh … I'm sorry … I did not catch your name, my good sir."

"That's because you were too busily derelict in your duties to ask it. My name is Chambers, and you are illegally holding several of my men. I *will* have them turned out, *immediately!*"

"Ah … Monsieur Chambers; you must be the 'Captain' your men speak of so affectionately. I am most sorry, Captain Chambers, but I may not release your men without first receiving the proper bail, or until they have been before the judge for sentencing." He shrugged and smiled apologetically.

But Nathan was not having it. Not today, "Look here, LeBlanc. I've heard all about your neat little 'business' going on here, but I'm not a paying customer. You're no more a real lawman than I'm a snake. I'll have my men out here in two minutes, or I swear by God, you'll regret it!"

But LeBlanc was used to dealing with all sorts, from drunken and belligerent longshoremen, to high-and-mighty gentlemen and government officials. He was not easily intimidated or bluffed.

"Monsieur, you will please show the proper respect for an officer of the law and will cease to make threats against my person. Or I shall be forced to use the legal powers of my station against you."

But Tom could see Nathan's control of his temper was now hanging by a thread.

"Tom, your watch … count off two minutes, if you please."

Nathan stood and stared down LeBlanc, as Tom counted off the time, calling out every fifteen seconds. LeBlanc stood still, arms folded, staring right back, a scowl on his face. But Tom could tell by Nathan's expression he was *not* bluffing. He wondered what would happen when the two minutes were up, but whatever it was, he was pretty sure he would enjoy it!

Tom read off the final count, "Two minutes, sir."

Nathan continued to stare at LeBlanc, but then seemed to relax and made a deep sigh. LeBlanc also appeared to loosen up slightly. Then, without warning, Nathan reached across the desk and grabbed LeBlanc by the lapels of his tunic. He stepped back, dragging LeBlanc up and over the top. Nathan pivoted and slammed the man's back into the brick wall next to where Tom and Billy stood. LeBlanc grunted then tried to squirm free. But Nathan was much stronger and had him thoroughly manhandled.

"Billy … Tom, hold his arms." They jumped to comply, and now LeBlanc couldn't move at all.

"You will pay for this, Chambers. I may not be molested in this manner; I am an officer of the law. My cousin is the presiding judge of the parish; he will lock you up with no key!"

"Shut your sniveling, lying mouth!" Nathan said, and punched him hard in the stomach. LeBlanc gasped and coughed but couldn't get enough breath to speak.

Nathan turned to Billy and reached out his hand, "Give me your hunting knife."

Billy reached inside his shirt and pulled out the knife he'd hidden there, the one the Captain somehow knew about. Without hesitation, he handed it to Nathan, handle first, the highly polished blade sparkling in the dimly lit room.

Nathan took it and put the point up against LeBlanc's throat. "I will have my men out … *now*."

"Or what … you would murder me right here, monsieur?"

"Oh no, I'm not going to *murder* you … that would cause too much trouble, even for me. No … but I am going to *hurt* you. We've been out West where things aren't so *civilized* as here. We've learned some very nasty ways of cutting a man from the Comanche, how to cause the most pain for the longest time without killing him. Of course, the victims aren't much the same *after*. And none too pleasant to look at."

"You *wouldn't!*"

By way of answer Nathan pushed the blade further up under LeBlanc's chin. Billy kept it razor sharp, so a small stream of blood oozed out. Nathan slowly dragged the knife along LeBlanc's skin, widening the cut. Blood now ran down into the collar of his shirt.

LeBlanc was used to threats, fights, and all manner of violence, but the look he saw in Nathan's eyes frightened him. And he'd heard the others talking casually among themselves about fighting Indians, so he knew that part of the story was true. Finally, he decided it was not worth literally risking his neck to call this man's bluff. Not for a few dollars in bail money.

"Very well, very well, monsieur! You may have your men. There is no need for this violence."

Nathan lowered the knife and motioned the men to move LeBlanc toward the barred door at the back of the office. LeBlanc blotted the blood on his neck with his shirt sleeve.

"The keys," LeBlanc said, "you must let me reach the keys."

Nathan reached up and took the key ring off its hook, but before allowing Tom and Billy to release him, he gave LeBlanc a quick, thorough search for any weapons. He turned out a small, but heavy club, the type a man would use to bash someone in the head from behind. He scowled at LeBlanc as he held it up, but LeBlanc shrugged his shoulders, as if it was of no significance. Nathan also found a short blade in a leather sheath which he also confiscated. The double-barreled shotgun LeBlanc had wielded at the tavern sat in a bracket on the wall behind the desk. Nathan walked over and grabbed it. It was loaded, so Nathan pulled off the percussion caps and pocketed them before returning the gun to its bracket.

He brought the keys over to LeBlanc and held them out. But as LeBlanc reached to take them, he said, "No! Show us which ones. *We* will open the cage."

So LeBlanc pointed out the key to the outer door and the one for the cell containing Nathan's men.

"Billy, do you know how to work this kind of lock?"

"Yes, Captain."

"Good. Please go fetch the men. Tom and I will conduct a little 'business' with Monsieur LeBlanc."

Billy took the keys, careful to take hold of the two specific keys he would need. He turned, quickly unlocked the outer door, and headed inside.

LeBlanc became nervous about what this other "business" might be, concerned Chambers may have decided to cut him up after all. But Nathan gestured for LeBlanc to return to his desk and sit.

"Now, you will write in your logbook there, that these men were properly fined ... let's say a dollar each, for 'drunk and disorderly' ... and legally discharged. But only the four men you brought in earlier. My other man, Mr. Wiggins, was entirely innocent; he came here for the completely legal and legitimate purpose of obtaining the others' release. My man Mr. Clark here will pay you and watch to make sure you record everything properly, and legally. You will make two exact, signed copies of the log entry, one of which we will take with us when we depart. I will deduct the money from my men's pay as just punishment."

"Well, it is *less* than the usual fine, but it would be ... within the proper legalities. But monsieur ... if you intended to pay the fine all along, why did we not settle this whole matter more amicably, with no need for threats or violence?"

"Because, monsieur, I didn't *want* to settle it amicably. And I *enjoyed* the threats and violence," Nathan answered, smiling for the first time since they'd entered the building, though not pleasantly to LeBlanc's thinking.

LeBlanc shook his head, and muttered, "*English!* I will never understand them," as he reached for his pen and ink well.

☽℘ℛℭℲ☽℘ℛℭℲ☽℘ℛℭℲ

Nathan was not much pleased with his men, and they knew it, so they followed along behind him, meekly and quietly. They *had*, it turned out, been "whoring and carousing, ending up in a stinking jail," the very thing Nathan had congratulated Tom for *not* doing. Except for Jim, of course; he was enjoying holding the high moral ground over the men and made sure they knew it.

Billy, who had followed along but stayed out of the trouble, was also still on the Captain's good side. But he couldn't understand what all the fuss was about. Now they'd gotten the men out, he considered the matter successfully resolved, so there was no point in worrying it more.

Nathan strode along at a great pace, puffing on a cigar as they walked. The road from Gallatin Street back to the hotel ran parallel to the waterfront a few blocks back from the river. The whole area was a thoroughly congested bustle of commerce—every kind of wagon and cart coming to and from the river; goods being steadily offloaded from ships and onto wagons, and vice versa, or being moved in and out of the multitude of warehouses that seemed to fill every square inch of real estate in the district.

They were approaching one of these warehouses, and could see a group of black men—obviously slaves—loading heavy sacks from out of a warehouse onto a wagon. As they neared the scene, they saw one of the men stumble beneath his heavy load, his sack falling to the ground and bursting open. A light-brown powder spread out over the ground—sugar.

They heard a loud voice from within the warehouse door, shouting, "Goddamn it! Damn, clumsy, useless, lazy bastard. That's cost the master good money, spilling that sugar. Goddamn! I'm gonna have to take that money outta your filthy hide."

They could see the black man cowering in fear, on the ground trying to scoop the spilled sugar back into the ruptured bag, to little effect.

A man strode out from the warehouse. He was holding something long and thin in his hand that appeared to be a buggy whip. He strode right over to the man on the ground and immediately thrashed him with the whip. The slave cowered and whimpered, but otherwise took the beating without complaint.

"Hey, you there! Stop that this instant!" Nathan called out, in his most commanding captain's voice.

The man stopped and looked up as Nathan and his men approached.

"And what business is it of yours, anyway?" he asked, in a surly tone.

On a good day, Nathan might have tried to reason with the man, and talk him out of his present course of action in a calm, and gentlemanly way. But this had *not* been a normal, good day for Nathan, first with the hotel clerk, and then with the crooked policeman.

"The business of *any* decent man ... and I'm *making* it my business."

The man looked at him for a moment with a puzzled expression. He noticed a tough-looking bunch of men accompanied the gentleman. But still ...

"Bugger off! This ain't none of your damned business, *sir!*" he said, turning his attention back to the slave and giving him another whack.

The next sensation the man felt was a strong hand grabbing the back of his shirt, followed almost immediately by his face hitting the hard cobblestones of the street. A hand grabbed him by the hair on the back of his head, and a knee pressed down hard in the middle of his back. He reached up to dislodge his assailant, but soon realized he had no leverage, and his adversary was *much* heavier and stronger than he.

The face of the gentleman appeared in his view. But the man no longer looked very gentlemanly.

"I was just now thinking you might have a different attitude if you were on the receiving end of some punishment. What say *you?* Nothing? Not surprised ... big mouth when you're the one holding the whip, not so big on the other end."

The slave foreman wanted to reply but couldn't get any breath. In fact, he realized he was having a hard time breathing at all; and the more he struggled, the harder the man pressed down on him.

Then a different man appeared in front of his face. It was one of the tough-looking fellows who'd been following along behind the gentleman.

"You know, if I was you, I'd listen politely to what the gentleman says, and stop trying to fight. The last fellow tried to fight him ended up stuck to a wall with a Bowie knife. Ah ... you should have seen it ... 'twas quite a sight. Took Big Stan over there three tries to pull the knife out."

A strange, foreign voice said, "*Nyet* ... was only *two* tries. But *was* difficult! And made *big* mess."

"Yep, that's right, only *two* hard pulls, now's you remind me of it, Stanny boy. *Oh!* I kept the fellow's gold tooth; cut it right out with my belt knife … well, he *was* all the way dead, of course; I figured he wasn't needing it no more. Got it right here in my pocket; would you like to see it? No? Well, maybe some other time …"

The warehouse foreman could only cough in reply, but he suddenly felt the pressure ease up, and then it was gone, and he could sit up. The gentleman had stepped back, and no longer looked at him; only the man that'd been telling the knife story was still looking his direction. The other tough-looking characters had formed a half-circle around the gentleman. They stood still, fists balled up, staring down the men looking out the warehouse door.

There were only three white men standing there, and they stayed well back, despite the predicament their foreman was in. They figured he'd gotten himself into it, so he could just as well get himself out. It wasn't worth getting beat up or killed over. Of course, with the help of their slaves they'd have had the newcomers badly outnumbered. But they never allowed slaves to attack white men for *any* reason, not even to defend their masters. It was the law of the land, strictly enforced and severely punished, so there was never any question of disobeying it.

Nathan turned and stared off down the street, as if his mind was suddenly elsewhere. He stood still, not saying a word, slowly puffing on a cigar. The foreman sat where he was on the ground, rubbing his sore head and catching his breath, not entirely sure of what to do next, fearing to reignite the wrath of the ill-tempered gentleman.

As Nathan stood there in quiet contemplation, a man in a fine dark suit came riding slowly down the street on a shiny black horse. The rider pulled up a few feet short of the group of men gathered in the street.

He looked down at Nathan and said, "I am Antoine Dubuclet." He paused for a moment, waiting for a response as if Nathan should recognize the name. Nathan gave him a blank look, so he continued, "This is my warehouse, and these are my men."

He spoke with a French accent, *Creole* rather than *Cajun*, Tom decided; his time spent with Adilida and her uncle had taught him to hear the subtle difference.

"Who are you, monsieur, and why are you molesting my people, and interfering with the conduct of my legal commerce?" the man continued.

"My name is Chambers. And I care nothing of your commerce, one way or the other. This man was beating a slave, for no good reason other than he's a sadistic bully. It is a gentleman's prerogative—nay, *duty* even, to put a stop to such doings when he sees them."

The rider turned his attention to the foreman who had gotten himself up off the ground and brushed himself off at his employer's arrival. "Is this true, Federman? Were you beating one of my slaves for no purpose, other than your own sick pleasure? That would be a serious dereliction of duty; a waste of the wages I pay you, not to mention the risk of damaging my valuable property."

"Oh, no, sir! Nothing of the sort! The fool has been getting lazy, and sullen of late. The 'last straw,' as they say, was he dumped a whole bag of your valuable sugar all over the street, as you can clearly see for yourself."

"Hmm ... *oui*, I can see this. And why aren't you busily cleaning it up, and salvaging what you can, rather than playing at fisticuffs with these ... *gentlemen?*"

"Well, of course, sir. I was going to get to that straight away, right after giving the slave, Teddy here, a good reprimand to straighten out his thinking, so to speak. But these ... *fellows* ... came along and jumped me. For no good reason!"

Nathan glared at him and the fellow looked down and shut his mouth.

"So ... Chambers, what say you to my man's tale? Is it true, or a lie?"

"It's true from *his* perspective, I'm sure, but—"

"Well, then! It seems to me you are in the wrong here, monsieur. Perhaps it is too much to ask you to apologize to Mr.

Federman, for your assault on him. But you can at least stand out of the way and let him continue with his business, no?"

"You care nothing he was beating one of your slaves, for a simple stumble? Something that could easily happen to any of us, through no fault of our own."

"If he was doing so, then in his judgment the punishment was warranted, and it may teach the miscreant not to do so again. I expect discipline and hard work from my slaves, or they will suffer the consequences. Besides, I don't see what concern it is of yours. Please do go about your business, monsieur, and leave *me* to *mine.*" The man turned his horse and started to ride back down the street in the direction from which he'd come, the conversation over.

"You sicken me, sir! Even cattle are treated better. I find your attitude disgusting," Nathan said with a growl.

Dubuclet stopped and turned his horse around. "I believe I have shown admirable restraint up 'til now, *sir!* But I will *not* be insulted, on my own property, in front of my own servants! Now you have invoked my wrath, monsieur, and this must be answered. Let us see how disgusted you are from inside a jail cell. Or when doling out a sizable fine for interfering with lawful commerce and interposing yourself between a slave and his master. I'm sure the parish judge will find such behavior quite reprehensible, no? Perhaps he will even deem it a flogging offense? *Oui* … I think that quite likely; the judge and I … well, let's just say we tend to agree on most legal matters. Good day, *sir!*"

This time he turned his horse and trotted off, not waiting for a reply.

Nathan stared after him for a moment, tossed down the stub of his cigar and stomped it out. "Let's go."

He set off again at a great pace, even faster than the one he'd set before. But after they'd gone about a block, and were no longer in sight of the warehouse, he raised his right hand for a stop. He turned and walked up to Jim, looking him in the eye.

"Firstly, I want to thank *you*, Mr. Wiggins … *most* sincerely."

"You're welcome, sir. Happy I could help," he answered, returning Nathan's serious look. He did not flash his usual grin but smiled with his eyes.

This puzzled Tom, "What did I miss ... thank him for *what?*"

Nathan paused a moment, then looked at Tom and said, "For timely reminding me ... what can happen when I lose control of my temper."

Tom nodded, now understanding what he'd meant. "But sir," he continued, "that rider, the slave owner ... did you see ... he was ... he was a ..."

"A black man? Shocking, isn't it? I'd heard black freemen sometimes acquired slaves of their own, especially here in Louisiana, but to see it in person ... How clear now is the lie we're doing these black men a favor by allowing them to be here, doing our labor. That fellow has no such *supposed* noble intentions ... his motives are only avarice and greed, as I'm sure he would freely admit, without the slightest hint of guilt."

"Well, sir, what now? Do you think he'll make good on his threats?"

Nathan paused before answering, "I don't know. But I don't want to wait and find out. After our experience with LeBlanc, it would not surprise me at all if this Dubuclet has the local parish judge on his payroll.

"I've finished my business here in New Orleans and was already feeling anxious to be on our way. And now I'm thinking we've about worn out our welcome."

After another pause, he said, "Tom, what time does the last train of the day, headed north for Mississippi, leave the station?"

Tom thought for a moment. He'd been checking on train schedules earlier this morning, to prepare for the next leg of their journey. "It's at seven ... no, seven thirty, sir."

After another moment's pause, Nathan said, "Gentlemen ... I mean to be on that train!"

ꚙꙮꙭꚙꙮꚙꙭꙮꚙꙮꙭꙮ

By the time they'd returned to the hotel, it was early afternoon. Nathan split them up, each to his assigned task that they might be ready to depart as quickly as possible. He was anxious not to miss that 7:30 train.

He sent Jamie and Georgie to see to the horses, to saddle them and load their gear.

Jim sent Billy back outside to do what he did best; keep an eye on things. If he saw LeBlanc, Dubuclet, or any of their men—or any armed men, for that matter—he was to come warn them immediately.

He sent William and Stan with Jim, giving them a special assignment: loading all their firearms; Nathan wasn't taking any chances on their trip down to the railway station.

When Jim asked what he and Tom would be doing, he answered, "Tom and I have a little unfinished business in the dining hall."

Tom gave him a serious look and said, "Are you sure about this, sir?"

"Of course, Tom; it's the *right* thing to do, and I wouldn't consider leaving town without doing it."

Jim looked from one to the other, with a puzzled expression, but Tom said, "It's … some *personal* business of mine. I'll tell you all about it later."

When they parted ways, Nathan said, "I'm afraid we won't be able to invite her to come along with us, Tom. Not under the circumstances; I'll not put her at risk. But feel free to ask her if she'll follow along later, as soon as she may."

"Yes, sir. You're absolutely right about that. There'd not be time for her to say her proper goodbyes and make any necessary arrangements, anyway. And once you start talking about loading the weapons, well … that's not any proper place for a lady."

They entered the dining hall and looked around. Nathan had a keen eye for such things, and was hoping to spot her from Tom's description, without him having to point her out. He was looking for a pretty young lady, nicely dressed, either seated alone, or with her Uncle Edouard, whom Nathan had already met. But after gazing around the room, he came up empty, so he turned to Tom to see if he had spotted her.

His heart sank. Tom suddenly had a dark, sullen expression. "What is it, Tom?"

"Fifth table in from the door, third from the right. Off-white dress trimmed in lace, embroidered flowers around the edges," he said.

Nathan counted off the rows until he located the table. He spotted the young woman wearing the dress even as Tom had described. He also immediately noticed the thing that had so clearly upset Tom. It was also, of course, the reason Nathan hadn't previously spotted her; he'd been looking for a young lady either seated alone, or with the older gentleman he already knew, and he'd seen neither. He had *not* expected to see her seated with another young man. She was presently sitting right next to a good-looking young gentleman, nicely dressed, older than Tom, but probably a few years younger than Nathan. He could see they were talking, and she leaned into him, squeezing his arm below the shoulder. She reached up and kissed him on the cheek. He laughed. From the way they looked at each other, it was clear they were very comfortable together.

"Oh. I see. An old friend, maybe?" Nathan asked, hoping he was misreading the situation.

"She told me she but rarely comes to New Orleans, and knows no one here, except her Uncle, of course."

"Oh," was all Nathan could think of to say. He could see Tom's face was turning red; he looked like a bomb about to explode.

"What will you do?" he asked.

Tom didn't immediately answer. Finally, he said, "What I would *really* enjoy doing is walking up and punching that fellow; very hard in his smug-looking face. Then keep on punching until I feel a little better."

"That's sounds more like something *I'd* do, than *you*, Tom."

"I said it was what I *wanted* to do, not what I *would* do."

Nathan said nothing, waiting for Tom to make the next move.

"I feel … she has played me false. That she convinced me she had true feelings for me but was only … *toying* with me. Getting me to fall for her … to … *fall in love with her.* Maybe since I never said it … never said I *loved* her … she has gone on to the next man. I don't understand …"

Nathan felt heartsick for Tom. He'd never really had his heart broken before, but he could imagine how devastating it must be — to suddenly discover the woman you were falling for, that you believed had true feelings for you, was so untrue.

"Will you confront her, for playing you false?"

Tom was quiet for a moment.

"No … no, if she has done this before, which one would have to assume … that fellow over there is just as innocent as I was. And … since she was expecting me to arrive … she must enjoy the conflict. In some demented way, she must like seeing men fight over her, to fire their emotions. No … I will turn and walk away. That will be the best revenge. It will tell her she meant nothing to me. That I was the one using *her*, and that she was nothing more to me than … than … *a common whore.*"

Tom was clearly distraught. He said the last phrase in almost a whisper, so softly Nathan was never entirely sure what it was he'd said. But when Tom turned and strode out of the room, Nathan made one quick glance back toward the young woman. She still sat at her table with the other young gentleman. He shrugged his shoulders, turned, and followed Tom out the door.

ಬಡಿಐೋರ್ಚಲ್ಬಡಿಐೋರ್ಚಲ್ಬಡಿಐೋರ್ಚಲ್

Adilida conversed with the young gentleman at her table in French, with the idioms and colloquialisms particular to the Cajun people.

Had they spoken English, it might have sounded like this:

"Oh, cousin! It is so *wonderful* to see you! What a brilliant surprise! Does your father know you're here? When did you arrive? Did you come by boat? How long has it been since we have seen each other? Two … three years?"

He laughed, responding, "Addie dear, you must slow down, or you will lose your breath! Which would you like me to answer first?"

She laughed, "Sorry, Philippe, dear. You so caught me by surprise, I don't even know what to say, other than … I am so happy you're here!" She gave his arm another squeeze and reached up to kiss him on the cheek. "All right, now you may talk!"

He laughed again, "Thank you, for your kind permission! It has, in fact, been three years, my dear since I was last home in Thibodeaux. And a whole year since I have seen father here in New Orleans.

"I arrived this morning by steamboat from Baton Rouge. I came straight here, guessing this would be where you and father would be staying. And when I asked after you with the concierge, he said you were seated in the dining hall, so ... *here I am!*

"I was hoping you would enjoy my little surprise; I can't wait to see the look on father's face as well! You see, I also needed to conduct a little business in the city. So when I received father's letter a few months ago, telling me when the two of you would be in New Orleans, I hatched my little plot—to be here at the same time as you. I was sure father would have more business to do than I would, so I thought I'd come keep you from being lonesome."

"Oh, Philippe, that was so thoughtful of you!"

"So, Addie, how has your holiday been so far? You have been here ... three days now?"

"Four, and this is the fifth. And yes, Uncle has been very busy with work, and I had been a little ... lonely. That is, *until yesterday.*"

"Oh? And what changed yesterday?"

"My dear Philippe! I am so happy to see you so I can tell you my marvelous news ... I have met the most wonderful man! He is intelligent, so very handsome ... and, oh, Philippe, you would not believe the things he has been doing. Out in Texas he was an Army officer, leading men out fighting Indians! Yes, real, live savage Indians such as we hear about in tales. In fact, he is here with a group of his fellow soldiers from out West. And apparently from what he tells me, one of these Indians joined their side, and has come with them. No, I have not met him yet, but Thomas ... that is the young gentleman's name, Thomas Clark, from

Connecticut. Anyway, Thomas says their Indian companion is a complete gentleman, but also a fearless fighter, like Thomas."

"Really? Oh, Addie, congratulations. This is *wonderful* news. When can I meet your Thomas?"

"Well, as a matter of fact, we should see him any moment now. We were to meet here for lunch at … what time is it, Philippe?"

He pulled out a pocket watch, "It is a quarter past one."

"Oh! He should have been here already, in fact, an hour ago. I wonder what may be keeping him …"

ԾჂᏣᏪԾჂᏣᏪԾჂᏣᏪ

After gathering their personal effects, Nathan and Tom met Jim and company downstairs, in Jim's room. He was there with Stan and William. The three of them had finished loading all the pistols, two for each man. Nathan said, "Load the rifle, also."

William grabbed the hunting rifle from where it leaned against one wall and started loading it. Before he'd finished, Jamie and Georgie arrived, announcing the horses were ready to go, and the hotel grooms would bring them around to the front entrance shortly. Jim and Stan distributed the guns to their proper owners, but when Nathan saw Jamie attempting the hide his pistol under his clothing, he said, "No, stop!"

Everyone stopped what they were doing and looked up at him.

"Gentlemen, sometimes a situation calls for a show of extreme force to demoralize the enemy and prevent a battle from ever taking place. I believe this is one of those times. Wear your weapons on the *outside*; all of them—even knives. The more conspicuous the better. And put on your very most serious, ready-to-fight faces. Anyone out there watching will think twice before confronting us."

Jim grinned, "Yes sir! It will be a pleasure, sir. Y'all heard him, boys; the more *conspicuous* the better."

But Nathan noticed Tom didn't smile and already wore his "ready-to-fight" face.

Then, as ordered, they all strapped their pistol holsters on outside their clothing, hanging their hunting knives off the opposite side as a counterbalance. Each tucked his extra pistol into the belt in front. Jamie even slung the hunting rifle up over his shoulder for good measure.

Nathan did likewise, wrapping his gun belt around the outside of his suit jacket, with the great Bowie knife on the left side. He still kept the small Colt hidden in his pocket, however—just in case.

When all was ready, they shouldered their personal baggage, and marched out to the foyer in a group. Their first stop was the hotel clerk's desk, where Nathan settled the bill. While he did that, the men kept a close eye on the room, watching for any suspicious activity. In return, they received a lot of curious looks; it wasn't every day a troop of heavily armed, fierce-looking men walked through the St. Charles foyer.

As he was finishing up his business, the hotel clerk said, "Mr. Chambers … I must protest the way in which you and your men are … *attired.* It seems to me this show of weapons is *most* inappropriate."

But Nathan took out a cigar, lit it, blew a puff, looked back at the clerk and said, "I beg to disagree, sir. Under the circumstances, this particular attire, is *most* appropriate!"

Jim, overhearing the conversation had a thought, "It surely gives new meaning to the term, 'dressed to kill,' don't it, sir?" He chuckled.

Nathan smiled, then turned and headed for the door. His men followed closely behind, scanning the room in all directions as they went.

They found their horses and the mule waiting for them in the street in front of the main entrance, all packed and saddled up. They quickly stowed their personal items, mounted their horses, and started up the street.

At the end of the block they turned left up a side street. Nathan would lead them in a circuitous route to the train station to confuse any watchers. They'd ridden less than two blocks from the hotel when Billy came trotting up.

"I have seen nothing unusual or suspicious, Captain. None of the enemies we know, and nobody else armed or threatening."

"Good. Saddle up Billy, and ride with us. We should all stick together the rest of the way, so none may be taken alone."

But Billy slowly shook his head, "No, Captain. I should *not* do that."

"What? What do you mean, Billy?"

"I will always follow your orders, Captain, even to death. But in this, I think I should do my *duty*, and continue to scout. The enemy knows these streets; it is his own territory. Even well-armed, we could ride into an ambush and be taken by surprise. Let me do my duty, Captain."

"He's right, sir," Jim said.

"Well, yes, maybe. But I don't like having a man out there alone, as he says, in enemy territory. If they were to take him, then what? It would make our situation extremely desperate."

"I do not fear being alone in enemy territory, Captain. I have done it many times amongst the Comanche; they are much fiercer than LeBlanc and his bullies."

Nathan sat his horse for a moment, puffing on his cigar, staring off down the street. Finally, he gave a heavy sigh, and said, "All right, Billy, we'll do it your way. Jim … please hand him down his pistols."

Jim complied and soon Billy was strapping on his holster and stuffing the extra pistol in front. Unlike the others, however, he hid his weapons inside his trousers, with his shirt hanging over top, since he was trying to remain inconspicuous.

"Billy … remember, we *must* be on that 7:30 train, no matter what. *All* of us. Do you understand?"

"Yes, Captain. I will meet you at the train. Seven and a half o'clock."

ജ്ഞരുന്നുജ്ഞരുന്നുജ്ഞരുന്നു

Sunday June 3, 1860 – Greenbrier County, Virginia:

Miss Abbey entered the church at her usual time, 9:00 in the morning. She enjoyed entering right before the service started so she'd not have to sit too long, nor be obliged to stand around making idle conversation. She preferred doing *that* after the service.

So if she arrived early, she'd stay in the carriage until the appointed time. It was a habit of longstanding; Jacob had originally started it long before they were married, and now she was so used to it she'd never considered doing anything else. And she'd never had to worry about finding a seat; Jacob, along with Percival Walters, had basically paid the entire cost of construction on the new Episcopal Methodist Church some ten years earlier. What had started as a neighborhood fundraising drive, had turned into a spending contest between the two men, each trying to outdo the other. As a result, the church was much larger and more sturdily built than originally planned, though it was still a simple, one-room country church, white painted on the outside with fine hardwood floors on the inside. There were plans to eventually add stained glass to the windows, but it had not yet been done. It featured twelve rows of pews, made of the same hardwood as the floor, divided by a wide center aisle with a narrower aisle up each side. Each pew could seat six adults, and by general understanding of all the parishioners, they'd allotted each of the two major donors a front-row pew—the Chambers on the right side of the aisle, and the Walters on the left.

And other families generally sat in the same seats every Sunday. So when Miss Abbey entered, she knew just where to look to give special greetings and waves to the women and families she was especially close with. But today as she moved down the aisle, trailed by three of the Mountain Meadows hands, Zeke, Benny, and Joe, the sullen looks she saw surprised her. Not the usual happy smiles, and warm greetings. Serious, concerned looks greeted her this Sunday. She could not imagine what had changed the usual demeanor of her friends and neighbors.

And when she reached the front of the church and turned toward her seats, she suffered a rude shock. Six men already filled the front pew. She recognized several as Walters' farmhands. They did not look up at her or acknowledge her presence but stared straight ahead. She looked over to the left of the aisle and saw Walters. He was in his usual place in the front-row seat farthest from the aisle. He was looking straight at her, neither smiling nor gloating—just that odd blank expression of his.

She found herself at a complete loss. She looked back at her men who also looked puzzled and out of their element. It was the young hand Zeke who finally reacted. Stepping around Miss Abbey, he leaned over and tapped the first man on the shoulder. "Hey ... buddy, them seats belong to my mistress here."

The man looked up at Zeke and scowled. "Ain't got her name on them. We was here first. Find some other seats."

By now the church had gone quiet. All eyes were on the confrontation brewing at the front of the room.

Zeke looked surprised, stood and whispered to Miss Abbey, "Me and the boys'll be happy to force the issue, ma'am ... if you like. Though it don't seem proper-like, fighting in church and all ..."

She looked in his eyes and could see he was quite earnest. He was ready to fight these men for her, though they'd be badly outnumbered—only three Mountain Meadows hands to six of Walters' on that bench, and another four on the other side of the aisle, not counting Walters. And Zeke was not an especially large man, though he was tall, and strong despite his lack of girth. But his loyalty and courage warmed her heart and helped relieve the discomfort of the moment.

She decided not to whisper her answer, but to say it aloud so all could hear, "No. Thank you kindly, Zeke. It is most gallant of you to offer, but I'll not instigate a fight inside the church. Let us find other seats in more ... *friendly* company."

She turned and walked down the aisle toward the back of the church. Several of the parishioners would not meet her eye as she walked, ashamed of what had just happened to her, she assumed. Others had red faces, and angry looks, but no one spoke up or offered to intervene on her behalf.

Although there were other seats available, she made a point of sitting in the very back row. The last several rows were typically empty on any given Sunday, aside from the occasional mother with a squirmy toddler or fussy baby. Today Abbey and her men had the back bench on the right side all to themselves.

Shortly after they took their seats, two young ushers in white robes came down the aisle and lit candles on tall brass floor stands at the front of the church. Then Pastor Blackburn arrived, proceeding deliberately down the center aisle before turning to face his flock from the front of the room. He had white hair, and was a bit heavy-set with a round face, though he typically had a serious demeanor. Typical of a pastor, he wore black robes, with white shirt sleeves at the wrists and a gold, silken, embroidered sash hung around his neck. He began his sermon, and if he noticed the change in seating arrangements, he did not react, nor give any sign this Sunday was anything other than business as usual.

ᛒᚢᛊᛟᚳᚱᚳᛒᚢᛊᛟᚳᚱᚳᛒᚢᛊᛟᚳᚱᚳᛒ

Three men sat their horses just inside the woods at the edge of the gravel roadway. From here they had a clear view of the intersection of this narrow road with the broader main east-west road to Richmond a few hundred yards away. In the other direction, up the hill was Mountain Meadows Farm. And though they could easily spy any traffic coming along the road, travelers could not easily see them in the shade of the thick woods behind tall bushes. If someone on the main road *could've* seen them, they might've been alarmed; they were a rough-looking crew, unshaven and ragged in dirty, travel-stained clothing and well-worn hats. But that was not the worst of it; all three wore pistols at their hips, and the largest of the three had a black patch over one eye. Rumors had spread in the past week about a series of roadway robberies by a one-eyed bandit and his men. But those incidents had occurred farther to the west, in the wilder parts of the county, so there was no particular concern around the "big town" of Lewisburg.

"How long we gotta wait?" one of the men asked the leader with the eye patch.

"As long as it takes. Why, you got somewhere better to be?"

"No … don't like sitting and waiting is all."

"The man said the church service ends at ten, and they always goes straight home after. So ... should be here quarter past ... half past at the latest."

"And you sure they ain't armed."

"Afraid of a little gunfight? *Pah!* Use what little brain God done give you ... you ever seen a man go armed to church?"

"No ... but ..."

"The man says the old lady'll have three or four farmhands with her, but none's expected to be armed."

"And we's fixing to kill the lady? What about her men?"

"Her men don't matter, but we'd best kill at least one, so it don't seem suspicious, like we was aiming for the old lady. The important thing is ... one of the men needs to get away, so's he can tell all about the 'one-eyed bandit.'"

The third man flashed a wicked smile, "The murderous bandit who's gonna suddenly disappear and not never be seen again?"

"Yep. That's the plan, and it can't happen too soon. I'll be happy to be done with it today; things're starting to get too hot around here. When I was in at the post office yesterday, I saw a wanted poster of the 'one-eyed bandit' up on the wall. It looked a little too much like *me* for comfort. I reckon once we're done here today a ride over to Richmond will be just the thing. With plenty of money in our pockets, and no one the wiser."

☙✲✺✲☙✲✺✲☙✲✺✲☙✲✺✲☙

At first, Abbey tried to focus on the sermon, but her mind kept returning to Walters' men taking her seats, the latest in a long series of slights and incidents intended to intimidate or frighten her into selling the farm. She might have entertained the offer at one point if Nathan had decided not to return. But she was just stubborn enough she'd not sell now even if forced to run the farm by herself. But fortunately, that was not the case; Nathan would soon be home. Only yesterday she'd received his telegram from New Orleans! Not much longer now ...

She fantasized about her son standing up to the bully ... maybe punching him square in his smug face! She smiled, then remembered where she was, and blushed. *Such thoughts in church!*

Please forgive me, Father … they have provoked me into un-Christian-like thoughts!

When the service ended and Pastor Blackburn made his exit, Abbey moved quickly to the door. She intended to head straight for her carriage and leave for home, forgoing her usual socializing with the ladies of the church. She had no interest in idle chit chat or gossip this morning. Her friends would understand, and those who weren't her friends … well, they hardly mattered anyway.

As she passed the pastor, he nodded his head and smiled, "Miss Abbey, a pleasure to see you again."

But she did not return his smile. She respected that he'd always taken pains to remain neutral in the feud. But now she was annoyed he'd said nothing and done nothing about this latest slight right in front of him in his own house.

"Pastor Blackburn," she said curtly and continued on her way.

She marched across the drive toward where Cobb stood next to her fine black carriage, the three farmhands hard on her heels. Cobb seemed surprised by her sudden exit from the church.

"Mistress … is aught amiss?" he asked.

"No. Yes! Oh … never mind, Cobb. Let's just go."

Zeke and the other men went straight to their horses, unhitched them, and prepared to mount up.

But as Abbey took Cobb's hand, preparing to step up into the carriage, she heard a voice call out behind her, "Miss Abbey … Miss Abbey … Abigail, dear … please wait!"

She recognized the voice of one of her best friends, Rebecca Walker.

Abbey sighed, and turned to face her friend, who was trotting across the drive, blue and white gingham skirts in her hands so they'd not entangle her feet.

Rebecca arrived out of breath, and red in the face. But Abbey could see she had a fire in her eyes, "It's not right what *he's* done in there, Abbey! I'm just … *beside* myself! After all you and Jacob have done for this church … it's scandalous, is what it is. I am *so* sorry, Abbey … I … don't know what to say!"

"It's all right, Becky. Thank you for your concern, though."

Just then Rebecca's husband John caught up to them, "Miss Abbey," he said, tipping his hat to her politely. "I agree with Becky; Walters has gone too far this time. I intend to get some of the others together and speak to the pastor about it, as soon as may be."

"Thank you, John. That's very kindly of you, but it's really unnecessary. Mr. Walters is ... *not* someone to get on the wrong side of; I should know. And besides ... my son will be home soon, and I have a feeling he'll have no difficulty dealing with our neighborhood bully."

"Oh! Truly? I never knew Nathaniel was coming home, Abbey. That's wonderful news, but ... I don't recall you mentioning it before," Rebecca said.

"No ... sorry, Becky, for not saying anything sooner. At first, I didn't know if he *would* come. And then ... well, I decided not to tell anyone because of ... well, anyway, the news is out now, so there's no reason not to speak of it."

"Oh, you must be so excited! Please, Abbey, won't you come to our house and share some tea with me? I would love to hear all there is to tell about Nathaniel and his journey. And also ... I'm sure it would do you good to talk to a friend about all the awful things Mr. Walters has been doing ..."

When Abbey hesitated, John added, "Yes, please do come to our place, Miss Abbey ... it's the least we can do after your disgraceful treatment this morning."

She could see the sincere pain and concern in his face, and ... it *would* be nice to tell someone about everything that's been happening—her fears and concerns about Walters, and her anxiety and worry for Nathan on his long, and potentially dangerous journey. At Mountain Meadows she had to be strong; she was in charge, and couldn't show weakness or hesitation, not even with Megs.

"All right, *yes* ... thank you, John, Becky. That would be lovely."

John turned toward the farmhands, who were politely standing by waiting for Miss Abbey to give the word, "You fellas are welcome to come as well. Though I doubt you'll be wanting any tea, I do have a beer keg I've just tapped, and it's a good'n."

This brought smiles to the faces of the young men, and Zeke answered, "Thank you, kindly, Mr. Walker. That beer would go down nicely after a hot ride in the sun, now you mention it. Much obliged."

It was two miles to the Walker farm, and Rebecca shared a ride with Abbey in her carriage. Once she started talking, Abbey found it a great joy and relief to tell all to her friend. She ended up spending the rest of the morning at the Walkers', and half the afternoon.

By the time her carriage passed the spot where the three men had been hiding earlier that morning, there was no sign of them — except for a small black eye patch, lying on the ground back in the woods where it had been discarded.

When Abbey returned to her house, she was in a much happier frame of mind, confident all would be well with Nathan arriving soon.

ༀༀༀༀༀༀༀༀༀༀༀ

Friday June 1, 1860 – New Orleans, Louisiana:

Nathan led his men on a very indirect route, even doubling back an entire block at one point to confuse anyone who might be observing and intending to lay a trap. Whether it was because of this, or for some other unknown reason, they arrived at the train station unmolested.

Nathan was feeling a sense of relief — that perhaps he had been overly cautious, if not down-right paranoid — when he noticed a group of men standing together on the train station platform.

He hissed at the others, "Look … there by that pile of baggage."

They all looked, and Tom said, "LeBlanc. And … hmm … I count eight men. And there could be others hidden among the crowd. Can't tell if they're armed, but I would assume so."

"Humph. I'd bet my entire card winnings from last night, they are!" Jim said.

307

"All right … let's bluff it out. Take it slow and easy, no sudden moves; we'll go about our business, purchasing the tickets, loading the horses, and whatnot. Keep an eye on them, and a lookout for anyone else looking suspicious. But don't pay them much mind, as if they are of little concern to us. But … for *God's sake*, whatever else you do, stick together! Anyone wandering off by himself now is likely to earn an extended stay at LeBlanc's hotel."

"Yes, sir!" they all answered.

"And has anyone seen Billy?" he asked.

Nobody had, and Nathan thought he denoted a worried expression on Jim's face. Well, hopefully he would show up soon or … *or what?*

They paid their fare and loaded the horses. LeBlanc and his men continued to watch them but made no move. And Billy had not appeared.

They stowed their baggage and secured their seats. Still no sign of Billy.

Nathan and company now stood in front of their train car. As they looked across the platform, LeBlanc walked toward them, followed by his men.

"Stand to!" Jim said, and the men all stood straighter, unbuttoning the safety straps on their holsters. Jamie took the rifle down off his shoulder, and held it in his two hands, across his chest. Jim made a show of loosening the extra pistol tucked into his belt.

LeBlanc, to his credit, showed no sign of fear as he walked straight toward Nathan. He did not carry his shotgun and appeared to be unarmed. He stopped ten feet away and held up his hand to halt his men.

"Monsieur Chambers, we meet again."

"LeBlanc."

"The parish judge has issued a warrant for the arrest of you and your men."

"On what charges?"

"Assault, disruption of lawful commerce, and interference between a legal slave owner and his property."

Nathan pulled out a cigar, bit off the end and spat it on the ground.

"You mean that shameless slaver, Monsieur Dubuclet? The man hasn't even the common decency to pretend his behavior is anything but nefarious and self-serving. He's more than happy to bind and brutalize men who've done him no wrong for the sake of a few dollars."

LeBlanc returned a wry grin, "Such matters are of no concern to me, monsieur. I am but a simple lawman doing his duty."

Nathan snorted a derisive laugh, then lit the cigar and took a puff before responding.

"You, a lawman? More like a lapdog. Paid to do Dubuclet's bidding, when you're not busy extorting drunks for bail money. You're nothing more than a petty thief and a slaver's errand boy."

LeBlanc scowled, crossing his arms across his chest. But he seemed disinclined to make answer.

Nathan took another puff on his cigar, then said, "Well then … it seems we have ourselves a little dilemma here, Monsieur LeBlanc. I intend to be on this train and leave the city *tonight*. And I don't especially care what you, your crooked cousin the judge, or his reprehensible benefactor Monsieur Dubuclet, have to say about it.

"So … once again, LeBlanc, you must ask yourself whether it's worth it … to cross me, when I'm in a position to do you *grave bodily harm.*"

LeBlanc had eight men with him, so the odds were slightly in his favor by pure numbers, even without additional men dispersed in the crowd, if any. However, he was well aware Chambers' men were all veteran Indian fighters, while his men were more used to bullying drunks. None had ever been in a *real* gunfight, including himself. For the sake of his own hide, he felt compelled to bow to the inevitable.

"Monsieur Chambers … for the record, I am placing you under arrest, based on the charges I have recited to you. And I will report you are resisting my legal attempts at securing your arrest by means of armed force."

Nathan stared him down, continuing to puff on his cigar. Then he said, "That'll be fine, LeBlanc; you do that. And if you wish to add, I threatened to shoot you and your men down in the street like the rabid dogs you are, I would be all right with that as well."

He continued to glare at LeBlanc until the lawman turned, gave a quick hand signal, and departed, followed closely by his men.

"Damn it!" Jim said, "Billy ain't here yet. How long before the train leaves?"

Nathan continued to watch LeBlanc and his men depart, so Tom pulled out his pocket watch and said, "It's ... seven twenty-five."

"Damn it. Goddamn it to hell!" Jim said, and spat.

"Yes, Mr. Wiggins, I agree with the sentiment, but there's no need for blasphemy."

"Sorry, sir. Of course, you're right. Sorry, just worried about Billy, is all."

"Yes ... as are we all, Mr. Wiggins."

Five more minutes went by, and no Billy.

"I'll stay behind, Captain," Jim offered.

"No! If Billy doesn't come, we *all* stay."

They waited for several more minutes. Now they could hear the engine rumbling, taking on a more urgent tone, as the fireman stoked the coals.

Three cars further down the line they could see the conductor talking to the passengers on the platform, urging them to take their seats on the train. A few more minutes passed, and now they were the only ones standing on the platform. The conductor had already passed their car, prodding them to board the car, which they politely ignored.

"Mr. Wiggins."

"Sir?"

"Take two men and go up front. See if you can *persuade* the engineer to delay the start. I still don't like splitting us up, but with three you'll be able to put up a good fight, if there's trouble."

"How much *'persuasion'* did you have in mind, sir? I doubt the engineer's gonna to be too agreeable to a *friendly request.*"

"Whatever it takes, Mr. Wiggins. We're already 'outlaws' in this town, so one more offense won't make much difference."

Jim smiled, "I like your way of thinking, Captain. Jenkins, Volkov … with me."

William and Stan stepped forward and followed Jim as he started toward the front of the train at a quick trot.

"Wait! Belay that, Jim!" Tom shouted, "Look, Captain …" He pointed to the gap between two of the passenger cars back toward the rear of the train. They saw a man jump off the connection hitch down onto the platform. He turned and headed their direction at a trot. It was Billy.

"Good!" Nathan said with a heavy sigh, "I'd just as soon not add 'train robber' to my list of dubious titles here in New Orleans."

Billy arrived at almost the same time Jim, Stan, and William returned.

"Good to see you, Billy," Jim said, "but you gave us a scare. What kept you?"

"Followed LeBlanc and his men when they left the station. Wanted to make sure they didn't double-back or try some other trick, so I trailed them for a few blocks. But they went in a straight line back toward the jailhouse and never stopped to discuss plans or change direction. So, I came back."

"Well done, scout! Thank you," Jim responded, beaming and giving him a warm pat on the back.

Billy looked puzzled. Nobody'd ever thanked him for doing his job before. He smiled, shrugged his shoulders, and said, "You're … *welcome?*"

After they took their seats, Nathan pulled something out of his jacket pocket; for once it was *not* a cigar, but his small, dog-eared traveling Bible. Jim smiled at him and raised a questioning eyebrow.

"In Psalms chapter thirty-seven, verse eight it says, *'Cease from anger, and forsake wrath: fret not thyself in any wise to do evil.'* After the day I've had, Mr. Wiggins, I believe I need a little retraining."

"Amen to that, sir. Amen to that," and then Jim *did* pull a cigar from his pocket and stuck it between his teeth, still grinning. To him, it'd been a very *good* day; *All's well that ends well, as they say,* he thought.

Chapter 10. Dire Forebodings

"Whenever I hear anyone
arguing for slavery,
I feel a strong impulse to see it
tried on him personally."
– Abraham Lincoln

Friday June 1, 1860 – New Orleans, Louisiana:

"I'm so sorry, my dear one. I understand how you are feeling. But let me tell you all I have learned, from asking around in the gentleman's club. It seems your Thomas, and his companions, were forced to leave the city in a great hurry, under some kind of duress. In fact, they walked through the hotel foyer with drawn guns in their hands, threatening anyone who came close. What? No, I do not know for sure why, but the rumors ... they are spreading like a fire in the wild. Some say their Indian companion caused some mischief that caused them to have to leave town. Others say they were actually outlaws from out West, and the law had finally caught up with them. So they had to leave quickly, or risk being hanged. Some even say the hotel clerk tried to stop them from leaving, but their leader threatened to shoot him dead where he stood.

"What do I think? Well ... having spent an evening with your Thomas ... I believe he is *exactly* what he says he is ... a soldier from the West, heading east to Virginia with his companions. Adilida, my dear, if you were to ask me what I think *really* happened, irrespective of the many rumors swirling around this hotel, I would say these men had some kind of run-in with the law, which in this town certainly does *not* make them criminals. In fact, from what I have seen and heard, the lawmen in this city are more likely to be criminals than the outlaws! Anyway, something happened forcing them to depart in great haste. And your Thomas had no time to say goodbye. Or maybe he had time, but wished to keep you out of the troubles he and his friends were in.

"Come, my dear, please *do* cheer up; I'm sure once he gets to Virginia he will write and tell you all about what has happened. Just you wait and see."

Adilida stopped sobbing and sniffling long enough to look up at her uncle and nod her head appreciatively.

I hope to God I am right about this, he thought, with a sinking feeling in the pit of his stomach.

ಐ⁊Ꝺ☾ℛ℃ℬಐ⁊Ꝺ☾ℛ℃ℬಐ⁊Ꝺ☾ℛ℃ℬ

Friday June 1, 1860 – Greenbrier County, Virginia:

"Hey, you fellas heard what people's been saying? That we's getting a new master?" Johnny asked. He spoke in the particular, low voice the field workers used to communicate with each other while going about their daily business. Through long practice he, like all the others, had perfected a way of talking that wouldn't project. He timed the words to match his movements and the natural noises he made while crawling along between the rows of tobacco plants, pulling out weeds. Although they didn't strictly forbid talk while working, the white farmhands became annoyed and peevish if there was too much of it. And it was never good to draw attention to one's self.

"No," Tony answered back, in the same soft voice, "ain't heard nothing. What? Miss Abbey up and sell the place, now the old master done died? Or she jump the broom with some new fella?"

"No, none of that … they be saying the *old* master … he got him a son who's coming back here so as to be the *new* master."

"Son? Ain't never seen no son. He ain't never been here, far as I can recall."

"No, Tony, he ain't. The way they tell it, the olders that is … the son left here long time ago when he's a young'n, back before us'en was even born. They say the old master got sore angry with him one day and sent him packing, and he ain't been back since."

"Oh. So why he coming back now, after all this time?"

"*Fool!* You know nothing about this-here world? With white folks, when the old man dies, the son gets all his things—house, farm, animals … us slaves. *Everything.*"

"Oh," was all Tony could think to say. Now that Johnny said it he understood it, but he'd never thought of such a thing before. He tried to imagine his own father, who'd passed when Tony was still a young boy, having anything worth giving to his son.

"What it matter to the likes of us, who the new master is?" Ned said, in his usual sullen tone. "One white man's same as the other."

"Well, that ain't true, and you knows it, Ned. Just 'cause you got that bad whipping that one time, don't mean all white men's itching to peel your hide. They say they's white folks, way up in them northern parts, reckons they ought to free us black men. They even got a fancy name for their selves … '*abo … something*' … well, anyway, it means they don't want no more slavery."

"Where you hear such nonsense, Johnny? If these white folks so keen on freein' us, why they ain't done it yet?" Tony asked.

"Cause they ain't no reason white folks would free slaves, when they can work 'em to death for nothing," Ned answered for him.

But Johnny was not so easily deterred, "I knows stuff 'cause I listens … and not only to the nattering in the cabins. If you pays attention when them white folks is talking, you learn things. And if you talks with the household slaves, and the grooms, who hears the white folks talking all day long, you can learn a bunch more."

Ned spat. "House slaves … no better'n whites. Coddling them slavers … kissing their babies. They makes me sick to look at. Why care what any white folks say, anyway? Things they talk on ain't none of our concern, and don't mean nothing to us-all."

"Well, I say you're wrong, Ned. Seems to me the more we knows, the better … though, I ain't figgered out the why yet."

Ned snorted a derisive laugh.

They continued pulling out weeds on hands and knees in the blazing hot sun while they talked. Sweat thoroughly soaked their shirts, and it ran down from beneath their straw hats, trickling down the sides of their faces in streams. Most men would consider

315

this job agonizing, back-breaking labor. But for these three young men, and dozens more black-skinned men and women spread around the farm, it was the normal, everyday, mind-numbing routine.

And tomorrow would be much the same. Same as yesterday, and all the days before.

ᏸᏇᏁᏣᏘᏔᏸᏇᏁᏣᏘᏔᏸᏇᏁᏣᏘᏔ

"What you hear 'bout the new master, Cobb?" Phinney asked, as he brushed down the mare he was working on.

"Not much, but what I did hear don't sound too good."

Cobb was in the next stall over picking a rock from the hoof of a gelding.

"Oh, what was that? I ain't hardly heard a thing 'til now."

"Well, only he was a troublesome child, when he's a little tyke. And he got in to having a mean streak, with an angry-bad temper when he growed a bit older. They say he was always a fighting with them other white boys and was fearsome big and strong for his age. Give out some terrible bad beatings."

"You're right, Cobb, that don't bode well for us lot."

"No, it don't. And they's worse. They say in his growed-up years he been away out in them wild lands with soldiers, killing Indians. And I hears them in the Army whips their own soldiers even worse than us slaves, when they has the notion."

"Wheeew …" Phinney whistled, "That sounds awful bad. The old master … well, he was powerful mean, and never spared the whip, that's certain. But a man like *this'n* … like to kill us, as soon as look at us. You're right, Cobb; it ain't sounding good."

But Cobb shrugged his shoulders, and said, "Well, no, it ain't. Though they's nothing any of us gonna do about it anyways, so may as well not worry on it. But I tell you a strange thing, Phin …"

"What that be, Cobb?"

"Well, though all this *sounds* bad … I don't know … but for some reason I have a good *feeling* about it. Like … well, like something's gonna change for the good."

316

"Well, Cobb, that's strange enough, all right. I sure hopes you're right on it, or at least not too far wrong."

"Me too, Phin, me too."

ଈୠଓଔଈୠଓଔଈୠଓଔ

"What be troubling you, Babs?" George asked, looking up from his meal. It was dark out, but he could see she had a worried expression, even by the light of the single candle set on a small shelf on the wall. They'd put their two little girls, Annie and Lucy, to bed a few minutes earlier. They were already fast asleep, breathing softly.

She came over and sat across from him at the small, simple wood table. "Oh … *nothing* really," she answered with a heavy sigh.

George set down his spoon and gave her his full attention. He knew her well enough to know when she said "nothing" that way, it really meant, "something!" They'd "jumped the broom" … five—or was it six years ago now? He tried to recall exactly, but the years and the seasons all seemed to run together in his mind. Babs would know it, but she'd be disappointed in him if he had to ask, so he never did.

"What is it, Babs, darling?" he asked.

She sighed again and said, "Look at our sweet little babies, sleeping there so peaceful-like. Like tiny angels, ain't they?"

George looked over at the two little girls, side by side with covers pulled up under their chins, sharing a tiny bed, "Yes, Babs. Whenever I looks at them, I reckon they's the most beautiful things in the whole world. Uh, next to you, of course," he added at the last moment, feeling like a man who'd narrowly avoided stepping in a large hole.

She scowled at him, shaking her head. He was always amazed how she made him feel like he'd said exactly the right thing but was still a complete fool … both at the same time!

"George, you ever think on what their lives will be like … if … if they'll be, *somehow,* better'n ours?"

"What you mean, Babs?"

317

"Oh, George! Can't you *see?* Your Daddy and Momma was slaves, and so was mine. So we was born slaves, and that we been our whole lives. And now we have babies of our own, so young and so sweet. Oh, George, it just … it just breaks my heart. Our sweet little ones is gonna spend their lives being … being nothing more than *slaves*, somebody's servant … somebody's *property!*"

"But Babs … why you wanna go saying things like that? You know it don't do no good, dwelling on such."

"It's just … what if'n this new master says we got too many women-folk on this-here farm, and he needs more men for to work the fields? He gonna sell them babies off to one of them awful slave traders, and we ain't never gonna see 'em again! Or, he sell *you* … or *me*, and break up our family. I been hearing all kind of frightful-bad things 'bout the new master. Who knows what a wicked, cruel man the likes of that gonna do!"

She buried her face in her hands and sobbed, saying nothing more for several minutes.

Babs rarely acted this way; she was normally the calm, level-headed one. It made him anxious, not knowing how to comfort her.

Worst of all, what she'd said was true.

This was the third place he'd lived, himself. When he was only a babe they had sold him away from his mother, so's he couldn't even remember her face or name. Then when nearly fully grown they'd sold away again, this time to Mountain Meadows. He'd been here ever since. The *old* master Chambers was a mean, hard man. George had worked harder here than he'd done at the last place. But some things at Mountain Meadows were better. For one, the cabins were much nicer. These had actual windows with glass, rather than gaps between logs to let in the light—along with the wind, rain, and snow. And the roof here kept the rain off, mostly, so long as one kept clear of the few leaky spots.

And, although Master Chambers' white farmhands laid on the lash with great regularity, they did so usually only to inflict pain, not to cause serious bleeding or lasting damage. The severe, crippling beatings had been rare, and they'd meted them out only for the most severe offenses, for which George was grateful. The last place he'd been, he'd seen several men killed by such beatings. One time he'd overheard Master Chambers telling the overseer never to do the hard whippings. He'd spent good money on them slaves and wouldn't stand anyone damaging or killing his valuable property. That made good sense to George. But many white men didn't see it that way. Guess they reckoned they'd just buy more black men from the slave traders or raise up more from babes.

He had also fed them better, and they always had adequate clothing, and a new pair of shoes once a year if they needed them. At his last farm a man might go months with no shirt to wear. And a few had no pants. He'd even seen new arrivals go out into the fields to work completely naked.

But there were always tradeoffs. At the last place, the master gave every Sunday off work. He said it was "against his religion," his servants working on the Sabbath. Since they didn't have to be in the fields at first light, they enjoyed their Saturday nights. It'd given them a distraction, with dancing, music, and other foolishness. Sometimes they'd sneak off into the woods and light a fire, singing and hooting it up 'til all hours of the night.

But old Master Chambers worked them every day, so there were no Saturday night shenanigans. He gave them one day off a year, on Christmas. It was a pleasure they looked forward to months before and talked about months after. Though Mountain Meadows took better care of its slaves than other places, he had to admit … it was more mind-numbing and tedious, because of the never-ending workdays.

And Master Chambers had rarely sold off his slaves. At the old place, they'd regularly sell off all the babies as soon as their mommas weaned them. It was a horrible thing to see; the younger women would scream and cry in heart-breaking misery. A few even jumped into the river and drowned themselves.

But after a while you'd get used to anything, he supposed. He'd not worried about slave traders for years until now. But when he thought about them selling off his little Annie and Lucy, he felt a cold chill in his heart.

He got up from the table and moved around to Babs' side, where she sat sobbing, covering her face with her hands. There wasn't another chair on her side of the table (they only had two in the cabin), so he knelt on the floor. He reached over and wrapped his big arms around her. She leaned into him, put her head against his chest, and continued to cry, long and hard.

Ⅎℂℂℂ

The young girl Rosa trotted toward the cabin, carrying a heavy bucket of water back from the well. She'd done it so many times she now did it with little effort. And she'd learned to time the swinging of the bucket with her strides, so she barely ever spilled a drop, despite going along at a brisk pace.

Not *so young* anymore, she decided. Just this spring she'd … well, become a *woman*. At least that's what the older women said, as she'd begun to have her "moon cycles," and they told her that's what it meant. She'd had other noticeable changes to her body as well in the last year, with small, but womanly breasts suddenly appearing, so she knew it was true. But she still considered herself a little girl, no different from a year ago, or two years.

And more changes were coming, this time not to her body. They told her she'd have to work in the fields this fall, come the harvest. They needed all able-bodied adults to pick the cotton, along with the older children. Even the white farmhands would join in. She wasn't looking forward to it; she'd seen how the rough cotton seed pods scratched and cut the people's hands until they'd come back home bloody. And they'd get up the next day to do it again.

Back at the cabin, Rosa set the bucket down on the kitchen table. Betsy, a large, full-grown woman, was cutting up turnips and dumping them into a pot for the midday meal. She was also watching over two babies and three toddlers, whose mothers worked out in the fields. As usual, Betsy started in on the latest rumors about the new master. It was all the talk around the farm these days. But what else was there? None of them knew anything of the wider world. If it wasn't happening on the farm, it wasn't something they knew about.

Most of the rumors sounded bad. Maybe even *really* bad. They said he was cruel and had a violent temper. That he'd been far in the West killing some kind of wild men out there. No one knew why. Possibly just for sport.

The slaves had hated and feared the old master—serious, sullen, never smiling, ever quick to mete out harsh discipline. Painful whippings were commonplace, severe beatings less frequent. But the rumors said the young son had been ill-tempered when he was younger. He'd made the old master look kindly by compare, and *nobody* much thought of the old master as kindly.

Nobody, that is, except Rosa herself, and she wasn't sure why. It was a mystery, but somehow … something told her it was a something she could *not* share with the others. For one, she felt they would think her foolish, and they would not believe her. But there was more to it, she was sure—something she couldn't quite name.

She'd only spoken with the old master a few times, but each time he talked to her he'd had a warm expression on his face. He seemed … almost shy. But that didn't make any sense. It was as if the great master didn't know what to say to the little slave girl, but wanted to say something … *friendly?* He'd ask after her health and if she was happy. She always answered back politely, as they'd taught her, saying only things that would please him, and never anything that wouldn't.

But she remembered one time he'd reached in his pocket and pulled out something wrapped in a small piece of cloth. He looked around, as if making sure no one was looking before he handed it to her. He said, "This is for you. Don't tell the others; just enjoy it yourself." Then he gave her a little smile, a quick pat on the head, and strode away. When she unwrapped it, she found a piece of hard candy. She did as he'd told her, and neither shared it with anyone, nor told anyone about it. But it was, without question, the most wonderful gift anyone had ever given her. And sometimes when she closed her eyes and thought really hard, she could still almost taste its wonderful sweetness. She still had the little square of cloth in which it'd been wrapped. She'd sucked all

321

the sweetness from it. Then she'd washed it and carefully tucked it away in the little bundle of her personal things she stowed in one corner of the cabin.

When the word had spread earlier this spring of the old master's passing, most of the slaves seemed either happy about it, or didn't care one way or the other. The people in the cabins did worry about what would come next, whether they'd sell the farm, whether they'd sell off the slaves together or separately, if they'd split up families, and so on.

She was apparently the only one who felt sad, as if he was a kindly old man nobody understood because he always showed his hard-outer shell, like one of those turtles down at the river. She'd felt the sadness for a long time and had wished she could talk to someone about it. But nobody would understand. She also wished to attend his funeral, down at the Chambers' family burial plot alongside the duck pond. But of course, she couldn't, it being for the white folks only.

She wondered if, despite everyone's fears, the new master would be like his Daddy, hard on the outside, like a turtle, but secretly soft and kindly underneath. She mulled it over for a long time before finally deciding she'd wait and see for herself. She'd long since tired of all the rumors and had long since decided they were probably all wrong anyway.

ೞಞೞಞೞಞೞಞೞಞೞಞ

Ganda, called "old Toby" by the white masters, addressed the small gathering. "I want y'all to talk on what you recall of the boy *Nathaniel*, from when he was a boy here."

For a moment, nobody spoke. The five "Elders" gathered in the small cabin for their regular meeting, convened to discuss anything of concern to the slaves on the farm. The white masters knew nothing about this meeting. In fact, the very existence of the group of Elders was the most sacred kind of secret among the farm workers.

Mimba took the lead as usual, "I recall he was a real mischief when he's a child. Running' wild about the place, getting into some kind of trouble or other. I remembers a time when he took

322

one of the little slave boys to go swimming' … or … fishing, or some such … down to the river, rather than doing his chores. The slave boy got beat, of course. But young master Chambers … well, I recall him standing and watching the beating, red in the face, like it embarrassed him, or made him angry, or … something."

"Yes, I remembers somewhat of the kind," Mussu said. "I also remembers when he was a tad older, I done seen him setting in to fighting with a neighbor's white boy. They was running a race, I recall. The other boy was losing, I reckon, so's he reaches out and trips young Nathaniel, and he falls hard, with a tumble. The other boy, well he stops and laughs. But our young master … I tell you, he comes up fighting mad, cursing, spitting, and swinging fists. 'Fore the white overseers come over to pull them boys apart, the other'n was bleeding outta nose and mouth, looking in a bad way. I reckon he'd other fights besides, but I ain't never seen 'em."

"That's right," said Camba, whose slave name was Naomie. She, like Mimba, worked the fields. "I also seen him having a terrible bad spat with the old master once. We was coming in from working end of day, me and some others. He and the old master was standing by the big old oak tree hard-by the cabins. Old master he's a pointing his finger at the young'n, giving out a bad scolding. The younger was … well, pert-near tall as old master, so's I guess he be a young man. Anyways, old master scolds him something fierce, we couldn't hear on account of what. Then, *Lordie!* That young'n gets angry and starts in to yelling right back at old master. And damned if old master don't just turn and stomp off in a huff. Well, you can well believe, all us workers was trying our best to look like we ain't never saw nothing. But I recall young master looking our way 'fore he left. It was as if … well, as if he was wondering if we agreed with him, or something. Strange 'cause … well, 'cause, why would young master *care* what we-all thought about it anyways?"

Ganda spoke again, "I done overheard the overseers saying Nathanial the man's been off soldiering somewhere to west, past where the sun sets. There he been fighting the wild men who lives out there … what the white men calls *Indians*, whatever they may be."

He shook his head slowly for a moment before continuing, "I am sore fearful this man may be a *terrible* bad master. A reckless child, an angry youth, and a wild, violent adult. It don't seem to bode well for our lot."

Then Juba, who went by the name "Betsy," said, "I don't recall much about the child. But … seems to me it ain't right to judge the *man*, by the *boy*. Ain't we-all … well … I don't know … more smarter, kinder, and whatnot, since we done growed? Maybe *he* smartened up, too. And softened; who's to say? Ain't we always complaining the white folks think they know us, on account of our color, and because we's slaves, without ever *really* knowing us? Now ain't we doing the same … thinking we know this man, when really we don't?"

But she hadn't swayed Ganda, "Look here, Juba; you've always been the sunshiny one among us, and that's always nice on the ears. But still, there's plenty to be worrying about, and not enough to hang our hopes on. And there's little enough we can do about any of it anyway. Except … well, except keep on doing as we been doing all these years."

"But, Ganda …" Camba said, "I agrees with Juba; it don't seem fair not to … well, not to at least give the new master a chance. Let him prove he gonna be good, or bad, or something ordinary in-between, before we starts in to working against him?"

The others nodded their agreement; Camba had made a good point.

But Ganda shook his head. "I can't agree. In the end, a master's still a *master*. He can beat, starve, and misuse us in any number of different ways any time he feels so. And, even if he treats us perfectly nice … well, he still working us hard and making his wealth off'n our sweat and blood and giving little or nothing in return. So in my book, even the nicest, gentlest, most kindliest master … he still a *slaver*. Ain't no creature, no matter how well fed nor kindly treated, don't want to come out when the cage door be opened."

Camba looked down but didn't respond. No one argued against Ganda's logic on that point.

"All right then, if there's nothing more to say, I'd like a vote on keeping on with 'The Way' or not."

Just the mention of *The Way* caused visions of his past participation to flash through his mind, loosening a bolt holding on the plow head, breaking off every tenth un-ripened cotton branch, skipping over hidden weeds. And acting slow and stupid when the master asked him a question. Leaning heavily on his cane and limping like an old invalid when in fact he felt perfectly fine.

Though a part of him knew it was justified, and everyone else was doing similar things, he still felt a twinge of guilt. No, that wasn't quite right. Not *guilt* exactly, more like … sadness or regret for never being able to do a good job at anything.

With an effort of will, he shook off his reverie and brought himself back to the present. "If'n the vote be 'no' on *The Way*," he continued, "then … well, then I guess we'll need to talk things through some more and decide just what that means. All in favor of keeping with *The Way* raise up your hand now."

It was three for and two against. Ganda wasn't surprised the two "nays" were Juba and Camba; they'd been more hopeful and had spoken for giving the new master the benefit of the doubt. They'd never fixed the number of Elders; it varied from time to time depending on deaths, illnesses, and whatnot, and on who the group considered ready for inclusion. The only firm rule was there'd be an odd number so there'd never be tied votes. The discussion and voting finished, they all rose, said their good nights, and headed off to their own respective cabins.

ᘒᘯᘍᘜᘒᘯᘍᘜᘒᘯᘍᘜ

The five household maids and two cooks sat around the kitchen table. It was the time of evening they all enjoyed, a little quiet comradery before bed. They'd cleared away the dinner, washed the dishes, and escorted Miss Abbey off to bed, so they had a few minutes of free time before turning in.

This evening the conversation had a more serious tone than was typical. There had been a general sense of unease … of an impending change that might not be for the best. Miss Abbey had

325

announced her grown son, Nathaniel, was returning after a very long absence, to be their new master. The rumors swirling among the field workers were also making their way through the Big House; the new master may be a monster.

"They say he used to beat the other white boys bloody, and even the old master was afraid of him when he got older," said Cara, a young maid.

"That's right. I was told Miss Abbey sent him away to a school for bad boys so's they'd punish him. But he done run away to go fight with the soldiers out in the West," Sally added.

"My goodness, I remember the boy," said Jeb, one of the cooks, whose gray hair was proof he was old enough for it to be true. "He used to run through this kitchen, snatch up something to eat, and run right out of the back door with a laugh ... like he done owned the whole place! And I remembers the master being three-shades-of-red furious at him. Oh, Lordie ... what a sight ..." He smiled and shook his head.

There was a long silence.

Jeb finally said, "Megs ... you been strangely quiet, but I recall you probably knew the boy best, having helped take care of him when he was a young'n."

Megs didn't immediately respond, as if deciding what she wanted to say. She'd not said much all evening, which was curious since she was neither shy nor reserved. Megs was not only the boss among the house slaves, but she was also usually the most talkative. She typically dominated any discussion at the table.

Finally, she said, "It's true, I knew him well back then. When I was only a young girl, they brought me into the Big House and trained me up to be a maid.

"One day the old master returned from Richmond, having married Miss Abbey over there. He was always a hard man. And no kinder to her than to any of us, from all I saw.

"So I reckon she was lonesome, and me being the same age as her, she took a liking to me. And ... well, I guess you could say we became friends, if such a thing be possible between a slave maid and her mistress. Anyway, when she got herself heavy with child, with young Nathaniel, she pulled me aside one day. She wanted to teach me my letters, so's I could help her teach the young child as he grew. I reckon she needed someone to help share her burden—the old master being of no comfort to her.

"So I reckon I helped raise the boy, teaching him reading and writing, among other things.

"Anyway … I can't disagree with anything y'all have said. I'd even say every word of it's *true*, as best as I know and can remember. And, I agree; it seems like our new master might be *very* bad for us—cruel, and of a bad temper. And *yet* …"

There was a long pause.

Sally finally said, "And yet … *what*, Megs?"

"And yet … he had a soft side, too. A kindness toward small animals, and helpless things. I remember he used to spend hours in Miss Abbey's flower garden watching them tiny birds who buzz about, sipping the juice from the flowers. He used to call them … what was it now? Oh yes, his 'brave little knights,' and say they was 'jousting with each other to see who would win the flowers.'"

She paused, and the others stared at her with blank looks, not understanding why the boy would refer to birds as "nights" nor what "jousting" meant.

She looked around the table and smiled, "Sorry—strange words from old books I used to read the boy. I also recall he'd spend hours laying out under that old Magnolia, gazing up at the flowers. He'd say they looked like a thousand purple stars. He also loved going down to the pond and watching them frogs and ducks swim around. I remember a time he got furious angry at the white farmhands when they shot a few of the ducks off the pond for supper. He was only six or seven, but he stood there with such a stern look, and gave them *such* a scolding … *oh, Lordie!* I reckon they never did it again after."

There was another long silence, the older ones trying to remember anything they could about the boy.

Finally, Megs said, "I know it all *looks* bad … but somehow … I feel *hopeful*. I can't tell why, but I feel things are going to get better, not worse."

Later, before going to her bed, Megs stepped outside for some fresh air and looked up at the stars. It was a moonless, cloudless night, with stars sparkling in a great, thick band overhead. *Like a thousand purple Magnolia flowers,* she thought and chuckled. The little boy Nathaniel would have enjoyed the sight, she was certain.

She walked to the veranda's edge and sat at the top of the steps. She recalled her own life.

Her early years, before coming to Mountain Meadows, were now a blur. She vaguely remembered a big, strong man who used to lift her up off the ground and call himself Daddy. Her Momma she recalled little better. They'd sold Megs off when still a toddler.

Now, nearly fifty years later, she couldn't even remember their faces. She decided that even if God brought them to life right in front of her, she wouldn't know them. No. Mountain Meadows was now her life—the only life she remembered.

She concentrated hard and remembered back as far as she could. The fear and emptiness when she first came to Mountain Meadows as a small child, not knowing why they'd taken her away from her Momma and Daddy. The endless tears. There were black women who'd been nice to her and comforted her. She remembered crying and crying until someone came and sternly said she had to stop crying and grow up. So, she had.

Her time spent living in the cabins was another blur. So routine, she reckoned there was nothing to stick in her memory. Except the day when one of the white farmhands had taken her by the arm, and said, "They's lookin' for another maid up to the Big House. Come along and see if they takes a likin' to you."

The next thing she remembered she was being taught how to make a bed. And they gave her a bed of her own, a hard pallet on the floor in back of the kitchen in the Big House. She never went back to the cabins.

But she sometimes wondered … what would my life have been out in the cabins? The field workers resented and distrusted her, same as all the other household slaves. *They think we-all live a pampered life, but they never think of what we give up for a little comfort. They think we've all gone over to the side of the white slavers, but in truth we are the least free of any slave, living under the same roof as the master and mistress, always under their watchful eyes.* After she'd become a maid, the slaves who worked the fields wouldn't speak to her. Even the same women who'd taken her in and comforted her when she'd first arrived, would no longer acknowledge her. She felt shunned by her own people.

For the thousandth time she wondered what it would have been like to meet a man out in the fields, to share *that* kind of love. And to … have a child? But reality interjected; it asked, *and what then, Megs? Would they have sold away your child, like they did you?*

She shuddered and shook her head to clear away those demons. *No … don't go there again, Megs,* she scolded herself.

Better to think about the one baby she'd had … young Nathaniel. The baby she'd held, sung to, and comforted when he cried. The starry-eyed little boy she read wild adventure stories to and played with out on the lawn and in the fields. The serious, diligent young man determined to learn his letters. Yes … he was the closest thing to her own child she'd ever had. Or ever would have.

But … what was he like now that he was a fully-grown man?

It was true … he'd been an angry, uncontrollable youth when he'd left. He hadn't even said goodbye to her … that still hurt after all these years, she realized. It occurred to her, for the first time, she'd loved that little boy more than anyone else in her life. What if he was now a cruel monster, like the others said he was?

She rested her head in her hands and sighed a heavy sigh. After a few minutes she leaned back, looked up at the sky and tried to empty her mind of all the vile, evil thoughts trying to take hold. She focused on all the good things she remembered of young Nathaniel. In the end, she settled on an even balance of good versus bad—enough so she could honestly say with some relief, *well, Megs … we'll just have to wait and see.*

ಬಃಞಂಲಃಞಜಃಞಂಲಃಞ

Sunday June 3, 1860 – On the Railroad in Mississippi:

They rode the train throughout the night after departing New Orleans, arriving in Jackson, Mississippi the following morning, just after nine. Nathan had finally relaxed a little, once they were no longer in Louisiana. He'd been uneasy at each of the four stops along the way, lest LeBlanc had telegraphed ahead to stir up trouble for them with the local authorities. But once they reached the train stop in Osyka, Mississippi at half-past two in the morning, it was no longer a concern, them now being in a different state.

It was now midafternoon; they were heading due north and were somewhere in the middle of Mississippi. Nathan pulled out his pocket watch: half-past four.

"Tom, any idea where we are?"

"Well, sir, according to the conductor, the little town we just left was *Winona*, Mississippi. You probably noticed the train station was all fresh wood; new construction—apparently just opened this year. So new, in fact, it doesn't even show up on the map I acquired in New Orleans. But from what I can tell, it's a few miles east of another little town called Middleton, which *is* on the map. That puts us a bit north of the middle of the state, and about 120 miles from Memphis. If we continue at our current pace, with roughly the same number of stops, I estimate we'll arrive in Memphis somewhere around half-past one in the morning.

"And … by pure luck I ran into a man at the hotel who'd come west from Richmond. He had a railroad map of Virginia he was willing to part with. The good news, Captain, is the railroad now extends to within fifty miles or so of your home, near a small town called Covington!"

"I know the place! My Daddy took me there once on horseback when I was a young man, though I can't recall now why we went there. Within fifty miles you say?! That's great news, Tom. It'll save us days and days on horseback from how it was in the old days."

"Yes, sir. But …"

"Yes?"

"The *bad* news is … we have to ride the train all the way to the coast at Richmond, before boarding the train heading back west. So … I estimate we have … well, *only* about a thousand and fifty miles, give or take a few, until we reach the end of the line!"

Nathan groaned and gave Tom an ironic smile. But Tom didn't return the smile, and once again seemed serious and thoughtful. Nathan felt sad for him, assuming he still suffered the effects of the incident with the young lady back in New Orleans. He feared Tom would be a long time getting over it.

But Nathan had his own worries. And being idle on the train, with nothing to do but watch the miles go by, seemed to bring them to the fore. What was going on back home? He couldn't seem to shake the feeling of dread.

He must have been scowling because Tom noticed and said, "What troubles you, sir?"

"I don't know, Tom. I've had this anxious feeling since we left Fort Davis. That something is amiss back home."

"Cheer up, sir. We'll have you back home to western Virginia shortly."

"Yes, I know. But for some reason I have a strong feeling I should have been home … *yesterday*."

He settled into his seat, pulled his hat down, and eventually nodded off into a dream-troubled sleep.

xxxxxxxxxxxx

Sunday June 3, 1860 – Greenbrier County, Virginia:

By accident, or luck, he had discovered a way to fulfill Mr. Walters' wishes concerning Miss Abbey. He had nothing against her personally; she was always pleasant enough. But there was good money in it, much more than they'd paid him earlier to cut the cinch on her saddle and plant the dead snake where it'd likely spook her horse. That was just intended to scare her, so she'd be more willing to sell the farm. This time they wanted her dead.

If he could pull it off, they'd pay him more than he'd earn working half a year at his normal job. And there'd also been the promise of employment—at a substantially higher rate than he was getting now—for the rest of his days, if you believed such things. By contrast, with the son returning home soon, there was no guarantee his job at Mountain Meadows would continue at all.

He'd discovered Miss Abbey invariably strolled around her flower garden on nice, sunny Sundays immediately after returning from church. And after her walk, she'd sit on the veranda to have her tea. But apparently, she didn't like her tea too hot. So the maids always served it out at her table a few minutes before she returned to give it time to cool. He'd learned this when he had business at the Big House one Sunday afternoon. Having quizzed one of the maids about it, he found it was a ritual, run like clockwork, so the tea would be at the right temperature.

This gave him a small window of opportunity. A time when the tea was left standing, unsupervised, while the maids were off attending to other duties. Just enough time, he'd decided, to slip arsenic into her tea. It was the perfect poison; odorless and tasteless, it produced symptoms—diarrhea, vomiting, abdominal pain—like any of a dozen different natural illnesses.

Though he didn't know the details, he'd come to understand there'd been some kind of plan to kill her the Sunday before. But something had gone wrong, to the point Miss Abbey had never even known of it. Walters was most insistent nothing go wrong *this* time, with Miss Abbey's son due home any day now. And Walters wasn't a man you wanted to disappoint.

So he waited in the woods as Miss Abbey walked out to the flower garden wearing a straw hat. Her head gardener accompanied her, presumably so they could discuss any work that needed doing as they walked.

He waited and watched. Shortly a maid came and laid out a white tablecloth, tea, and various treats on a table in the shady part of the veranda by the back stairs. As soon as the maid walked back inside, he came out from behind the bush and strode briskly across the lawn toward the house. He resisted the temptation to run—if someone saw him running it would be extremely suspicious; but a brisk walk simply showed a man going about his normal business. His biggest worry was that the maid would come back, having forgotten to deliver some item or other, or a gardener would come around the house on an errand. But he reached the back stairs encountering no one. So far so good.

He took the stairs two at a time and walked up to the table. There he stopped and took another look around, reaching into his vest pocket for the small vial of liquid he'd placed there. It contained arsenic powder dissolved in water.

He leaned over the teacup; steam rose from the hot contents. He removed the stopper from the vial, reached out and started to pour the contents into the cup. He flinched and pulled back the vial when he heard the door open behind him and a voice say, "Mr. Sickles!"

He quickly stoppered the vial and returned it to his pocket before turning around. It was the head maid, Megs.

"Mr. Sickles ... is there something I can do for you, sir?"

Damn the bad luck, he thought, wondering how much poison he'd already dumped into the cup. He'd carefully calculated the amount in the vial so as to appear as a natural illness and not look suspicious. He figured he'd emptied about half into the cup but couldn't be sure the dose was yet enough. He needed another shot at that teacup!

But Megs was the *one* maid he couldn't intimidate nor immediately send running off on some errand, because of her privileged position with Miss Abbey—not to mention her stubborn demeanor.

"Oh, hello, Megs. No, no ... I ... had some business to discuss with Miss Abbey and was hoping to catch her at tea. Do you know when she's expected to arrive at table?"

"Well, she's out in the flower garden right now ... I reckon she'll be here in ten minutes or so, if you'd care to wait. She don't much like being disturbed when she's out among them flowers."

"Yes ... fine, I'll just wait for her here," he said, pulling out a chair and taking a seat. Whenever the maid went back about her business he could get on with his. But he noticed for the first time she had a broom in her hand, and instead of returning into the house, she started sweeping the veranda. Sickles silently groaned in frustration. It might take her hours to finish sweeping. He'd need to think up a reason to make her leave.

"Oh, Megs ... I'm not much a one for tea, but I would appreciate a cup of coffee, if you would."

"Yes, certainly, Mr. Sickles. I shall fetch you a whole pot of coffee, if you please."

"Thank you; that would be fine."

Megs turned, walked to the back door, and opened it. Then, to Sickles' surprise and disappointment she called out, "Sarah, come here now, if you please."

A moment later the maid Sarah stood in the back doorway.

"Go on into the kitchen now, and brew Mr. Sickles a pot of coffee, then bring it 'round here with a cup when you're done."

"Yes, ma'am. Will there be anything else?"

Megs looked over at Sickles, "Can we bring you anything more, sir? Something to eat, perhaps?"

"No … and never mind about the coffee. I've just remembered … an urgent matter that needs tending. I'll speak with Miss Abbey later."

He stood, turned, and stalked off the veranda. He hoped there was enough arsenic in the tea to do the job; only time would tell now.

There was still a week or more before the son would likely return, so in the worst case he'd just have to find a way to give her another dose …

After Sickles disappeared around the corner of the house, Megs turned back to Sarah and handed her the broom. "Here, you can put this away now. Turns out I'll not be needing it after all."

"But Megs, you know I done swept this part of the veranda earlier this morning."

"Yes … I know," she nodded at the younger woman, who returned a puzzled look, shrugged, and took the broom.

<End of Book I>

If you enjoyed *Road to the Breaking*
please post a review.

ENIGMA
ROAD TO THE BREAKING BOOK 2

As they reached the valley floor, and the road flattened out, they saw ahead of them a row of people standing still, lining both sides of the drive. Men, women, and children of all ages and sizes, with black faces—the slaves. Nathan swallowed a lump in his throat; this was the moment he'd thought about, dreamt about, and dreaded the entire journey.

How would they react to his return? Were they anything like he remembered? It was all so hazy in his memory. His world had changed since he was last here. It'd been another lifetime, another person—not himself. And yet ... he could remember sneaking off to the river with a couple of the young black boys to swim and go fishing. Running, climbing, swinging from a rope into the water, laughing uproariously! And the boys suffering punishment later while he was forced to watch. Was it a dream, or had it really happened oh, so long ago?

The men on horseback leaned forward, looking around with curiosity. At a time when an adult slave might sell for fifteen hundred dollars or more at auction, this group represented more wealth than most men would earn in a lifetime.

Tom whistled quietly, turned to Jim and whispered, "I knew the Captain's family had wealth, but this?" He shook his head. Jim nodded and grunted his agreement.

But for Nathan, the economic value of these people was the furthest thing from his mind. As they walked their horses between the rows of people, he looked down at their faces. None looked back. In the days before their arrival he'd replayed this moment in his mind a hundred times, the expectant faces looking up at their new master with curiosity, wondering what he'd become in his years of absence. Maybe a shy smile or two, or a look of recognition, which he might return in an encouraging manner.

But this ...

He felt his earlier excitement draining away. Face after face looked straight at the ground, never looking up at him, never meeting his eyes. Too afraid, too humbled, too downtrodden to even glance up to see how their new master looked, or what might be his demeanor.

He suffered a growing sadness, a wave of depression and hopelessness that threatened to darken the otherwise bright day of his homecoming. After the last two days of hard travel by horseback, Nathan had pulled out his dress clothes this morning for his arrival. He wanted to make an impression on his new "employees," both black and white. But now he felt foolish for the thought. These people didn't care how he looked; they had no reason to.

Acknowledgments

Thanks to:
Joel Osteen
—*that it **could** be done*

And
K.M. Weiland
—*how it **should** be done*

But especially
My friends and family
—*why it **has been** done*

Speaking of friends and family ... I'd like to thank the following individuals for assisting in the writing and editing of *Road to The Breaking*, including reading the beta version and providing invaluable feedback: Angela Thompson, Bruce Wright, Charlie Carman, Craig Bennett, Gay Petersen, Jeff Kaye, Larry Zinkan, Leslie Johns, Marilyn Bennett, Mike Bennett, Nick Bennett, Patricia Bennett, Rachel Bennett, and Tessa Wyrsch.

And special thanks to my editor, Ericka McIntyre, who keeps me honest and on track, and my proofreader Travis Tynan, who makes sure everything is done correctly!

And, last but not least (at all!), the experts at New Shelves Books; my trusted advisor on all things "bookish," Keri-Rae Barnum, and the guru Amy Collins!

Get Exclusive Free Content

The most enjoyable part of writing books is talking about them with readers like you. In my case that means all things related to *Road to the Breaking*—the story and characters, themes, and concepts. And of course, Civil War history in general, and West Virginia history in particular.

If you sign up for my mailing list, you'll receive some free bonus material I think you'll enjoy:

- A fully illustrated ***Road to the Breaking* Fact vs. Fiction Quiz.** Test your knowledge of history with this short quiz on the people, places, and things in the book (did they really exist in 1860, or are they purely fictional?)

- **Cut scenes from *Road to the Breaking.*** One of the hazards of writing a novel is word and page count. At some point you realize you need to trim it back to give the reader a faster-paced, more engaging experience. However, now you've finished reading the book, wouldn't you like to know a little more detail about some of your favorite characters? Here's your chance to take a peek behind the curtain!

- I'll occasionally put out a **newsletter with information about the Road to the Breaking Series**—new book releases, news and information about the author, etc. I promise not to inundate you with spam (it's one of my personal pet peeves, so why would I propagate it?)

To sign up, visit my website:
http://www.ChrisABennett.com

ROAD TO THE BREAKING SERIES:

Made in United States
North Haven, CT
25 March 2025

67234401R00207